W9-BFG-299

PASSION'S PRISONER

Talen advanced. He was ready for anything—except her speed. She came at him like a pouncing ice wolf, right fist swinging. He dodged the blow, but she toppled him to the bunk with a quick blow behind the knees and an arm across his shoulders.

He could have fought back, but he didn't. He was where he wanted to be. His bed. Admittedly, he liked the press of her breasts against his back, the profoundly female muskiness of her scent filling his nostrils.

The loose shackle snapped around his wrist.

Adrenaline kicked in. This wasn't part of the bargain. But an undefined, deeper urging kept him from wrestling her for control of the master key. Deciding that Kari Solis needed an unexpected ending to her scheming, he waited for the right moment.

As soon as she slapped her sequencer onto the shackle binding her other hand, Talon knocked the key away. It popped loose from its magnetic grip, bounced twice on the floor, then rolled toward a section of open grating.

"No!" Kari burst out. Desperation swelled in her chest.

She lunged for the disk, but the chain brought her up far short of her goal. Pain registered as the shackle cut into her wrist.

"You know, Princess, if you wanted us to get closer, all you had to do was ask."

Kari's eyes snapped open. Her breath sucked in a gasp of dismay. She had been so wrapped up in the loss of her goal, she'd forgotten the more immediate consequence of her aborted escape attempt.

Talon was shackled to the other end of the chain.

LOVE SPELL ✦ NEW YORK CITY

LOVE SPELL®

March 1997

Published by

Dorchester Publishing Co., Inc.
276 Fifth Avenue
New York, NY 10001

The name "Love Spell" and its logo are trademarks of Dorchester Publishing Co., Inc.

Printed in the United States of America.

Chapter One

"I don't like the looks of this, Beryl," Talon said grimly as he guided the *Nighthawk* toward the space station's narrow portal.

A puff of air ruffled his long brown hair, warning him just before his companion settled lightly on his right shoulder. Beryl folded her shimmering wings. Out of the corner of his eye, Talon watched her head turn toward the starboard viewport. Her clawed feet tightened their grip on his flight suit. Her black-eyed gaze riveted on the cause for concern—a Lochnar battle cruiser on final approach to Star Alpha's main hangar bay.

Their view was cut off as the *Nighthawk* entered the station. Thank the stars he always used the auxiliary bay, reserved for delivery of supplies, rather than the main hangar. Otherwise he would be trapped right now, vastly outnumbered, and targeted for capture and transport to a Lochnar prison.

Or rather, the brute squad would try. Six years ago he'd vowed they would never take him again.

A series of warbles and trills, overlaid with a note of worry, filled his ear. The translation of Beryl's question simultaneously communicated to Talon through telepathy.

"Lochnar soldiers?"

"Yes, though it doesn't look like they're here to enjoy the entertainment facilities, does it?" It wasn't unusual to see Lochnar soldiers at the orbiting complex, but only those

9

on leave were welcome, and they arrived in shuttles. The proprietors of Star Alpha adamantly maintained the space station's neutrality. Soldiers were expected to mingle peacefully with traders and freighter crews, even tolerating the Rebels as long as politics were left planetside. They sure as hell didn't drop in aboard a solar-class battle cruiser.

Beryl trilled softly. She threaded her left hand through the close-cropped hair over Talon's temple. Her other hand tugged at the stiff collar of his dark blue flight suit.

"Don't worry, little jewel," he reassured the Sylph. "I doubt they're looking for me. I'm not that much of an annoyance these days."

"Smugglers always annoy the Dynast. Leave, we must."

"You know we can't do that," he said firmly. "Not yet."

Beryl sprang from his shoulder onto the ship's console. She crossed her arms tightly over her chest. Her jewel-tone coloring—from the emerald green at the base of each wing blending through varying shades into a vivid blue along the edges—shimmered vibrantly in the console lighting. Delicate green scales completely covered the tiny body that was humanoid in appearance except for the hairless head and four-fingered hands and feet.

"Not safe here. Like to catch you, Lochnar soldiers would. Reckless human." Her wings twitched. *"Why always must I watch for you? Without me, the Dynast would have caught, mayhap killed you long ago."*

Talon arched one thick eyebrow. "Rather huffier than usual today, aren't we?" he countered, though common sense did dictate he pivot the *Nighthawk* on its hoverlifts and blast back out the way he had come. But there was someone here in even greater danger than himself.

"You know Rand asked me to meet him and, unfortunately, he's already here." Talon gestured toward the viewport. Another spacecraft, the same model as his own, was parked in the bay. Only the midnight-blue and gold coloring of Rand Markos's ship distinguished it from the black and silver *Nighthawk*. The Rebel High Commander was already here . . . unsuspecting, unprepared. "I have to warn him, even if I do make it a hard-and-fast rule to navigate around Rebel business. I'm not leaving until I know he's safe."

Beryl's wings drooped, a sign of reluctant acceptance. The Sylph had a soft spot in her heart for Rand.

Talon's hands tightened around the finicky hoverlift controls. The leather of his fingerless black gloves stretched taut over his knuckles. With a rock-steady grip, he maneuvered the sleek ship in the limited confines of the hangar bay.

The landing skids settled onto the metal deck with a clank. The sound, jarring after the silence of space, grated against nerve endings on full alert. He set the ship on stand-by.

Unbuckling his restraints, Talon jumped up from the pilot's seat and grabbed his weapons from their bulkhead mounts. He pressed the sheath containing the dagger to his upper right arm—hilt down for easy access. The bands snapped around his biceps. A magnetic grip held the blade in place. The dagger's hilt was fashioned like the head of a Valken bird of prey, with hooked talons forming the hand guard.

He clipped the *Singh Dubh* sword to his utility belt, hanging it over his left hip. The name, meaning *flame of fury*, fit the weapon—the blade and the flaring crossguards were etched with leaping tongues of fire.

Between clenched teeth, he muttered, "Only for you, Rand."

His fist hit the control for the hatch.

"Stay out of sight until I get back," he ordered. To amend for his harsh tone, he gently stroked the edge of Beryl's wing.

She grasped his finger. *"Come back quickly. Worry me, and very angry will I be,"* she warbled irritably.

"A more terrifying prospect I can't imagine. Believe me,

11

I intend to find Rand and drag him out by his ear if I have to."

He left the cabin and bounded down the hatch ramp, emerging beneath the belly of the ship.

The stale, flat smell of manufactured atmosphere assailed his senses. Though the recycled air on his own ship wasn't much better, at least he didn't have the added unpleasantness of ozone burn, nor the resin odor from newly molded shipping crates.

Three back-to-back smuggling runs had kept him in space longer than usual. When he finished here he'd avail himself of a short sojourn on the planet below. A couple of days spent hiking one of Serac's massive glaciers, breathing in the pure, oxygen-rich atmosphere, squinting his eyes against the painfully blue sky, would help purge the dark emptiness from his soul.

For those few days, at least.

The hatch ramp closed. The pressure lock hissed shut, sealing the ship against intruders . . . just the way he liked it.

Talon headed for the nearest exit. The door whisked open. Bringing into play special training from his childhood, he moved soundlessly into the network of passageways that criss-crossed the wheel-shaped space station, his goal the centrally located Stargazer tavern and gaming hall.

He was more than halfway to Rand's rendezvous site when the clomp of boot heels jolted him into battle readiness.

Five men stepped into view from a side passageway, blocking his path. The tallest was dressed in a maroon flight suit, the other four in nondescript gray crew uniforms.

Runagate hell, Talon swore inwardly. As if he didn't have enough trouble with a Lochnar patrol aboard.

He watched Jhase Merrick's brows arch against the maroon silk band that held his shaggy mane of black hair in place. Jhase's hard mouth tilted in a sardonic grin that held no humor yet plenty of anticipation.

The timing couldn't be worse. Talon had known there would be a reckoning for his previous encounter with Jhase but, dammit, not now. Their last altercation had ended with Talon sticking a dagger through the other smuggler's thigh. Though it was Jhase who'd escalated their competitive animosity into a challenge, the man's pride was at stake. No one but Talon had ever defeated the tall, powerfully built captain of the *Vagabond* in a fair fight.

Talon tensed as Jhase approached, his men flanking him, two on either side. The other pilot's stride almost, but not quite, concealed a lingering limp. Talon shifted smoothly into a defensive stance.

"Talon," Jhase greeted him, using the only name anyone knew.

A brief nod was Talon's only warning, that and the dual hiss of swords being drawn. The two outside crewers leapt forward and attacked. Metal clanged as Talon blocked the blows with the forearm guards encasing his arms from elbow to wrist. A kick to one crewer's solar plexus dropped the man to the floor, fighting for air. Talon grabbed a fist-ful of the other's jumpsuit and slammed him against the wall. He yanked out his Valken dagger and pressed it to the shocked man's throat.

Instead of following up the attack, Jhase's deep laughter reverberated off the walls. "Excellent," he said with grating enthusiasm. "Now I know the last time wasn't a fluke."

Talon snarled a curse. He backed away from the wide-eyed crewer, the instrument of Jhase's manipulative game.

The crewer's gaze shifted to Talon's gloves. The reaction was all too familiar, Talon thought bitterly, but at least among fellow smugglers the response was one of curiosity rather than open hostility. There were many ex-convicts in this profession. Most chose to display their scars like a badge of honor.

Talon glanced at the knotted scars marring the backs of Jhase's hands, an eternal reminder of the mutilating procedure used to strip away the tattoos delineating a man or woman's family Line. Lochnar policy for criminals, political or otherwise. Steal a man's identity. Talon's hands curled into fists, his knuckles straining against leather. These men would be startled to know why he chose to wear gloves . . . and he'd make damn sure they never found out.

"I don't need to be tested, Jhase," Talon said acidly. A ticklish ribbon of sweat trailed down his chest. He slid the dagger back into its sheath.

Jhase laughed again. "I love to see those lightning-quick reflexes of yours at work . . . on someone other than me, that is. Crimony, but it's a thing of beauty." He signaled the remaining two men to help their still gasping shipmate up from the floor. "I have every confidence in your defensive ability, but someone has to help keep you sharp, Talon. Now that you've bested me, your reputation is too intimidating. No one will challenge you. Wouldn't want to see you get soft, mate."

"There's not a worry of that. Have I provided you with sufficient entertainment today?"

"Couldn't have been better."

"Spare yourself any more demonstrations."

Jhase's grin disappeared, acknowledging the warning. "I've been thinking, mate. There's not a man in the solar system to match your fighting skills or smuggling savvy. Hell, not even me, though I'm the better pilot." Talon's right eyebrow arched. Jhase continued, undeterred. "I propose we form a partnership. Together we'd create a hell of a shipping enterprise."

"Not interested."

Scowling now, Jhase jammed his thumbs into his utility belt. "Crimony, your independence is excessive. I'd sacrifice last month's profits to know why you're so adamant about keeping to yourself." His gray-eyed gaze shifted to Talon's hands.

Even Jhase wasn't immune to speculating. Talon rubbed one thumb against the soft leather. "I have my reasons."

Persisting, Jhase said, "Think it over before you make a—"

"Sorry to cut this short," Talon interrupted, "but I have business to attend to." *Before the head start I have on the Lochnar patrol deteriorates any further,* he added inwardly.

Jhase's wrist commlink clicked rapidly. "Must be the man I left with the ship," he muttered. He switched it on, saying irritably, "This better be good, Ellis."

"Cap'n. Tell me you're on your way back to the *Vagabond*," the voice pleaded.

Talon, in the process of moving past the others, hesitated. Any information from the main hangar could prove valuable.

"What's the problem?" Jhase asked sharply.

"Two squads of Lochnar soldiers jes' got off one of them mama-have-mercy battle cruisers. A woman is leading 'em, Cap'n. A woman! Those twelve stiffs are leaving the bay right now. My nerves are as twitchy as that time the ion cannon overloaded."

"Calm down, Ellis. We'll be right there." Jhase switched off the commlink and swore. "Now she's raiding Star Alpha. As predatory as a catamount, that one."

"Who?" Talon demanded.

Jhase eyed him dubiously. "Kari Solis, the Dynast's daughter. Where have you been for the past couple of weeks?"

"In space, providing you competition."

"Well, she arrested both Tewfik and Sirr'han. It was quite a fight, from what I hear. You know those two lousy ship-thieves and their crews stay well armed, even though phazers are obsolete. Appears the rumored training she's undergone for the past ten years has paid off. Her dear old

15

daddy, our beloved dictator, has finally decided to turn her loose. Lucky us."

Talon's worry deepened, blowing a chill wind through his soul that rivaled any storm across the ice fields of Serac.

"We're out of here," said Jhase. "I'd suggest you make a speedy exit, as well, before you run across that Lochnar patrol."

"I appreciate the warning, but I think I'll stick around."

Jhase fixed him with a probing gaze, then shrugged. "Suit yourself. Maybe you'll get caught and I'll be able to pick up the *Nighthawk* from impound at a bargain rate. If I can't have you as a partner, I might as well get that sweetheart of a ship," he finished with a wink.

"Keep fantasizing," Talon countered dryly. "That's as close as you'll get to owning my cruiser."

At least the Stargazer didn't appear any different than usual, Talon thought as he stepped into the huge circular room. A typically relaxed and noisy crowd, apparently unaware of any cause for concern, filled the more than eighty tables.

The gaming hall had an atmosphere of wealth that fooled many a gambler into thinking this was the place to circumnavigate the gritty hard work it took to survive the competitive space-trade and the burden of Lochnar taxation. The decor capitalized on the best characteristics from the three habitable planets. The carpet and upholstery, fashioned of green Taki silk, were from Verdigris, as were the round tables of black calamani wood. The massive bar, which curved along the wall to Talon's left, was carved of polished lava topped with slabs of gold marble from Serac. A mural dominated the wall behind the bar, depicting contrasting scenes from the desert and jungle regions of Avernus. Teeming with animal and plant life, the mural held patrons' attention while the bartenders shorted the drinks.

Booths lined the viewports opposite the main entrance, beyond the busy gaming tables. From space, Serac presented a deceptively serene picture. It rotated in its thirty-two-hour day like a ball of glittering white quartzite, its pristine beauty tarnished only by the equatorial belt of brown tundra. The blue-green of plankton-rich ocean peeked out occasionally through gaps in the ice permasheet.

Serac offered few resources to exploit . . . apparently the reason the Dynast had never wasted money or soldiers on an invasion. Either that, or in the twenty-three years since Myklar Solis conquered the solar system, he hadn't dared to challenge the Mal'Harith warrior clans on their native world. He might arrogantly call Serac part of his dominion, but Lochnar soldiers were conspicuously scarce there.

An excellent reason for the largest faction of Rebels to call the ice planet home.

Talon quickly found Rand Markos at a table on the far side of the room. Rand's gaze connected instantly, as if he instinctively knew Talon had entered the room.

Talon felt a rare measure of peace wash through him at the contact. It eased a bit of his loneliness, at the same time making him more acutely aware of his isolation. Only Rand knew of his flaws and accepted him nevertheless. The hardships they had shared growing up would have been enough to draw them close, even if they weren't brothers.

No one knew they were brothers. Despite Rand's urgings to the contrary, Talon adamantly intended to keep it that way. Rand shouldn't have to share in his shame.

Though they were similar in both looks and physique, Talon exploited the differences to conceal their relationship. Rand's short, dark blond hair and hazel eyes contrasted well with Talon's shoulder-length brown hair and brown eyes. Brushing his fingertips across his jaw, Talon sought reassurance in the coarse feel of the two-day stubble he always grew for their meetings.

He worked his way across the room, frequently forced to turn his lean hips sideways to slip between the crowded tables. He slid into the chair on his older brother's left.

"I was beginning to wonder if you'd make it," said Rand.

"Rand, we—"

"How'd you manage to maneuver the *Nighthawk* into that narrow slot I left you in the aux hanger bay?" Rand interrupted. He stretched out in his chair, crossing his legs at the ankle with an air of rangy casualness. He took a sip from his tankard. "I don't know whether to be impressed or skeptical. Did you hire some hotshot copilot?"

Talon retorted automatically. "I had more room to land than you think. You're sadly out of practice. Too much time spent on the ground, not enough in space."

"I'm a better pilot than you'll ever hope to be, upstart." Rand's handsome face spread in a broad grin. One didn't have to search deeply to see the charm and intelligence that had earned him a place as the most highly respected leader among the Rebels. But staying close to Rand meant being part of the Rebellion. In Talon's case, that would be tantamount to suicide. They both knew it. So they tread separate paths, seldom seeing one another. It was better that way, Talon reminded himself harshly.

When he spoke again his voice seemed overly rough. "We're canceling for today. There's a Lochnar patrol aboard, and it doesn't look like they're here for the gambling."

Rand stiffened. Before he could respond his attention was snared by two men crossing the room, glasses in hand.

Talon disliked the note of recognition in his brother's eyes. "You know we keep these meetings private," he snapped. "You've combined this trip with Rebel business, haven't you?"

Rand's neck reddened slightly, confirming the suspicion. "Now that you mention it, I was scheduled to meet someone here later, a mining engineer named Bayne who claims to have some valuable information."

A meeting with a spy. The feeling of dread twisted deeper in Talon's gut. "Dammit, Rand. We've got to get out of here."

The two men approached the table. Talon knew the moment Arden Jamero recognized him; he was treated to the full, caustic force of the blond lieutenant's scowl. Tall, lean to the point of being thin, Arden projected the grim-faced hardness of a man familiar with struggle and disappointment, unlike his shorter, dark-haired companion, who had the eager look of youth untempered by experience. Wes Torquil, Talon guessed. At their last meeting Rand had mentioned grooming the new recruit.

"Let's go," Rand ordered when they reached the table.

"What? We just got our drinks," Arden protested.

"I'll explain later." Rand started to rise.

Talon clamped a hand over his brother's shoulder, holding him in place. "Too late," he whispered in warning. "Have your men sit down, slowly, before they draw unwanted attention."

Arden, with his back still to the door, retorted, "It'll be a hot day on Serac before I take orders from you, smuggler."

"Do it," hissed Rand. "We have company."

Arden glanced over his shoulder and complied quickly. Wes followed suit. Ten Lochnar soldiers, led by a woman, stood just inside the main entrance.

There were only two exits from the Stargazer. The front one was blocked. The other door, though only three tables away, was too far to reach without blatantly inviting pursuit.

Six of the ten soldiers started across the room, stopping to scan the recognition plate of each patron. Though the robust, noisy gambling hadn't diminished, the patrons' jovial attitudes were now more of the deliberate, I'm-innocent variety. The other four soldiers and their leader hovered near the main door, clearly demonstrating that no one would be leaving just yet.

From Jhase's description, the woman could be none other than Kari Solis. Talon watched her from beneath lowered brows. Why did she claim his attention more than the immediate danger of the approaching soldiers? Was it the athletic grace of her body as she gave orders, the hint of raw energy behind each gesture?

She was clad completely in brown, right down to the leather pants and calf-gripper boots shaping her long legs. Her helmet was a seldom worn style with cheek-wings clipped together in the front. Only her eyes were visible. The helmet, the sword, the torso armor custom-kilned to fit over her slender figure, the forearm guards—all were made of prized cinnadar metal. Flecks of gold and orange mica glittered in the polished brown surfaces.

Arden shifted restlessly. "We should make a break for it."

"Great way to admit guilt," Talon scoffed. "Besides, I've heard there are twelve soldiers in this patrol. I see only ten. The other two could be waiting to intercept anyone leaving."

"Perhaps they're not after Rebels," Wes ventured.

Rand grunted his doubt. "Who's the woman?" he asked softly.

"Kari Solis," Talon murmured.

"Sweet everlasting," said Rand, finally sounding worried.

"The best way to avoid their notice is to appear totally unconcerned. Like everyone else in the Stargazer."

Arden muttered, "Even if they're searching for Rebels, our false Recog plates should conceal our identities."

"And if they suspect who we really are, what then?" whispered Wes. "There's eleven of them and only four of us."

"Three," Arden corrected with a hostile glance toward Talon. "Don't you know the smuggler's reputation, Wes? He has no commitment to the Rebellion. In fact, Talon aligns himself with no cause. He's the definitive Neutral."

"Causes are fickle, shifting, distorting over time," Talon countered coldly. "In the end, it's only the integrity of the survivors that matters, not the vainglory of martyrs."

Arden's breath let out in a hiss. "Don't try that tarpan dung on me. It won't change my opinion. You play it safe while we take all the risks."

Out of long habit, Talon bit back his initial reaction and remained silent, refusing to rise to Arden's bait. It would be easier, however, if Wes didn't look so wide-eyed and expectant, waiting to see how Talon would retaliate.

"Shut up, Arden," Rand snapped. "Talon is a friend."

"I don't know how you tolerate—" Arden persisted.

"His life is for him to do with as he pleases."

"It obviously pleases him to run away from any conflict," the lieutenant grumbled, then looked deliberately away.

Rand leaned close to Talon's ear. "Why don't you let me tell them? Why do you allow this abuse?"

"I'm used to it by now," Talon muttered low enough for only Rand to hear. "Besides, you know why. You're the only one who does. If my secret becomes general knowledge, I'll prove a pathetically easy target for Lochnar soldiers, or one of my more ruthless competitors, for that matter."

"I understand, dammit, but I don't have to like it."

The six soldiers had worked their way halfway across the room. Rand fidgeted with his sword. Talon thanked the stars that phazers were a thing of the past. Arden and Wes were so nervous, the slightest provocation would have erupted into a barrage of phazer fire across the crowded room, creating pandemonium and frying innocent bystanders. But the only known fuel for the warehoused weapons had been depleted twenty-three years ago in the Dynast's bid for domination.

A delicate balance of power had existed between the dictator's forces and the Rebels since then, with neither side claiming a decisive advantage . . . a balance undergoing a dangerous shift, if finding Lochnar soldiers at this traditionally neutral space station was any indication.

The two missing soldiers entered the Stargazer, dragging a small man with thinning red hair. The man cowered when they brought him before Kari Solis.

An uneasy premonition nipped at Talon. "Would that happen to be the man you were supposed to meet?"

Rand groaned. "That's Bayne, all right. Looks like things are about to turn sour, boys."

The prisoner pointed a shaky finger at their group. Solis turned sharply, her alert posture one of anticipated triumph. With a curt command, she redirected the six soldiers.

Rand went rigid. "That's it. They're coming this way. Get out of here, Talon. It's me they want."

"No."

"Dammit, Lochnar soldiers fight dirty. While you're engaged in sword battle with one, another may sneak up behind."

"Exactly why you need me to watch your back."

"This isn't your fight. I don't want your help."

Talon rose from the table. "Then I'll just have to create a fight of my own. Be ready to take advantage of the diversion."

"Curse it all, get back—" Rand snapped, too late.

Talon worked his way down the side of the room. The advancing soldiers, intent on Rand and his lieutenants, gave him only the most cursory of glances.

Not so Kari Solis, whose gaze followed him steadily. Her dark eyes narrowed above the cheek-wings of her helmet. Talon forced himself to ignore the nerve-tingling sensation from that assessing gaze, concentrating instead on the two tables of gamblers he was nearing. Freighter crewers were notoriously suspicious. And they should be, if Bhut Camargue was up to his old tricks.

Talon stepped close to one particularly broad, burly fellow whose stacks of value tokens was running quite low.

"Did you realize," he offered smoothly, "that Bhut Camargue is sitting at the table behind us with a convenient view of your cards? He's perfected a nice technique of transmitting their face value to your opponent in the black flight suit."

The man in the glossy black suit flushed angrily. "Who asked you to nudge in, Talon?"

"If you'll recall from a few weeks back, I have a compulsion for honest games. Don't I, Bhut?" he added in a harder tone, without turning around.

A string of expletives came from the other table.

The burly man glanced up at Talon, his beefy expression one of dawning understanding. "They're cheating me?"

"You catch on fast, my friend."

Talon stepped back as the man surged to his feet.

"Cheating!" the crewer bellowed. He grabbed the man in the black suit, dragged him bodily across the table, and sent him sailing into the center of Camargue's adjacent game. The table collapsed with a crash. Cards and value tokens scattered.

Talon knew the rougher, fringe elements of his own people, the Jem'Adal. They couldn't resist the thrill of a good fight.

Chaos broke out all around him, spreading like a volcanic shock wave across the room. Rand, Arden, and Wes used the confusion to dart toward the side door. Kari Solis barked a pursuit order. The four soldiers at her side followed the Rebels. The odds shifted in Rand's favor, however, as the original six were caught in the middle of the melee, three of whom were knocked down within seconds. Trust freighter pilots to grab an opportunity to lay low the Lochnar soldiers who constantly harassed their shipping routes. The two men holding the spy backed away, wary lest the violence swarm over them.

That left only Kari Solis between Talon and the front door.

* * *

Kari clenched her fists in fury. The man identified as Rand Markos was slipping away. The four soldiers she'd sent after him would not be enough. She hadn't studied Markos—his little-known history, his almost untraceable habits—to have her efforts at tracking him down go to waste.

The disreputable-looking fellow striding in her direction was to blame, the one in the dark blue flight suit who'd precipitated this chaos.

A smuggler. She recognized the type. With disdain, Kari noted the stubble darkening his square jaw, the boldly arrogant stride. He was one of a diminishing number, thanks to her recent efforts, of rogue pilots who flouted Lochnar authority.

His gaze locked with hers. Brown was normally her favorite color, but in his cold, intense eyes the hue lost all its warmth. A tingle of awareness went down her spine. Kari attributed it to adrenaline. Her hand went to her sword.

Just let him try to get past her.

Brawny arms closed around her waist from behind.

"Hey, sweeting," said a scratchy voice that reeked of ale. "I'll bet you aren't so prickly without that helmet. Come here and I'll show you something really worth watching." With a grip like durasteel, despite being stumbling drunk, the stranger dragged her into the crowd.

Cold anger energized Kari. Her response came as naturally as breathing. A sharp jab with her elbow, a grunt of pain from her assailant, and she was free to pivot and slam a fist into the man's vulnerable nose.

"Leave it!" she barked at the six struggling soldiers, her husky voice rising above the racket. "Join the others chasing the commander and his men. Now! Fail to bring them back, and every one of you will be reassigned to the refuse compactors."

The soldiers still standing helped their fallen comrades to their feet. All six wrenched away from the fight and scrambled through the side door in the wake of Markos and his men.

Disgusted, Kari fought her way back toward the main entrance. Blazes, the smuggler was gone! There must be a way to intercept him. His interference risked the entire operation, nullified her careful planning. If he had some connection to Markos, he wasn't going to get away. Who in blazes was he?

Her gaze locked on a bulky figure slinking toward the exit. Now there was someone who might give her some answers.

"Camargue!" Kari shouted. The man stiffened and turned slowly. She crooked a finger at him. He approached with obvious reluctance. "Don't be in such a hurry. I have a few questions."

His lips stretched over yellowed teeth in a wan imitation of a smile. "Glad to help ya', Jemara Solis," he said tightly, using the formal title.

"Ah, you know who I am."

"Well, you're gainin' a bit of a reputation around 'ere." His ruddy complexion reddened even more. "I mean, we all know to tread lightly around ya."

"We? You must mean smugglers and thieves," she said silkily. "I've had my eye on you, Bhut Camargue."

He swallowed hard. His blond beard twitched.

"But I'd consider it in your favor," Kari continued, "if you would tell me who that man was—the one who busted up your game."

The hunted expression was replaced by one of swift anger. "Ya mean Talon? That slimy son of a tarpan?" he said acidly, equating his competitor to one of the smelly, pig-like creatures that rooted through the undergrowth of Verdigran forests.

Kari drew in a quick breath. Talon. She recognized the name of the notorious smuggler. The one man whose records were more incomplete than those of Markos. Neither man had a captoimage on file. She'd imagined Talon

25

looked more like . . . well, Camargue: slovenly and ugly. He was anything but, which only heightened her suspicions. How was he linked to the Rebels?

"I've heard Talon pilots a ship called the *Nighthawk*," she prompted.

"Yeah. A black-and-silver DX16 T-class cruiser. Ya can't miss that honey."

"And is he a Rebel?" she asked pointedly.

"Well, Jemara, there's a question with a lot of value to it," he hinted, rubbing his bearded cheek. He couldn't see the scowl behind her helmet, but he must have read her answer in her eyes, for he paled and added hastily, "For you, though, I'll make a gift of it." He leaned closer and said in a low voice, "I'd say it's a sure thing. Besides being a real loner, whenever he's here he spends a lot of time with that Markos fellow."

"What about the gloves? Rather uncommon, wouldn't you say?"

"Sure are. Most of us aren't ashamed to show our scars." He raised his own hands to demonstrate his point.

Kari's mouth tightened. Convicts. What atrocity had Camargue committed to deserve having his family Line stripped away? More to the point, what had Talon done? She glanced proudly at the elaborate, colorful tattoos decorating her own hands, her father's crest on her right hand, her mother's family symbol on the left.

"You may go, Camargue."

He wasted no time in taking her up on her offer.

A ship of the *Nighthawk*'s make had definitely not been in the main hangar bay when she arrived. That left only one place to land—the smaller bay on the station's planetside. Better yet, there was a shortcut there, a utility tunnel used for delivery of freight to the Stargazer.

Kari ran toward the bar, smiling. She'd known memorization of Star Alpha's schematics would pay off.

Two prime arrests in one day. The anticipation flowed

like potent *Bar'okh* wine through her blood. Father would be pleased.

Locating the doorway concealed in the mural, she took off through the narrow, dimly lit tunnel.

Chapter Two

Kari burst through the access opening at the far end of the tunnel, emerging into the auxiliary bay behind a stack of crates.

The only person visible was the female ops controller in the booth built high into the wall opposite. The exterior bay doors far to Kari's right were open, though the magnaseal force field kept the vacuum of space safely locked away. The nearly transparent shield glittered blue, as if embedded with gemstones of rare kaelinite.

Two ships were parked side by side on the deck. Kari blinked, making sure her vision was clear—except for color, the ships were identical. The far one was painted blue and gold, but the near one . . .

Every sense on alert, she fixed her attention on the black and silver *Nighthawk*. Its sleek body, gleaming in the overhead lights, sloped forward to a point almost like a beak. The slanted oval dome in the starboard side of the cockpit, backlit by the ship's console lights, resembled a predatory eye. Slightly down-curved wings swept backward to align with the thick aft section and its powerful stardrive jets.

The perfect smuggler's ship, fast, elusive . . . like its pilot. But the mystery would end once she had Talon in custody, Kari vowed. Her gaze scanned the bay. So where was he?

Just then a door far to her left slid open. Talon charged through. His lean, muscular body moved with power as well as grace. Her shortcut had worked better than anticipated.

As he ran, he barked a command into a commlink embedded in his forearm guard. With a muffled hum, the hatch ramp beneath the belly of his ship started to lower.

But the DX16 wasn't equipped with an audio-prompted hatch release, Kari's logical mind protested.

She glanced sharply toward the cockpit of the ship. There must be someone else on the *Nighthawk*, though the few information cels she had on Talon indicated that he was a maverick, a complete loner, without benefit of partner or crew. She had to capture him before whoever was on board came to his aid. Drawing her sword as she ran, Kari darted beneath the ship and blocked his way to the open hatch.

Talon skidded to a halt. A dark eyebrow arched insolently. Kari's anger escalated sharply, despite her best efforts to remain cool and professional.

She snapped, "Talon, I'm taking you prisoner for suspicion of conspiring with the Rebellion."

"Don't count on it," he corrected coldly. "I value my freedom too much to rot in a Lochnar detention cell."

"It looks as if you have experience in that area." She glanced pointedly at his gloved hands.

"All the more reason to prevent it from happening again," he said softly, barely audible over the hiss of his sword sliding from its sheath.

Kari attacked.

He parried. The clang of opposing weapons reverberated through the hangar bay. She struck again and again. Talon met each slash of her blade, either with his weapon or with a block from his forearm guards. Only once did she penetrate his defense, her sword slipping across his raised forearm. He ducked his head to the side, though not quickly enough to avoid a shallow cut across the left corner of his jaw.

He sucked in his breath and leapt back. His hand jerked

29

reflexively to his cheek and came away with blood-tipped fingers.

"Dammit," he growled, glaring at her.

"I doubt that nick will prove fatal," Kari said acidly. "But if you don't surrender, I'll give you something that will."

He repaid her sarcastic threat by going on the offensive for the first time, forcing her back.

Exhaustion from wielding the heavy sword crept up on Kari. Usually by this point in a fight she had handily defeated her opponent, whether computer-simulated or real. But Talon was countering everything she threw at him, deftly working her out of position while he backed up to the *Nighthawk*. She cursed as he took one step, then another, toward the ramp. Hounded by frustration, she gave into rage and went wild with her next swing, arcing it down from over her head.

His sword arm shot up, catching her blade high overhead against his own. Before she could step back and break free, Talon kicked up his left leg, planted the sole of his boot flat against her chest, and shoved.

She stumbled backward, thrown completely off balance by the surprise move. Her sword clattered to the deck as she threw her hands back to catch herself. She landed hard on her rump.

For a moment she sat there, incredulous, appalled by the indignity of her position and the fact that he had outmaneuvered her.

"I think I like you better this way, Princess," Talon taunted, then backed up the ramp.

With a throaty cry of rage, Kari lunged to her feet. She snatched up her weapon as she came off the deck, though she knew it was too late. He stood just inside the ship, legs braced apart, the heel of his palm poised over the hatch release. Despite the blood dripping down his neck, his gaze sparkled with unmistakable satisfaction. A smile slanted across his face.

How she despised that arrogant grin.

The hydralator mechanism whirred, the hatch ramp closed swiftly, and he was sealed beyond her reach.

Kari slammed her now useless sword into its sheath. "Oh, no, you don't," she whispered tightly. "You won't get away that easily." She pivoted sharply on her heel.

Talon dropped into the pilot seat of the *Nighthawk* and snapped the restraints around his torso.

"Strap in, Beryl," he warned. "I'm throwing her into full throttle the moment we have launch window." The Sylph slipped into her small seat bolted to the console.

He fed his clearance code into the hangar bay's computer, then punched up the request for shield-lock launch.

Nothing happened.

The force field that should have dropped in around him—to seal off the inner bay from the vacuum of space as the outer shield opened—failed to appear.

Talon looked sharply at the director's booth built into the wall to port. The ops controller, an attractive brunette, stood behind the acrylic bubble. Her silver jumpsuit, nipped in at the waist, accentuated her shapely figure. He switched on the comm.

"What the hell is going on, Deni?" he exploded.

"You haven't dropped in to see me this trip, Talon."

He bit back an oath. "You were on duty."

"That hasn't stopped us before," she purred, brushing her straight black hair back from her face.

"Next time, okay? In case you haven't noticed, I'm in a hurry. Now, give me the blasted launch—"

"Hey, sweetie, I would if I could," Deni broke in, shrugging with palms upward in a gesture of futility. "I'd like to claim the credit for keeping you here, but that accolade goes to your friend over there. She just entered an override sequence into the deck-level terminal outlet, some code I've never seen before. I'm locked out of shield control. Where did you pick up that scrawny bitch, anyway?"

"It wasn't by choice, I promise you. Perhaps I can reverse her ploy. What happened to the code she entered?"

31

"I didn't catch it. It went by too fast. That's the problem with having to rely on Lochnar technology for your computer systems. Maybe I can recall it for you."

"No!" he snapped. Deni snatched her hands back from the keyboard as if she'd been burned. "She probably set it for auto-erase in case of ops intervention."

"Then what—"

"I might be able to get to it through the back door," Talon interrupted. He keyed in a command. "I'm going to download the entire log to the *Nighthawk*'s computer." He watched the long list of entries scroll down his screen, in no discernable order—every blasted minor system entry on Star Alpha, from a reorder on Serakian white brandy for the Stargazer to what the station master had for dinner. He groaned.

"What's the matter?" queried Deni.

"Damn. Aren't these entries time-stamped and sorted?"

"Well, they are sorted by priority code, then function—"

"Next to useless. It'll take time to sift through this mess, time I don't have." His clenched jaw only intensified the icy feeling of helplessness pressing up under his breastbone.

"You know, Talon," Deni murmured, leaning forward with a sly smile, "it's a real shame what an ion disrupter beam could potentially do to an ATX-2 force field. I keep telling Admin to upgrade to a model that would maintain its field integrity under that kind of negative charge disruption, but they only say the possibility of that happening is too remote to justify the cost."

Talon drew in a deep breath, stunned by what she was suggesting. "Are you sure, Deni?"

"For you, Talon? Anything."

He ignored her provocative smile. No doubt repayment of the debt would be the foremost topic of conversation next time he saw her. "What about the *Stormhawk*?"

"I have a level 9 magnetic lock on its landing skids. It's not going anywhere, sweetie."

"You'd better keep a tight hold on it. Rand will take off my hide in tiny strips if his precious ship is sucked out into space. He and his men should be close behind me."

"Don't worry. I'll keep it safe for him."

"That leaves us with one other problem. What about our uninvited guest?"

"What about her?" Deni quipped with exaggerated innocence.

Talon hesitated. Opening the bay to the vacuum of space was certainly one solution to the problem of Kari Solis. Lost without a trace . . . that was a mild way of phrasing it. A warble of agreement came from beside him.

"You, too, Beryl? I'm surrounded by bloodthirsty females." The Sylph responded with a series of indignant chirps. "No, Jemara Solis doesn't deserve to die just because she cut my cheek, and you'll have to wait until we're away before you tend it. If we don't get out of here right now, we doubtless won't be able to leave at all." He started up the ship's hoverlifts. With a muted roar, the sleek spacecraft rose a meter above deck level, facing the exit.

"Sound the alarm, Deni. Give her sufficient warning to get behind the airlock door. Tell me when she's clear."

The emergency claxon sounded, pounding its ear-splitting rhythm across the hangar bay. Twin red warning lights on either side of the control booth pulsed in alternating flashes. Talon keyed in distance, charge capacity, everything necessary to calculate the impact of the ion disruption he was about to unleash. It would destabilize the force field for perhaps three seconds, if he was lucky, providing a small window to punch the *Nighthawk* through. If he miscalculated . . . well, he wouldn't have anything more to worry about. Ever again. He reached for the control.

"She's not moving, Talon," came Deni's voice over the channel. "Perhaps she thinks it's a bluff."

He expelled an oath that made Deni flinch, then switched off the comm. "All right, if she needs extra motivation to get her shapely, stubborn little backside out of here, I'll give it to her."

The hum of the *Nighthawk*'s engines increased in volume as he pivoted the ship ninety degrees to face Kari. He switched on the normally disabled alert beacon on the ion gun. The blue light started flashing, its reflection blurred yet unmistakable in the polished metal wall behind her.

She stiffened, her tension clearly defined in the lean, muscular line of her thighs beneath the brown leather pants. Her hands curled into fists. Suddenly she reached up and wrenched off her helmet.

Talon's breathing stopped.

A thick cascade of dark hair tumbled down across her shoulders. Red highlights shone in its depths, leaving Talon wondering whether the color was truly such a rich auburn, or if it was simply a trick of the flashing red lights.

Damp, curling tendrils of hair clung to her temples. Her expression of cold fury accentuated the classic lines of her face—the high cheekbones, the slightly squared chin, and the bold arches of dark eyebrows pinched together at the center. Despite her mouth being tightly compressed, he could distinguish the sensual curves of her lips. Green eyes sparking with intelligence also promised retribution. It would be a mistake to refer to her face as delicate . . . it would be criminal to fail to call it beautiful.

Such beauty was lethal, for she intended to steal away his freedom.

Talon's eyes narrowed with cold determination. His hands shifted over the ship's controls. Kari watched him intently through the cockpit window. Apparently she detected the new resolve in his attitude, for her chin jerked up and her hand shifted to the hilt of her sword. Let her believe he meant to blow her into space.

After offering a casual salute with two fingers, as if he were bidding her an aloof farewell, he began pivoting the *Nighthawk* again toward the exit. This time, he noted with gritty satisfaction, she took him seriously. With a glare that should have melted durasteel, she dove through the opening into the service tunnel and sealed the door.

Talon faced the inviting emptiness of space. All that separated him from escape was a deceptively clear barrier, one that could crumple his ship into scrap metal.

He fired the ion beam, then punched the ship's throttle in synchrony with the calculations designed to intersect the shield at its weakest moment. The acceleration pressed him back into the seat. Beryl let out a squeak of protest.

Bluc fire snaked across the force field. The integrity was definitely disrupted, but how big was the hole? Talon clenched his teeth as the *Nighthawk* neared the shield, half expecting his ship, and himself, to be obliterated into flaming shards of debris. Static crackled from the console and crawled through the hair on his forearms, but there was no explosion.

Just when he thought they must be safely through, a heavy blow, and then another, jarred the ship in rapid succession.

Talon jerked at the sounds of impact. He braced against the inevitable explosion. Instead, the diamond-studded velvet of space opened before him. They were free of Star Alpha and still intact.

So what the runagate hell had hit the *Nighthawk?*

Talon craned his neck to look aft through the oval starboard viewport and found his answer. Half a dozen shipping crates, tumbling uselessly through space, receded in the distance. The vacuum he had created upon blasting through the outer shield had sucked out every loose article in the hangar bay.

Beryl trilled an anxious question.

"Don't worry, little jewel, we're still in one piece. Those were only shipping crates that struck us." He punched the engines into full drive.

The click of Beryl's tiny restraint belt caught his attention. She climbed nimbly out of her seat. *"Attend to your cheek I must,"* she insisted.

"In a minute. I have to contact Rand first. He should have reached the *Stormhawk* by now. I have to share our little exit tactic before Kari Solis traps him in the hangar bay."

He tuned the channel to Rand's commlink. Nothing but static. Talon's jaw clenched as he reached for an illegal device installed under the console. One touch to the power cell and he was tuned into the Lochnar military channel.

It took only seconds to hear the unthinkable. Rand and Arden, as well as Bayne, had been taken prisoner. Wes, wounded in a fight with the soldiers, had been sent to Star Alpha's medic facilities. The three men had been hauled onto the Lochnar battle cruiser. Talon circled the station, tense, watchful. Within minutes a blip of light marked the launch of the other ship, its destination named as Narkwar prison. A hellhole built into the surface of one of Avernus's lifeless moons . . . a place Talon had sworn never to see again.

Kari Solis had sent his brother to the horror of Narkwar.

He couldn't attack the battle cruiser without risking injury to Rand, or worse. Cursing his helplessness, he tracked the Lochnar ship until it entered the first floating station of the interplanetary Corridor. The ship's running lights vanished as it accelerated into the artificial wormhole.

Twelve hours to Verdigris, another fourteen on the next jump through the Avernus Corridor, time enough for Kari Solis to engage in a favorite Lochnar pastime . . . torture. Biting back a roar of rage, Talon turned the *Nighthawk* toward Serac. The Rebels would have to listen to him if they wanted their high commander back. They needed him, because he knew things about Narkwar they couldn't begin to imagine. And he needed them.

Talon looked at Beryl. He didn't have to ask if she'd understood the Lochnar message. Her sad expression focused the fear within to a sharp ache in his chest.

"We'll get him back," he whispered hoarsely.

"From Narkwar, yes. Freedom your gift to Rand will be," Beryl warbled with a note of determination. *"Please to wipe away that mess,"* she added with a sniff, indicating the blood still dripping steadily from his lacerated cheek.

While he used the sleeve of his flight suit to comply, Beryl fluttered her wings rapidly. A cloudy white gelatinous fluid oozed from pores at the base of her wings. She gathered the nectar into her hands and kneaded it into a paste. Then she flew up to perch on his left shoulder. Talon tilted his head to provide her better access to the cut.

She prodded the abused flesh. He winced and bit back a complaint. *"Not too deep. Is good,"* she trilled softly.

As Beryl gently worked the paste into the cut, Talon tried not to think of what Kari Solis and Narkwar prison could do to Rand while he recruited the necessary men for the rescue team.

He failed miserably.

The brutal, unforgiving landscape of Serac stretched out before the *Nighthawk*, white and more white, the monotony of the permasheet broken only by the jagged spines of mountain peaks swathed in glaciers.

Only Serac's geothermal nature enabled it to be more than a frozen rock in space. Submerged volcanoes kept sections of the ocean free of ice and rich with life. Ancient lava tubes, volcanic ruptures in the bedrock, glacial melt carving away the limestone over the millennia—all combined to create an extensive system of underground caverns. Both humans and native animals dwelled primarily below ground, avoiding temperatures that could hit 120 below on the surface.

Talon hovered the ship over a huge gray circle in the ice underlit by a orange glow in its center—a "blister," one of thousands dotting the surface of the planet. Blisters formed where a geothermal pool melted away most of the permasheet, creating an open atrium with a cover of ice thin enough for light to penetrate. The heat from beneath counteracted the cold from outside, maintaining a delicately balanced environment.

This particular blister harbored the secret Rebel base of Inclement, its only entrance through an adjacent cavern. Access through the tunnel was barred by a hidden shield positioned to obliterate any unauthorized invader. Talon knew it was there because he'd helped Rand choose the mount locations for the shield generators. Runagate hell, he'd helped design this whole damned place, though no one other than his brother knew. Now he couldn't get in. Seething with frustration, he cursed the irony of the situation.

The comm crackled to life, finally receiving a response from his persistent hails.

"What do you want, Talon?" The voice, hard-edged as a lash, belonged to Kjell Timor, Rand's second-in-command.

"I need your help."

"Like I give a damn," Kjell retorted. "Neutrals aren't welcome here, even a friend of Rand's. I'm not even going to ask how you found this place. Just manage to lose it again before we shoot you down."

"Not a chance, Kjell. Rand and Arden have been captured by Lochnar soldiers. We have to get them out."

"And you just expect me to believe you?" the other scoffed. "We've had no such reports."

"That's because it just happened. I was there," Talon countered through gritted teeth. "Why else would I come here?"

"We'll check out your story. If it's true, we'll take care of it ourselves. We have men who can handle the job."

"I don't doubt it. That's why I came to you. The question is, do they know their way in and out of Narkwar prison?"

"Narkwar?" The channel hissed with a string of curses. "We'll manage," came the terse reply.

Talon's temper skated dangerously close to the edge of a very deep, very dark chasm. "You don't stand a chance without me and you know it," he growled.

"I'll be blunt, you blasted smuggler. The fact that you were with Rand when he was captured is friggin' suspicious. How do I know you didn't turn him in for some hefty reward?"

That did it. There was only one way to make Kjell listen. And only one way in. Talon switched off the comm.

He hauled back on the *Nighthawk*'s controls, gaining altitude. A quick check of his scanners verified that no one was beneath the ice cap. Rebels used the blister atrium only for storage of supplies. They preferred the security of the deep caverns for their living quarters, where they were shielded from scanner penetration by meters-thick rock.

Banking the ship, he headed down. One impact torpedo should do the trick.

He hit the firing mechanism.

The explosion sent a cloud of shattered ice fragments into the air. The center of the blister cap cratered. Massive shards broke free and crashed to the floor of the atrium. Talon plunged the *Nighthawk* through the devastation, immediately turning the ship into a spiral path around the inner walls of the atrium before heading straight for the adjoining cavern.

Chapter Three

Perimeter defense guns began firing. Talon took out the two guns at the mouth of the cavern, dead on, with two shots of his ion beam. The gunners leaped back as white charges swarmed over the weapons, temporarily disabling them. The remaining two guns, farther inside the dimly lit tunnel, met a similar fate.

Lights came on everywhere as he landed the *Nighthawk*. A group of Rebels raced toward the ship, weapons drawn and ready. Kjell, recognizable by his light blond hair, was in the lead.

The Rebels would either listen to him now . . . or kill him. Unfortunately, the latter was the more likely scenario of the two.

Time for any advantage he could lay his hands on. He wrenched open a storage bin in the floor and pulled out two of his most treasured belongings. The pair of shiny silver forearm guards, uniquely etched with his Line crest, were the only remaining evidence of his lineage.

Removing the plain metal bands he normally wore, Talon snapped the heirloom pair in place. Beryl flew to his shoulder as he opened the hatch. She ignored his frown and dug a death grip into his flight suit with her claws, making it clear he'd have to tear her loose to leave her behind.

Grimly, he descended the ramp, hands in the air away from his weapons. Kjell stepped forward, lifting his sword-point to Talon's throat.

"You're a dead man," Kjell said softly. His hard brown gaze gave credence to his reputation as the most aggressive pilot in the Rebel fighter squadron, with the most kills to his credit.

Talon didn't flinch. "You want proof that I can be trusted? Look," he challenged, raising his wrists.

Kjell's furious gaze flashed between the tell-tale etchings. The moment his brows arched incredulously in recognition, Talon lowered his arms before the Rebel could note that the Valkenbur Line crests boasted the slight difference in design reserved for a second son. Everything depended on Kjell believing these once belonged to Rand.

"You think Rand would have entrusted these to just anybody?" Talon whispered.

Kjell glanced over his shoulder. The white crackle of the ion discharge was just beginning to fade. "You knew the exact location of those guns. How?" he demanded.

"I helped Rand design the defenses of this place. How else do you think I knew its one weak point?" He gestured toward the outer atrium. Brutally bright beams of sunlight slanted through the ravaged ceiling, turning the settling cloud of ice particles into a gleaming silver cascade.

"Dammit, Talon, you made a mess," Kjell snarled.

He shrugged. "Ten to twelve hours of a fine mist water spray from above and the blister will restore itself. Then I suggest you set up extra shield generators beneath the ice cap."

"You know too damn much for my peace of mind. I need to have a serious talk with Rand about this."

"You won't be able to, unless we get him back."

"Yeah," Kjell muttered. "Yeah, you've made your point. But Narkwar? Dammit. Come on." He jerked his head, then spun on his heel and strode deeper into the cavern.

"We're in, Beryl," Talon murmured as he followed. "Too bad the worst is yet to come."

She warbled in unhappy agreement.

* * *

41

"What of Talon?" taunted Naill.

Kari's irritation flared. Naill, her half-brother, had obviously debriefed the soldiers who accompanied her on the mission. She certainly hadn't mentioned Talon's escape. As usual, Naill was bent on pointing out her shortcomings in front of their father. Even when he could find no fault in her, he delighted in making up lies.

"He's just a smuggler," she shot back, "and by all reports an avowed Neutral. He's never allied himself with the Rebels."

"Fact or assumption? How very convenient, when the point of disagreement has slipped away and cannot be tested."

Kari's eyes narrowed as Naill moved across the expansive communal room to stare out the huge window that stretched from floor to ceiling. His quarters aboard the *Regalia*, the Lochnar military stronghold in orbit about Verdigris, were equipped with the station's largest viewport. The sparkling starlight outlined his tall, slender frame. His hair, thin mustache, and neatly trimmed goatee were as black as the infinite expanse beyond.

"There is no proof Talon has done anything worse than transport contraband cargo," she insisted.

Turning, Naill commented silkily, "Yet you tried to take him prisoner. Now why is that?"

Gritting her teeth, Kari looked to her father. Myklar disliked their bickering so much, he had separated them ten years ago by taking Naill to the *Regalia* and leaving her on Verdigris with a houseful of guardians and trainers. She had been fifteen at the time. She had seen Naill seldom since then, but she had an excellent memory when it came to malicious bullies.

For now, however, Myklar stood neutral, seeming content to let the sibling confrontation run its course. His attention was devoted to a long wall bristling with a display of weapons. He stood with hands clasped behind his straight back, his head with its silver-laced black hair and full beard tilted up to admire Naill's collection of Halflinger daggers, helix-horn swords, primed crossbows, and obsolete phazers.

To the casual observer, Myklar seemed totally preoccupied. But Kari knew he was listening intently. She crossed her arms over her chest, determined to brazen out Naill's taunts. She wouldn't miss this opportunity to prove herself to her father.

"Talon initiated the brawl that almost allowed Rand to escape. When I tried to detain him, he resisted. I thought it best to bring him in for questioning."

"Then why is he not here, enjoying our hospitality?"

"He got away," she snapped. "My soldiers were busy subduing Markos and his men."

Naill snorted. "One lowly smuggler, and you couldn't handle him yourself? A lot of good all your elaborate training has done. Perhaps Father has wasted his efforts on you."

She took a step forward, prepared to demonstrate some of the mocked training by wiping the satisfied smirk from her half-brother's face. Myklar's deep, resigned voice interfered.

"Enough, both of you. Naill, your bitterness is quite tedious. Kari identified and trapped Markos when your men failed to even get close to the High Commander for the past two years." He turned to her and nodded. "You have done well, daughter."

The nod from the Dynast was little more than a dignified inclination of his head, but Kari understood its significance. Her father was proud of her. Her chest swelled with pleasure. After all these years of desperately seeking her father's approval and falling short because he always expected more, he was finally satisfied with the results of her training.

She couldn't resist a gloating glance toward Naill. Their rivalry had been too intense to pass up the opportunity. A muscle twitched at regular intervals along one cheekbone of his lean, hawkish face.

"What do you wish me to do next, Father?" she asked eagerly.

"I realize you have just arrived, but I want you to follow your men on to Narkwar prison and keep an eye on our prisoners."

"Do you suspect the Rebels will try to break them free?" Myklar's graying eyebrows shot up. "Out of that fortress? They wouldn't dare."

"Then why send me there? Surely there must be more important things for me to do?"

"That is my wish," he said firmly. "The warden has sent me very sketchy reports over the last few months. I suspect portions of them may have been falsified. I intend removing him as soon as I can find a suitable replacement. In the meantime, I need someone trustworthy to oversee the situation."

Kari winced. Narkwar was hardly the assignment she would have chosen. Then again, anything capable of provoking that delightful expression of fury on Naill's face was worth a few sacrifices. If it would increase Myklar's confidence in her—

"Yes, Father. I will leave immediately."

"Excellent."

Naill's snide tone interjected, "Don't let your woman's sensibilities melt you into a puddle of sympathy when you see those poor, pathetic shirkers in the detention blocks."

"I'm a soldier first, Naill."

"That remains to be seen," he retorted with a sneer.

Turning away before he could manipulate her into another argument, she stormed to the door. If there was ever a piece of tarpan dung disguised as human, it was Naill.

She punched the activator button with a force that threatened to shatter the cordite covering, but she didn't care. Perhaps a bit of damage could begin to repay the cruel taunts and dirty tricks Naill had used to plague her growing years.

On second thought, that much damage would necessitate disabling the *Regalia* and sending it plunging from orbit to crash into Verdigris.

Her headlong march was halted abruptly when she saw the small man blocking her exit.

"Penn," she greeted the new arrival with a curt nod of her head that, hopefully, displayed her total lack of enthusiasm. Penn Tebrooke, or Naill's shadow as she thought of the man, generated almost as many feelings of disgust as her half-brother.

The Gent'Sian bowed. "Jemara Solis." As he straightened, his sandaled feet peeked out from under his shapeless cream-colored robes. "Welcome to the *Regalia*. I am pleased to learn of the success of your first series of missions."

Gent'Sians were always unfailingly polite. Kari gave Penn that much credit, even though it was a smarmy, self-serving type of courtesy. She critically eyed the copper-skinned man, who stood no taller than her nose. Penn was human, all right; Gent'Sians were descended from her own race, the Jem'Adal. All humans in the solar system were byproducts of the aggressive colonization by the Jem'Adal two centuries ago. However, 180 years of isolation and selective inbreeding among a group preferring to focus completely on intellectual development had generated its own race.

Penn was typical of the Gent'Sia, with his frail body and enlarged head. His thin, pale hair marked a strange contrast to his copper-tinted skin, which had come from generations of ingesting water and plant life from the iron-rich regions of Avernus. He was also typical, Kari thought with disdain, of the race that had evolved intellectually to the point of being unable to defend itself physically. Gent'Sians were very good at ingratiating themselves to the Jem'Adal, who were quite capable of providing the needed protection.

Kari couldn't understand how her father and Naill tolerated the subtle ego-stroking at which Penn and his kind excelled. It was nauseating, really, but they seemed to thrive on it.

"Thank you for the compliment, Penn, though I'm sure you didn't tap into your shallow supply of sincerity to come up with that one. Now, get the blazes out of my way."

She waited until the slender man stepped aside, then continued down the hallway. Long since, she'd discovered it didn't pay to be polite to Penn. Any kind word tended to make him think she was succumbing to his oily, diplomatic charm.

"She is not as capable of command as I." Naill vented his frustration the moment the door closed behind Kari. He faced his father, struggling to control his rising temper.

"True," agreed Myklar. "That will change over time, however." The lines at the corners of his eyes deepened as he smiled slightly. "You may have noticed it is already changing."

"She hasn't my experience. You place your trust in a novice."

"Trust. Now there's a key word." Myklar lifted a knuckler from the assortment of weapons on the display wall. His hand smoothed over the heavy metal ball with its short handle. "I have absolute faith in Kari's loyalty. She will obey my orders explicitly. Sometimes I'm not so sure of you, Naill."

"I'm your son. Of course you can trust me, Father."

Myklar tilted his chin down and gazed at Naill from beneath bushy brows, until his son had the aggravating urge, quickly stifled, to shift from one foot to the other. "I'll keep that in mind," rumbled Myklar in a wry tone.

"She has bewitched you," Naill snapped. "You cater to her every need and train her to succeed you as Dynast. All for the sake of your own archaic beliefs . . . and that woman." He stepped forward and plucked a primed crossbow from its wall mount. When he pressed his middle finger to one of the three broad-tipped arrows the sharp point pricked his skin. He sucked the trickle of blood.

"You had best be careful how you speak of Kari's mother, Naill," warned Myklar stiffly. "I have beaten you for your attitude in the past. You know I would not hesitate to do so again. Do not despoil Isolde's memory with your jealousy."

"For thirteen years you have worshiped the memory of a woman who did not love you," Naill persisted furiously, "who very likely hated you for destroying her family in your ascent to power, though she never voiced her bitterness. A woman who gave up living when Kari was twelve, and walked into the forest on Verdigris to die. For this you deny your son his birthright."

"Enough!" roared Myklar. "Before my military might ousted the consular family from power, the Lochnar Line hadn't a hope in rotting hell of ascending to a high title. The Khazanjian Consularship remained unbroken for nearly three centuries. Kari is acceptable heir of both bloodlines. It is an advantage you cannot hope to duplicate in the hearts of the people. They fear me, but when I die this entire solar system will erupt into war if you succeed as Dynast."

"You give me no opportunity to try," cried Naill. He jerked the crossbow to his shoulder, aimed it at one of the overstuffed chairs grouped in the center of the room, and pulled the center trigger. The largest of the three arrows embedded deep in the chair with a muffled thunk.

Myklar didn't even blink. "Accept it, Naill, for I remain firm in my decision. Kari will be Heir. I will tolerate your attitude and your bitterness for now, since it has the beneficial effect of honing your leadership skills. But beware; my patience will only stretch so far, even for you. If you attempt to tell her the details of her family's downfall, of which even you are unsure, you will find my revenge swift and sure. I leave for now to inspect the construction of the *Viceroy*, in orbit about Avernus. The completion of the new military station will strengthen my hold upon the planets."

With that, Myklar turned sharply and left the room.

Naill stood in silent rage, his frustration like a corrosive acid eating away at his insides. His hand clenched on the cold metal of the crossbow. He gave in to the impulse to whip the weapon into firing position again. The two remaining arrows joined their mate in the hapless chair. The crushing anger receded a bit. He rehung the empty crossbow on the wall.

Penn drifted out of the shadows.

"It never fails to impress me, Lord Naill, the courage you display in standing up to your father. A lesser man would cringe before Myklar's reputation of ruthlessness."

"My father has mellowed, Penn," Naill muttered in disgust. "He forgives Kari a mistake that five years ago would have occasioned a beating for any minion who botched an assignment. Regardless of what Myklar says, without capturing that slippery smuggler Talon, her mission was incomplete."

"Perhaps age and the burden of responsibility weigh heavily upon Myklar, dulling the ruthless edge," offered Penn. He folded his arms into the bell-shaped sleeves of his robe, the picture of dignified serenity.

"Regardless of the reason, Father is going to ruin everything," Naill snarled.

"But soon all that will change."

"Yes. Yes," Naill repeated slowly, taking a deep breath. "My plans are going forward well, aren't they, Penn?"

"Yes, Lord Naill. Your strategic brilliance is beginning to gain the expected results."

"Bayne is a definite glitch, however." He began to pace. "I managed to manipulate my father into capturing the man, though I didn't expect Myklar to send that little bitch.

I'm unsure how much Bayne knows of my plans. I cannot risk him talking."

"Indeed not."

"And that blasted rebel, Markos. How much does he know?"

"Uncertain, my lord. Apparently Jemara Kari intercepted Bayne before he could meet with Markos, but there is no way of knowing what communiques they had prior to that."

"Exactly, Penn. I cannot risk either of them leaking a hint of my plans."

"Shall I send a special request to your man inside Narkwar prison, my lord?"

Naill stopped abruptly. "I wish we could. It would be so much simpler that way," he muttered. "Unfortunately, my father has sent Kari to Narkwar. The little bitch will rush back screaming of treachery if she arrives to find her prisoners dead. If only there was a way to keep Markos and Bayne alive, yet totally incapable of rational thinking, much less talk."

"May I suggest your recent discovery as an alternative?"

"Ah, yes," drawled Naill in long, satisfied tones. He laughed deeply. "Perfect. I knew that substance would prove useful, though I lost three of my men before I realized the source of the symptoms. Once again you have provided me with inspiration, Penn."

The Gent'Sian bowed. "I do try to be useful, my lord."

"She will be leaving at any moment. Send a ship after her through the Corridor, at an anonymous distance, with a special delivery for Narkwar."

Chapter Four

"We're in!" Quinn cried triumphantly. "I have satellite linkup with Narkwar's system."

Talon's mouth twisted in a grim parody of a smile. He wished he could share the enthusiasm of the young Rebel, who couldn't be any older than nineteen. But Rand was imprisoned in the moon fortress now visible through the cockpit window, and the members of the infiltration team might die in the rescue attempt. Talon's arguments for leaving Quinn behind on Serac had been ignored, particularly by Quinn himself. The lad had been recruited on this mission for his talent in pirating computers.

"Wow, Talon, this override code is great. Narkwar Central is not even aware of the breach. I can scramble the guards' shift duties. Hey, you want me to electronically unlock all the detention cells in the prison at one time?" Quinn looked up expectantly, his fingers poised over the keyboard. Eager blue eyes blinked at Talon from between strands of lanky hair.

"Slow down, kid. Don't tinker with anything that could draw unwanted attention. Those are real guards, with real weapons, we have to slip past to get to Rand and Arden, not just names on a duty roster. Just stick to the agenda I gave you, all right?"

"Sure, Talon," Quinn agreed with a shrug. "What was the override code again? I didn't see you enter it the first time. Boy, I can really crack some first-class systems with this baby."

"Afraid that won't be the case."

"What do you mean?"

"Let's just say it's classified."

"Ah, no, Talon, say you don't mean it," Quinn said in obvious dismay. His fingers moved furiously across the keyboard, trying to recall the code Talon had entered on their approach.

"Don't bother, kid. I set it for auto-erase."

"You don't intend to share it with us?" challenged Kjell from the pilot's seat. His angry glare never left Talon's face as he set the ship on auto-approach and stood up.

The other four members of the team, seated about the cabin, shifted restlessly. And why shouldn't they be nervous? The barely leashed hostility between himself and Kjell had simmered ever since the confrontation at Inclement. Very likely things would have come to blows by now if Talon hadn't made the twenty-six-hour trip from Serac alone, rendezvousing with the team once they reached the far side of Narkwar moon, where he left the *Nighthawk* in synchronized orbit.

"Sorry; trade secret," Talon answered evenly. "Besides, I can't guarantee the code's reliability or longevity. It's override clearance might be deactivated at any moment."

"Where, exactly, did it come from?" Kjell persisted.

"From a . . . friend on Star Alpha. That's all I can say. Smuggler's code of confidence. You know how it goes, Kjell."

"If it was anyone else other than Rand in there, I wouldn't trust you. But for some reason you want him out as badly as we do, so I'm willing to take the risk. Though, as far as I'm concerned, you're a poor bet under the best of circumstances."

Talon tasted the bitterness of truth and resented it. Kjell had no tangible reason to trust him. And he was a risk, more than they knew. "Fair enough. And don't worry—I'll disappear once Rand is safe," he offered sarcastically.

"How do you know so much about Narkwar, when no

one imprisoned there has ever lived to tell about it?"

"Another trade secret, I'm afraid," Talon said deliberately, knowing it would annoy the Rebel second-in-command. It worked. Kjell spun away, swearing under his breath.

"Narkwar is hailing us, sir," whispered Quinn, disrupting the tense atmosphere in the cabin.

Talon turned and leaned forward eagerly, one hand braced on the console, the other on the arm of Quinn's chair. "Transmit the identification code you pirated from the shuttle's computer."

Quinn complied.

The comm crackled with static, then a voice came from the surface. "Lochnar shuttle Tarsus X-L-niner, this is Narkwar command central. State your origin and business."

Talon answered, "Got a little present for your warden. Three Rebel prisoners we picked up on Serac."

"Really? I hear it's difficult to dig those cowards out of their bolt-holes. Where did you find them?"

Talon glanced over his shoulder. A grin tugged at his mouth. "With their zipstraps undone, making yellow snow."

"My, those Rebel shirkers are getting careless lately. We'll soon run out of detention cells." The prison comm engineer laughed, enjoying his own lame joke.

Talon fully appreciated the sight of Kjell's fierce scowl.

"You're cleared for landing, Tarsus X-L-niner. Deliver your prisoners to Detention Block 4."

"Acknowledged." Talon switched off the comm to cut transmission. "You still have computer linkup?" he asked Quinn. The kid nodded. "Good. So, where are they?"

Quinn queried the system. "Detention Block 6. Cells Two, Three and . . . Rand's in Nine."

"You're a natural at this, kid." Quinn beamed at the compliment. "Now, switch our orders from Block four to six so we can deliver our 'prisoners' to the right place. Identify all security camera grids in the guardroom and hallways of Block six, plus the ones in our boys' cells. Enter freeze-image commands across all targeted grids. And a disable on the alarm would be convenient. Any problem with that?"

"Nope," muttered Quinn in a distracted tone. "I'm on it. You want me to sabotage the shields for our exit?"

"Kid, I like how you think. If I'm ever looking for a protégé . . ."

Quinn glanced up with a wistful expression. "I wish I was going after Rand and Arden with you."

Talon's smile vanished. "No, you don't," he said flatly. "Besides, we need you to maintain the craft for our escape."

Kjell took the controls again as the shuttle swept down across the brown, pockmarked surface of the moon. The ship rapidly approached the stark tan walls of the prison built into the side of an immense crater, and shot through the brightly lit opening of the hangar bay. As Kjell set the ship onto the deck, Talon clipped a black utility belt over his slate gray flight suit and adjusted the shoulder strap diagonally across his chest.

"Beryl, time to go."

"This is idiotic, Talon," protested Kjell as he set the ship on standby. "We can't take a Sylph along. She'll draw attention like a beacon with those sparkling scales."

"No, she won't. Watch." Beryl flew to his chest, stretched her body along the diagonal strap, and folded her wings back in a smooth, seamless line. With a tiny shudder that rippled along her scales, the Sylph turned the same black as the leather to which she clung.

"Stars in heaven," breathed one of the Rebels in amazement.

Kjell let out a low whistle. "The perfect camouflage. I didn't know they could do that."

"How much time have you spent around Sylphs?" asked Talon.

"Next to none. As you know, they're exceedingly rare."

"Yeah, right," Talon said sardonically. "Beryl will be able to smell or hear any guards better than we can. She also has a mission of her own. We've heard rumors that the warden, Urkanis, has a Sylph at the complex. He has a nasty hobby of cultivating exotic plants from Avernus, each with its own variety of poison. He gets his thrills from experimenting with various derivatives on the prisoners. But he can't keep the plants thriving without a Sylph, can he, Beryl?"

She purred a muffled warble of agreement against his chest. He ran a gentle hand down her folded black wings.

"Too late for me to argue about it now," Kjell grumbled.

"Exactly." Talon pressed the hatch release.

Three of the soldiers fastened specially modified wrist restraints behind their backs. The team descended the ramp into the stale, cold air of the hangar bay. Two prison guards, in drab brown suits, eyed them with only token interest. Quinn closed the hatch and remained on the shuttle.

The team struck out with their three prisoners under escort. Halfway to their destination, Talon dropped a little behind the others, then stopped. He could feel the tension in Beryl's tiny body. He didn't need to hear the words in his mind to know the direction of her thoughts.

"Yes, little jewel," he murmured. "That's the passageway to the warden's quarters. Are you sure you'll be okay?"

"Get her I must."

"I know," Talon agreed softly. "Just make sure you meet us back at the ship on time."

Beryl's light weight pressed against his chest as she pushed off. Her color flashed back to a vivid blue-green, a bold contrast to the bland tan background of the walls, as she flew down the hall and disappeared around a corner.

She was going into danger, alone. Talon tensed with worry and the urge to help her, but Rand needed him more. Just as he caught up with the others, the team boarded the turbolift to Detention Block 6.

One good thing had come from his incarceration at Narkwar; he had found Beryl here. She had been the prison warden's "pet," trapped on Verdigris and brought here. The grim environment and the cruel purposes of the plants she tended were slow death to a Sylph's soul.

Talon had rescued her from a sad, short future by taking her with him when he escaped. Beryl had used her nectar to treat the wounds he'd suffered during the escape. There was no doubt she'd saved his life. She insisted he had saved her's.

He had gained a companion in his lonely life, albeit one whose bossy temperament sometimes made him feel like tossing her out the airlock. She had gained a protector and someone who indulged a Sylph's second love, next to tending growing things—the ability to fly beyond where their own wings could carry them.

The guard on duty in the main corridor of Detention Block 6 stepped forward with a frown, apparently ready to question their right to be there. Kjell silenced him with a quick blow to the neck. The other four Rebels slipped through the doorway of the guard station. The sounds of a struggle were brief, with no shouts of warning. Talon's mouth tilted in a wry grin. The members of Kjell's handpicked team were worth their weight in raw kaelinite from the jewel mines of Avernus.

Talon bent to the unconscious guard in the corridor and plucked the key sequencer from his belt. As the Rebel soldiers reemerged from the guardroom, he attached the small, flat disc to the lock panel of cell 2, where it clung magnetically as it clicked off the electronic combination. With a muffled clank, the metal bolt released.

Talon pulled open the door.

Arden jerked to a sitting position on his cot. He fixed Talon with a look of stunned surprise. Talon thought the reaction odd, until he realized that he was the last man Arden would expect to come to the rescue. Regret left a bitter taste on Talon's tongue. Yet another thing of value was missing in his life—having the respect of his brother's men.

"Are you coming or not?" Talon snapped, disgusted at his own yearnings. He turned away.

Arden leapt to his feet, following close behind. Talon detached the key sequencer and started toward the adjacent cell. His reach was brought up short as Arden gripped his arm.

"What is it?"

"I'm not sure what you'll find in there," Arden warned.

A chill ran down Talon's spine. There was no mistaking the genuine dread in the other man's voice. "Why? What did you see?"

"Nothing. They haven't removed me from my cell since we were brought here. It's what I've heard since last night. Screams, curses, pounding on the wall. Gave me the creeps."

"You're saying he was tortured?"

"I don't know." His grip on Talon's arm tightened. "Please tell me that's not Rand in there," he pleaded hoarsely.

"No. Prison files record this as Bayne's cell." Arden relaxed noticeably and released his hold. Talon felt no such relief. A sense of horror rippled through him as he glanced down the hall toward Rand's cell. Bayne's capture had been a coup for Kari Solis, but Rand was the real prize. Though a sense of urgency tore at Talon to hurry to his brother, he suddenly did not feel adequately prepared to face what he might discover in his cell. He had to confront the lesser demons here first.

He unlocked and opened the cell door.

Bayne sat huddled on the floor, whimpering. His red hair hung limply about his face. His eyes shifted with an expression of unfocused panic. The cot and table were overturned. A mangled chair had been used to gouge scratches in the wall.

Talon knew exactly how Arden felt. The hair along his nape tingled.

"Bayne?" he whispered.

The prisoner's head jerked up. His eyes focused, but not with a lucid expression. Surrounded by white, they appeared more like those of a cornered wild animal than a rational man's.

"Who are you?" Bayne rasped.

"Rand's friends. We've come to get you out of here."

The man scrambled to his feet and cowered deeper into his corner. "Liar," he accused with a plaintive moan. "You've come to kill me. I know it. I've known it all along."

Talon frowned. "The prison guards wish to hurt you, not us. We're here to help."

"Liar. You've murder in your evil hearts. I'm unarmed, helpless, and you know it," Bayne said breathlessly, his voice accelerating and rising in pitch with each accusation.

"What's the matter with him?" Talon heard one of the men whisper behind him. "Did the torture drive him mad?"

"No," Talon said darkly, "this is something different." He swallowed hard. Would they find Rand in this same condition?

Kjell stepped forward, taking a stride past Talon. "Relax, Bayne. I realize you don't recognize Talon, but we've met."

"I know you. You're the devil," Bayne cried. "You enjoy my pain and suffering, don't you? The only one worse is that bastard, Naill Solis. Well, when his grand plans are finalized you'll all destroy one another. No more Rebellion. No more anything," he taunted, laughing.

"What grand plans, Bayne? Are you referring to the new Lochnar station, the *Viceroy*?" Talon demanded.

"I won't tell! You'll steal what I know, then torture me."

Stepping forward again, hands raised palms up in a gesture of nonaggression, Kjell coaxed, "Bayne, let us help—"

With surprising speed that caught every Rebel in the crowded room off balance, Bayne leaped forward and grabbed Kjell's sword from its sheath. With an almost incoherent shout about not undergoing any more suffering, he swung at Kjell's skull. The Rebel's left arm shot up to block the blow. The clang of impacting metal resounded through the room as the blade came up short against his forearm guard.

Bayne stepped back and raised the weapon again.

"Kjell!" Talon shouted, then tossed his sword to the unarmed man. Catching it by the hilt, Kjell struck a defensive posture.

Bayne lunged again, this time for his chest. The Rebel leader countered. Instead of recovering for another strike, Bayne continued to drive forward with his weapon lowered. Kjell tried to pull back at the last instant, but the smaller man spread his arms and allowed his momentum to impale him on the sword.

Bayne smiled slowly before his eyes closed for the last time, as if death were a great release. His body slumped to the floor, sliding free of Talon's blade.

Kjell bent to wipe the blade on Bayne's jumpsuit. He rose and returned the sword to Talon.

"Sorry, Talon," he said raggedly. "I didn't mean to bloody your blade for such a vile purpose."

"It's better than dying," Talon responded gravely as he sheathed the Singh Dubh. "You had no choice, Kjell. There was no doubt he meant to kill you if he found an opening, or any of us, for that matter." He looked down at Bayne's crumpled body, then added in a hoarse whisper, "And there was no way of knowing he meant to throw himself on the sword. Runagate hell, what so haunted the man that he would take his own life?"

"What will Rand say?" Kjell said grimly. "The information Bayne carried died with him."

"I think we'd best worry whether Rand will be capable of saying anything at all," Talon bit out. A chilling silence filled the room as the Rebels grasped his meaning.

Talon gladly left the grim scene in Bayne's cell.

"This is it," he said tensely as they reached cell 9. He unlocked the door and stepped anxiously into the room.

Not the smartest move he'd ever made, the thought registered as 190 pounds of solid muscle launched at him from the side. The collision knocked him flat to the floor. He lay unmoving, not so much from the impact as the incredulity of seeing his own brother, snarling like a crazed animal, reaching for his throat. Not until hands like durasteel manacles cut off his air and pinched off his carotids did Talon realize this was really happening. He grasped Rand's wrists in desperation.

"You thought I was just going to wait in here until you came to kill me?" Rand shouted. "If I die, you'll die with me!"

Kjell and two of the Rebels recovered from their shock and pounced on Rand, dragging him loose. Their commander, apparently no more able to recognize his men than his brother, lunged frantically against their hold and let loose a string of oaths.

"Let him go," Talon rasped, struggling to his feet and massaging his bruised throat. Fear that they might hurt Rand—or that Rand might hurt himself—tied his gut into knots. The debacle in Bayne's cell filled him with cold terror of a repeat performance.

The Rebels released Rand. He retreated against the far wall and faced Talon in a half-crouch, breathing hard, his eyes narrowed. Though he seemed ready for battle, he also trembled violently, his hands clenched spasmodically, the muscles of his throat working as he swallowed over and over.

Talon signaled the men to move away. As they backed out of the cell, Talon handed his sword and Valken dagger to Kjell. They shared a look of concern and perfect understanding. Kjell hustled his men, and their weapons, beyond Rand's reach, leaving Talon alone with a wild-eyed maniac who was almost a stranger.

"Rand," Talon urged in a soothing tone. "It's some kind of drug, isn't it? Whatever it is, you've got to fight it. Don't let it beat you. We're here to free you, to take you home."

With a roar, Rand lunged for him again. So much for the diplomatic approach, Talon thought bitterly as he quickly dodged to the side. He swung his fist in a hard right cross, all the more powerful because of the desperation behind it. He had to get Rand out of this hellhole. Pain lanced through his fist as it connected with Rand's square jaw. The force of the blow slammed his brother into the wall, where he slid to the floor.

Heat pricked behind Talon's eyes as he stared down at his unconscious brother. Blinking rapidly, he soothed the raging anger clawing at his insides and calmed his fears with promises of vengeance. That auburn-haired witch was responsible for this. He was going to hunt her down until he could wrap his fingers around her mercenary little throat.

"Stars," hissed one of the Rebels as the group reentered the cell. "What's wrong with him?"

"I don't know," Talon said thickly as he donned his weapons again, "but I'd suggest we get him out of here before he wakes up. We'll never make it back to the shuttle if the liberated prisoner keeps insisting on attacking his rescuers."

Kari stepped into Narkwar Security Central and prowled restlessly before the triple-decker row of video screens. The operator eyed her nervously. Not surprising, after the raging argument she'd had last night with the warden, Gar Urkanis.

She paused before the screens projecting from the detention cells of her three prisoners. Arden lay on his cot with his fingers interlaced behind his head. Bayne sat huddled in the corner, cowering. Her dislike of the cowardly man increased.

She eyed Markos at length as he sat on his cot, both hands shoved into his thick hair, his gaze fixed on the floor. Despite his role in the Rebellion against her father, Markos was one man she was coming to respect. With dignity, and an extreme stubbornness almost matching that of Talon, the commander had withstood the intense interrogation she'd begun after her arrival at Narkwar.

Urkanis had insisted on taking over the process, using his own methods . . . without her present to interfere. She'd refused, of course, which led to the argument that had reverberated throughout the detention block. Urkanis had taken perverse pleasure in predicting that her father would be most displeased with her lack of success.

A shiver ran through Kari at the thought of facing her father's anger. Still, she couldn't bring herself to torture Markos. There was no dignity, no honor, in putting a man through enough physical punishment that he betrayed his friends. She preferred the direct approach. Though it might take longer, she would find the Rebel factions without any leads.

Her gaze narrowed as she regarded Markos. He didn't look well. Perhaps she should check on him. It didn't seem natural, the way he was sitting still for so long.

In fact, he hadn't moved at all.

Kari glanced sharply at the other two screens. Arden and Bayne hadn't shifted so much as a centimeter. "Move over, you idiot," Kari snapped at the video operator. He quickly complied, staring at her as if she'd lost her mind.

She queried a log of command entries for the past twenty minutes. There it was, a freeze-image command on certain cam locations, as well as a disable on the alarm system. Everything was authorized by her own override code, the one she'd used at Star Alpha. Kari went rigid, pure fury tightening every muscle.

Talon was here.

Her clenched fist struck the top of the console. She tried a reset on the alarm. The computer refused. Blazes, locked out by her own code. Talon was going to pay dearly for this.

"Where's the manual alarm?" she barked at the operator.

He pointed mutely at a lever in the wall next to the door. She rushed over and yanked it down. A rhythmic, teeth-grating siren began sounding throughout the whole complex.

"I want a squad of guards to meet me at Detention Block 6 in two minutes. Forget the ones stationed there. They're obviously out of commission. I'll take my own men as well."

"But—"

"Do it!" she demanded, then slammed out of the room.

The operator eyed his screen, choked as he saw the freeze-image commands, and hit the comm to the central guardroom.

"Alarm!" yelped Arden needlessly.

"Talon, hurry," hissed Kjell.

"It's too late. The guards will easily cut us off if we take the obvious route out." Talon looked at the expectant faces around him. Six men, unfamiliar with Narkwar, who were counting on him to find a way out of this tangle for themselves and Rand.

"Take the alternative route I mapped out for you. I'll draw them away with this." He used his dagger to slice through a wristband strapped to the unconscious Rand's forearm. "It's a tracker. They'll think I'm Rand, and follow."

"You must be joking," protested Kjell. "You don't stand a chance by yourself."

"I did it once. I'll do it again."

Kjell stared at him. "You were imprisoned at Narkwar?"

"Three years."

A new understanding dawned in Kjell's eyes. "Then

come with us, man. You don't want to get trapped here again."

"What chance do we stand taking on the entire prison garrison?"

"Next to none," Kjell agreed grudgingly. "How are you going to get out?"

Talon thought of the *Nighthawk*, in orbit on the far side of the moon. "I'll steal a ship and get back to my own. Don't worry. Take Rand to Serac. Boreas has the best med facilities. Leave the moment you get him aboard the shuttle."

With a grim nod, Kjell ushered his team out. Two of the men dragged Rand with his arms looped over their shoulders. Kjell turned just as the others preceded him down the hallway. "We'll give you eight minutes to meet us at the shuttle."

"Like runagate hell you—"

"What about Beryl?" Kjell cut him off sharply. "You want us to abandon her?"

Talon's jaw clenched. "She'll want to go back to my ship."

"We'll swing around and drop her through a docking sphincter, same way we picked you up."

"Thanks," Talon said gruffly.

"Just make it to the shuttle on time. I don't want to explain to Rand why you didn't come back with us."

"The signal leads here? Are you certain?"

"Yes, Jemara Solis," the prison guard answered. He held the palm-sized tracking unit out before him, panning back and forth at the juncture of two passageways. "Down the left," he whispered tensely, then moved in the indicated direction.

The other five guards from the squad that had met her at Detention Block 6 hurried after him. Kari and her own men—five soldiers who had accompanied her to Narkwar—followed more cautiously with swords drawn. The

Rebels were capable of violence, as demonstrated by their killing of Bayne.

The lead man with the tracking unit stopped. He moved the device to the left, then the right; then he turned full circle before pausing with a crease of confusion on his brow.

"I've lost direction. The signal is indistinct, as if—" the guard murmured, pausing to look around his feet.

"As if you were standing right on top of it," Kari finished for him. She glanced up at the grating overhead, commenting dryly, "Or right underneath. Captain Benkyr, would you mind?" she said to the ranking officer of her own entourage.

The captain grasped her about the waist, lifting her up until she could slip her fingers through the metal grating. When he lowered her again Rand's wristband was cradled in her palm.

The six prison guards burst into action. Three of their squad, boosted up on the others' bent knees, ripped open the grating and cautiously poked their heads through the ragged opening in the ceiling, stun wands and swords poised and ready.

Kari rolled her eyes in disgust. "This was a deliberate plant, gentlemen. I'm sure our quarry is long gone." She tapped the commlink clipped to her breastplate. "Security Central, respond. Have you found their ship yet?"

"A shuttle docked in Bay Two, but it's Lochnar, and it transmitted the right approval codes for prisoner delivery."

"The ship, as well as the codes, were obviously stolen," Kari responded irritably, thinking that her own carelessness with her code had handed a decisive advantage to Talon. "Get at least a dozen men down on the deck to surround the ship. Now."

The comm clicked, with no response from the Security operator. There was a moment of static; then it clicked again.

"Jemara Solis," came a new, unwelcome voice. "This is Warden Urkanis. What the hell is going on?"

"A Rebel team has broken Rand Markos out of his cell."

"Ridiculous. You must be mistaken. Security is too tight."

"Nevertheless, Markos is missing from his cell. Are you suggesting your men misplaced him, or that he just walked out?"

"Of course not," Urkanis said with a snort. "Markos is in no condition to—"

Kari frowned when the warden failed to finish his comment. "What do you mean?" she prompted suspiciously.

"Nothing. Well, never say I'm not cooperative. I've dispatched a squad of men to watch this suspicious shuttle."

"Only six men? That's absurd. Double the guard."

"I'm sorry, but my only other available squad has been given duty elsewhere. Something of value to me has disappeared."

Kari swore under her breath and switched off the comm channel. The prison guards watched her expectantly. Between clenched teeth, she commanded, "Get down to Bay Two. Keep anyone from boarding that blazing shuttle."

"They were useless, anyway," commented Captain Benkyr as the resident security trotted off.

"Agreed." She tightened her grip on the wristband. "Someone created a diversion with this tracker, someone who is trying to draw us away from Markos. I want that man caught."

The captain nodded crisply. "Which way, Jemara?"

She paused, then murmured thoughtfully, "He's separated from his group. His expected escape route is cut off. Which is the only ship on this rock worth stealing?"

"Ours, in Hangar Bay Three." Benkyr straightened abruptly as he grasped her meaning.

"Exactly. Let's go."

They caught a turbolift down to Bay 3, just in time to find Talon with a panel open beneath the *Artemis*, attempting to cross-wire the hatch. He spun around and drew his sword. Her soldiers pulled their own weapons and attacked him, five against one.

Though the odds were hopelessly against him, Talon fought furiously, injuring two of her men before the captain broke through his guard. A hot surge of horror—something she didn't understand, should not have felt—rushed through Kari the instant she saw Benkyr gather momentum for his lunge.

"No!" she shouted. Benkyr froze, stopping just in time. "I want the smuggler uninjured." She stepped forward. "Well, Talon? Do you wish to stay in one piece, or play the martyr?"

Though his eyes flared with animosity and defiance, Talon couldn't fight the fact that Benkyr's blade hovered a hair's breadth from his belly. He dropped his sword. The men leaped forward and grabbed him by the arms, forcing him to his knees.

Her commlink beeped. Kari tapped it impatiently.

"What is it now?"

"Jemara." Despite the background noise from the hangar bay, Kari recognized the voice of the guard with the tracking unit. "I'm afraid we're too late. The Rebels escaped on the shuttle."

Kari swore under her breath. "Track them."

"Uh . . . we can't, Jemara. The craft has circled around behind the moon. In such close proximity, the gravity fields completely distort our sensor scans."

"Urkanis has sent out pursuit vehicles, I trust."

"Well, no. Some computer override has set all craft on standby. The engineer says they're locked into a maintenance check. If he interrupts the sequence, the computer will assume system failure and route them into complete shutdown."

"Why am I not surprised?" Kari retorted. She plucked the prison commlink off her armor and dropped it on the floor, grinding it beneath her boot heel. Her own ship wasn't even initiated for launch sequence. By the time they cleared the hangar bay the Rebels would be long gone. Rand Markos was lost to her, thanks to this son of a tarpan. She turned slowly to face Talon. The satisfaction in his unflinching brown gaze thrust deeply into her growing sense of failure.

"No doubt you realize how much trouble you're in," she said with every bit of hostility she was feeling.

"The thought has crossed my mind, Princess."

"Stop calling me that," she snapped.

"A little unpleasant reminder from our first meeting, eh? You know, I have only one regret from that encounter."

"Just one? I have several. And what would yours be?"

"Instead of just knocking you flat on your backside," he growled, "I should have kissed you. Long and hot, with a lot of tongue-tunneling to see if there really is a woman beneath that soldier's garb." His insolent gaze traveled over her from neck to toe. "Though I doubt it."

Something ripped through Kari's chest at the insult. She could swear it was a physical pain, which was ludicrous. Words couldn't cause such hurt. Nevertheless, before she realized what she was doing, Kari lashed out with her right leg in retaliation. The side of her boot caught Talon across the jaw with an outer crescent kick. He sagged forward against the soldiers' grip.

She threaded her fingers through his brown hair. The unwelcome thought intruded that his hair was amazingly thick and soft. Her mouth flattened in a cynical line. Anything so sensually pleasant was a waste of nature on this troublemaker.

Lifting his head to confirm that he was, indeed, unconscious, she noticed, with a strange sense of relief, that she hadn't broken the skin on his ruggedly handsome face. Her eyes narrowed at the neatly knitted wound from their last encounter. He had healed quickly, without need of sutures. Grinding her teeth, Kari let his chin fall back against his chest.

She glared at her men. The smiles twitching at the corners of their mouths disappeared instantly.

"We're taking him with us. It's a fourteen-hour trip through the Verdigran Corridor to the *Regalia*. Make sure he stays unconscious the whole way, even if you have to drug him. I've had all I can take of his sarcastic tongue." She stopped cold. Her own choice of words, combined with Talon's threat, crafted a mental image of herself imprisoned in his strong arms, his tongue aggressively exploring her soft mouth and sending her senses spiraling out of control like an Avernian desert whirlwind. She shook her head, jarring loose the disturbing image. Irritably, she added, "Begin an immediate scan for his ship. The *Nighthawk* must be close by. I want it. Take it under tow once we've launched."

Chapter Five

Talon realized where he was within a few moments of waking: a detention cell. He was no longer at Narkwar, however. The cells in the moon prison were lined with tan, opaque eracylite. Here he was surrounded by polished black metal. There was only one other Lochnar stronghold where he could be: the *Regalia*.

Well, if someone had to be captured during the Narkwar raid, it was best him. He hoped Rand, Beryl, and the others had gotten away safely. It was agony not knowing their fates.

He sat up on the narrow cot and discovered how they had transported him. The auburn-haired witch had drugged him. That was the only explanation for this lingering light-headedness. Adrenaline would burn the last of the drug from his system if he could just get his hands on her.

The cell door clanked as the electronic bolt slid back. The door swung open, revealing a pair of wary-looking Lochnar guards, one carrying an armed crossbow and the other a long sword. He smiled wryly. The guards regarded him as a threat. If only they realized he was barely functional at the moment.

"Jemidar Solis wishes to see you," said the crossbow guard.

Talon's smile faded. "The Dynast?"

"No. His son, Naill."

Worse and worse. Talon eyed their weapons warily and

cautioned himself not to make any sudden moves. "Does Jemidar Solis intend to offer me the use of his personal lav?"

The other guard snorted. "Not likely, smuggler."

"Then I suggest you let me use the facilities here first."

The two guards eyed one another uncertainly. "Suppose so," conceded the first. He raised his crossbow, aiming it at Talon's chest. "But don't try anything foolish."

Talon stepped through the door and steered a wide course around them, well clear of the tips of their weapons. Without Beryl along, he didn't want any wounds worse than the ones to his pride, though he couldn't resist adding dryly, "Didn't know an unarmed man in the lav was so dangerous, fellows."

That crack earned him a punch in the back.

It took the two guards, plus four additional men waiting in Naill's quarters, to wrestle Talon to the floor, strip him almost naked, and secure him with shackles hanging from the ceiling.

They were gone now, dismissed by Solis. Only Naill and his Gent'Sian lackey remained, standing before a wall bristling with an assortment of weapons.

Talon, his arms stretched straight overhead, glared at the two men. Thank the stars they hadn't bothered to remove his gloves; otherwise the hard edges of the metal shackles would have cut into the heels of his hands. He wondered why his flight suit had been stripped away, leaving only the skintight black shorts from waist to midthigh. The mystery intensified as the Gent'Sian touched a control panel and water poured down from the ceiling.

The cool liquid ran down Talon's arms, through the curling hair on his chest, and pooled in a puddle under his bare feet.

Naill moved to stand in front of him, his eyes glittering with obvious anticipation. "So good to finally meet you, Talon."

"The pleasure is all yours," Talon snarled.

Naill smiled lazily. "Satisfy my curiosity: Why do you choose smuggling rather than fighting for the Rebellion?"

"Only fools risk martyrdom. There's no profit in heroics."

"Ah, the most basic of motives. Money."

"I'm a very basic sort of fellow, Solis. Uncomplicated in the extreme. Hardly the type from whom you'd hope to extract any valuable information," Talon said meaningfully.

"On the contrary, you must be quite complex if you can successfully lead a team to break Markos out of Narkwar." Naill stroked his goatee. "And kill Bayne."

Talon's muscles twitched in surprise. "We didn't kill him. He attacked us, then threw himself on my sword."

"Indeed. How very convenient for me."

Convenient? Talon's jaw clenched. What did Naill mean? Bayne's dire warning of a grand scheme came back to haunt him. Had those words been more than the fevered rantings of a madman?

"By the way," Naill added, interrupting Talon's speculation, "how did you manage to successfully navigate in Narkwar?"

"Three years there helps a fellow learn his way around."

Naill blinked, betraying his surprise. "You were interned at Narkwar? Odd; my information cells don't reflect as much. But then, my history on you doesn't go back more than six years."

"Just goes to show you're not infallible."

Naill's face hardened. "Prison certainly explains the gloves. Those types of scars are so disfiguring, wouldn't you agree? And so much of a man's identity is lost when the badges of family lineage are burned away," he added maliciously. He moved to a small table in the center of the room and set the shackles' key sequencer down, tapping it with his forefinger, a deliberate taunt if there ever was one. "Besides, after we finish here I'll know every detail about you, all the way back to your insignificant birth."

"I won't give you that satisfaction, you bloody shirker," Talon snarled. His temper was cratering, despite his best efforts to rein it in. It infuriated him that Solis had found an old hurt and shame to exploit. *Where's your self-control?* he cursed himself. *Naill plans to do enough damage to your body without you allowing him to screw with your mind.*

"Oh, you'll talk all right," Naill corrected smoothly. "Penn, bring in the voltaic lizards."

Talon stiffened as the Gent'Sian left the room. Now he knew why Naill had drenched him in water—and it wasn't so he'd take a chill and die slowly of lung congestion.

"A couple of pets of mine."

"I'm familiar with them," Talon responded hoarsely.

Penn returned, wheeling a cart carrying a large, insulated box. Well, Talon told himself firmly, voltaics were preferable to instruments of torture that specialized in drawing blood.

Naill lifted out one lizard, careful to grip it around the wide rib cage. The animal, over half a meter in length, dangled placidly from his hand. Scaleless, it had a thick, nubby skin that provided camouflage in its native environment of Avernus. This one was gray with black speckles, but Talon had seen them in every color ranging from olive green to rust brown. Its golden eyes were set in a broad, triangular head. The long gray tail possessed a chain of black nodules down either side.

Talon had always thought voltaics handsome in their own way. Harmless, they ate only other reptiles, small mammals, and birds. But nature had provided the peaceful creatures one advantage to compensate for their slow-moving physiology; their tails could emit an electric shock sufficient to knock a man flat on his back. Just a touch was all it took. What damage would a prolonged charge cause? Apparently he was about to find out.

"Just in case you were wondering, Talon, they are hungry. And you know what happens when a voltaic is seeking food."

"Runagate hell," Talon hissed under his breath.

Naill walked over and placed the lizard on Talon's left calf. With sticky toes that could carry a voltaic up a smooth durasteel wall, the animal climbed up the side of Talon's thigh. The sensation was almost ticklish. He tensed when Naill dangled a small chunk of meat above the voltaic's nose. Its tail curled downward and wrapped around Talon's knee and upper calf.

The jolt flung his head back and spasmed the muscles of his neck. He couldn't release the contraction on a single muscle in his body—he sure as hell couldn't breathe. Death was a tingling, cold current ruthlessly conducting through his wet body. Too much of this and his heart would fail.

Naill dropped the food into the lizard's mouth. The flow of electricity stopped abruptly as the animal chewed contentedly.

Talon's body sagged in relief.

Naill grinned. "Anything you'd care to tell me?"

"Nothing you'd care to hear, shirker," Talon ground out. He took a deep draught of blessed air. "Besides, you don't want me to talk too soon. Easy capitulation would spoil your fun."

"Very astute. Penn, bring me the other lizard."

Talon swore inwardly as Naill set the other voltaic, this one a deep burgundy, against Talon's chest. Its front feet clung to his collarbone, its back feet to his ribs. He forced himself not to flinch as its tail snaked halfway around his waist.

Another piece of food appeared in Naill's hand. The lizard on Talon's chest responded, sending a vicious jolt though him. The voltaic on his leg joined in out of jealous hunger.

For the sake of his pride Talon was grateful his scream locked in his muscle-spasmed throat.

When Naill quit teasing the lizards, rage filled Talon,

leaving him more shaken than had the voltaics' charge. Rage not only for his own pain, but for the harmless, stupid animals Naill was manipulating for his own vile ends.

"Solis, you're a dead man," Talon said in a low snarl.

"Oh?" Naill laughed. "Markos is in no condition to return the favor of rescue, and you have a decided lack of friends in the right places. There is nothing, and no one, to help you."

Kari stormed down the passageway, thumping her fist against her thigh with each step. She tossed her head, a minuscule expression of her fury. Her heavy braid whipped the side of her jaw. Irritably, she flipped it back over her shoulder.

She had gone down to the detention block to check on Talon. That runagate smuggler was so elusive, she wasn't sure she trusted even her father's well-trained guards to keep a proper eye on him. Sure enough, he was gone, but not of his own volition.

Naill had pulled rank and hijacked her prisoner.

He knew she would never allow this private interrogation, which was why he conveniently forgot to mention it. She punched the button to his quarters with her fist. It cracked. Good.

She stepped into the room and came to an abrupt halt.

"What the blazes do you think you're doing, Naill?" she exploded as she took in the scene. The sight of Talon dangling half naked, reddened strips encircling his waist and leg, filled her with a gut-wrenching fury. She knew the pain the lizards could inflict, having once accidentally come in contact with a voltaic's tail. But beyond the obvious, there was something horribly wrong about seeing a man with Talon's excessive pride a victim of her half-brother's sadistic games. A painful memory arose in her mind's eye—herself as a nine-year-old child, her wrists bound, and Naill laughing as he dropped Batak cave spiders in her hair. She could still hear her own shrieks.

"Interrogating the prisoner, of course," said Naill. He turned, the picture of smug satisfaction. "Something you should have been doing. Yet another failure to exercise your duty."

Naill was still a bully, but she was no longer a helpless, cowering child. Ten years of training had seen to that. She strode forward, growling, "I'm warning you, cut him down."

"I think not."

"He's mine, damn you."

Naill raked back his hair, pushing it off his glistening forehead. The room smelled unpleasantly of sweat and the intangible element of sadistic excitement. "Since when is any Lochnar prisoner your exclusive property?"

"I have prior claim on him. You have no right."

"If you have a protest, I suggest you take it up with Father."

Kari's hands fisted with the growing urge to hit something, preferably Naill, but he would only call his men to throw her out. "You know perfectly well he's still away inspecting the *Viceroy*. His aides tell me he won't be back for three days."

"What a pity. Why don't you send him a message?"

"Transmitting a message has to wait until the station orbits to this side of Avernus. That's seven hours from now. I'd wager my sword you're already aware of the delay. Put Talon back in the detention cell until then. We'll let Father decide."

"I think not," Naill repeated coldly. He moved to the weapons display and took down a Haflinger dagger. Turning it so light flashed from its red metal surface, he ran a thumb lightly across the edge of the broad, curved blade. "This prisoner is a valuable source of information. I'm very close to breaking him."

Kari met Talon's gaze squarely for the first time since entering the room. Stubborn pride and anger glared past the pain in his eyes. She knew he would not be broken. He'd die first.

Guilt flashed through her. This was not what she'd intended. Talon might be a blazing runagate, but he didn't deserve to die this way. And Naill certainly didn't deserve to be handed a victory. Yet the only way she could force him to release Talon was to pit her loyal soldiers against Naill's personal guard, which would create a battle aboard the *Regalia*. Kari cringed to think of her father's reaction to such a debacle.

She couldn't force her hand, but she could use deception.

Moving close to Talon, she carefully avoided the twitching tails of the voltaics. She swallowed convulsively as she faced that broad chest of lean, hard muscle and curling hair, so near she could feel the warmth radiating from his skin. There was no denying he was put together with an artist's touch, though his magnificent physique had more than its fair share of scars.

Keeping her body positioned between Talon and Naill, her hand stole to her waist. Hidden in her utility belt was the injector wand, containing the last of the tranquilizer, which she'd tucked away as they left the *Artemis*.

"I'll certainly never admit you're in the right, Naill," she said, slipping the device into the cradle of her palm, "but Talon did cause me to lose Markos and Bayne. I want revenge. This is as good a way as any for him to die."

She injected Talon with the tranquilizer. His jaw flexed.

"Too afraid to face me on equal terms?" he said softly, his voice vibrating with hostility.

"Just hold on until the next voltaic charge," she whispered. "It will be more convincing that way." She spun away angrily. Blazes, must he always be so uncooperative!

Naill glared at her as she headed for the door. A sense of urgency drove her. She had much to prepare and little time.

"Just save the body for me, Penn," she snapped as she

passed the bowing Gent'Sian on her way out.

Talon stared in stunned fury at Kari's departing back. After his painful struggle against Naill's cruelties she had finished him off in one swift stroke. What else could she have injected except poison? Runagate hell, he hated that woman.

He searched for the pinprick hole in his chest, undetectable since injector wands closed the flesh as they withdrew. It didn't matter. Even if it had created a gaping hole, he'd die from the poison before he bled to death. His vision began to blur.

Naill approached with more meat. Talon felt a chill spread through his system. Lethargy claimed his ravaged body.

"Bloody shirker," he snarled at Naill one last time before the voltaics sent their electric jolts through him. By the time their greedy mouths had been filled Talon had blacked out.

Kari watched from the Security Central video room while Naill, unable to torture an unconscious prisoner, let out a bellow of rage. She smiled grimly. His tantrum looked quite ridiculous from the dual angles of the two ceiling-mounted cams.

Penn moved to Talon's side and gingerly removed the two lizards. Avoiding a pacing Naill, the Gent'Sian replaced the two voltaics in their box. A rare ripple of amusement flashed through Kari as Penn cautiously dumped the remainder of the meat in with the lizards . . . when Naill wasn't looking, of course.

Activating the cameras had been simple. Because they were normally disabled she doubted Naill would even consider the possibility. She'd also been lucky to find a lifelong comrade of her father's on video duty, a man she'd known since childhood. With any other guard she would have been obliged to offer some pretext to order him from the room. With Tislan, she just said she wanted to spy on Naill and he'd left with a chuckle.

He wouldn't have laughed if he knew what else she planned.

She needed some leverage against Naill. Surely she could find something dirty if she looked in the right places. Bringing up a 3-D data map on the computer, she located Naill's file deposit. She requested a condense and download, then ejected the thumb-sized cylinder and tucked it into her utility belt.

Now, one more task to accomplish. She searched the archive of video slips for the *Artemis*'s docking pad and passageways en route. Though she had learned a trick or two from Talon at Narkwar, she would do him one better than freeze-image commands. She loaded the archived slips into the selected units and switched from record to play. Everything looked completely innocent. *Regalia* business as usual . . . old business.

That done, she checked the cams in Naill's quarters once more, just in time to see him storm out. Penn followed. Timing was critical now. Kari shut off the spy cams and snatched up a master key sequencer. This should take care of the shackles.

After checking in both directions down the passageway to make sure no soldiers were in sight, Kari slipped into Naill's quarters. There was no telling when he and Penn would return.

Talon still hung from the ceiling shackles. The fact that Naill had abandoned him there, suspended like an animal carcass in meat storage, generated a caustic burn of anger. Kari moved quickly to his side, a new injector wand gripped in her hand. The offensive smell had departed with Naill. Talon's scent was a sense-tingling combination of musk and spice, not unpleasant . . . if one liked something that blatantly male, she amended quickly.

He raised his head slowly. She recoiled in surprise. He

was supposed to be out cold. With amazement, she realized he had struggled his way back to consciousness, even now fighting the effects of the tranquilizer.

His bloodshot eyes regarded her with a feral expression. "Wait until I get my hands around your scrawny neck," he said in a rough voice she barely recognized.

"Not likely in this millennium, smuggler," she retorted with swift anger. "You are still my prisoner."

"I thought Naill had usurped your questionable authority, and dear old daddy wasn't here to slap his hand," Talon snarled.

Kari ground her teeth. He seemed to take great pleasure in provoking her. "That's about to change." She reached forward.

He flinched away from the wand, as if it were another voltaic lizard. "Going to kill off the evidence, eh? Didn't the first dose do the trick?"

She hesitated, understanding dawning slowly. "You thought I was trying to poison you?" she protested.

"What else? It would fit your pattern to date."

Kari jabbed the wand into his side with more force than necessary. The muscles across his ribs and stomach tightened. He clenched his jaw. She hoped he was biting back a groan.

"For your information this is the antidote for the tranquilizer I gave you earlier," she snapped. "You should be back to your typically charming self in just a few minutes."

She drew her sword and reached up to spring the mechanism over his head. The chain slithered out of the ceiling, barely avoiding hitting Talon as he staggered to one side.

"Watch out for the chain," Kari warned belatedly, smiling with false sweetness.

Talon stood with legs braced apart, swaying slightly. The metal clinked as he massaged the circulation back into his arms. He glared at her with undisguised contempt.

Kari bit back the urge to reveal her plan of secreting him beyond Naill's vindictiveness. He was her prisoner, for galaxy's sake. She certainly didn't owe him any explanations.

With her sword cocked at a warning angle, Kari took the black flight suit draped over her shoulder and shoved it at him. "Here. I swip—er, borrowed this from Supply. I don't know where yours is. Put it on, unless you prefer to display your flesh for the entertainment of the *Regalia* crew."

"If it would embarrass you, it would be worth it," he said sourly, but he reached for the clothing. He raised his wrists. "Any brilliant suggestions on how I dress with these things on?"

She frowned. "They have to come off anyway. You'll draw unwanted attention as we move through the station."

"Am I allowed to ask where we're going?"

"To my ship, the *Artemis*, then down to the surface of Verdigris." That much he would find out soon enough, anyway.

"Aren't you worried your delightful brother will follow?"

"He wouldn't dare. Where we're going, everyone is faithful to me. Naill is disliked intensely there. Hold your arms out straight."

Talon complied. Lifting her blade so it pointed lethally at his abdomen, she reached into her utility belt for the master key sequencer. She used the small electronic disc to unlock both shackles. Talon let the chain drop to the floor.

He stretched. The need to ease cramped muscles was a logical result of his ordeal, Kari told herself, which didn't prevent her gaze from traveling down the perfect symmetry of his chest, lean hips, and muscular legs. The straight lines of his flight suit had hidden much. The black undershorts hid nothing . . . or rather, hid just enough to keep her from flushing red.

He flexed his arms, his face rigid with obvious discomfort. She stared at the bunching muscles . . . sizing up her opponent, of course. The argument had a hollow ring to it.

He stumbled as he stepped into the borrowed suit, almost going to his knees. She reached out automatically with her left hand, then snatched it back before he could look up and see the gesture. Even if he was still groggy from the drug, Talon deserved to fall flat on his face after all the trouble he'd caused.

He moved to the chairs grouped in the center of the room, still unsteady on his feet. Bracing a hand on top of a small table, he bent to retrieve his scuffed boots. Then, with one hand gripping his boots and the other tucked in his pocket, he returned to her side. He clumsily grasped the right boot and aimed his foot, missing twice before he found the opening. Kari bit back a sarcastic comment about sitting down before he collapsed, but he managed. He bent to retrieve the chain and draped it around his neck, tucking it inside the suit before adjusting the zip-straps.

"What do you want that for?" she scoffed.

"A souvenir," he drawled.

She snorted. "You are strange. Hurry up."

Kari glanced nervously at the door. They were ready to go. Now came the tricky part—getting him to the *Artemis* before Naill discovered he was missing.

She caught a flash of movement out of the corner of her eye. Disbelief held her motionless for a heartbeat, one instant too long in allowing Talon to gain the advantage. He grabbed her right wrist and twisted her arm at a vicious angle behind her back. Her sword dropped from pain-numbed fingers. He hooked his arm around her throat and pulled her back against his chest.

"Don't move," he whispered. The quiet tone carried more menace than a shout. "Don't even think of yelling for help or I'll squeeze off your carotid until every cell in your brain turns blue from lack of oxygen."

Fury flashed through her. The weakness, disorientation—it had all been an act to lower her guard. And she had fallen for it like a rank novice. She was learning, too late, that the smuggler deserved high marks for sheer chicanery.

"Where's my gear?" he growled.

"In my quarters."

"Take me there."

"Why the blazes should I?"

"Because if you don't, I might give in to this nagging urge to break your deceitful neck," he said softly against her ear. The warmth of his breath sent a tingle racing down her back.

She squirmed against his hold. Pain shot through her bent arm. No one knew she was here. There was no one to come to her aid—or witness how her plan had backfired, thank the stars.

She'd get herself out of this. Fighting him wasn't the solution, however. His strength and agility exceeded those of any man she'd ever dealt with. The resultant battle would alert the *Regalia* crew. She might as well deliver him to Naill, for all the good she would have accomplished. Blazes. She'd do anything to prevent that, even let Talon believe he was in control of the situation. Her goal was to get him off this station. If he succeeded in actually escaping, that was preferable to Naill torturing him to death before Myklar returned. Later she would recapture him at a place and time of her choosing.

"Get moving." He shoved her out in front of him, then snatched up her sword. "And no detours."

Kari led him through the passageway to her quarters. She watched for an opening. He offered none. She could feel his alertness like pins pricking across her shoulders, a sensation he reinforced by nudging her with the sword every time she hesitated. Even if she wanted to alert Security, her own tampering with the video cams mocked her.

When they reached her door he pushed her into the room . . . and looked about in obvious surprise.

Heat rose into her cheeks. She hadn't considered this

invasion of her privacy. This was a room few people saw, with its comfortable sofas of burgundy Taki silk arranged around a low oval table carved from blue marble. The plush cream carpet sported a swirled design in burgundy and blue. A painting of an Avernian mountain range bathed in the glow of a fiery sunset, and another of a Verdigran waterfall, graced the walls. Hardly the austere quarters of a soldier.

"I just saved you from Naill," she snapped, drawing his attention away from the bold yet feminine decor. "You have a disgusting way of expressing gratitude."

"I'm sure you'll understand if I hold off on the genuflecting until later," he drawled. "Something tells me you're just saving me to serve me up to a bigger predator. Your father, for instance." His voice was chilly when he added, "I'm no longer in a forgiving mood, much less a grateful one, since I found Rand at Narkwar with his brains scrambled, you kicked me in the face, and your brother used my body as an electrical conduit."

"What do you mean, you found Markos with his brains scrambled?" she scoffed.

He covered the short distance between them with the speed of a striking whip-serpent. He grabbed her upper arm and yanked her close. The touch of steel against her hip choked off her initial reaction to fight back. Even in anger, he maintained his vigilance. She glared at him in mute defiance.

"When I broke Rand out of that cell," Talon said acidly, "he was suffering from drug-induced paranoia, alternating between fits of terror and homicidal panic. He tried to strangle me, though he believed he was acting in self-defense."

"Nonsense. He was fine shortly before that. I saw him."

"Well, Princess, he sure wasn't fine when I got to him."

Warden Urkanis's odd statement pricked at her memory. *Markos is in no condition—* Perhaps it was true.

"I didn't do that to him," she denied emphatically. She

chewed on her lower lip, suspicions growing, for neither did Urkanis have sufficient reason to act on his own.

Talon stared at her mouth. Kari belatedly realized what she was doing. Slowly, so he wouldn't interpret the action as a sign of self-conscious weakness, she let her lip slide from between her teeth. A muscle twitched in his cheek.

With a low growl he released her so abruptly she staggered back. "I may be a fool, but I believe you," he snapped. "Something so cruel and underhanded doesn't seem your usual straight-on, tactless, bull-headed style."

"Thank you for your twisted faith in my integrity," she countered sourly. Thinking the style sounded all too familiar, she hinted, "Any other culprit come to mind?"

"Yeah, your half-brother," he acknowledged gravely. "He said something about knowing Rand was incapable of rescuing me."

"If Naill was responsible, then why are you bullying me?"

His gaze held all the warmth of a Serakian blizzard. "If it weren't for you, Rand would never have been caught and I wouldn't have been a convenient victim for your brother's sadistic little games. Besides," he added, "I harbor a natural dislike for anyone who kicks me in the face."

"Happens often, does it?" she shot back.

"Where are my clothes?" he demanded, ignoring the jibe.

"I'll get them for you," Kari offered quickly. She headed for a low cabinet beneath the waterfall painting but was brought to an abrupt, painful halt by fingers hooked into the base of her braid. Talon turned her head. A slanted grin transformed his dour expression into something almost appealing. Amusement glittered in his eyes, enhanced by gold flecks in their brown depths. An odd sensation fluttered through her belly.

"Such eagerness to help. I'm touched," he said wryly. "However, you've yet to do anything voluntarily, so I suspect my weapons are in there as well." Still keeping a firm hold on her hair, he guided her over to the cabinet and nudged it with his toe. The door slid open, revealing his sword, dagger, and other belongings. "You're as persistent as you are wily, Princess, I'll grant you that."

With escalating resentment, she hissed, "I'm much more, smuggler. I succeed at anything I try. I'll catch you again."

"Though I've had a great deal of practice at eluding pursuit, the prospect of your heel-biting tactics is a compelling reason for leaving the solar system. The exploration companies pay well, and I love a challenge, but don't expect me to be happy about it," he growled. "I've worked hard over the years, despite certain obstacles, to build a business and a life for myself. With a bounty on my head, that's all gone now. Everything."

"I'm getting all weepy," she retorted with cutting sarcasm.

Steady pressure on a stinging scalp forced her to her knees. "Clasp your hands behind your neck," he snapped.

He left her no choice. Though he released her hair, she couldn't attack from this awkward position without providing ample warning. He donned his own weapons, then slung her sword from his utility belt. The Valken dagger, quick and deadly in his skilled hand, was an even worse threat than the sword.

"How do you plan to get out unnoticed?" she challenged. "The *Regalia* is bristling with security cams."

"Yeah, but isn't it odd we haven't been swarmed by guards? Been tinkering with the video system, Jemara Solis? Daddy won't be pleased."

Blazes, how she hated him. The emotion was complicated by an odd excitement shimmering through her veins. He was a worthy opponent, she couldn't deny that . . . worthy of being beaten.

He pulled her over to the computer console against the rear wall. "Bring up the docking records for all hangar bays."

She sat down and punched the keys extra hard. The list of spacecraft appeared.

He bent forward to examine the logs. "The *Artemis*, you said? There she is. Hangar Bay Nine. Status reads ready for—" His head jerked around to stare at her. It wasn't hard to guess what he'd discovered. "How the hell did the *Nighthawk* get here?"

"We took it under tow and brought it through the Corridor. By the way, you have a tidy little lock-out system installed," she probed, watching for his reaction. "No one's been able to break it. The hatch reseals every time the techs decipher the combination, almost as if someone were issuing manual resets."

He smiled. "That's what I wanted to hear. Well, time for me to go. Can't say it's been fun," he quipped. He ripped open the zipstraps and began to pull out the chain.

Kari suddenly realized why he'd saved the chain. He intended to bind her with it. Her heart began to race.

"All right," she agreed, urgently plotting a new strategy. "Where are we going?" If she could keep from being chained, she stood a chance of jumping him before he boarded his ship.

"We? Oh, no, I'm not fool enough to take you any farther."

Much more of dealing with this runagate smuggler, Kari fumed, and frustration was going to eat a hole right through the pit of her stomach. "If I leave you to your own devices, you'll only succeed in getting captured again. I disabled some cams, true, but not along the direct route. Only I know the way." She cocked her head and gave him a superior smile. "Or perhaps you'd rather turn some corner and run smack into a squad of soldiers."

A muscle twitched in his cheek. "You know, the notion of a hostage is growing more appealing by the moment," he responded in that silky, confident tone she was growing to despise—particularly because the deep, masculine tenor vibrated right to the core of her spine. He tucked the chain back inside the suit and shoved her toward the door.

The passageways were relatively silent. Not recognizing the few soldiers they did pass, Kari felt compelled to stay quiet. She could only trust her own men. Then there was the small matter of the dagger hidden at her back. They reached the bay to find it deserted except for three men in the director's booth.

"Guards given others duties?" he commented wryly. "I sense your manipulative touch again. Very clever."

She fumed in silence.

After a softly spoken command into his wrist commlink the hatch ramp of his ship hummed open.

This was it. She couldn't jump him—the point of his dagger seemed to anticipate her every move. *He won't hurt you*, an internal voice whispered insistently. Don't be a simkin, she scoffed in response. The man's life is at stake. He'll do whatever is necessary to gain his freedom.

Hunting him down would have to wait, a duty she would pursue with unequaled persistence and enthusiasm. Now, however, it was time to minimize her losses.

"It will appear I aided in your escape voluntarily."

"I know." She thought she saw a flash of regret in his eyes. What a ridiculous notion.

"You can make it look as if you forced me," she urged.

One eyebrow shot up. "In case you hadn't noticed, I have forced you. But you want me to make it obvious for Naill's sake, no doubt. What do you suggest? There's still the chain."

"You'd enjoy that, wouldn't you?" she retorted with a sneer. "No. I want you to hit me."

His brows dropped into a scowl. "You must be joking."

"Of course I'm not," she said impatiently. She tilted her head and thrust her chin out. "Leave a convincing bruise."

He stared at her, unmoving, his face like stone. She cleared her throat and glanced pointedly at his right hand. It curled into a fist, the leather across his knuckles stretching taut, but still he didn't move. They didn't have time for this, she thought irritably.

"I can take it, smuggler. You think after all those years of rigorous training I haven't been hit before? This can't be worse than other blows I've experienced. Come on."

Talon took a step closer. Kari braced herself, locking her hands behind her back so she wouldn't instinctively throw her arms up in self-defense. She felt wide open, vulnerable, but at least it would be over quickly. It was worth it to defy Naill.

Talon swore viciously. Instead of swinging at her face, in a series of lightning-quick moves he jammed the dagger into its sheath, grabbed her arm, and whipped her around against his chest. A rough hand clamped over her lips, cutting off her gasp of surprise. He hauled her up the ramp and into the *Nighthawk*.

Chapter Six

Talon dragged Kari up the ramp, cursing himself as a galaxy-class idiot with every backward step.

Though he couldn't ask for a better hostage than the Dynast's daughter, it was more hazardous to take her with him. She was dangerous—more crafty, agile, and persistent than any woman he'd ever known—waiting for the opportunity to jump him. Which could happen soon, considering his almost debilitating headache and the exhaustion encroaching on his battered body.

All because he wasn't able to dredge up the resolve to hit her. It should have been easy, considering all the agony she'd caused him. But when she stood there with her chin out-thrust, so proud, defiant, and—yes, dammit, so beautiful—he'd felt like claws were digging into his arm to hold it back.

Her statement about receiving worse blows in the past had finally done him in. For some insane reason that infuriated him, arousing a burning resentment against her family.

He couldn't leave her behind to face Naill's vindictiveness, not after she'd saved him from a slow death by electrocution.

Reaching the top of the ramp, Talon uncovered her mouth. Her whipcord tension passed between their compressed bodies like a supersonic vibration, tingling up the arm he'd clamped around her midriff, increasing his awareness of her tenfold. He knew she waited for an opening . . . he would have. He yanked out one end of the chain and snapped a shackle around her right wrist.

"Liar!" she burst out, trying to wrench free of his hold.

"You wanted it to look as if I forced you to aid in my escape," he countered, battling to contain her struggles in the narrow entryway. "Taking you hostage ought to do it."

"You promised to hit me instead."

"I'm still considering the idea, but I'll save it for later," he snapped in frustration. He couldn't even free a hand to reach for the sheathed dagger.

"I won't let you chain me!" Her left fist slammed into the side of his head. The ache at the base of his skull exploded upward, driving spikes of agony through his brain.

Sweat trickled down his temples. Dammit. Maybe this wasn't worth it, after all. He didn't really need Kari to get off the *Regalia*. He still had her override code—at least he hoped it still worked—and with the *Nighthawk*'s superior speed he could be gone before the Lochnar pilots scrambled a pursuit.

He ought to shove her down the ramp and be done with it.

Kari lashed backward with one heel, catching his right leg just below the kneecap. Hot needles stabbed through the joint. He stumbled forward, swearing as the movement enabled her to plant both feet against the bulkhead and shove, hard. Talon slammed against the opposite wall, his grip still tight around her waist. Something blunt jabbed into his shoulder blade.

The hatch ramp came to life, starting to rise. He'd fallen against the control. The hatch thumped shut. A muffled hiss marked the closing of the pressurized seal.

Well, that decided the issue. He was stuck with her now.

"Runagate hell, woman," he snarled in her ear. "I'm going to have to hurt you if you keep struggling. Hold still, dammit."

"No!" She dropped her center of gravity abruptly, reaching back to grasp him behind the head.

Before she could flip him over her shoulder he slammed her against the bulkhead with his full length. Her firm backside fit snugly into the curve of his body. She squirmed, wriggling against exactly the wrong place. Talon swallowed hard as his flesh hardened unexpectedly. He ground his teeth.

How the hell was he going to get her into the ship's cabin? He might as well kiss his freedom good-bye if he had to fight a raging catamount every step of the way.

He pressed his knuckles hard against a major nerve along the side of her neck. Though the method was quick, it was not without some initial pain before the victim blacked out.

She whimpered. The sound sabotaged his anger. The unexpected guilt caused him to frown in annoyance.

She sagged against the bulkhead, slipping into unconsciousness. He swung her limp body into his arms. She was light, and supple as the buttery soft leather of her pants. Tendrils of hair, pulled free from her braid during the struggle, clung to the perspiration along her jaw. One auburn lock trailed across her cheek and stuck to the corner of her mouth. In the dim lights of the entryway, it looked like a bloody gash. For some reason that bothered him. Talon lowered his head and brushed the offending lock aside with his chin.

He swore and jerked his head up. Was he a complete simkin? He had to get rid of this troublesome woman as soon as possible.

He carried her down the short passageway and kicked the cabin door open.

"Beryl? Where are you?" Though there was no response, he had no doubt she was on board after Kari's comments about the ship's lock resetting. He'd taught Beryl that little trick. Kjell had succeeded in transporting the Sylph to the *Nighthawk*. Talon glanced toward the special alcove, enclosed in smoky gray cordite, built into the portside rear corner of the cabin. The small arbor was a bit of native jungle for Beryl. She must be in her nest, asleep in her finely interwoven hammock of leaves and aerial roots. He would check on her once they were away.

He turned to the right and jabbed a panel with his elbow. The ship's only bunk lowered, unfolding from the bulkhead. The legs locked into sockets in the deck. With a hiss, the mattress inflated from a canister of compressed air mounted on the wall.

He laid Kari in the middle of the bed, wondering where he was going to sleep. If he didn't get some quality rest soon, he'd no doubt collapse. At least once they safely entered the Corridor to Serac he wouldn't have to worry about any pursuit overtaking them—all ships were pulled through the grav-well tunnel at the same speed, regardless of engine capacity.

He wound the chain around the bedframe and snapped the other shackle to her left wrist. Remembering the key sequencer she carried, he unbuckled her utility belt and tossed it over the back of the copilot's seat, beyond reach. His hand dipped into his own pocket, fingering the second sequencer he'd pilfered from Naill's quarters when he'd reached for his boots.

Setting both swords aside, Talon dropped into the pilot's seat. He keyed for launch and transmitted Kari's override code to the Bay 9 computer. The familiar start-up rumble of the *Nighthawk*'s powerful engines surged through his body, beating in time with the thrumming of his blood. He closed his eyes and briefly savored being home again.

A puff of air ruffled through his hair. Beryl settled lightly on his shoulder.

"*A paying passenger, is she?*" Even telepathically, the Sylph could convey a huffy tone.

"Don't get cute with me, Beryl. I'm not in the mood."

The Sylph sniffed. "*Ask, was all I did.*"

"Right. I'm well aware you dislike any guest aboard the ship, particularly human females," he countered dryly. "Strap in. I'm punching the ship out of here. I hope."

"About time. Dislike this place, I do," Beryl retorted, then flew off and disappeared again through the small access panel built into the wall of the arbor.

Talon glanced after her, a frown creasing his brow. Beryl usually liked to sit up front at launch.

Well, he didn't have the luxury of wondering what she was up to now. Tension gripped every muscle as he waited for shield-lock clearance . . . or the alarm to sound and his bid for freedom to be choked off. Uncertainty made the wait seem like a damned eternity. His pent-up breath exhaled in a rush with the welcome hum and thump of shields beaming into place. The yellow go light shone on his console. The exit window was open. His head pressed back against the seat as the *Nighthawk* accelerated.

Their launch went unchallenged at first, but that wouldn't last. Pursuit was inevitable. He kicked in the distance-crunching stardrive the moment they were clear of the *Regalia*.

The first relay station of the Verdigris-Serac Corridor came into view, floating in open space like a massive flower. Solar collector panels bristled beneath like a dense nest of sepals, while the two broad arms curved solemnly upward to meet at the top, forming a circle. In his father's time it would have taken in excess of four months to travel from Verdigris to Serac. The man-made relay stations, established in their solar orbits thirty-two years ago to create artificial worm-holes between planets, shortened the trip to twelve hours.

Stars blurred as Talon navigated the *Nighthawk* into the mouth of the Corridor.

He glanced back at Kari's sleeping form, sprawled on her side on the bunk. Despite the hostility churning inside, his gaze lingered over the graceful curve of her waist and hip. What was he going to do with her? After ensuring that Rand was all right he'd have to leave her on Serac or Star Alpha. Not that it mattered either way. The life he'd struggled to build was over. Thanks to Kari Solis, he was a fugitive . . . again.

"And you just let the ship take off?" Naill shouted into his commlink. "Without a thorough check? Without clearance?"

A trembling yet insistent voice responded, "Jemidar Solis, the *Nighthawk* transmitted—"

"You imbecile! Do you realize the prisoner, Talon, must have been aboard that ship? He certainly can't be found anywhere on the *Regalia*. What is your name and rank?"

"Tech-Major Cuirn. Sir, I respectfully submit that—"

"Be prepared to surrender your director's duties in Bay Nine as soon as I send a replacement," snapped Naill impatiently. "Then return to your quarters prior to demotion in rank."

A pause, then a sigh at the other end. "Yes, sir. However, I still maintain there was a good reason for the decision."

"Tech-Major, your persistence is annoying me a great deal. A soldier who cannot own up to his mistakes is unworthy of the privilege of being an officer aboard the *Regalia*. Understood?"

"Perfectly, Jemidar Solis," came the audibly stiff reply.

"Good." Naill reached to switch off his commlink. His wrist was caught in a gentle grip by a copper-skinned hand.

"Sometimes, my lord, interesting tidbits of information come from the most unlikely sources," Penn said softly. He nodded toward the commlink.

"As usual, Penn, you are the governor of my temper," Naill murmured. Louder, he added, "Cuirn, are you still there?"

"Yes, Jemidar."

"My anger is understandable, considering the regrettable fact that my prisoner has just escaped. I may have been a bit hasty, however, in excluding your input. What were you trying to say?"

"I had authorization in allowing the *Nighthawk* to launch, sir." The vigor had returned to Cuirn's voice.

"Authorization?" Naill glanced sharply at Penn. "Feel free to be more specific, Tech-Major."

"The smuggler's ship transmitted a launch code at the highest level. I had no choice but to let it go."

"Very interesting. Initiate a data search to identify the owner of that code."

"I already have, sir."

"Indeed. And what did you find?"

Cuirn hesitated before answering with evident reluctance, "The code is a private clearance assigned to Jemara Kari."

A slow smile spread across Naill's face. That particular answer couldn't have played any better, or harmonized any more perfectly with his purposes, if he'd orchestrated it himself.

"Do not concern yourself, Tech-Major. We can assume Talon stole the code from my half-sister. Notify my Interceptor pilots immediately. Link me to all four cockpits, on a private channel, when the ships are ready."

"Begging your pardon, Jemidar, but aren't you concerned that Jemara Kari is aboard the *Nighthawk* as a hostage?"

"No," Naill responded decisively. "As a matter of fact, I saw her on my way back to my chambers. She was entering the deck four simulation chamber, no doubt to practice her swordsmanship with the variety of opponents she has programmed into the computer."

"That is a relief, sir."

"Do not concern yourself, Cuirn. I will deal with the situation. Just carry out the orders I gave you. And Cuirn?"

"Yes, sir?"

"I regard your initiative in researching the code as a point in your favor. I might reconsider the demotion."

"Thank you, Jemidar Solis," Cuirn's voice responded crisply.

With a sly smile, Naill switched off the commlink. He could easily picture Cuirn jerking to full attention at the last. He had a rare skill in handling his father's men.

Penn's voice slipped into the silence. "I sense the story of Jemara Kari's whereabouts is a fabrication."

"One of my best, don't you think?" Naill chuckled. He stroked his goatee as he glared at the empty chain hook in the ceiling. "Someone evidently freed Talon. Who else but Kari? She wanted her prize back, so she took him. That knowledge will remain our secret, Penn. If the Interceptor pilots suspect Myklar's daughter is aboard the *Nighthawk*, they will refuse to blow up the ship in a suitably spectacular fashion. And that is exactly what I intend for them to do, with a few incentives to sweeten the kill for the successful pilot."

"Do you think it possible she accompanied him willingly?"

"The way she despises the man?" Naill scoffed. "Either she's piloting the *Nighthawk* with Talon as prisoner or her plan backfired and he took her hostage. The end result will be the same. Though it's a shame my pilots will destroy the ship before Kari and the smuggler kill each other. That would have been entertaining to watch."

She would have given anything, Kari fumed silently, if Talon's escape from the *Regalia* hadn't been so easy. He didn't deserve easy. He deserved to be drop-kicked into a deep tank surrounded by hungry voltaic lizards, long tails dangling in the water, electric jolts at full charge.

She glared at his back from where she sat cross-legged on the bunk. Talon lounged, seemingly oblivious to her presence, in the pilot's seat of the *Nighthawk*. His legs, crossed at the ankle, were propped up on the edge of the console. His gaze was locked on the viewport and the unnatural blackness of the Corridor's grav-well tunnel.

They had been underway for an hour, heading toward the ice world. Though she'd always wanted to visit Serac—

not just study information cels on its harsh climate and strange wildlife, or view projections of its rugged, surreal white landscape in a simulation chamber—she didn't care for the circumstances of her first trip. A hostage, in chains. How galling.

Her gaze shifted to Talon's right hand, where he manipulated a token coin. He'd been doing the same blazing thing since she'd regained consciousness and purged her fury with some choice remarks on his character—none of which he acknowledged with the slightest word or gesture. She wasn't sure why she watched him, except that there was something mesmerizing in the way he walked the gold coin across his knuckles, then flipped it up with his thumb and snatched it out of midair. He didn't miss. He didn't drop the coin, not even once. His deftness aggravated her temper. She impatiently shifted position, trying to get more comfortable.

The chains rasped across the frame of the bed.

The coin hit the floor with a sharp ping.

Kari held her breath. Talon retrieved the coin, then resumed his exercise in dexterity. Had she discovered a way to get under his shagya-thick hide? She tested her theory by clanking the chains again. Though he flipped the coin high and caught it without a hitch, his hand fisted so tightly, the knuckles stood out against the leather of his glove.

So, he disliked the rattle of the chains. The sound probably reminded him of his painful experience in Naill's quarters. The knowledge gained her little beyond the opportunity to provoke him, which was fast losing its appeal. He was a very unresponsive target. Kari sighed.

She lapsed into sulky silence and examined her prison. There was enough room in the cabin for two people to maneuver without bumping into one another, which intensified the mystery of the Lochnar techs' inability to break into the *Nighthawk*. She had believed someone was on board manipulating the lockout mechanism, but Talon couldn't have kept a crew member hidden. The only visible oddity was the enclosed area to her left—apparently an arbor. She could see the faint outline of vines and leaves against the almost opaque cordite. Why would a smuggler have a garden aboard ship? Otherwise, the cabin's design was standard fare. The front was dominated by the console, faced by the pilot and copilot seats, behind which was the bunk. A lav took up the starboard rear corner of the cabin. A compact meal station was built into the bulkhead to her right. The only oddity there was the presence of two food preserver units mounted on the wall, rather than the one expected for such a small crew.

For the hundredth time her attention strayed to her utility belt, draped over the copilot's seat. She rubbed her fingertips together. They itched with the knowledge of the master key tucked in one pocket. There was also the small matter of the cylinder containing Naill's files. Had Talon noticed it? She couldn't allow him access to the sensitive data.

Talon couldn't maintain his vigilance forever. She would escape and recapture him; that much was inevitable. Right now she was too tired and beaten down to give it much thought. She hadn't slept at all, come to think of it, since Narkwar prison.

Kari gnawed on her lower lip. Failure was not an option. Myklar would send her back to Verdigris, away from him and everything she'd strived for, back to her childhood home and a renewal of the lonely, grueling training. He rightfully expected much from her training by the best master warriors in the Lochnar army. And once Myklar suffered a disappointment, she would have to work three times as hard to regain his trust.

Kari sighed and leaned against the bulkhead, straightening her cramped legs. The silk of her shirt clung damply to her back and chest like an amphibian skin beneath the torso armor. The edges of the metal pressed uncomfortably against her collarbone. Though the armor had been custom-made to fit her to perfection, the thing had never been intended to wear for hours on end.

Removing it suddenly became a priority. She reached to unfasten the clasps down one side. The wrist shackles rasped sharply against the cinnadar metal.

Talon swore under his breath and stood abruptly. She froze. He stepped around the pilot's seat and came toward her. Kari braced herself for a verbal raking over, intending to give as good as she got. He looked down, his expression inscrutable.

"Hungry?" he asked gruffly.

She blinked. It took a moment for her surprise over the mundane question to wear off. She bit back the initial urge to throw a *no* back in his face. *Face it, Kari, you're starving.*

"I might be," she responded cautiously.

"Well, I certainly am," he muttered, turning toward the meal station. "I plan to have a solid meal, then a shower. After that, some sleep."

A shower. Kari shrugged her shoulders, trying in vain to pull the clinging silk free from her skin. A shower sounded heavenly . . . solar-heated water beating the soreness from stiff muscles, caressing her face and neck—

Talon pulled open a deep drawer, distracting her from the vulnerable longing, and tugged out a clear bag full of shriveled, dark shapes. Vegetables, and quite an assortment from what she could see. Not exactly the nutritious luxury she would have expected from the rough-hewn smuggler. Talon selected a handful, piled them loosely in a large bowl, and shoved the bowl into the rehydrator. Two minutes later the unit pinged. He pulled out a bowl of plumped, lightly steaming vegetables.

Setting the bowl on a small table that folded out from a slot in the wall, he called, "Beryl, food's ready. Are you going to come out of there long enough to eat?"

Beryl? The mysterious crew member? Impossible, Kari thought. No one could have stayed hidden this long. Her speculations were cut short as an access panel in the arbor wall opened. A vibrant, blue-green creature flashed across the cabin.

Kari's mouth dropped open. A Sylph. After growing up on Verdigris, she ought to be able to recognize one of the rare forest creatures. They were highly prized by horticulturists in cultivating specialized gardens. This was Talon's crew?

The Sylph landed on his shoulder. Her wings folded in a relaxed pose, as if she sat there often. Glaring at Kari, she ran one hand through Talon's hair in a gesture that struck Kari as blatantly possessive. Just as abruptly, the Sylph flew down, grabbed the bowl, and headed back toward the arbor.

"Hey," Talon protested, "I didn't mean the whole bowl, you little pirate. Bring that back here." The Sylph stopped just outside the open panel and, fluttering awkwardly with the weight of the bowl, emitted a complex dialog of undecipherable warbles and trills. Talon listened intently, then suddenly his dark eyebrows shot up. "You have a what? A guest? Runagate hell, I'd forgotten all about that. Well, not forgotten, actually, but I thought Kjell and the others had taken her with them to Serac."

The creature chirped, evidently excited.

"A he?" Talon responded, his expression stunned.

With a tiny smile and a flip of her wings, Beryl disappeared with the bowl. The panel closed.

"A male? Damn, it's not even mating season. Beryl, are you sure you know what you're doing?" He started toward the arbor.

"A Sylph!" Kari burst out, halting him in his tracks. "Only the elite class on Verdigris are allowed to keep Sylphs."

He glared at her. "I'm fully aware of the rules."

"You poached her," Kari accused, fighting a twinge of envy. The Sylph obviously communicated telepathically with Talon, an honor their species bestowed only on humans they liked and respected. This particular Sylph must be deranged.

"Beryl is with me of her own free will."

"Oh, that's rich. I can't imagine any being with a modicum of intelligence going anywhere with you. At least, not willingly." She raised her shackled wrists for emphasis.

A muscle twitched across his cheek. He glanced at the arbor, then pivoted sharply and headed back to the meal station.

"What? Aren't you going after her?" Kari taunted.

"She's entitled to her privacy." He dumped more vegetables into another bowl and shoved it into the rehydrator. Slamming the door, he muttered sourly, "Just like everyone else."

The implication was clear. Kari smiled with false sweetness. "Next time I'll be sure to knock before I so eagerly, and voluntarily, board your ship." The rehydrator pinged again. Talon pulled out the plumped vegetables and divided them between two plates. He was just reaching for a sifter of *tangchitt* seasoning when she added, "Just to show my good intentions, I'll be more than happy to debark at the first opportunity."

"Even over a desolate ice field on Serac, with temperatures well below zero?" he asked softly. He seasoned his food.

"Anything is preferable to my current circumstances," she countered. Warily, she eyed the *tangchitt* sifter as he held it motionless over her plate. An overabundance of the seasoning was known to cause a very unpleasant skin reaction. If she wanted to eat, maybe she should stop provoking him.

"I'll keep that in mind." He sprinkled her food with a small amount, then handed over an eating spear and her plate.

She balanced it on her crossed legs. Talon pulled out a folding chair and sat down at the table.

"If you didn't poach Beryl, where did she come from?"

"I rescued her six years ago at Narkwar, from Gar Ur-kanis."

Kari snorted. "Stole, you mean."

His eyes narrowed. "No, liberated, just like Beryl rescued the other Sylph on this last little sightseeing trip."

Stabbing a lavender *elodea* with the two-pronged fork, Kari conceded, "I can't fault you for taking her. Urkanis is a cruel son of a tarpan, hardly deserving of a Sylph." Talon gave her an odd look. Realizing she'd come dangerously close to complimenting him, Kari amended hastily, "Then again, neither are you."

He jabbed his spear into a *ribos* bean.

She pointed at his gloves, saying sarcastically, "Were your Line insignia burned away at Narkwar because you were a convict, or did your family disown you even before that?"

"A ritualistic Shunning?" He gave a bark of laughter that held no humor, chilling rather than warming the atmosphere. "That's entirely possible, considering things I've done over the years . . . if they'd lived long enough. But my father died in Myklar's war. I was eleven at the time. My mother passed away shortly after," he finished in a hard voice.

"Your parents were part of the resistance, then."

"My father was an officer in the *rightful* government, the Consularship. You can bet they resisted the takeover by your tyrannical father."

"He ousted a weak, ineffectual government suffering from a pathetic degree of infighting and brought order back to the solar system," Kari snapped back, her tone equally antagonistic. Her palms began to sweat. Impatiently, she rubbed them against the bedding.

"Is that what he told you? The infighting is true. As to the rest, you've been seriously deluded, Princess," he snarled.

"And why should I believe you? You're an unaligned convict, a rogue pilot who doesn't believe in any cause other than his own convenience. An avowed Neutral, remember?"

"Just because I choose not to actively take sides in the Rebellion doesn't mean I don't believe in the Rebel cause."

"That's treasonous talk, Talon."

"Well, I can hardly be in more trouble than I am already."

"Exactly. Kidnapping the Dynast's daughter rates high on the penalty list, I'm sure, though no one's ever been fool enough to put it to the test."

He stood abruptly and slammed his unfinished plate of food onto the table. "I'll be in the lav."

"What about when I need to use it?" she grumbled, yanking on the shackles. His scowl deepened. "Hadn't thought of that, eh?"

He stormed through the narrow door of the lav, then emerged a second later with—of all things she didn't want to see—a portable waste unit. Setting it down on the floor next to the bunk, he shot her a scathing look. "That ought to do for now."

Before she could summon a suitable comeback he disappeared into the lav.

Kari caught her breath when he closed the door. Now was her chance. Quickly, she set her plate aside and slid off the bunk, stretching out as far as she could reach. The toe of her boot came up just short of her dangling utility belt.

The lav door opened a crack. Kari froze. Instead of Talon emerging to catch her in the act, the Lochnar flight suit came sailing out to land in a heap in the middle of the floor. Before the door closed again, she caught another flash of black drifting downward. He'd shed his undershorts.

He was naked in there.

Of course he is, you fool, he intends to shower, she admonished herself. But logic did nothing to alleviate her strange shortness of breath. The most ridiculous question popped into her mind: Were his buttocks a smooth white, a particularly striking contrast to the dark, hostile depths of his brown eyes, or the deep bronze of his skin?

Shaking her head in disgust, she wrenched her thoughts back to important matters. Her gaze locked on a small lever at the base of the copilot seat. The recline mechanism. Of course! If she could just trigger it, the seat would tilt back and freedom would be within her grasp.

Chapter Seven

Talon did this on purpose, Kari thought furiously. He'd left her utility belt tantalizingly close but physically inaccessible, no doubt to deliberately torment her.

She lay along the deck, arms straight overhead, stretched to the limits of her body and the chain. The recline mechanism on the copilot's seat remained barely beyond the toe of her boot.

She bit her lip, concentrating, trying to ignore the pain of her breastplate digging into her shoulders. It was no use. The torso armor robbed her of the flexibility needed to stretch those last few centimeters. Growling with impatience, she sat up and rapidly unfastened the clips down the sides, then pulled the armor off over her head and shoved it under the bunk.

Only a bit more length; that was all she needed.

The idea started as a whisper in her mind, then rushed in with the force of a Verdigran cliff-top waterfall. Kari tugged her boot half off, until her foot was just above the leather ankle, and stretched out again. She kicked with the loose heel, a clumsy tactic born of desperation, but it worked. The boot heel struck the lever. The chair reclined backward. Triumph surged through her veins as the utility belt moved within reach.

Struggling to calm her breathing, Kari gingerly lifted the belt free with her other foot. She kicked the recline mechanism once more, returning the copilot seat to its upright position. Everything looked normal. Good. Anything that would allay Talon's suspicions might gain her a few precious seconds.

She again sat cross-legged on the bunk and grasped the belt in her eager hands. They shook with a sense of urgency. She felt a hot flash of annoyance for the unfamiliar reaction, though it wasn't hard to guess its source . . . before Talon, she'd never known a man with the physical and mental potential to stop her.

Pulling out the sequencer, she attached it to one shackle.

Talon tilted his head back and closed his eyes, letting the shower spray pound on his face and course its soothing path down his battered body. Even the muscles in his cheeks ached. At least the headache was diminishing. Leaning back a little, he shifted the stream to his neck and shoulders. Blessedly warm water sheeted down across his groin in a gentle caress and snaked in ever-changing rivulets around his thighs.

He could stay in here forever.

Unfortunately, he couldn't afford that luxury, though he deserved it. A drain on the main tanks would overload the water recycling system. And he needed sleep, which meant his bunk. The last thing he wanted was to spend the night passage in the pilot's seat. A bit of a problem, there—one with auburn hair and a temper that would intimidate a catamount.

He reached for the gel-foam dispenser, then swore when he saw black through the spray. He'd forgotten to take off his gloves. Runagate hell, he must be farther gone than he thought. It was a good thing he kept several pairs.

After undoing the zipstraps around his wrists, he peeled off the soggy leather and dropped the gloves over the shower door.

Filling his palm with blue gel, he began to work the substance into a lather along his arm. He paused, staring at the back of his hand. His lips compressed into a tight line. With familiar, gut-wrenching regret, he ran his thumbs over the smooth, unmarked pale skin on first one hand, and then the other. A harsh laugh escaped, as short and violent as a clap of thunder. Kari envisioned his hands as brutally scarred, marred forever by the cruel acid-burning process of tattoo removal. Surprise, Princess, he thought bitterly, but he knew he mocked himself.

Just as he did every day of his life, Talon wished fervently that his hands were mutilated. Anything would be better than this shameful nakedness, the flawless skin underlaid by sinewy tendons and blue veins. His hands should be proudly decorated by Valkenbur Line tattoos almost identical to Rand's, with the small difference in design afforded a younger son. Instead he had nothing— no lineage, no identity. Only what he knew in his heart of his past and his family, only the reassurances Rand offered with a brother's love. His Mal'Harith mother, Etana Markos, had always reassured him that those things would be enough.

They weren't. Perhaps they would have been, if his father hadn't abandoned his eleven-and thirteen-year-old sons by choosing to martyr himself fighting against Myklar's forces. If his mother hadn't subsequently died so sad, so young. If he didn't have to hide his shame and conceal his past for the sake of survival.

Talon washed vigorously, forcing his thoughts to how his bare hands had gained him one thing . . . anonymity. Even at Narkwar, where they'd ridiculed his status as lower than a bastard, they hadn't known how to record a prisoner with no identity. Talon had refused to be linked back to his deceased family, or to Rand, by providing a name. As far as Lochnar records were concerned, Talon hadn't existed . . . at least not until he'd escaped the prison and created a reputation as a rogue pilot.

A sense of unease began to creep up on him. He disliked not having Kari under his watchful eye. But what could she do, chained? He massaged the tense muscles along the back of his neck. Knowing her resourcefulness, if she wasn't trying something, she was in the planning stages. At least the ship's console was well beyond reach. Any manipulation of the controls, the slightest deviation from their course through the Corridor, and the *Nighthawk* would disintegrate against the intense gravity walls of the artificial worm-hole.

Feeling increasingly restless without knowing why, Talon stepped out of the shower and toweled off hastily. He postponed the idea of a shave, instead tugging on spare gloves and the baggy, tie-string pants he typically wore on board. He didn't even take time to don a shirt before wrenching open the door.

"Hurry, hurry," Kari whispered tightly as the tiny lights on the master key flashed, searching through the library of combinations, taking longer than a sequencer coded specifically for these shackles. She glanced repeatedly at the lav door, checking for the critical sound of running water.

Without warning, the shower stopped.

No, not yet! She bit down on her lower lip. The yellow light on the sequencer beamed. The shackle clicked open. She was half-free.

She was just transferring the disk to the other wrist when the door opened abruptly. With a muffled yelp, she jerked her hands and the utility belt behind her back.

Talon stepped out. Kari froze, staring. His bare chest gleamed with a lingering sheen of moisture. Tiny sparkling droplets emphasized the sculpted shape of his muscles.

Her concentration slipped.

And so did the sequencer—right from her fingers, dropping onto the bedding behind her back.

Biting back a startled curse, Kari met his gaze and smiled. She wasn't sure where the grin came from, only that every muscle in her body was tense with nervousness.

Her cheeks locked in a smile while her fingertips searched blindly for the small disk.

There was something definitely in the works, Talon thought suspiciously, if Kari Solis was grinning at him.

The unwelcome wish—that she would offer him such a brilliant smile under other circumstances—jumped up to bite him. It was the change in her, dammit. The unexpectedness of it was wrecking havoc on his equilibrium. Though removing her armor shouldn't make such a difference, it did. He tried to recollect how dangerous she could be but failed to distract his attention from the way her silk shirt clung to her breasts, revealing the delicate tips of her hardened nipples. She looked soft, downright feminine, welcoming. The woman rather than the soldier.

It was all a lie, of course.

For once, logic failed him. It wasn't there to keep his imagination from running rampant, nor prevent the throbbing of his blood from keeping pace. Her breasts were fuller, more rounded than expected, yet still in perfect proportion to her sleek, athletic build. They had drawn to taut peaks because of the cabin temperature, no doubt. He could feel the chill touching the dampness over his own suddenly heated skin.

He took a step forward. Kari's smile faltered, breaking the spell. Talon's common sense returned.

She was up to something. Whatever her intent, he was going to put a stop to it. He'd discovered a perverse side of himself that enjoyed causing her difficulty—for revenge, of course, though there was something invigorating about the way anger pushed color into her cheeks and ignited sparks in her eyes.

When he advanced on her, he was ready for anything—except her speed. She came at him like a pouncing ice wolf, right fist swinging. He dodged the blow. Before he could fully recover his balance she toppled him to the bunk with a quick blow behind the knees and an arm across his shoulders.

He could have fought back, but he didn't. He was where he wanted to be. His bed. Admittedly, he also liked the press of her breasts against his back, the profoundly female muskiness of her scent filling his nostrils. A fellow could do worse than share a bed with such a uniquely beautiful woman . . . even if she would prefer to see him dead. Since the weapons were locked away the worst he could get was a few bruises.

The loose shackle snapped around his wrist.

Adrenaline kicked in. This wasn't part of the bargain. But an undefined, deeper urging kept him from wrestling her for control of the master key. A quick glance at the discarded Lochnar flight suit, with the other sequencer secretly tucked in one pocket, reassured him that freedom lay within reach any time he chose. Deciding simultaneously that Kari Solis needed an unexpected ending to her scheming, he waited for the right moment.

As soon as she slapped her sequencer onto the shackle binding her other hand, Talon knocked the key away. It popped loose from its magnetic grip, bounced twice on the floor, then rolled toward a section of open grating.

"No!" Kari burst out. Desperation swelled in her chest.

She lunged for the disk, but the chain brought her up far short of her goal. Pain registered as the shackle cut into the tender flesh of her wrist, but her attention was focused on her freedom dropping through the grating and out of sight.

She closed her eyes. The throbbing in her wrist was as nothing compared to the agony of failure. Still trapped. Her mouth felt as if it were coated with Avernian volcanic grit.

"You know, Princess, if you wanted us to get closer, all you had to do was ask."

Kari's eyes snapped open. Her breath sucked in on a gasp of dismay. She had been so wrapped up in the loss of her goal, she'd forgotten the more immediate consequence of her aborted escape attempt.

Talon was shackled to the other end of the chain.

His brows arched. "What, nothing to say? That doesn't seem like you."

"I've come to the conclusion that I'm simply having a blazing nightmare," Kari muttered sourly, racking her brain for a way out of this dilemma and seeing none. She sat on the opposite end of the bunk, as far away from Talon as possible.

Talon's gaze flashed to her shackled wrist. "You little idiot," he snapped. "Was it worth cutting yourself?"

"Yes! Anything to get away from you," she said acidly, though inwardly she was appalled to finally notice the blood smeared around her wrist and trailing down her hand. The cuts on either side were almost half a centimeter deep.

"Beryl!" Talon shouted. "Get out here. I need you."

"The Sylph? What can she do?" Kari scoffed.

"Wait and see."

Beryl emerged from the arbor.

"Bring me a wrap bandage," Talon ordered. "And hurry."

Disappearing into the lav, the forest creature emerged a moment later with the bandage clutched in her hand. She flew over to land on Talon's knee.

"Jemara Solis is bleeding, Beryl. She needs your help."

As Kari wondered what the Sylph could possibly do, Beryl crossed her arms over her shiny green chest and broke into a cacophony of indignant chirps. It wasn't hard to guess that she was protesting the idea of giving any help to the enemy.

"Drop the jealousy, little jewel," Talon interrupted in a soothing tone. "It doesn't become you. It's in your nature to help anyone in need. Besides, Kari is a guest on the *Nighthawk*."

Kari and the Sylph snorted in unintended unison.

Beryl glared at Kari; then suddenly she seemed to droop, warbling sadly.

Talon's brows snapped together. "What do you mean

111

he's ill?" He glanced sharply toward the arbor. "What's wrong with him?"

The Sylph chirped, ending in a throaty clicking noise.

"Salt deprivation?"

Beryl nodded.

"Damn Urkanis, that irresponsible shirker. You know we've run out of your store of loose salt, Beryl. I was planning on replenishing it at our next supply stop. Any other salt is prepackaged in the meat. And I don't have to ask if a Sylph can stomach meat. Will he be okay until we get to Serac?"

The response came in pitiful tones. Kari didn't need to hear Talon's interpretation to know the answer was not encouraging. She turned away, concealing any outward expression of the worried, sinking sensation in her chest. Sylphs were so rare, so very unique and precious.

"Runagate hell. There's nothing I can do to get us there any faster," Talon growled. He slammed the heel of his palm into the bulkhead.

Kari jerked back around, startled more by the vehemence and frustration in his normally cold, cynical voice than by any measure of violence.

He gestured toward her wrist. Gruffly, he muttered, "Beryl, do something about this before she bleeds all over my damn ship."

Kari's mouth opened to utter a blistering retort, only to stop short when Beryl began fluttering her wings rapidly.

"Sylph nectar?" Kari exclaimed, recognizing the gelatinous secretion the creature gathered from the base of her wings. "But they use their nectar to nourish plants."

The Sylph kneaded the substance into an opaque paste, then pulled open Talon's loose fist by two of his fingers. After slapping the paste onto his palm, Beryl flew off to the arbor with an indignant flip of her wings.

Talon frowned after the disappearing Beryl, then turned his attention back to Kari. "It also contains a natural healant. It'll stop the bleeding. Here," he said, reaching for her arm.

Kari jerked away.

"Can't you even cooperate with something meant to help you?"

"How do I know it will help? I'd be a fool to trust you."

"I'm not giving you any choice, dammit." Without warning, his free hand shot forward to snatch her forearm in a viselike grip. He jerked her against his side.

A jolt of awareness rocketed through Kari. Tucked under his muscular arm, pressed against the hard, warm side of his naked chest, she felt a tingle cascade through her body. It centered in her belly, a nervous fluttering.

Talon smeared the nectar paste into her cuts.

"This stuff must come in handy for someone with as many enemies as you have," she said sourly, retaliating for the strange, unwelcome feelings his proximity invoked.

"Exactly. Beryl has to patch up my wounds every other day. She can barely keep up with all the battles I'm in."

"You're only trying to cheer me with thoughts of your demise," she countered smoothly.

Talon's eyes narrowed in warning. He pushed the shackle up her forearm. The bleeding had already slowed significantly. Kari struggled to hide her amazement over this unknown—except for Talon's insufferable insight—use for Sylph nectar.

He fastened the bandage loosely around her wrist, then pulled the adjusto strip. The bandage shrank until it fit snugly over her lacerations.

"I suggest you not be so eager for my death, Princess. You'll only find yourself shackled to a corpse."

She raised her bandaged wrist, fist clenched. The chain rattled. "What do we do about these?" she demanded.

"We'll just have to share the bunk for now."

"What?" she croaked. "That's your grand solution?"

"No, it's my practical alternative. May I remind you, I didn't create this situation." He yanked off his boots. "I've

113

had a rough day, in case you hadn't noticed. The time of night passage has arrived and I intend to take full advantage of the Corridor trip to sleep. Perhaps I'll have an idea by morning."

"Sleep? Here? Impossible."

"Not at all. I just close my eyes, shut out all the unpleasantness around me—most particularly you—and let exhaustion take over."

"Shouldn't we be searching for some way to free ourselves?"

"I might not find a way out of this dilemma *you* created until we're nearing the Corridor exit," he pointed out bluntly.

"That's over ten hours from now." Her voice came out in a hoarse whisper.

"Exactly. All the more reason to sleep for at least part of the time."

"I'm warning you to keep your distance, smuggler. Don't even consider touching me."

The threat, as if she expected him to pounce on her any second, sparked a flare of anger in Talon. The memory of how his thoughts had steered in exactly that direction earlier—when hers obviously ran completely counter, finding him repulsive—didn't help his temper.

"No problem, Princess," he jeered in a silky, ominous voice. "You may have the looks of the women in your mother's Line, but you certainly haven't the desirability or the compassion. You needn't worry about any advances from me. And if I decide I'm going to sleep in my own bunk, I'm damn well going to do exactly that. Any more arguments?"

Kari stiffened. "None," she answered coldly. "I'll just sleep on the floor." Putting actions to words, she slipped carefully around him, avoiding any contact, and sat on the floor with her back to the wall.

"Stubborn woman. Suit yourself." Talon slammed his fist into the malleable foam headrest, shaping it for his head and neck. He flopped on his side, facing away from Kari. And he'd been worried about sexual tension keeping him awake? He'd obviously been without a woman for too long. He steadfastly clung to that thought as he closed his eyes, trying to purge the delectable memory of Kari's full lips turned down in a pout. Exhaustion did the rest, pulling him with unexpected swiftness into the dark abyss of sleep.

In offended disbelief, Kari listened to Talon's deep breathing drop into a low, even rhythm.

He had fallen asleep, just like that.

Any decent person would have tried harder to convince her not to attempt sleep on this cold floor. Not that she would have listened, of course.

The memory of his verbal attack lanced through her, despite her best efforts to shore up her defenses. How dare he compare her so unfavorably to the women in the Khazanjian Line! Lacking in compassion and desirability? She glared at the rumpled softness of Talon's dark hair, trying to build up sufficient righteous outrage to counteract the trembling that plagued her insides and caused her jaw to clench.

Because, worst of all, he was right.

Compassion had been vigorously trained out of her. Myklar considered it an unacceptable weakness. Kari felt out of touch with the very notion of compassion, unsure of its meaning. Desirability she understood all too well, having frequently felt the lack thereof. Men had never shown an interest in her. All her life she'd been too tall, gangly, awkward. Now that maturity and training had transformed her awkwardness into skill and agility, men found her too independent and intelligent. Attractiveness never was one of her strong suits.

It was true, damn his observant hide. She wasn't lovable.

After all, her own mother had abandoned her.

Kari winced, violently shying away from the thought.

115

Down that path lay only heartache and loneliness. Squaring her shoulders, she tried to explain away the sharp stinging behind her eyes, ascribing it to exhaustion. After all, she'd long since purged those old doubts. Dead memories had nothing to do with the pressure in her head, or the sinking feeling in her gut.

She blinked. Moisture spilled over her lower lids, twin hot trails of unfamiliar vulnerability.

No. She couldn't be crying. She never cried.

A tiny sniff interrupted the stillness of the cabin, and it didn't originate from her.

Kari didn't move, not even to wipe the dampness from her face. Another sniff sounded. Something moved near the arbor. The dim lights from the console reflected off scales, jewel tones of blue and purple. Not Beryl, with her blue-green coloring.

The male Sylph had come out of hiding.

Kari watched in fascination, afraid to move lest she spook the elusive Sylph. He pushed off from the open access panel, straining his wings in flight toward her. He immediately began to falter. Kari jerked forward, cursing the chain that prevented her from helping, muscles straining in sympathetic support for his weakly fluttering wings. She gasped in dismay when he tumbled to the deck with a little thump. He rose to his feet, then walked the rest of the way with an uneven gait.

She held herself perfectly still, despite her growing excitement and a touch of apprehension. What seemed almost like a dream became remarkably real when he stepped onto her right foot. He grasped the laces on the front of her boot and climbed them like a miniature ladder. Her knee served as a perch.

He leaned forward. Kari battled the instinctive urge to pull back as the tiny face drew nearer. Did the Sylph intend to bite her? What did he want? She remained motionless, however; otherwise she might startle him into flying away. In his present condition he could injure himself with another fall to the deck.

He came close . . . and licked the wet trail of tears from her right cheek. His tiny tongue was warm and rough. Kari held her breath. She'd forgotten about the tears.

The salt. Of course. He desperately needed the salt. Apparently, the Sylph's sense of smell was so acute, he had picked up the faint scent of her tears from inside the arbor.

He licked her other cheek, then settled back to sit on her knee. He cocked his head to one side.

"More?"

Kari's heart thundered in her chest. The question had taken shape in her mind, unhindered yet nonthreatening, like a gentle caress. He was communicating with her telepathically. She stared at him, enthralled.

His head cocked the other direction. *"More to offer me?"*

Kari blinked, coming to her senses. "No, I-I'm sorry. I never cry, you see," she whispered, determined not to wake Talon. "I wouldn't know how to call forth tears. I'd like to help you more, but—" The wonder of the experience choked off her words, swelling in her chest until the pressure was almost painful in its glorious excitement. Her vision blurred. Before she realized they were there, fat tears rolled free. The Sylph warbled softly, leaning forward to help himself, then sat back on her knee. More tears came. He ignored them. Embarrassed, Kari scrubbed away the last remnants.

"My thanks."

Soft warbles and chirps accompanied his mental message, soothing sounds, deeper in tone than Beryl's. Kari began to relax. "You're welcome. Will that be enough?"

"Yes, until at Serac we arrive."

"Good. I mean, I don't think there's any more anyway. Crying is not a normal thing for me. It's a waste of energy to feel sorry for myself."

"All creatures deserve moments of sadness and reflection."

Kari's short, chopped-off laugh emerged more like a

grunt. "Not the Dynast's daughter. I can't afford to show signs of weakness. A leader has to be diligent and strong, always."

" 'Tis too hard on yourself, you are."

"What's your name?" she asked, deftly changing the subject.

"Oberon."

"Can I touch you, Oberon?" she ventured in a whisper.

In answer, he stood on her knee. Tentatively, Kari ran a finger across the purple edge of his graceful wing. Bolder, yet still gentle, she did the same down his blue torso. He felt like silk, the scales were so delicate. A smile worked its way across her mouth. It was then that she realized her hand was trembling.

Kari pulled it back quickly, curling her hand into a fist. "I must be tired," she said, feeling compelled to excuse her weakness.

"Exhausted, you are. Why do you not sleep?"

"Not blazing likely on this hard floor."

"Why do you deprive yourself of comfort in the bunk?"

"Because Talon's in there," she exclaimed.

"Left space for you, he has."

Intending to scoff at the very notion, she glanced cynically at the sleeping pilot. But it was true; the inner half of the bunk was still open. Talon could have covered the entire bunk in a casual, selfish male sprawl. A small consideration on his part, or coincidence? The idea of laying down was all too tempting. Kari moistened dry lips with the tip of her tongue.

"I couldn't," she whispered hoarsely.

"Talon is the only one who deserves comfort, then?"

"Of course not. If anything, he deserves to sleep in the brig," she hissed. "Too bad the *Nighthawk* doesn't have one."

"Then why do you deny yourself? 'Tis your own stubbornness, Kari of Khazanjian," the Sylph retorted.

Startled by the scolding tone of his mental message, it

118

took a moment for Kari to grasp the full import of his statement. He began to turn, gathering himself to launch into flight, when she whispered frantically, "Wait! How did you know who I am? Did Beryl tell you?"

"No. 'Tis because you have the look of your mother, Isolde."

"You knew my mother?"

"Yes, when she hid with us for the last of her days."

Then he flitted his wings and disappeared into his refuge.

Swearing, Kari lurched to her knees. Us? Other Sylphs? Then her mother hadn't wandered aimlessly into the forest to die. Isolde Solis had gone to the Sylphs.

Mother, why didn't you take me with you?

The old, haunting question cried out with a child's voice deep inside. Kari pressed her fist to her ribs, driving back the tormenting tightness and pain within her chest. No, she would not succumb to those worn-out doubts, the never-ending questions with no answers.

She sagged, weary to the marrow of her bones. It was all too much to deal with now. Tomorrow she'd demand more of the story from the Sylph. Her face warmed as realization struck—her father's tactics would hardly work in this situation. One couldn't interrogate a creature who communicated only by choice. Without the telepathic link, any explanation the Sylph provided would seem like so much garbled nonsense, no matter how musical.

And the last thing Kari wanted was to estrange the enchanting fellow. She wanted to touch him again, to experience the odd intimacy of sharing thoughts with a creature so very different from herself.

She'd think about it more after sleeping, when she was stronger. Her decision was made. As Oberon said, why should Talon be the only one allowed any comfort?

Leaning forward on hands and knees, she watched his face, probing for any sign of wakefulness—a flexing muscle, a flicker of an eyelid. If the runagate smuggler even hinted at being awake, she'd . . . well, she'd probably knock him over the head and ensure herself some deserved sleep, and a bit of revenge in the bargain.

When he didn't betray so much as a twitch, she permitted her gaze to wander, searching for faults. Her examination lingered over his broad forehead, prominent cheekbones, and square jaw. By the time she reached his ears, her irritation was mounting. She should be able to criticize his blazing ears . . . most men had rather ugly ears. Aha, now there was something. His nose was too bold, an outward indication of his blatant arrogance. And his eyebrows were far too thick, even with that stately arch. Before, his mouth had appeared hard, almost cruel. Now, softened in sleep, she could see a sculptured fullness to his firm lips.

She broke off the examination abruptly, irritated by the unruly direction of her thoughts. Okay, so he was attractive, she admitted grudgingly, in a barbaric sort of way. Thankfully, however, she didn't fall in with the pathetic lot of women who reputedly found Talon's looks appealing.

Kari crawled, ever so stealthily, onto the bunk and lay down. She held her breath, then let it out slowly when nothing happened. The rigidity in her body released one muscle at a time. Her thoughts began to drift.

What had Oberon meant by saying her mother had hidden with the Sylphs? Why would Isolde Solis need to hide?

Talon awoke the instant he felt Kari's weight settle onto the bunk behind him.

It took all his willpower not to jerk upright and reach instinctively for his weapons, responding with reflexes so ingrained they might as well have been genetically encoded. He lay perfectly still, knowing any sign that he was awake would send her flying out of the bunk quicker than . . . well, suffice it to say, a merkaat wouldn't bolt any faster if someone burned its long, clawed toes. The wait taxed his patience to the limit. After an inordinately long time her breathing evened out.

He turned over slowly. Propping up on his right elbow, he faced his unexpected bunkmate. She lay with her back to him, as close to the bulkhead as she could get. His mouth slanted in a wry grin. Even in sleep, she maintained maximum distance.

He stared at Kari's shadowed silhouette. The ebb and flow of her breathing lifted her chest in a soft rhythm. This way, at least, she was more woman than soldier. Her claws were sheathed.

Talon lowered his face into the curve of her neck and breathed deeply. He closed his eyes and allowed her scent, spiced with the slight tang of salt, to fill his senses.

He picked up her thick braid and rubbed it between his thumb and forefinger. So soft. The color appeared almost black in the darkened cabin. Without sufficient light to reflect the deep red strands, the fire in her hair was subdued, much as sleep temporarily tamed her hot temper. He stroked her hair against his upper lip.

A shudder rippled through him unexpectedly, awakening nerve endings he thought numb from exhaustion. His hand stretched out toward her. What could it hurt? She'd never know. He might as well enjoy this aura of softness about her, because it would certainly disappear the moment she awoke.

He traced her graceful outline, his palm hovering at the very edge of her radiating warmth . . . a safe distance, a rational distance. From her shoulder, down to the deep curve of her slender waist, up over gently flared hips—

He reached her thigh. His lower arm trembled with the urge to make contact. The heat of her invaded his palm. His hand lowered, seemingly of its own will, to rest lightly on her upper thigh. Even through the leather pants, he could feel the resilience of firm legs and buttocks. His breathing reversed unexpectedly, drawing in on a long, ragged intake of air.

121

Drawing back with a scowl, Talon lay down with a grunt of self-disgust, still facing her. This was insane. The woman hated him. The feeling was mutual, of course, when she was awake and he was treated to the full, acidic force of her antagonism.

And the biggest, most lethal trap of all was to give credence to the ludicrous idea that her temper and hardheadedness hid a passionate nature.

Chapter Eight

Instinct prodded Talon awake just before the Corridor exit. There was nothing new about that. What made this time very different was waking to discover an expanse of creamy skin and a curve of long, luxuriously thick auburn lashes directly in his line of sight.

Sometime during the night passage Kari had turned over. How had she managed that without waking him? Sleep should have been fitful, at best.

He must be losing his edge.

Slowly, with the same care he'd give to not disturbing a venomous whip-serpent, Talon eased back a little from his volatile bunkmate. If she awoke and found him this close—runagate hell, the resultant explosion would likely knock the *Nighthawk* off course.

She murmured softly, unintelligible little sleep mutterings. The sound somehow made her seem more approachable, the natural woman emerging through the misty world of dreams. Talon wondered what type of dreamworld Kari Solis retreated to in her sleep. Did she capture smugglers and defeat the Rebels single-handedly?

She sighed just then, a uniquely throaty sound of feminine contentment. His mouth quirked upward at one corner. She didn't seem to be waging any battles at the moment. He hesitated, stealing the opportunity to examine her intriguing, beautiful face in repose, untainted by her typical frown of hostility.

Her free hand reached forward, seeking blindly. Her fingers fanned across his bare chest; her palm grazed over one nipple.

Talon clenched his teeth. He might have been able to crush his body's response to that first innocent contact, but she repeated the intimacy with a touch of pure velvet. The sensation speared straight for his core, slicing through his defenses, leaving an insidious breach for desire to invade. It stormed in, hot and demanding, hardening his manhood in a rush.

Kari's eyes opened slowly, the long lashes brushing against her cheeks as she blinked sleepily. She was obviously only half awake, disoriented, since she wasn't trying to claw his eyes out.

Her tongue slid out, gathering her lip between her teeth. The lower half of her luscious mouth—that infuriatingly full, provocative lip—escaped bondage slowly, slipping free of her white, even teeth. The sight drew him like a magnet. What would it feel like to kiss her? He leaned forward to find out.

The ship's proximity alarm went off, warning of the imminent Corridor exit.

Green eyes flew open. Outrage sparked. Instinct clamored for Talon to jerk back, but his body seemed curiously sluggish. Though he saw the blow coming, it seemed to unravel in slow motion, as if it was happening to someone else, or in a dream.

He woke up quickly enough when her fist connected.

He rolled off the bed, furious. How could he have been gullible enough to believe that soft, approachable look could be remotely real? Everything about Kari Solis was a disaster. One minute he reveled in the molten heat pooling in his loins, anticipating covering her teasing mouth with his own, the next he was trying to draw a ragged breath into his gut-punched body. Pain. She served it up to him in generous doses. Perhaps pain was just what he needed, believing for one idiotic moment that there was any warmth or passion beneath that prickly exterior.

Snatching up the Lochnar flight suit from the floor, he pulled out the reserve key sequencer and slapped it onto his shackle. Time for the volcanic fireworks to begin.

"Where did that come from?" she exploded, right on cue.

He glared at her through narrowed eyes. "It's the original sequencer for the shackles. I just happened to pick it up on our way out of Naill's quarters," he answered sourly, giving full rein to his sarcasm. The lock clicked open.

"You mean you had it all along?"

"You figured that out all by yourself? Impressive."

She opened her mouth, then shut it with a click of her teeth. When it opened again her withering tone conveyed her opinion of his intelligence. "Then why didn't you use it?"

"I just did." He lifted his free wrist to demonstrate.

"I mean last night," she snarled.

He shrugged. "I know what you mean. I used it when I chose to, after guaranteeing myself a good night's sleep."

Talon stepped toward her, shackle in hand. She recoiled, her expression as wary as a wounded animal's. A caustic feeling of revulsion spread through him at being cast in the role of torturer and jailer.

Cursing under his breath, he attached the key to her shackle. The snick of the opening lock was distinctly audible in the sudden silence.

For once Kari was struck speechless. She stared at him in disbelief as the hated metal restraint dropped from her wrist. She briefly considered diving at him, but his aggressive, ready stance told her that would not be a wise move.

"Why are you doing this?"

"I'm proposing a truce, Princess. Promise you won't try to escape and I'll abandon the temptation to parade you, shackled, through the tradeport of Boreas."

Her chin jerked up a notch. "You're suggesting I cooperate? Seems to me you're getting the better end of the bargain."

"I intend to put you on a shuttle for Star Alpha after I've finished my business on Serac. Satisfied?"

"*Willing* and *hostage* aren't exactly compatible terms, are they," she drawled, matching his cynical tone.

He let out a heavy sigh. "You don't seem too keen on the idea. Perhaps—" He stepped forward.

"All right! Anything to keep free of that blazing chain."

"I have your word, then?"

"Yes," she bit out, almost choking on the answer.

"Good."

"Just remember, the truce only lasts until your business is completed. Any time after that, you're fair game."

"Your threats are too damn frequent and bloodthirsty to be forgotten," he said between clenched teeth.

"Not threats, promises." The fire in his eyes warned her to back off, but wounded pride overrode common sense. "What about you? How do I know you won't renege and drag me back aboard?"

"Oh, don't worry," he said with deadly calm. "I'm motivated—quite eager, in fact—to be rid of you. I've regretted every moment since I brought you aboard the *Nighthawk*."

Kari wanted to retaliate with a vicious taunt of her own, but unexpectedly her throat closed off and her chest hurt, as if she'd swallowed a spiny seed pod from the *chaq'tu* tree.

Talon continued. "I'll put you on that shuttle, but not until I'm ready to leave Serac myself. Obviously, I have to make sure I stay one step ahead of you from now on."

He looked her over slowly, making her acutely aware, and furiously resentful, of every centimeter of smudged skin, sweat-stiffened clothing, and mussed hair.

"The lav is at your disposal, Princess. Use it. We have twenty minutes until atmosphere penetration. You'll need to be buckled into the copilot's seat by then. Any problem with that?"

"None whatsoever," she retorted sourly while struggling

to conceal her surprise, and then her secret pleasure. A shower!

Kari reluctantly turned off the water jets. Talon would likely drag her out by her hair if she didn't hurry.

Steam lingered in the lav, coating everything in a slick, dull sheen. After toweling off briskly she donned her plain brown bustier. The cool, smooth silk lining felt good against her heated skin. She lifted her pants down from the wall hook and discovered her utility belt hanging underneath them.

She snatched the belt down, dismay overriding the embarrassment of knowing Talon had entered the lav while she showered. The greater worry was the safety of the data cylinder. She tore open the pocket. The cylinder was there. She sagged in relief. Soon she'd be able to examine Naill's files, at Star Alpha, if not before. She wriggled her still-damp body into her pants and boots, then clipped on the belt. She looked around for her shirt.

It was gone. Why, that lousy pirate!

She stuck her head out the door. Talon sat hunched over the console. The blue-white curve of Serac dominated the viewport.

"Where's my shirt?"

"Hanging on the door," he said without turning around.

She looked up. A blue tunic, richly embroidered in black around the cuff and hem, hung outside. "That's not my shirt."

"True. It's mine."

Kari blinked. He intended to loan her his tunic? There must be some catch. "I want my own clothes."

"This is the ice planet, remember? You'll freeze in that wispy silk thing. The tunic's woven of quivote. Wear it."

She started to protest, then stopped, intrigued. Quivote. She'd heard of the prized material, woven from the hump-hair of the huge shagyas that grazed Serac's borderlands of tundra and loose snow. The talent for combing and weaving the fragile hair was a secret jealousy guarded by the Mal'Harith.

She stroked the tunic, then did so again to make sure her senses weren't fooling her. It was unbelievably soft. How would it feel against her skin? Well, logically speaking, being too cold would slow her reactions and put her at a disadvantage.

Talon watched Kari's reflection in the viewport, expecting her to grind his offering beneath her heel. Instead, a shapely arm slipped around the door. Then a bare shoulder peeked into view. Talon swallowed convulsively. She stroked her fingertips down the tunic. His chest muscles flexed. Stars, you'd think he was wearing the blasted thing! He closed his eyes in self-defense. When he opened them again the tunic was gone.

Kari donned the garment, sighing over the luxury of material softer than any she'd ever known. Too big, but she wasn't swamped by it. She rolled up the cuffs and peeked out the door.

Talon was still busy at the console. Beryl sat on his shoulder. Now was her chance to check on Oberon. Kari crept toward the arbor. Closing the small access panel, she opened the human-sized door and slipped silently into the Sylphs' domain.

The delicate scent of NightGlory flowers twined pleasantly around her. Violet blooms cascaded from a profusion of vines, anchored to the walls by aerial roots. Fiber-optic cables fed light from outside the ship. There was barely room to stand.

Oberon climbed nimbly down from a nest of interwoven leaves and roots. He squatted on a thick vine hanging at eye level. Kari hugged her arms about her waist, cherishing the bubbling feeling of joy that came from just watching him. Each shimmering blue and purple scale was as colorful as a tiny jewel.

"Are you all right, Oberon?"

"Yes."

Drawing a deep breath, Kari ventured into unknown territory. "What did you mean by saying my mother 'hid' with the Sylphs?"

"Asked for refuge, your mother did."

"Refuge? Why?"

"Reveal the reason, Isolde did not."

"I don't understand," Kari murmured, mostly to herself. She shook her head in wounded confusion. "Why would Mother need refuge? Father gave her everything her heart desired. And if she had stayed where she could have been given the best medical care, she might have lived."

"Perhaps all will be made clear when you come."

"Come? Come where?"

"To Verdigris, you must."

"You can certainly count on that," Kari said in an emphatic whisper. "Escape from Talon is top priority. Home is where I should be right now, preparing my ship and crew to chase that reprobate to the end of the solar system . . . on my terms."

"Not to your home; to mine. Isolde left something for you."

Kari stared at him in blank shock. Oberon couldn't have said anything more designed to throw her off balance. She had only a few small mementoes of her mother—a bracelet, a hair comb, a dagger etched with the Khazanjian crest—things she'd barely managed to conceal from Myklar's rage when he discovered his wife gone. Myklar had ordered everything destroyed, unable to bear the bittersweet sight of his beloved wife's belongings. Was there more? Other treasures, more personal things that could help resurrect the memories she craved? More importantly, a message of some kind, any kind, explaining why a grieving twelve-year-old daughter had been left behind.

Realizing where her raw emotions were taking her, Kari forcefully shrugged the excitement away. She shouldn't care. She refused to let it matter. Very likely she would discover painful proof of a mother's lack of caring.

Nevertheless, she croaked, "What did she leave?"

"This I do not know. 'Tis sealed in a chest, left in our keeping. 'Tis an honor among us to guard Isolde's legacy."

"How many Sylphs are there in this place?"

"When last I was there, almost four hundred adults. There were many young, as well."

Kari gasped. "Is there just one of these . . . Sylph kingdoms?"

"No. Many, there are. I speak only of my home."

And Sylphs were thought to be exceedingly rare. How elusive were creatures who managed to conceal their number from their human neighbors for generations, perhaps thousands of years? True, they occupied the most inaccessible parts of the Verdigran forests, the remote ends of the vein-canyons too narrow for human dwellings, but the accomplishment of such secrecy was stunning.

"How did you end up at Narkwar?"

"Saved a young female from an adheso-net, only to become entangled in the sticky fibers. Eight months have passed."

"But it's illegal to trap Sylphs! They're supposed to come of their own free will."

"Yet, it is done," Oberon communicated with the first sign of anger she'd heard from him. *"Sylphs like the company of humans, enjoy tending the variety of plants they cultivate, but only those humans of warm spirit. Not all humans are of warm spirit, Kari of Khazanjian,"* he finished in a warning tone.

Kari gnawed her lower lip. How right he was. Gar Urkanis was a prime example. How it must have pained Oberon, not only physically but deep in his complex soul, to be under Gar's control in that grim place. So where did Talon fit into this formula? What had he done to earn the loyalty of a Sylph? It just didn't fit.

To cover her resentment-laced confusion, Kari asked, "Where is your home?"

"A special place of safety. A sacred place to Sylphs. Betray

its location to others, you must not," he said sternly.

"No. No, of course not. I would never reveal your hiding place." The thought of Oberon entangled in a net, his wings useless, his freedom stolen away, was making her feel ill. She couldn't bear for that to happen to others. "But if the location is secret, how will I find it?"

"Show you the way, I will."

The door to the arbor swung open.

"There you are," came a deep, resonant voice.

Kari pivoted to face Talon. He filled the doorway, the outline of his broad shoulders distorted by the shape of Beryl crouched on one side and a tunic tossed negligently over the other. He was still bare-chested . . . dammit. He had shaved, revealing the full impact of his rugged good looks. Worst of all, the zipstrap up the front of his black pants was only half done, exposing a *V* of dark hair below his navel.

"What are you doing in here?" he demanded.

"I—" she began, then faltered. Her thoughts seemed to be spiraling down a black hole, dominated by images of dark hair and sleek muscles. The sweet smell of flowers competed with the spice of shaving gel, but the true victor was the subtle musk of raw masculinity.

Oberon leapt from his perch onto her shoulder. The slight impact jarred her back to her senses. The Sylph wrapped his left wing around the back of her head.

Talon's eyebrows shot up. "Runagate hell, the Sylph's connected with you."

Connected. Kari liked the term. Her mouth curved in a smile as she answered defiantly, "Yes, he has."

Her jailer's expression hardened noticeably. "Must be due to his weakened condition. Sylphs only connect with people they like and respect. I thought he would be more discriminating."

Anger spurred Kari into taking a step forward. She glared belligerently into Talon's set face. "Too bad I can't be so choosey about whom I talk to."

Beryl interrupted the escalating series of insults by erupting into a staccato series of chirps and whistles, an obvious scolding tone directed at Oberon. The male Sylph countered the jealous tirade by stroking Kari's damp hair.

Beryl's lecture halted abruptly. With a strangled little squeak, she pushed off Talon's shoulder and disappeared. Talon ducked his head to the side, dodging a flurry of purple wings as Oberon followed. The Sylphs' abrupt exit left the two humans alone, nose-to-chin.

They were entirely too close.

The realization slammed into Kari, causing her breath to come shallow and fast. She should take a step backward, but her damnably unresponsive feet seemed rooted to the floor. The silence raked across her nerves as Talon's piercing gaze searched her face . . . for what? And why didn't he make one of his cynical comments? Yes, that's what she needed. Then anger would enable her to move. But, uncooperative wretch that he was, he uttered not a word to trigger her natural defenses. Instead, his hand lifted toward her unbound hair.

The movement was slow, nonthreatening. His splayed fingers slipped into her damp hair. His warm fingertips brushed the cool skin behind her ear. An odd melting sensation invaded her legs, leaving them weak and trembling. Of all the insane things, she felt like leaning into him, pressing her hands to the flat planes of his abdomen, feeling that crisp hair curling against her palms.

His head tilted toward her.

The first bump that rocked the ship didn't earn any notice. It fit right in with the leap of her heart and all the other foreign sensations she was experiencing.

The second bump deserved complete attention. Talon's head snapped up.

"Dammit, the nav-computer's taking us into the atmosphere." He grabbed her arm. "Come on, we have to strap in."

He tugged her, still dazed, into the cabin. She dropped

into the copilot's seat and buckled the restraints. He yanked on his tunic—a duplicate of hers, except his was black with silver embroidery—then strapped into the pilot's seat. The Sylphs retreated to the arbor, still bickering.

Kari braided her hair during the rough ride into the atmosphere, more to conceal stealthy glances at her shipmate than to keep herself occupied. Talon seemed totally engrossed in his task, as if nothing significant had just occurred between them. It irritated her that he had apparently easily dismissed what just happened, while her insides were still quivering.

He banked the *Nighthawk* fifteen degrees as they approached the surface, flying almost straight into the glare of the rising sun. The golden rays turned the flat plain of snow and ice crystals into a glittering spectrum of refracted color.

A huge circle, darker than the surrounding ice, appeared ahead. Its center glowed orange.

"The blister city of Boreas," Talon explained.

"That's the access tunnel?" she asked, indicating an opening in the ice well away from the semi-transparent blister cap.

"The entrance to the inter-planetary hangar bay, yes. The hangar for the local shuttle is on the opposite side. Both are approximately thirty meters beneath the surface. They can only be reached through the tunnels."

He proceeded to demonstrate, heading the ship straight down through the gaping maw of the main entrance. What followed seemed to Kari a chaotic, slipheed ride through twisting tubes of glistening white. Each turn threatened an imminent crash. Only when they emerged into the hangar and Talon switched to hoverlifts did she realize her nails were digging into her seat. She didn't know whether to snap at him or praise his piloting skills.

She quickly lost interest in either, caught up in the wonder of Boreas's link to the rest of the solar system. The hangar, a majestic cathedral with a high domed ceiling of opaque white, bustled with the activity of a busy tradeport. Spacecraft of all varieties lined the ice walls. Men scrambled about loading or unloading cargoes. Tradesmen gestured emphatically as they dickered prices. Talon set the *Nighthawk* down in an open slot.

While the ship powered down he opened a storage bin in the floor and pulled out a thick fur coat, matching hat, and a pair of serrated metal plates. He pressed the plates to the bottom of his boots. Clamps snapped into place, transforming the soles into bristling rows of teeth.

"Sorry I have only the one pair of spikebits. You'll need to hold on to my arm as we walk." Slanting her a wary look, he added, "unless you prefer to slip and fall flat on your backside."

Kari welcomed the jibe, grateful for the return to their usual thrust-and-parry. It was a familiar battleground, safer than the new and unsettling feelings that careened through her body when he touched her. "I'd rather go home bruised from head to toe," she retorted.

Talon scowled. "I'll buy you some damned spikebits of your own. Now, try this on." He shoved the coat at her.

Kari reached out, prepared to push the coat back in his face, until her fingers sank into the fur. She hesitated, drawn by the luxurious feel, curious as to its source. Though slightly rough-textured, the long creamy-white hairs were dense and warm. "What kind of pelt is this?"

"Catamount."

Startled, she glanced up. His revelation triggered memories of lessons on the huge feline predators: Serac's native nightmare, complete with curved fangs and vicious claws. "I've heard few men have successfully hunted catamounts. They must be a very difficult kill."

"This one was, but when a catamount is attacking you don't stop to think about statistics."

Kari's hands clenched convulsively in the fur, suddenly sure this had been his kill. What kind of courage did it take to face something so primitive, a creature whose only goal was to spill blood and dine on your flesh? "Are they really as big as they appear in the capto-images?" she whispered.

"Bigger. Try it on," he insisted.

"No." She dumped the coat back in his arms.

"You are the most unreasonably stubborn woman I've ever met!" he exploded. "What's wrong with the coat, Princess? Is it contaminated because I've worn it?"

"No. But if I wear it, what will prevent you from being cold?" she said quietly, surprising herself with the comment, particularly because she meant every word.

The anger vanished from his eyes, replaced by uncertainty. He looked away, then back again. His gaze searched her face, no doubt expecting signs of insincerity. In that moment he seemed almost . . . vulnerable.

"Then I'll just carry it for now," he finally grumbled, turning away. "We can both freeze, like idiots. Let's go."

A smile tugged at the corners of Kari's mouth. This uncertain, almost boyish side to Talon was an intriguing contrast to his typical competent arrogance. "What about your spikebits? Aren't you going to take them off? If we're to leave the *Nighthawk* on such equal terms, you should be prepared to slip and fall on your posterior, too."

He looked over his shoulder. His right eyebrow arched sardonically. "One of us has to show some common sense."

Excitement bubbled up in her chest. Appalled, Kari realized she was about to laugh. She sobered instantly.

"You first," he said, indicating the hatch with a nod.

After descending the ramp Kari stood beneath the ship and looked around curiously. People moved in and out of the hangar, walking or riding ice skimmers. Tunnels opened in every conceivable direction. The clomp of Talon's serrated boots sounded after a minute. She turned to get an eyeful of muscular thighs and the outline of his sword, with her own strapped to the outside of the sheath and his dagger in place on his arm.

135

Very clever, Talon, she thought with reluctant admiration. He'd waited until she was outside before revealing where he'd hidden the weapons. A missed opportunity. Then again, not. She'd given her word.

"So many tunnels. How do they manage the work involved?" she observed as they moved toward one of the smaller, less-trafficked exits. Keeping her footing wasn't that difficult. The ice was so chewed up by spikebits it was like walking on dry powder rather than something slick and treacherous.

"Hoarworms carve out the tunnels. They're perfect for the job. Just harness their natural burrowing behavior and direct them where to carve a passageway."

Kari turned to search the cavern.

Talon chuckled. "Don't worry; if one was in the hangar you would have spotted it. Adult males max out at about nine meters, females at seven. Even newborns are as long as you are tall."

She followed him into the tunnel. The floor was definitely slippery here. Head down, Kari concentrated on her footing. The last thing she wanted was to end up in an ignoble sprawl on the floor, providing Talon with amusement. She didn't notice he had stopped until, suddenly, she walked right into his broad back. It was like hitting a wall. Her boots slipped. She started to fall. He caught her around the shoulders, steadying her against his side . . . so close. Her heart accelerated.

"Look," he said softly.

She did, and gasped. The entire tunnel was blocked by a giant white bristle pad, the lower half dominated by a gaping mouth with three rows of sharp teeth, above and below. High over the mouth were a pair of oval-shaped blue crystals as large as her head. Opaque membranes passed over the blue eyes as the creature blinked. Captoimages didn't do a Hoarworm justice.

"Somewhat intimidating at first encounter, aren't they?" he commented.

She shivered, not from the cold but the shocking warmth of his breath against the side of her face. "Don't be ridiculous," she snapped. "I simply dislike having my path blocked by something that looks so distinctly . . . immoveable." She squirmed out from under his arm.

"You've got that right. One doesn't move a Hoarworm. One coaxes it gently to undulate out of the way. No legs, you know, just a series of thick, powerful muscles along its belly that propel it with a natural wave motion. A Hoar can move along at a pretty good clip when it wants to." He gave her a grin she could only refer to as calculating. "Want to pet it?"

Kari snorted before she could prevent herself. "And where am I supposed to put my hand among all those teeth and bristles?"

"Like this." He moved forward and pressed his hand to the area of bristles just above the Hoarworm's gaping mouth. Curling his fingers into the dense thicket, he stroked downward.

"See, she likes to be scratched," Talon urged. The creature gave a gurgling noise, something like a purr, that resonated against the solid walls of the tunnel. The sound tempted Kari to grin. She bit the inside of her cheek instead.

"Your turn." He stepped back, challenge in his gaze.

She reached out. Two vertical slits, each longer than her hand, flared open. She froze. "Let me guess. That's its nose."

"She's sniffing you. A Hoarworm's sense of smell is acute."

Kari waited until the slits closed again. She wouldn't want her hand to accidentally disappear inside there. Then she sank her fingers into the bristles. Though stiff, the hairs were surprisingly smooth and springy. With her back to Talon, she allowed herself a smile while she stroked gently.

Suddenly the slits flared open again. The Hoarworm

took a sharp intake of breath; then a blast of air exploded outward with enough force to knock Kari backward several steps.

The narrow tunnel rang with Talon's deep laughter. Kari fumed as she brushed dry, spiny ice crystals from her clothes.

"I suggested you scratch her, not tickle her nose and make her sneeze," he finally managed.

Something snapped at his latest taunt. Her vision flared red to match the heat in her skin. She swung at Talon. He caught her wrist and jerked her against him.

Her soft breasts crushed against his hard chest. There was no armor between them, no shield at all. An odd, frightening heat curled through her.

"You meant that to happen, just to embarrass me!"

"How was I to know your touch was so gentle the Hoarworm would find it ticklish? If you were honest, you would admit it was funny." The glint of humor faded from his eyes. Softly, he added, "I'm not like Naill. I only meant to tease you."

His voice was husky, appealing. A subversive little voice within cried out for her to believe in his supposed sincerity, to trust him. It was impossible. He was the enemy, her captor. She pushed at his chest. He let her go.

A slender youth slipped around the Hoarworm. He saluted them with the short, blunt rod he carried in one hand. The boy nudged the Hoarworm in the jaw with the instrument. The great beast turned, revealing a huge body completely covered in thick white hair and undulated away down an unfinished side tunnel. Sounds of crunching ice began immediately.

The Hoarworm's exit opened the main tunnel, allowing a frigid blast of air to sweep through. The chill cut through Talon's tunic, pricking at his skin. He heard Kari's sharp intake of breath. She crossed her arms tightly, pushing the graceful mounds of her breasts even higher.

Her soft flesh against his blue tunic, dammit. Talon bit

back a groan. In the future, every time he wore the garment it would remind him forcefully of her tempting curves.

"Cold?" he asked roughly.

He expected her to deny it. She surprised him by nodding. He shook out the coat and wrapped it around her. When she tried to shrug free he gripped her shoulders.

"Don't. Just wear it until we get to the blister atrium. Then I'll buy you a coat of your own." He released his hold before she could show her distaste of his touch again.

"That's not—"

"Consider it compensation for your trouble."

"You know I'm thinking in terms of a much larger payback."

"Since I intend to deny you the satisfaction of recapturing me, now or in the future, you'll have to settle for the coat."

"I hope you're cold," she said waspishly.

His mouth slanted in a self-mocking smile. Cold? His galloping libido still spread warmth to every extremity of his body, and one in particular. He'd consider himself lucky if just being close to her didn't cook him alive.

Chapter Nine

Boreas.

He'd been here a thousand times. But today was anything but mundane. Talon was seeing the tradeport city through new eyes.

Kari looked about with wide-eyed fascination when they emerged in the blister atrium. Sensing her eagerness, her childlike wonderment, he experienced a compelling urge to take her on a lengthy tour and show her all the amazing adaptations for life on the ice world. The open, vulnerable look on her face enhanced her beauty to the point that it hurt for him to draw breath.

He couldn't, of course. She was the enemy. He had to find Rand before he went crazy wondering what had happened to him. Kari would have to settle for the abbreviated tour. He grasped her arm and led her across the dense, pale yellow grass that composed the natural floor of the atrium, toward the buildings stacked against the opposite towering wall of ice.

The bubbling caldron of the geothermal pool dominated the center, creating and maintaining the delicate balance of this sheltered world. Nothing existed within a four-meter radius of the boiling, orange-gold water, so intense was the heat. Beyond that, much of the atrium floor was given over to agriculture. A variety of plants grew in concentric circles, nourished by the constant temperature and the mineral-rich soil. All were pale pastel in color, due to the filtered sunlight.

The buildings offered the only vibrant color. The prefabricated structures, attached to the ice and stacked three levels high, were constructed of dual-pane walls filled with an insulating, color-encoded gelatin. If the owners grew bored with their home's decor, they could liquify the gelatin and change the color. The residences and service buildings were connected by an elaborate network of walkways, ladders, and lifts.

Facing the buildings was a double row of vendor stalls where the real commerce of Boreas took place. Every conceivable ware was offered, from food to jewelry to clothing. Talon made two brief stops to take care of replenishing their food and salt supplies, including same-day delivery to the *Nighthawk*. Then he paused at a dealer with shagya wool goods.

The vendor, a beautiful young woman with waist-length blond hair and blue eyes, was easily recognizable as Mal'Harith.

"Hello, Talon," the woman said with an inviting smile.

Kari's eyes narrowed and shifted suspiciously between the two. For some ludicrous reason, Talon was suddenly glad Janna was not one of the women he'd taken to his bed.

"Good day to you, Janna. My friend here is in need of a coat, hat, gloves, and a pair of spikebits."

"I am not!"

Irritably, he pointed out, "The expense will put a drain on my already strained credit accounts. And if you intend to hunt me down on Serac, you'll need the proper gear."

"In that case, I accept," Kari declared, much too agreeably. Janna handed her a hat. She yanked it down over her ears.

Kari was defiant, daring, infuriating . . . and delightfully feminine with her face framed by the fluff of brown and white hair. This was insane. Not only was he attracted to a woman who regarded him as a prize to be delivered to

141

her father, his obsessive lust was getting progressively worse.

She reached for the coat. Without thinking, he snatched it up first. "Here, allow me." He stepped behind her and helped her put it on. Sliding his index finger beneath her braid, he ran his knuckle up, then down the nape of her neck, before tugging her hair free of the collar. Warmth radiated from her soft skin. He felt a delicate shiver ripple through her body.

"It's lined with quivote," he murmured against her ear.

"I . . . I noticed."

He willed her to look at him. The slightest turn of her head would bring her lips within kissing distance of his eagerly waiting mouth. She foiled his ploy by slanting a wary glance out of the corner of her eye. Finally, realizing Janna was staring at them curiously, he pulled back.

"Talon," Kjell called, interrupting the charged silence.

Talon turned to watch the Rebel second-in-command hurry toward them. Kjell Timor would know where to find Rand. Too bad Talon had to endure characteristic Rebel hostility to discover his brother's whereabouts.

"Stars, man," exclaimed Kjell. A grin flashed across his lean face. If that wasn't surprising enough, Talon felt his hand grasped in a vigorous shake. "Damn, I'm glad to see you, Talon. When you didn't follow us through the Corridor I was sure you'd been caught. Arden and I were meeting just now, making plans to go back for you, when Quinn burst in with the news that the *Nighthawk* had landed. Had to come see for myself." Kjell clapped him on the back. "How the hell did you get away from Narkwar?"

Talon's voice failed him, stolen away by shock. Where were the usual taunts, the derision? Kjell intended to risk his life to rescue him, a smuggler? Hope flickered, a tiny flame.

"It's a long story, one not very flattering to my ingenuity. Where is Rand? I want to see him before you take him home." Talon carefully avoided mention of Inclement, although the base would be nothing more than a name to Kari. Only Rebels knew the frequently changing coordinates of their highly mobile bases.

"He's in the med-lab. Seeing you will definitely lift his spirits." Kjell turned to Kari. "Who's the lovely lady?"

Talon recognized the blatant appreciation in Kjell's gaze, the male speculation. He felt a flash of irritation.

"Her name is Kari," he answered gruffly. "She's . . . in charge of a shipment I've arranged this trip."

"Really," Kjell drawled. "Procurer or client?"

"The former. Her family has been in the procurement business a long time. Isn't that right, Kari?"

Her family was in the procurement business, all right . . . whole planets and populations, not some paltry cargo. It was a naughty play on words designed to go over Kjell's head and draw Kari's attention back to himself. Where the demon urge to say it came from, he hadn't a clue.

"Indeed," Kari countered softly. "My family specializes in procurement. We're quite good at it, too."

Her gaze challenged his from beneath the smokey curve of her lashes. Talon felt a charge of excitement sweep through his body. He wanted to continue their verbal swordplay, see where it would lead. He wanted to kiss her so much he longed to tell Kjell to go stick his head in a snowdrift.

Talon quickly steered the conversation away from the deep pit he was digging for himself. "How is Rand?"

"Still pretty shaky," said Kjell. "The toxin finally wore off about three hours ago."

"Runagate hell, he was in that condition all this time?"

"Sorry. There was nothing we could do, other than strap him down to keep him from hurting himself . . . or us."

Swearing under his breath, Talon turned and snatched up Kari's newly acquired gloves and spikebits. "Thanks, Janna. You know where to charge it. Later, Kjell."

Leaving both people with their mouths gaping over his abrupt departure, he grasped Kari by the arm and strode urgently to the med-lab. When they entered the structure he signaled to a young med-tech.

"Keep my friend company, will you? She's never been to Boreas. If she tries to wander about, she might get lost. Or she might be mistaken for a Lochnar spy and be executed by the Rebels," he said half-jokingly. He gave her a warning glance, conveying a reminder of her oath as well as the fact that she was not among friends here. Then he headed down the hall.

The dimly lit recovery room was a marvel of soothing atmosphere and clean, crisp sanitation. The gelatinous coloring within the walls had been swirled into a marbleized pattern of forest green, cobalt blue, and cream, colors known to stimulate the body's own healing mechanisms.

The effect was lost on Talon when he saw his brother.

Rand lay on a body-conforming flexion bed. Everything about him bespoke crushing exhaustion. His hazel eyes focused on Talon from sockets so shadowed they looked bruised.

Someone was going to pay dearly for causing Rand such suffering. Since Naill was beyond reach—fortunately for him—Talon channeled his anger into self-disgust. Somehow he should have prevented this nightmare from happening to his brother.

"It's all right, Talon," said Rand, apparently sensing the direction of his thoughts. Though his voice was hoarse, it held an underlying strength that was reassuring.

Talon grasped Rand's hand. The weakness in his brother's normally brutally affectionate grip disturbed him deeply. He used his other gloved hand to enclose their clasped fists.

Talon said thickly, "I trust they found someone here who cooks well enough to put some weight back on you. I could do better than you've managed so far." They released hands.

Despite his efforts to tease a smile from Rand, it was

regret that flashed in those somber hazel eyes.

"Talon, I—" Rand began, then ground to a halt. He swallowed hard. "Kjell and Arden described what happened at Narkwar, how I tried to strangle—"

"They shouldn't have told you," Talon interjected harshly.

Rand's mouth slanted in a wry grin. "I sort of insisted."

"Forget the whole damned incident. All that mattered was successfully getting you out of there."

"I wish I could have done the same for you," Rand murmured.

"You didn't have the resources back then. And you pulled me out of enough scrapes before my internment at Narkwar to last a lifetime. How are you feeling, besides bloody awful?"

"He's doing quite well, considering," answered the physician, who chose that moment to enter the room.

"Did you find what caused the paranoia?" Talon demanded.

"Yes, indeed." The man turned aside and used a pair of tongs to lift a tiny object from a table. "The toxin was contained within this ampule, which was implanted under the skin of the high commander's inner thigh. The ampule was designed to slowly feed the toxin into the bloodstream, which is why the effects lasted so long. Evidently, the substance is a very strong hallucinogen, inducing severe paranoia and masking out the more reasoning brain functions, including memory."

"What do you mean, evidently? Surely you've tested it."

"Unfortunately, the substance was completely absorbed into his system before we could discover its source. There was nothing left in the ampule to test." The physician's disappointment was evident. "I do not know whether the toxin is natural or synthetic, where it came from, or even if we could have produced an antidote. Luckily, it wore off."

"I see." A chill worked its way under Talon's skin. This

could happen again. "Thanks for all your help. I'd like to talk to Commander Markos alone." The physician nodded and left.

"Rand, do you remember Kari Solis?"

"How could I forget? The woman was responsible for stealing my freedom. Stars, but she was determined to capture me."

"She still is."

Rand snorted. "Oh, and she told you this? When? Over a drink at the Stargazer?"

"No. At Narkwar," Talon muttered, despising the half truth. He'd never lied to his brother before, but he wasn't sure how Rand would react if he discovered Kari was in the next room.

"Sweet everlasting, Talon, what happened? Where have you been?" Rand demanded, his voice rising.

"Don't bother asking. I have no intention of telling you . . . yet. Suffice it to say you need to leave Boreas immediately, and live more underground than ever before. The woman's determined to hunt both of us down. She won't quit."

"Then we have to do something to stop her."

Talon stiffened. He had the means to stop Kari. He could turn her over to the Rebels . . . who would cage her and use her as a bargaining chip. But more disturbing, even frightening, was the knowledge that there were always extremists when a cause was at risk, even among the Rebels, men who might hurt her. An almost violent wave of possessiveness swept over him. No one would touch her, or influence her destiny, except him.

Or was his brother even proposing—? Furious, he snarled, "What do you suggest I do, Rand? Wait until she's aboard a ship smaller than a battle cruiser, then shoot it down?"

"The *Nighthawk* certainly has the firepower."

"Is that what you really want?" Talon probed fiercely.

"No, dammit," Rand shot back. He raked his hand

through his already mussed hair, then added roughly, "No, I don't."

Thank the stars he hadn't misjudged his older brother. The lessons from their mother still held sway: fight only when provoked, use their special skills only to defend.

"Rand, there's one thing I need to know. Was Jemara Solis responsible for your . . . condition? for the drug?"

"She did a damn good job of interrogating me, but I don't think she knew about this. She had a violent argument with Urkanis outside my cell concerning the cruelty of his preferred methods. When he came in later, with his slimy little lab-tech and four guards, and a nervous compulsion to glance repeatedly over his shoulder, I didn't think he had her blessing. I draw a blank afterwards, but that part I remember clearly."

Talon closed his eyes briefly, startled by the intensity of the relief washing through him. She hadn't lied to him.

He had to leave. If anyone recognized Kari—It was time to get her out of there before disaster struck.

"What aren't you telling me?" Rand asked suspiciously.

"Believe me, you don't want to know."

How very subtle of Talon, Kari thought bitterly, to give her a watchdog without labeling him as such. The young med-tech grinned sheepishly at her.

"Bored?" he asked sympathetically. "Sorry there's nothing here to entertain you. It's only a med facility."

She smiled back at him. "Do you have a computer I can borrow for a few minutes?"

"Yeah, I guess. I doubt you'll find our data repositories interesting, though. They only contain medical data, and even then they're a bit sketchy. We aren't allowed access to all the medical data stored in the Lochnar systems."

"That's all right. I brought my own," Kari reassured him, pulling the thumb-sized cylinder out of her utility belt.

He shrugged. "Sure, why not?" He showed her to a computer.

147

"You saved me from a tedious wait. Thanks."

"I'll leave you to . . . well, whatever it is you're going to do. Call if you need anything. I'll be right over there," he said, pointing to another station.

He moved away, freeing Kari to slide her cylinder into the reader. With a mounting sense of urgency, she sorted Naill's files by date and read six of the most recent ones. They contained nothing more than mundane Lochnar business. Kari forced her right hand to uncurl before she hit the keyboard. Blazes, time was not a luxury right now! Maybe she should just eject the cylinder and wait until she got to Star Alpha. No, one more file; just one. Issuing an open command on the next file, she clenched her teeth in expectation of another disappointment.

A window popped up instead, requesting a password.

Kari's heart rate jumped. A password-locked file? There was something here; she just knew it. She tried likely combinations as fast as her fingers could enter them, drawing on Naill's obsessions, his prejudices. Nothing worked.

Damn. She preferred open, honest confrontations, not this sly pilfering of secrets. She should program Naill into the *Regalia*'s sim-chambers as an opponent. He'd probably be flattered, considering that he hated her as much as she despised him.

Kari stilled. If Naill really wanted to protect this file, he'd have chosen as a password the last thing anyone would expect.

She typed in her name. The file opened.

Talon's voice filtered down the hallway.

No! Frantically, she tried to scan the document. In her haste, the words blurred into utter nonsense. Only one phrase stuck in her mind . . . *hijack the shipment*. Damn, what was that supposed to mean? She had to stop before Talon caught her.

She ejected the cylinder and popped it into her belt, then quickly moved away from the computer, trying to look nonchalant.

Talon came around the corner. At his expression, Kari forgot her own excitement. The planes of his handsome face had hardened until they were as stark and unyielding as bare cliffs of windswept slate. His eyes looked black, their depths boiling with fury and the promise of retribution. She no longer doubted. Rand Markos had been drugged, or worse, poisoned.

Mercy, did Talon blame her? Here was vengeance incarnate.

Talon grasped her upper arm. "We're leaving. Your shuttle awaits, Princess."

She followed, too grateful for the reprieve to complain about the manhandling. He didn't intend to throttle her here and now.

Outside, they were greeted by a low, moaning wail. "What is that awful noise?" she exclaimed.

"Boreas's version of an alarm. Anything more strident risks shattering the ice cap." Kjell came racing up. "What's going on?" Talon asked urgently.

"We've got incoming Lochnar Interceptors from the Corridor."

"How many?"

"Four."

"Did you retrieve the *Stormhawk* from Star Alpha?"

"Right after we got back," Kjell said reassuringly.

"Then get Rand out of here."

"Exactly what I had in mind." Kjell gripped Talon's shoulder in a brusk gesture, then ran into the med facility.

"Come on; we've got to get to the *Nighthawk.*"

Kari planted her feet and jerked back against his hold. "You're joking, right? My rescue is on the way."

He swung her around to face him and gave her a quick shake. "If you'd demonstrate some intelligence, instead of just bull-headed defiance, you'd figure out those ships are most likely sent by your half-brother . . . after both of us, dammit. Or do you think he applauded your helping me escape?"

"I prefer to believe they are from my father, sent to hunt you down like the runagate you are," she exploded defensively.

"Think, Kari. I heard you tell Naill that Myklar's on the *Viceroy*. These ships are less than an hour behind us," he countered with quiet, penetrating logic.

Kari glared at him, teeth clenched. She hated the knowledge in his fathomless brown eyes, the quiet surety that he wasn't the only one in danger. Would Naill dare to hurt her? Myklar was beyond reach. Her men had no idea of her whereabouts. She hadn't been this alone, this exposed, since . . . Images of the cruel, potentially dangerous tricks Naill had played on her as a child arose in her mind, making her mouth go dry.

Unexpectedly, Talon released her arms and stepped back. The loss of his touch left Kari feeling bereft, as if she'd lost a safehold, her best protection against a menace that was growing more malevolently possible the more she thought about it.

"Go ahead, leave," he said roughly, "if you feel it's safe."

"I'm not afraid of him!"

"I never said you were. But this isn't about fear. This is about strategy, facing the enemy at a time of your own choosing."

"And where am I supposed to devise this strategy? Aboard the *Nighthawk*, with you hovering over me as jailer?"

"Unfortunately, no," he retorted, then swore. She followed his angry gaze to find two pair of men clad in black armor, the customary garb of Naill's Interceptor force, emerging from the main tunnels to the hangar bay. "We're cut off. Come on; we'll have to try for the intercity shuttles," he said urgently, heading in the opposite direction.

"Hey, what are you doing? You can't take that!" a voice boomed across the comm after they leaped into a Serakian shuttle and slammed the hatch closed.

You've obviously never dealt with Talon, Kari thought wryly.

"Just watch me," Talon muttered, fulfilling her expectations of the whatever-it-takes mood she was coming to recognize.

The stern engines roared. The small craft surged forward. A short, frantic ride through the ice tunnel gave way to a brilliant blue sky and unblemished white landscape. Talon veered north, rapidly putting distance between themselves and Boreas.

Powerful engines roared overhead, paralleling their course. *So much for getting away unnoticed.* The shuttle's hull shuddered with sonic vibrations as the other ship shot past. Kari looked up to glimpse the Solis Line crest emblazoned in gold across the underside of the dark red, triangular-shaped craft.

The comm erupted into an ear-piercing whine. She recoiled in pain and disconnected the channel.

"They're jamming us," Talon confirmed.

He didn't need to elaborate. She knew the drill.

Interceptor pilots typically jammed all signals before shooting down an enemy ship. No prisoners.

Her fingers curled stiffly into her palms, longing to grip the weapons' controls in her own fighter. This paltry craft had none. Her fate depended on a miracle . . . or Talon.

"Tell me you have a plan in mind," she said tightly.

"I'm heading for those mountains, rough terrain. That ship is designed for space combat. I'm going to try and maneuver him into making a mistake by staying close to the surface."

"Isn't there something we can use against them—anything?"

"No, I—wait a second." His brow creased. "Maybe—"

The Interceptor banked sharply and headed back for them, growing rapidly in size and threat. It made a second pass overhead. Kari watched it turn again, slowing its speed for attack. They'd be overtaken before reaching the mountains.

"Talon, you better think of something quick."

"I'm working on it," he muttered while manipulating a strange set of controls on the console.

Something jarred the ship. "Blazes!" Kari swore, recognizing the flight path turbulence of an impact torpedo. A narrow miss. An explosion flared on the surface ahead. They sliced through a rising column of smoke.

The Interceptor roared past them into the distance, then executed another 180-degree turn. Kari's mouth went dry. The Lochnar pilot, in all likelihood, wouldn't miss this time. To make matters worse, something was going wrong with the shuttle. Odd vibrations shuddered through her seat.

She looked sharply at Talon. "What is that?"

"Anchor harpoons. I'm lowering them from their wing-berths. They're normally fired vertically into the ice, anchoring the ship on slopes, but I thought a horizontal firing position might come in handy." His eyes glittered. His mouth curved up at the corners in an oddly anticipatory smile.

Kari stared, speechless. Harpoons? What damage could harpoons inflict on a fast ship constructed of durasteel?

The red ship raced toward them, at the same altitude, directly on course for a head-on collision. The other pilot was trying to intimidate them. Kari held her breath.

Talon pulled back on the controls, gaining altitude at an abrupt 45-degree angle. Just as quickly, he dipped the nose of the shuttle on an intersect vector with the approaching ship. The Lochnar pilot dropped altitude to compensate. Talon fired the harpoons. The two heavy metal, barbed arrows hurtled straight for the Interceptor's cockpit. Kari caught a glimpse of the startled faces of the pilot and navigator as they reacted instinctively, dipping the ship to avoid the threat.

They were too low.

The fighter's wing-tip hit a snowdrift with enough force to crack the wing. It bellied into the surface with a horrendous grinding noise, sending up a spray of shaved ice and snow. A slight turn sent the crippled ship into a tumble, overturning it four times before coming to rest in a snowbank.

"Runagate hell!" Talon swore viciously.

His tone shattered Kari's bubbling sense of victory. Following his furious gaze, she saw another Interceptor dropping through a thin bank of clouds to the rear. An explosion near the stern nearly knocked the ship out of the air. They abruptly lost power in one engine. A hard knot of dread twisted in her chest.

"I think," Talon growled, "it's time to hide the shuttle."

"Don't land! They'll blast the area where we go down."

"Not if they torpedo the wrong spot. We'll just have to provide an alternative target."

"And just how do you propose to do that?"

"Jettison the engine cores."

"They'll be able to tell the difference between smoking engines parts and the main body of the craft!"

"Not if the engines are half buried in snow. There," he said, pointing ahead. "That's what I'm looking for."

Five huge ridges of sparkling snow, running parallel to one another, stretched across the shuttle's path directly ahead. Rock jutted upward from the last two, like dorsal scales along the backs of some great, lounging mythical beasts.

"Brace yourself," Talon commanded. "We're going through the first ridge."

"Through?" she yelped, sitting bolt upright. "Blazes, I'm going to die acting as copilot to a raging lunatic! What if it has a core of solid rock like those others?"

"The swirling winds typically mold drifts well out from a natural barrier, like sand dunes on Avernus. Those first ridges have the look of loosely packed snow, nothing more."

"How can you possibly be sure?"

"I didn't say I was," he muttered.

"This is terrific, just terrific. And if you're wrong?"

Muscles rippled up the length of his jaw. "Then we won't have to worry about torpedoes, will we? There won't be enough wreckage left to target. We'll only get one chance at this. You're in charge of jettisoning the cores. Hit the release the moment we punch through the drift."

Kari groaned aloud, agonizing over her lack of choices. Talon's plan, however ludicrous, was their only shot at survival.

She unlocked the lever, then gripped it with both hands. Her heart thundered, trying to push its way into her throat.

Talon leveled the shuttle just below the dorsal rim of the first ridge. Sparkling snow engulfed the viewport as they hit. Kari rammed the jettison lever as her body was thrown forward. A muffled explosion, marking the eject of the engines, jarred her senses as the shuttle broke through again into golden sunlight.

Kari barely had time to blink as the ship's momentum hurtled it toward the next ridge. They hit, punching deep into the wall of white. Then there was nothing but pain and blackness.

Chapter Ten

Unrelieved black.

That's what Naill found so appealing about the *gal'tur* bird perched next to his chair—not a spot of color in its feathers or hooked beak, nor in the curled plumage of its long tail. He admired the consistency of the creature, garbed in the perfect camouflage for hunting its night prey in the jungles of Avernus.

Naill fingered the plumed tail, then plucked out a choice feather. The bird squawked in protest. It erupted into flight, only to hit the end of its tether and return to the perch.

Settling deeper into the chair, Naill stroked the feather along his jaw. He ignored the spectacular sight of Verdigris in favor of the plans whirling through his mind. He wasn't sure how long he had sat there when the door to his quarters hissed open and the reflection of a familiar figure materialized in the viewport.

"What is it, Penn?"

The Gent'Sian glided forward, his hands tucked in the sleeves of his robe. "A message from your Interceptor pilots, my lord. They tracked the *Nighthawk* to Boreas, where they cut Talon off from his ship. Though he managed to slip away aboard an intercity shuttle, they pursued the vessel and shot it down."

Naill slowly brushed the feather across his smiling lips. "Excellent. What about survivors? Is it a confirmed kill?"

"Unfortunately, our craft are not equipped with ice runners for a landing. The shuttle crashed into a ridge. Our pilot then, to use his words, 'obliterated' the area around the smoking wreckage. He insists survival would be impossible."

"I despise snap judgments," Naill said acidly. "Tell the pilots I still prefer to keep Boreas under surveillance. They are to keep an eye on all traffic exiting the tradeport."

"Shall I tell them to look for something in particular?"

"Yes, for any activity concerning the *Nighthawk*. I dislike having it sitting there, still available, almost as much as I dislike not having a body count. Better yet, have one of the pilots and his navigator stay in the tradeport and keep an eye on the ship, subtly, without antagonizing the locals."

"For how long?"

"Until I say otherwise. And Penn . . ." Naill continued, pausing in his leisurely stroking to fix the Gent'Sian with an intense, expectant gaze. "Was Talon alone?"

"They spotted a woman boarding the shuttle with him, though they were too far away to see her face. They believe she was Mal'Harith, since she was clad in a shagya coat and hat."

"Interesting," Naill murmured. "Such a tragic accident."

Penn bowed. "I concur with not taking the conclusion for granted, my lord, but from all appearances they are both dead."

"Let us hope so. If not—" Naill hinted coldly, breaking the quill of the feather between his fingers. "Tell my men I will not tolerate a second miss."

"We made it, Princess," Talon said, knowing it would provoke her. It worked, thankfully. Color returned to her ashen face.

"I'd say that was a matter of opinion," Kari growled. She leaned back, wincing and pressing a hand to her chest, where the restraints had prevented her from slamming into the console.

"Admit it—I was right. Those first ridges were only snow."

She turned to glare at him. Her eyes flashed green fire. Here was the Kari he knew. Talon stifled a smile of relief.

"You just got lucky, you risk-taking, maniacal barbarian!" she exploded. "I will never, ever, fly with you again. Find another copilot. Find another hostage, for that matter. I'm leaving. Just try and stop me."

Talon didn't utter a single protest when she wrenched open her restraints and stomped across the cabin. He didn't need to. The door slid open to reveal a solid wall of snow, bringing her dramatic exit to a grinding halt.

"How the blazes do I get out of this crate?" she snapped.

Talon chuckled. "It's nice to know I'm still needed."

She rounded on him in a fighter's stance, beckoning with her hands. "Laugh just once more, please. I'd love to have an excuse to kick you across the jaw again. Come on, do it."

Talon rose and bore down on her. She stood her ground, chin high, refusing to be intimidated even when he reached over her shoulder to press the door mechanism and seal off the frigid air and dripping melt. He stayed in that position, his right arm braced alongside her head. Damn, he admired her courage.

Adrenaline pumped through his system from their near brush with death. Even that couldn't compare to the invigoration of confronting this hot-tempered, auburn-haired vixen.

"You're welcome to try," he said softly. "I deserve a little satisfaction this time. At Narkwar I didn't have an opportunity to defend myself."

He expected her to retaliate. Instead, her gaze probed his face, lingering on his mouth. The hostility drained slowly from her eyes, softening their green depths with . . . what? A look of invitation? Talon scoffed inwardly. Maybe in the wildest reaches of his imagination or, more accurately, his libido. There it was again—that dangerous, suicidal urge to kiss her. A risk-taker; that's what she'd called him. So be it. He leaned forward until his mouth was mere millimeters from hers.

Pausing, he gave her a chance to draw back. His abdominal muscles drew taut, responding to the growing heaviness in his loins as well as the likely threat of another punch to the ribs.

She didn't move, didn't strike. Her breathing quickened, blowing a tiny tempest against his mouth. The mystery of whether her fire could become passion tantalized him mercilessly. Her eyelids lowered halfway, shielding her expression. Was there uncertainty or calculation in that hooded gaze?

A few precautions were in order. He needed to maneuver her into a position where she wasn't free to draw his sword. Dropping his braced arm from the wall, Talon captured her left hand and folded it behind her back, interlacing their fingers. Her gaze flashed upward to meet his, her expression cautious but not angry . . . yet. He exerted pressure, drawing her to him. She countered with more than token resistance, but when his arm flexed insistently, she relented gradually, her radiated warmth slowly merging with his heat.

Talon almost groaned aloud when they made contact. Her body—all sleek, firm lines and soft curves—fit so snugly against him. He moved their joined hands lower, over her tailbone, pressing her hips intimately against his hard length. No doubt her obsession with capturing him just escalated to having him gelded.

He could feel her trembling. A good sign . . . maybe. He was charting dangerous, unexplored territory here. Always before he'd felt in control with a woman, confident of his ability to give physical pleasure. Kari was an utter enigma, threatening yet intriguing, a puzzle he was suddenly determined to solve.

He intended to start with a gentle, exploratory kiss. But when he claimed her mouth, raw hunger took over. Her lips were softer than the finest quivote. She began to return the kiss tentatively, surprising him. He greedily demanded more.

His tongue teased the closed line of her lips, hoping for a more intimate invasion. Her lips opened hesitantly. Slowly, he penetrated her heat, savoring every slight advance across the battleground. The hostility was still there, fraught with risk. He didn't care. All that mattered was the sensual, intoxicating taste of her mouth, the burgeoning excitement of possession, the strange, growing feeling of possessiveness. Kari would be his, whether she wanted to be or not. The real battle had just begun.

The light scrape of her teeth triggered a new, strident warning. If she decided to bite him, it wouldn't be a little love nip.

He tensed, almost retreating, but then her free hand slid tentatively inside his coat and up his back. He was a randy fool, he thought as he wrapped his other arm about her and deepened the kiss.

The floor abruptly tipped beneath their feet.

Kari gasped. Talon's head jerked up.

The melt. Damn, he'd allowed lust to distract him from more immediate concerns. The friction heat from the shuttle's hull was melting the snow around them. As soon as the hull cooled—

He stepped back, feeling dazed, torn between the aching needs of his body and intruding reality. Kari slipped away like a whisper on a breeze. Runagate hell. Talon closed his eyes and pressed his fist against the rough metal of the bulkhead.

His voice was ragged when he spoke. "I'll start digging our way out. If I don't, the melting snow will freeze around the ship and seal us in. Why don't you break out the survival gear?"

Kari stole uneasy glances at Talon while she pulled out the packs. His body worked with a tireless, rhythmic motion of muscles and sinews as he shoveled snow and packed it down. His mouth compressed in a tight line. There was nothing hard about that mouth when he kissed her. The intoxicating stroke of his tongue generated the most amazing—

No! She didn't want to think about the tingling that still raced across her nerve endings. Okay, she thought grudgingly, so she found him attractive. It was simple lust, nothing more. Lust was a mindless thing. Her wits had temporarily deserted her, that's all, due to the stress of the crash.

It changed nothing, of course. Talon still deserved to be locked up for aiding the Rebellion. She would make it happen. It would just be . . . harder now, somehow. She checked the supplies in the pack, then yanked the zip-straps closed, suddenly angry.

Talon's shovel broke through to the outside. A white-gold shaft of sunlight slanted through the hole like the blade of a sword straight from a weapon-maker's forge. He climbed up the tunnel and pushed out the remaining barrier of snow. The freshest air she'd ever smelled swept into the cabin. She didn't know how to describe it, except that it was crystal clean compared to the metallic, recycled odors of shipboard life or the smells of dirt and forest on Verdigris.

They shoved the two packs outside and crawled out. Talon shrugged into the larger of the two—the one containing the thermo-tent—then handed her the supply pack.

"How far?" Kari asked tentatively, not really wanting to break the awkward silence that had descended between them.

"After that speed chase?" He snorted. "We've got a two-, maybe three-day trek back to Boreas. Not good."

The day was clear and windless as they set out.

They trudged for hours, forever south, with Talon in the lead. Kari forced the discomfort from her mind—the weight of the pack, the stinging cold in her feet—and dog-

gedly kept moving. Serac had its own kind of beauty, uncomplicated and serene. Except for the crunch of their spikebits, the stillness was complete. She could feel at peace in this land, if it wasn't for the fact that their gear included only the one thermo-tent. She would have to share with Talon. She tried not to think about it, but there was little else to occupy her thoughts.

The alternative, freezing to death, was slightly less appealing.

They struggled down a long slope of knee-deep snow. Beneath them stretched a broad, flat valley where the ice was smooth and slick, the covering of snow only a thin veneer. The color was different as well, Kari noticed with a frown.

"Why is the ice tinted blue here?"

"We're going over water," he said without turning around. "It's the Serakian Strait. One of the passages linking the North and Equatorial seas. Didn't your training cover geography?" His question had a hard, biting edge to it.

What was his problem? The derogatory question immediately fired her own anger. "Didn't your education include manners?"

"My education was notably different than you'd expect, with no room for such luxuries as manners," he retorted bluntly, with a wealth of meaning behind his words and no effort to elaborate. "Quit lagging behind," he snapped over his shoulder.

That did it. Kari slowed her steps, increasing the distance between them over the next half hour. Though he said nothing, he glanced back with gratifying frequency.

Suddenly the ice beneath Kari's feet darkened, creating the disorienting sensation that she walked across a bottomless void. The shadow passed. All was a normal blue-white again.

Kari blinked and tried to calm her fluttering pulse. Her eyes were playing tricks on her, that was all . . . too much endless expanse of white. Snow blindness, perhaps?

Another massive shadow skimmed by, as if a storm cloud passed overhead, except the sky this afternoon was almost painfully clear and bright. She swallowed hard. Something very strange was going on, either with the ice or her own vision. Logic argued that there was nothing to worry about. The ice here must be at least two meters thick.

The first impact knocked her off balance. Kari bit back a cry as a huge star splintered outward, deep beneath her feet.

Talon spun around with a thunderous frown. He started toward her with a stride that quickly accelerated into a run.

The next blow flung Kari to her knees.

"Rammer whales!" she heard him shout. "Run, Kari!"

The ice shuddered as the onslaught from below escalated. She struggled to her feet, only to watch ice erupt into the air between them. Huge slabs broke free, opening a fracture in the surface, separating as a massive nose shoved through.

An explosive sound slammed against Kari's ears as the muscle encircling the whale's blowhole released its grip, expelling the animal's breath. She watched in morbid fascination as the blowhole distended, drawing air back in with a rushing sound that rivaled a battle cruiser's engines.

The size of the whale was stunning, the extra boney ridge on the crown of its nose impressive in its ramming power. The dark gray of its skin contrasted sharply with the white landscape.

Slowly the behemoth sank below the ice. It pivoted as it descended, turning to show an eye the size of a Verdigran serving platter and a terrifyingly huge jaw studded with ivory teeth.

Kari heard the cracking of ice behind her, to her left and right, followed by more explosive rushes of air as the school of whales burst through to take greedy gulps of air.

She floated free on a slab of ice, cut off from escape.

The world tilted as another head surfaced, knocking the ice askew. Kari screamed. She dropped to her stomach and clawed at the hard, slanting surface. The spikebits failed to find a grip. Somewhere above the cacophony of whales and her own gasping breath, she heard Talon shouting her name.

She slid down toward an icy oblivion and certain death. She would freeze to death in that water within minutes . . . if the whales didn't eat her first.

She hit water and went under. The freezing cold slammed into her with the force of a fully charged stun wand. Maybe, she prayed, this would be a relatively quick death.

No such luck. With horror, she watched the blurred image of a massive nose approach from beneath. Blazes, she didn't want to be crushed between those conical teeth. She closed her eyes.

It nudged her floating body. Kari would have whimpered, if her throat wasn't stiff and her oxygen-starved body feeling as if it was about to burst. The tentative push changed to a full-fledged shove as the whale propelled her through the water. She expected the jaws to open any second, swallowing her whole.

Instead, the whale pushed her clear of the water, a soaked rag doll plastered to its nose. Water cascaded in all directions, like surf receding from a rocky shore. The whale's head tilted. She rolled off to land on solid, stable ice.

Kari groaned from the impact. Suddenly she was gulping sweet, blessedly dry air. Struggling to a sitting position, she gazed upward in awe at the whale. She could swear there was intelligent interest in its eye—viewing her as an intriguing oddity, no doubt. The gentle behemoth sank out of sight.

Talon dropped to his knees beside her.

"The whale. It saved . . . my life," Kari rasped.

"Runagate hell! Of all the stupid—" Talon snarled. He began peeling off her soggy coat.

The fury in his voice surprised her. "Didn't you see?"

"How could I miss it?" He pulled off her boots, muttering, "It pushed you out of the water, the most amazing damned thing I've ever seen."

Kari gazed blissfully at the muscles rippling across Talon's bare back, thinking that life had never felt so precious and she had never seen a man more beautiful. Her eyes widened in shock. Was he completely insane? He'd stripped off his coat, shirt, even his boots. Why would he do such a thing? She prepared to launch into a blistering scold when he began tugging down her pants.

"What the . . . blazes are you . . . doing?" she gasped, appalled. She tried to slap his hands away, only to find her arms too numb to do more than flutter ineffectually.

"If I don't get these wet clothes off quickly, they'll freeze to your skin. A bloody mess trying to get them off after that. Then we have to get you warm before hypothermia sets in."

"You mean . . . I could . . . still . . . die?" she forced out between chattering teeth.

The expression in his eyes was solemn, even gentle as he paused to look at her. "I won't let that happen. Just cooperate with me for a change, all right? I know what I'm doing."

"Why . . . no shirt?"

He didn't answer. Her gaze discovered the rope tied around his waist, followed its length to the pick embedded in the ice. He'd planned to go in after her.

"It would have been . . . suicide," she said unsteadily, shaking more from the idea of what he'd almost jeopardized than the cold.

He didn't pretend to misunderstand her. "Probably."

"Put on . . . your shirt . . . idiot." Kari concentrated on the soft swirls in his brown hair to hide the crushing embarrassment as he systematically stripped her down to her bustier and the tiny slip of underwear she wore.

"In a minute," he muttered. He wrenched a thermal blanket from the pack and wrapped it around her shivering body. With a quick flick of the igniter valve, he sent warmth spreading through the fibers interwoven into the wool. She felt ridiculously relieved when he yanked on his own clothes.

Pulling her knees to her chest, she let her body absorb the blanket's luxurious, life-affirming warmth.

He'd reacted in record time to strip off his encumbering clothes and prepare to dive into the brutal water, with the slim hope he could pull them both back up a slick wall of ice. He was a lunatic. Yet, if anyone could have succeeded, Talon would have. The quiet surety of that belief left her feeling disoriented, drifting in a void between her new discoveries and what she had been trained to believe about this man and others like him. Talon was . . . different . . . than she'd expected.

She watched him silently while he moved away from the whale pool and set up the tent. The sea giants stayed, surfacing frequently between the ice floes with the deep pop and hiss of their blowholes, storing up oxygen for the next stage of their migratory path. Kari wondered how far they could travel under ice, how long till they reached open water.

In short order Talon had all the essentials unpacked and the heater working at full throttle. Then he strode purposefully toward her and scooped her into his arms, blanket and all. He deposited her gently in the tent.

He was strangely distant, refusing to meet her eyes, his face set in granite planes.

"Thank you," she said stiffly.

"Yeah, sure. I'll dry out your things," he responded in a gruff tone, then stepped outside the tent.

Chapter Eleven

He was a long time in returning.

Kari occupied herself by unraveling her braid and spreading the auburn strands to dry. She peeled the damp wrap bandage from her wrist. Noting with interest how neatly her cuts were healing, she tossed it aside. Curious stuff, that Sylph nectar.

The light faded to gray, warning of approaching night and a falling temperature. She frowned, annoyed by the niggling concern that unfurled and grew over Talon's continued absence. Why should she care? She fidgeted with the heater's thermostat, then unpacked the supplies and arranged them in the corner.

The flap opened. Kari yanked her blanket over her scantily clad body, holding her head high and proud despite feeling at a distinct disadvantage.

Talon stopped in the opening and stared at her. Abruptly, without comment, he tossed her dried clothes in a heap at her feet. Then he was gone again.

Kari glared at the closed flap while she donned her tunic and pants. A battle raged inside. She despised feeling gratitude where he was concerned. Resentment was so much easier.

It grew increasingly like this when Talon was near. Her emotions degenerated into chaotic upheaval, her temper escalated into something she couldn't control, her heart gave odd lurches, leaving her breathless. In the beginning, she thought it was because she hated him. Okay, so that no longer held true. She'd learned to . . . tolerate his company.

She picked up her coat. The utility belt fell free.

"Oh, no," she cried out in dismay. Not the data cylinder! The water, the cold—Her freak incident with the whales might have destroyed her only leverage against Naill.

Though the leather was still damp, the zipstraps and linings were designed to be waterproof. She tugged out the cylinder.

A palm lantern lay among the supplies. Grabbing the metal ball, she thumbed on the switch and played the light over the silver surface of the cylinder. Two tiny spots marked where the reflective sheen had dulled to a flat pewter. Blazes! Dozens of files could be unreadable in those damaged sectors.

For the second time in as many days Kari felt the foreign urge to cry. Hot moisture gathered under her lids. She couldn't confront Naill without proof. The key lay hidden in this cylinder, she knew it. If only it wasn't destroyed.

The tears never fell. She bit her lip in determination. A damaged cylinder needed a sophisticated computer to salvage files. Star Alpha wasn't the answer. The station relied on Lochnar technology for its systems. They were not sold the best.

The perfect solution awaited in Boreas's hangar bay. The *Nighthawk*'s computers were more than adequate for the job. She also had unfinished business with Oberon. If Talon disappeared and took the male Sylph with him, she would never learn the secrets locked for thirteen years in her mother's box. She must get to Verdigris and Oberon's secret kingdom.

Now, how to convince the *Nighthawk*'s pilot that his violently reluctant passenger was suddenly eager to go back on board?

Impossible. Even if he believed her, she was the last person he wanted on his ship. There was only one solution.

She would have to steal the *Nighthawk*.

*   *   *

Talon deliberately lingered over the simple task of preparing a meal. He squatted before a compact flame-unit, boiling desiccated vegetables and *tarwanto* meat in melted snow until they were palatable. The surrounding temperature, now at 15 degrees, was dropping rapidly. The cold served its purpose, numbing the extremities of his body, particularly a certain part of his anatomy in need of some serious cooling off.

He closed his eyes, too exhausted to fight the images any longer. Though fear for Kari's safety had been uppermost in his mind when he peeled off her soaked clothes, he wasn't blind. The picture of her exquisite body, her skin drawn taut from the cold, was seared into his brain. The memory of her drying hair, flowing about her shoulders like a sinuous melding of fire and shadow, tormented him with a repetitive fantasy. He dreamed of burying his hands in its silken length, stroking her cheeks with his thumbs, and gently kissing the down-turned corners of her sensuous mouth until she clutched at him in pure feminine need.

All his adult life he'd exercised complete control over his body, using it as an instrument to pleasure women and himself, mastering it with the same proficiency he used in piloting his ship. Tonight that control eluded him. Hell, it had been slowly whittled away ever since he had dragged Kari aboard the *Nighthawk*.

He wanted her.

She was the last woman in the whole blasted universe he should desire. She sought to lock him up where he'd never see the stars again. His spirit would shrivel up inside of him. Only death was a worse fate.

If only he could forget how she'd returned his kiss, how ironically right she'd felt pressed up against him. As much as the memory tantalized and teased, firing a gnawing hunger, it also infuriated him. Images of slowly awakening passion were completely at odds with their tumultuous relationship.

Talon lurched to his feet. He shut down the flame-unit and carried their food inside.

She had braided her hair and dressed. Her gaze was hooded as she sat cross-legged on the blanket. The warrior was back.

He put the plate in her outstretched hands. She looked up at him. Her eyes reminded him of the jungles of Avernus—dark green depths concealing a variety of dangers, death masking its threat with a veil of beauty.

How appropriate.

They ate without speaking. During the brittle silence, Talon reminded himself forcefully of every grievous wrong she'd done him. Though resentment grew, another part of him watched for the slightest sign of encouragement.

There was none. When it came time to sleep she crawled beneath her blankets and turned her back to him.

He lay awake a very long time, burning.

"Is there any chance we'll make it to Boreas by nightfall?" Kari asked hopefully the next morning as they trudged, once again, across the monotonous white terrain.

"Afraid you'll be forced to share yet another night in the tent, Princess?"

His snarling tone confirmed what Kari already knew—Talon was in an excessively foul mood this morning. She should be the snappish one, considering how much sleep she'd lost. Her muscles were stiff. Her head ached. Irritability clawed at her nerves, though she couldn't pinpoint the cause. After all, Talon had been very considerate, keeping to his own side of the tent. He'd made no attempt to touch her with those long-fingered hands, whose supple strength couldn't be masked by gloves.

Succumbing to her temper, she retorted acidly, "If there's no other choice, I suppose I must. I can think of

worse fates . . . like falling down an ice crevice and breaking my neck."

Talon didn't answer. Instead, he kicked the ground,
sending up a spray of snow that caught on the breeze.

Kari brushed the light coating of white crystals from her
visor, deriving some satisfaction from knowing she'd gotten under his skin.

The sun was nearing its zenith when Talon suddenly
dropped to his belly and peered over the crest of a drift.
He signaled Kari to do the same. Ankle-deep snow
crunched beneath her stomach and elbows. More snow
worked its way inside her cuffs. Cold shivered up her
arms.

The dark red hull of the downed Interceptor ship appeared alien and ominous in the primitive landscape. Its
wings had broken up on impact, but the cockpit was intact
. . . and open. Two sets of tracks headed south.

"Come on," he said.

They clambered up on the twisted metal stub that was
once the port wing and looked inside. Empty. Both pilot
and navigator were indeed gone, apparently having survived the crash without serious injury. At least they hadn't
been able to call for help. The comm and other controls
were shorted out, blackened by electrical fire.

Kari looked at Talon. "What now?"

"We head south, as planned. Any blister city other than
Boreas would be too far." He reached into the cockpit and
came out with a Lochnar crossbow and a packet of arrows.

Kari eyed the weapon with misgiving. "If they left that
behind, they must be adequately armed."

"Apparently. This bow is one of the heavier models,
though. They probably didn't want to lug the extra weight
along with their survival gear. Big mistake." He slung the
weapon over his shoulder by its strap. "With the wide-
open terrain on Serac, a crossbow is often your best choice
of weapon."

Kari glared at him. Talon fairly bristled with weapons,

a stark contrast to her unarmed state. She felt practically naked without her sword. In her more distracted moments, she'd almost forgotten she was this man's captive. The reminder backhanded her in the face.

They walked onward, over terrain that grew increasingly rugged. After five hours Talon stopped abruptly at the crest of a rise. He turned back, grasped her arm, and steered her west.

"Change in direction," he said grimly.

"Why? I thought you said that way was the shortest."

"It is, but we're taking a slight detour. Don't argue."

She wrenched free of his grasp and stepped back. She'd put up with enough surliness from him, not to mention the infuriating way he expected her to blindly obey every command. "Not unless you tell me precisely why."

He scowled. "Believe me, you don't want to know."

"Is there something dangerous over that rise we should avoid?" she insisted, standing her ground.

"Not anymore," he said darkly.

"Then I don't see the problem."

He slipped the hood of his coat back. "It's apparent my opinion isn't worth a nugget of Avernian copper around here. If you're so determined to see, then go see."

Kari gritted her teeth as she climbed the low rise.

When she reached the top she saw supplies—Lochnar survival gear—scattered everywhere. The packs had been ripped open, strewing damaged gear over an area about six meters square. And blood. Lots of blood stained the snow. Though there were no signs of human remains, it was pretty obvious what had happened to the Interceptor crew. Kari shuddered, not wanting to imagine the animal, or animals, that had done this. Another example of survival of the fittest on this violent world.

She walked slowly back to where Talon stood. He regarded her with raised eyebrows. She said with stiff pride, "I've decided to listen to your suggestion. Let's go the other way."

He snorted and jerked his hood back into place.

An eerie wailing suddenly disrupted the otherwise silent landscape. Without warning, Talon raced up the long incline behind them. Kari followed.

At the top the ground ended abruptly in front of their feet, dropping off in a steep incline of solid ice. Outward from the base of the drop Kari could see the source of the panicked wailing. A huge catamount had a young Hoarworm by its stubby tail, attempting to pull it from its burrow. The Hoar had puffed its body full of air, trying desperately to cling to the inside of the tunnel, but it was evidently losing the battle. The shaggy white-blond catamount, which stood almost two meters at the shoulder, had the advantage of strength and hunger.

Talon armed the crossbow.

"You'll never hit it at this distance," she warned..

He snapped the crossbow to his shoulder and fired. The metal arrow speeded downward. Kari watched first in disbelief, and then in admiration, as the arrow was embedded in the catamount's hip.

A yowl of fury exploded upward from the scene. The great cat released the Hoarworm, which disappeared into its burrow. As the catamount twisted to bite at the arrow, Kari could see the sun glinting off its smooth wet fangs. The barbed arrowhead kept the weapon firmly in place. Another nerve-raking scream of rage rolled across the terrain.

The catamount spotted them. It bounded to the base of the slope, snarling. Whether from intelligence or intuition, it apparently understood the source of its pain. Using its dagger-sharp claws, it began to climb up the incline.

"Runagate hell! It's coming straight up," Talon shouted.

"Didn't you know it could do that?" Kari yelped.

"Not with an arrow in its hip." He shoved her into motion, away from the morbid fascination of the cat performing the seemingly impossible feat of climbing slick ice.

The cold air bit at her lungs as she ran. Another roar

sounded behind them, chilling the rest of her insides. Shock jarred through her as Talon unexpectedly skidded to a halt.

"What are you doing?" she gasped, stopping.

"It's coming over the top. If we don't face it now, it will simply pull us down from behind. You can't outrun a catamount."

He armed the crossbow again, then opened his coat and pulled out her sword. At first she thought he meant use it in the fight, until he held it out to her.

She grasped the hilt. His eyes were tense, wary, but he didn't hesitate to release the weapon into her control. The sudden, illogical urge to reassure him that she wouldn't use the sword against him surged into her throat, but the words refused to form. Slashing the blade through the air to warm up her arm, she sliced away confusing emotions at the same time.

Talon rapped out orders. "I'll draw its attention. You come in from a rear angle and go for the base of its ribs. And whatever you do, don't get in the path of those paws."

"Count on it," she agreed wholeheartedly. The image of those curved claws ripping through her flesh was all too vivid.

With another roar, the catamount pulled itself up over the edge. Talon whipped up the crossbow and fired. The arrow pierced the thick fur, plunging into its chest, but the cat didn't go down.

The beast lurched forward, noticeably weakened but still out for blood. Though the shafts of two arrows jutted out from places that would have felled a smaller animal, the catamount seemed hardly phased. Its broad head was set low in its massive shoulders, emphasizing the anatomy of an animal Serakian nature intended as a killing machine. Its tufted ears twitched furiously. Gleaming yellow eyes promised death.

Kari separated from Talon. As promised, he drew th beast's attention. She came in from the side. The great c wasn't so easily fooled. A raking paw drove her back.

They repeated the tactic several times, with the same discouraging results. Talon was in the greatest danger, though he proved amazingly nimble at dodging the vicious swipes.

Suddenly, the muscles of the catamount's hind legs bunched.

"Talon!" she screamed in warning.

The beast sprang. Talon dove to the side at the last second and rolled, coming immediately to his feet on the opposite side. He swung his sword in a mighty arc and sliced through the cat's left hamstring. Its hind leg crumpled.

Though its hindquarters were handicapped, the catamount twisted its upper body in a whipcord reaction, trying to get at its attacker. Desperate to stop it, Kari drove her blade into the cat's opposite shoulder. Talon tried to spin away at the same time. Not far enough. The sound of teeth ripping through Talon's coat reached Kari from over the animal's back.

Horror seared through her like a blast from a ship's stardrive exhaust. A cry of denial erupted from her chest.

Enraged, gripped by the need to retaliate, she pulled her sword free and plunged it between the predator's ribs. The catamount jerked, releasing its death grip on Talon, then slowly sank down onto the bright red snow.

Kari rushed around the dying animal.

She stumbled to a halt. Talon was alive, swearing vehemently while he shrugged out of his shredded coat, his face ashen. Kari was surprised her shaky legs held her upright. Her own skin must be identical in tone to Serac's predominant color.

Talon whipped off his tunic and turned his naked back to her.

"Any blood?" he demanded, his voice rough, strained.

Her fingers trembled as she moved his sweat-dampened air aside. Nothing, thank the stars. A centimeter closer d the fangs would have—Unable to resist, she smoothed her hand across the muscular planes of his miraculously undamaged skin, feeling the nubby roughness of old scars against her palm. His beautiful back didn't deserve any more injuries.

Talon stiffened, muscles flexing. Belatedly, Kari realized the intensity of his heat meant her hand must be ice cold in contrast. She snatched it away, embarrassed at causing him further discomfort. He pulled his tunic over his head.

He turned and gripped her shoulders. "Are you all right?"

He was asking her, when a moment before she'd feared he was mortally wounded? Hoarsely, she whispered, "You are so blazing lucky, it's unbelievable."

His mouth tilted in a wry grin. "You know, you faced that catamount with more courage than most men."

"Are you going to skin it? Another coat in the making. Looks like yours needs replacing," she joked, desperate for a distraction from the way his warm approval melted her insides. And the way he looked at her . . . as if he found her attractive, maybe just a little.

The muted roar of spacecraft engines cruelly shattered the fantasy. Kari turned, numb, feeling as if she was being sucked into a nightmare as she spotted the dark red outline of another Interceptor cutting through the clouds.

The ship screamed by overhead. A torpedo struck the ground ten meters behind them, exploding with a deafening blast. A cone-shaped cloud of debris shot into the air. Chunks of snow and ice rained down, pummeling them.

"Come on," Talon yelled, grabbing her by the wrist. "Let's make for the Hoar burrow. It's our only chance."

The only shelter around, Kari acknowledged as she raced alongside, but could they reach it in time? The Interceptor lined up on its next approach.

The thunder of another ship invaded the space overhead, descending at attack speed. No, no, no! Her head rang with unuttered cries of frustration and fear. They could never avoid both ships in this open terrain. She looked at Talon.

He was grinning. To make matters worse, he winked at her.

Stunned, Kari stumbled and fell into a snowdrift. His outstretched hand appeared immediately to pull her to her feet.

She punched him in the chest and screamed, "You're a lunatic! They mean to kill us, and you're laughing!"

"It's Rand!" he shouted back, still smiling as he cupped her cheek and turned her gaze skyward.

A blue-and-gold ship roared past. The Interceptor broke off its attack vector. It banked hard in a defensive maneuver, then came around, transferring its deadly intent to the newcomer.

The *Stormhawk* executed an impressive series of aerial acrobatics, dodging the Interceptor's first sally of torpedoes, then returned fire and blew the Lochnar ship out of the sky.

Talon tackled Kari into the drift, shielding her body with his own. All around them snow popped and hissed, steam rising from fallen pieces of hot debris. The ground shook as the main body of the craft went down half a kilometer away.

Talon propped himself up on one elbow and gazed down at her. The warmth of his breath melted the snowflakes on her cheeks. Kari felt caught in a net, bound by the intensity in his gaze, wondering what he intended to do next. She didn't have a chance to find out. The *Stormhawk* slowed nearby and switched to hoverlifts, stirring up a white storm.

With a scowl, Talon rose and helped her up.

They retrieved their fallen gear while the victorious ship landed. As they approached the fallen catamount for their weapons, Talon moved ahead with long strides and pulled Kari's blade from the cat's chest. He hung it once again from his belt with a meaningful glance at the *Stormhawk*.

The significance wasn't lost on Kari; he was protecting Rand Markos . . . from her.

They faced each other, stiff and unsure where moments before they'd teamed up in perfect, natural unison. Kari felt the widening gulf between them, like a wound that drained part of her energy and soul onto the snow. "Would you return my sword if Rand wasn't here?" she asked shakily.

His expression was inscrutable. "I don't know."

His lack of trust pierced right to her core, shattering something fragile that had been taking root. How could she ever have allowed herself to think of him as something other than the bitterest of enemies? Between clenched teeth, Kari growled, "Smart move, but my chance will come."

Muscles rippled up his jaw. His gaze chilled.

The hatch ramp lowered. Rand came rushing out, snapping, "Dammit, Talon, you scared the everliving out of me. All that blood on the snow; I thought—" He broke off abruptly. "What the hell is she doing here?"

"Did I forget to mention? She's my hostage," Talon snarled sarcastically, grasping her arm. Kari glanced at him sharply, surprised by his utter lack of gratitude for their rescue.

Rand didn't seem to notice, responding furiously, "You expect to stay Neutral this way? I let you out of my sight for a couple of days and you not only plunge into the middle of the war, you escalate—What are you doing? Don't take that woman on my ship!"

"You're going to take us back to Boreas, where I'm going to put her on the next shuttle for Star Alpha," Talon warned in a tone that did not invite argument.

Rand seemed unimpressed. "So she can start hunting us down?"

Halfway up the ramp, Talon turned. Quieting suddenly, like a lull on a storm-tossed sea, he said softly, "She saved my life, Rand." He held up his coat. Light filtered through the shredded holes. "If she hadn't attacked, the cata-mount's fangs would have cut through a lot more than my coat. Even Beryl couldn't have helped me with wounds that severe."

Rand sobered. "Sweet everlasting," he murmured hoarsely, but then his flashing hazel eyes darkened. "The discussion we had in the med-lab . . . she was with you, wasn't she? You had a chance to stop her, even then."

"What would you have me do, Rand?"

Kari watched the two men intently, and not just because she was the subject of the heated debate. It was the way they argued. Jem'Adal males very rarely felt so free to demonstrate their anger or frustration. More than that, strong emotions reverberated behind the words, an intensity, an understanding that bespoke a special, long-term familiarity.

This was the first time she'd seen Talon and Rand in close proximity. The similarities between them became very apparent as her perceptions broadened, eliminating the little, insignificant differences. Her heart pounded with the thrill of discovery.

Talon and Rand were brothers; she was sure of it.

And they didn't want anyone to know.

The Rebel High Commander turned to glare at her. "You intend to make my life miserable, don't you?"

How else could she answer, except with the truth? "My job is to hunt down any threat to the Lochnar dynasty, and I'm very good at what I do."

Rand swore violently.

Talon's grip tightened on her arm. "Let's go. The sooner we send her home, the happier she'll be. Isn't that right, Kari?"

"With a few detours," she muttered under her breath.

Chapter Twelve

Talon watched the *Stormhawk* disappear into the tunnel that exited Boreas's hangar bay. He hated those occasions, however rare, when he and Rand parted company in anger.

He shoved his fists into the pockets of the shagya coat Rand had loaned him. His spikebits grated against the ice floor as he pivoted to face Kari. There was just enough time to get her on the last scheduled flight to Star Alpha.

Two of the original four Lochnar Interceptors were still unaccounted for. They could be waiting for him right now, eager to see him in a body bag—or worse, determined to return him to Naill for that privilege.

Escape beckoned. Beryl, responding to a call ahead on the commlink, was putting his ship through preflight sequence. Even from the wide center aisle where Rand had dropped them off, he recognized the distinctive hum of the *Nighthawk*'s engines.

Nevertheless, Talon had a strange, infuriating reluctance to put Kari aboard the shuttle, or any ship for that matter, where he couldn't be assured of her safe delivery. If his hunch proved correct, she was in equal danger. Naill was depraved, greedy, and power-mad enough to want her out of the way.

Runagate hell. What else could he do but send her to Star Alpha? She'd made it abundantly clear that she wanted to be shed of his company as soon as possible. And he couldn't keep his guard up forever.

The bottom of his pockets threatened to rip out as he stood rigidly, though he knew he'd made the right decision. Boreans moved all about them in pursuit of their daily business, loading and off-loading cargoes. But the noise and bustling activity faded into the background when his gaze was drawn to a man who stood in the shadow of a small ship. The man's coarse wool cape was the inexpensive kind visitors often purchased. Though no one else considered the man worth notice, to Talon he seemed as out of place as a fleshy Batak cave spider on hot Avernian sand.

Unease skittered across his nerve endings. He'd survived by his instincts too long to dismiss the internal warning.

The man raised his arm and spoke into a wrist commlink. Talon responded instantly to primitive emotions that centered not on his own safety but on protecting the woman beside him.

"Where are we going?" she demanded in her most arrogant Lochnar tone when he urged her into a run.

"To the *Nighthawk*."

The tradeport's siren sounded its low, warning wail, which could mean only one thing . . . incoming Lochnar ships.

Some of the Boreans didn't even blink. Others erupted into a mad scramble. Most tradeports on Serac were hotspots for smuggling, and Boreas was no exception. Those engaged in business on the leeward side of Lochnar law frantically finished loading their cargoes and closed their ships for an abrupt departure.

The *Nighthawk*'s hatch ramp lowered without Talon's prompting. Beryl must be watching.

After hitting the *close* button he charged into the cockpit, Kari right on his heels. Both dropped into their seats and strapped in. The Sylphs, responding to their blatant sense of urgency, were already disappearing into their alcove.

Talon grabbed the controls. Was he leaping from one

deathtrap into another? At least outside he could maneuver, fight.

He eased the hoverlifts into play. The ship didn't budge. Frowning, he forced more pressure into the jets. The *Nighthawk* shuddered, yet still she didn't lift free. He shut down the hoverlifts and was back on his feet in an instant.

"What is it?" Kari demanded.

"They bolted the ship down. We can't lift off."

He wrenched open the storage compartment in the floor and pulled out a Mal'Harith battle axe. The curved blade, and the viciously sharp pick that balanced it on the opposite side of the handle, were fashioned of finest durasteel. Kari watched him with an intensity that made his shoulder muscles draw tight as he gripped the weapon and rushed out of the ship.

The Interceptor emerged from the entrance tunnel at the far end of the huge cavern. It moved forward slowly, like a malevolent red-skinned carnivore stalking its prey. Talon swore.

Four Borean ships lifted off, jockeying for position in a desperate bid for the exit tunnel. Their clumsy attempt at escape blocked the Interceptor, buying Talon precious seconds.

Two chains, each bolted deep into the ice, looped around the *Nighthawk*'s landing skids. He rammed the pick into one of the links, then threw all his weight against the handle. The link parted, barely enough. He slipped the chain loose.

Just as he swung the weapon, embedding the pick deep into the other chain, the last of the smugglers vanished into the exit tunnel. The Interceptor was free to move. It maneuvered into the center isle, hovering little more than a meter above the cavern floor as it approached the disabled *Nighthawk*.

Desperation drove untapped strength into Talon's arms. The link stretched, slowly. He yanked the chain away.

The blast of the *Nighthawk*'s hoverlifts knocked him to

his knees. The belly of the ship, his ship, rose beyond reach.

Kari was deserting him.

Hell, what did he expect? He'd handed her the perfect opportunity to escape.

"Kari!" he bellowed in raw fury, leaping to his feet.

The Interceptor started to pivot the 90 degrees needed to face him. A blinking light announced the arming of a torpedo.

He was about to be blown to cosmic dust. At least Kari would get his ship, Beryl, and Oberon safely away.

Abruptly, the *Nighthawk* halted its ascent. It lowered again, just until the ramp poised at chest level. Not pausing to question providence, Talon tossed the axe inside the ship, then leaped upward to grasp the ramp and haul himself inside. His heart surged into his throat as the ship accelerated straight up, rushing toward a collision with the ceiling of the cavern.

The unleashed torpedo exploded against the cavern wall where they had been. The resultant fireball flung out massive chunks of shattered ice. The force flipped over spacecraft in the adjacent parking slots, magnifying the destruction.

He closed the ramp, then slammed against the wall when the *Nighthawk* stopped without warning. At least Kari had the sense not to crash his ship into the ceiling. The rear propulsion engines roared. He struggled to the cockpit, bracing his hands against the walls, shouting at her to let the computer navigate them through the twisting exit tunnel.

They shot into the atmosphere. Relief, as expected, proved a short-lived luxury. The Interceptor emerged in pursuit.

"Move," he growled at Kari, capable only of monosyllables at the moment, at least where she was concerned.

She obliged quickly, wisely vacating the pilot's seat.

They broke free of Serac's atmosphere, the Lochnar ship

hot on their tail. Then he spotted it—the last Interceptor, outlined against the faint starlight of space. Laying in wait, ready, it fired two torpedoes simultaneously. Talon rolled the *Nighthawk*, narrowly avoiding both. He dodged under the ship and accelerated. Both Interceptors raced in pursuit, one right behind the other. He headed back down.

"Talon, are you nuts? The atmosphere will slow us down!"

He ignored her. Adjusting his vector at the last second, he bounced the *Nighthawk* off the planet's shimmering envelope. It was a bold move, a dangerous move, something the Lochnar pilots wouldn't anticipate. He counted on them adjusting too late.

It worked. The first ship imitated his move, bouncing off at the same angle . . . directly into the path of the other Interceptor. They collided in a fiery explosion.

Silence dominated the cabin as Talon put the ship on auto-navigation. His hands shook. Fear damn well wasn't the cause.

Time to deal with that incident back at the hangar.

He succumbed to the fury, the sense of betrayal, that still roiled around inside him. Leaping to his feet, he ripped off his coat and flung it aside. He slammed his hands against the armrests of Kari's seat, trapping her there.

"You were trying to steal my ship, damn you! Admit it; you intended to leave me at Boreas."

"Yes," she whispered.

"Then why did you hesitate? Not only would you have been free of me, you had the chance to swipe my means of escape. After that you might have hunted me down at your leisure."

"I couldn't—" She hesitated, swallowing hard.

"Couldn't what? Bear the idea of being separated from me?" he jeered.

She didn't deny it, surprising him. Instead, she searched his face, her expression baffled, the muscles taut around her eyes. "I just . . . couldn't leave you to them."

"Why?" he insisted, determined to have an answer that made sense. "Because only you deserve the privilege of capturing me?"

Something sparked in her green eyes, burning away the look of confusion. Her chin tilted stubbornly. "Exactly, smuggler. You're mine, and no one else can have you."

The claim, though uttered angrily in an entirely different context, sent a shiver of sensual anticipation through his body. He'd like her to have him, all right . . . in his bed. He leaned forward slightly, mentally plotting a course to her mouth, the same way he'd chart a course to any stellar destination.

"I need you," she murmured.

He stilled. Anticipation arced like lightning in his loins, though he didn't understand why he felt an equal thrill, a tightness, in his chest. She couldn't mean what he hoped.

"What do you mean?" he asked huskily.

"I need you to take me home. No other place is safe as long as Naill is after me."

He was burning with desire and she merely wanted a lift home. His eyes narrowed. "I can't take you back to the *Regalia*. You've called me a risk-taker; you're wrong. Everything I do is carefully weighed against the danger to my hide, and taking you back to the *Regalia* goes light-years beyond reckless abandon."

"I'm not suggesting you return me to the station. Verdigris will do nicely."

"The planet's surface?" he burst out. "You consider that safer? Runagate hell, woman, the place is off limits to anyone not dutiful to the Lochnar Dynasty."

"Not near any city. That should alleviate your concern. You owe me," she reminded him bluntly. "For saving you from the catamount. For getting you out of that mess back there."

"And how does your debt to me fit into that formula, Princess?" he asked silkily. Her eyes widened. "Ah, I can see you've forgotten how I saved you from freezing to death, not to mention helping you avoid Naill's hit-squad. I owe you nothing."

She caught her lower lip between her teeth. Stars, he hated the impact it had on him every time she did that. When it was an unconsciously provocative gesture he felt broadsided with a surge of lust. When it betrayed vulnerability, like now, he felt the most frightening urge to cup her cheek in his hand and kiss away the demons. She looked down, but not before he saw a sheen in her eyes. Tears? The contrast was like a kick in the chest. Transport to Verdigris obviously meant a great deal to her.

"Why don't you tell me the real reason, Kari?"

Her hands curled into fists on her lap. "I have to travel to Oberon's Sylph kingdom. He said my mother left something there for me. I have to find it." Her gaze lifted, her eyes two fathomless pools of confusion and pain, haunting reminders of the lost little girl she must have been when her mother disappeared.

He felt suddenly helpless in the face of her silent plea.

"All right, I'll take you," he said gruffly. Straightening, he turned to the console. They were almost upon the entrance to the Serac-Verdigris Corridor. He took the ship in.

When he turned back her expression was wary. "There must be a hitch," she said accusingly.

"You're right. You'll owe me," he countered. Tension was knotting inside him. His gaze fixed on her lips.

"What kind of payment are we talking about?"

"Let's start with this."

He pulled her up and into his arms before she could protest. He claimed her mouth hungrily, crushing her lips beneath his own. His hands pushed her coat free until it fell in a heap on the floor. Caution and passion intertwined in a hopelessly complex tangle in his brain. So he let them go, funneling all his concentration into the one thing he could understand . . . the fierce, unbearable longing to feel

185

his bare body pressed against hers, to caress her with his hands and mouth until she whimpered and clung to him, to bury himself in her.

This was insane. Kari wouldn't let this go on. Each microsecond he expected her to wrench away, then treat him to a knee in the groin. He greedily stole every bit of taste and velvety texture while he still could. His hands urgently explored the sleek lines of her back before pleasure could erupt into pain.

Instead, she parted her lips and welcomed his tongue into her mouth, creating a shockwave so intense at first that he thought she had simultaneously delivered a bruising blow.

His legs were turning to water, but not from agony.

Refusing to break contact with her mouth, he swept Kari into his arms and carried her to the bed, then tumbled backward with her on top of him.

He turned, trapping her legs beneath his own before she could change her mind and flee. She didn't seem interested in leaving. Her hands slid beneath his tunic to caress his chest. The tentative explorations were a bit clumsy, betraying her lack of experience, but Talon felt he would melt from the sweet passion of it. Clothes suddenly became an aberration, alien things to be purged from this feverish dream world of desire.

He yanked off his utility belt, sword, and dagger sheath, retaining enough sense to toss them into the open storage bin. His tunic, jerked off over his head, sailed into oblivion. When he unfastened Kari's belt she stiffened, but she relaxed again when he dropped it to the floor. Her tunic was next. She didn't resist when he pulled it off. Talon paused, savoring the sight of her breasts curving over the top of her brown bustier.

His thumbs moved restlessly over the stiff material. "Show me how to take it off," he said in a throaty whisper.

Her gaze—dark, enigmatic, skittish like a wild animal poised for flight—held his while she guided his fingertips to the fasteners at her back. Each hook he released drew a tiny gasp from her mouth. Each innocent sound of untapped desire tore through his body like a blast wave, building his own excitement to a fever pitch. He captured her mouth in a ravaging kiss.

The bustier came loose in his hands and he tossed it aside. Her breasts were warm, resilient and ever so soft as they filled his hands. He didn't want to release her mouth, but he felt compelled to taste the silken texture of her flesh. He dipped his head to kiss the womanly curves and flick one firm nipple with his tongue. Her back arched. Two delicate fists locked into the hair at the base of his skull, rigid yet painless.

He traced circles around the puckered tip with his tongue, pressing deeper into the sweet fullness of her breast. When she shuddered, answering quivers rippled through his body. He drew the crown of her breast into his mouth, simultaneously cupping his hand over her woman's mound.

"Stars," she said raggedly as a shiver rippled through her body. Lightning rocketed to his toes. He had speculated that passion lay untapped beneath her fiery hair and temper, but he'd never anticipated such an intense response, such a sensual heat.

It caused him physical pain, this inability to touch her completely. The pants mocked him, yielding her heat but not her full essence, preventing him from seeking out her soft petals.

He sat up and reached for her boots. Her hands smoothed over his back while he worked, tracing the outline of muscles, the hollow of his spine. Tentative fingertips lingered over old scars, touching them with exquisite gentleness. Fancifully, he imagined a special healing in her touch. It had been a long time . . . forever . . . since anyone offered him tenderness. A powerful shudder sank into his core, one that went mysteriously beyond sensual pleasure.

When he'd succeeded in pulling off the boots he turned and yanked off her pants with a throbbing sense of urgency.

"Talon," she whispered, clutching at his upper arms.

He'd never heard a sound so sweet as his name from her lips. The hint of worry gentled him, though, reminding him to go slowly.

He lay alongside her, making her forget her doubts in another melting kiss. His fingers slipped into the triangle of dark curls, seeking the center of her passion, feeling triumph in the dampness that awaited him. When he touched the tiny nub her hips came up off the bed. He circled his finger, absorbing her feminine moans into his mouth, glorying in the restless, reaching movements of her body, the clenching of her hands on his shoulders. He desperately wanted to give her what she sought.

He eased his body between her thighs, covering her with care, then pushed slowly into her tight channel. She watched him with the same silent, unnerving, stimulating intensity. Her tense body opened in tiny degrees to accommodate him . . . until he encountered her maiden's barrier. It was as he'd suspected—he was her first. A sublime gift, treasured all the more because he couldn't understand why she had offered it to him.

There was no way to avoid the inevitable. He imprisoned her face lightly between his hands, forcing her enigmatic gaze to stay locked with his, willing her to understand the significance of their joining as he broke through with one swift stroke. Her lower body jerked in reaction, muscles twitched around her eyes, but she did not cry out. His brave Kari.

He caressed her stiff body with his hands, coaxing the pain to fade, seeking forgetfulness for her and forgiveness for himself. The wait was agony for him. Her sheath clenched him so tightly, he thought he would die from the sweet torture of it.

She bit her lower lip. "Don't," he murmured thickly. He

teased it free with his thumb, then caught its fullness between his own teeth, nibbling it before claiming her full
mouth.

She began to relax. He pulled back, then sank into her
velvety heat again. Her eyes widened in wonder. She caressed his cheek, feather-light, in an unexpected display
of tenderness.

He forced himself to stroke slowly, holding back until
he felt her respond, felt her body welcome his, rise to meet
his with increasing confidence and urgency. Her legs
wrapped around his waist, gripping tightly. Suddenly he
felt worthy, no longer half a man, unaligned, an outcast.
She trusted him to guide her safely through a universe
shimmering with a startling brilliance, pulsing with sensation and the pounding of his frantically quickening
rhythm. He had to trust her as well; it had never been like
this before, his emotions as involved as his body.

"Kari." He whispered her name with reverence when her
internal tremors reverberated through his body, her cry of
release trembled against his mouth, and their world
erupted into a supernova.

Talon gathered a sleeping Kari into his body, spoon
fashion. Taking a deep breath, he filled his lungs with the
satisfying combination of her unique scent and the lingering smell of their lovemaking. She sighed and snuggled
closer.

He needed to lock up the weapons . . . he would, in a
minute, when she wasn't so wonderfully warm, when she
didn't fit against him like a cast returned to its mold. Unaware, he slipped into the deepest, most peaceful slumber
he'd known in years.

Kari awoke to the sound of muffled thumps and chirps
coming from the alcove. She raised her head, brows
creased in concern. It seemed the Sylphs were chasing
each other around their miniature jungle. She propped

herself up on one elbow, prepared to go check on them, when the sounds softened to low, throaty warbles.

Her face heated in the darkness of the cabin. Apparently the Sylphs were engaged in their own sexual romp. She turned carefully within the warm weight of Talon's arm and studied the faint outline of his body.

How could she have been so wanton, so completely divorced from reality? It had taken only one touch, one kiss, and her body had surrendered to a stirring deep in her soul, something forbidden, beyond her experience yet sweetly familiar.

She'd wanted to forget he was the enemy.

The worst part? She'd do it again if she had the choice. Despite a lingering soreness, she ached to repeat the sensation of Talon's intense masculinity surrounding, claiming, filling her. She tingled with the intoxicating knowledge of his one vulnerability . . . that with her hands, her mouth, she could drive this powerful man over the edge.

She couldn't think of him as an enemy . . . not now, not after she'd shared her body with him and offered him part of her soul.

The console lights sparkled like stars. Memory intruded on her fantasies, whispering of duty. This was the perfect opportunity to view Naill's files, while Talon was asleep.

Like a wraith, she eased from the bed and threw on her tunic and pants. The material rubbed softly against her bare, sensitized nipples, setting off little sparks of lightning that centered between her thighs. A tremor passed through her.

Holding her breath, she inserted the data cylinder into the computer and retrieved Naill's password-protected file. It opened, thankfully undamaged. But as she read its contents, horror gripped her. After twenty-three years of searching, Lochnar engineers had discovered a new vein of neryllium ore on Avernus.

Once processed into gel form, neryllium could be used

to fuel hand-held phazers, as well as the powerful laser cannons laying dormant in every ship in the solar system.

And Naill intended to hijack the first shipment of ore to use in a military coup against Myklar.

Naill was willing to destroy Myklar in his impatience to claim the Dynasty. With shaking hands, she opened a comm channel to the *Regalia*. Her father had to be warned.

Just as suddenly her panic began to calm . . . conscious thought returned . . . a hint of logic. She shut off the comm. The full implications were beginning to sink in.

Did Father know of the mine? She couldn't tell from the note. The word *hijack* disturbed her . . . deeply. Naill wouldn't need to steal the ore if it was exclusively his operation, carried out without Myklar's knowledge or approval. Loyalty battled with the evidence at hand. Did her father intend to use the neryllium to equip his soldiers?

The balance of power was about to become a pathetic fallacy. The Rebellion would be crushed, annihilated. It was the goal she'd been trained to pursue since childhood, but at what cost? Thousands would die. Lochnar soldiers would hunt down the Rebels like animals. Feeling distinctly ill, Kari rubbed her damp palms against her tunic. Even if the Rebels were still faceless enemies to her, which they were no longer, she couldn't abide the wholesale destruction of human lives.

Suddenly she felt alone, cut adrift in the immense vastness of the universe, unable to trust anyone, not even her father.

There was only one solution: She had to destroy the shipment herself, blow it up so no one could use it. At the very least she had to stop Naill's coup attempt. Though the mine would remain intact, she could leak word of its existence, provide the Rebels time to plan, to escape the solar system before enough new ore could be mined.

Frantically, she checked the note for the shipment date. Three days from now. Just three days before the massive cargo ship launched from Avernus. If she could get to her base on Verdigris, she could collect her ship, CX-15 explosives, and be on her way to a rendezvous with the freighter. Simple.

Blazes, this was madness. She dropped her head into her hands, spearing her fingers roughly through her hair. In that moment she hated Naill vehemently. Even through all his cruel, sadistic tricks during their childhood, she hadn't felt this strongly. Despised him, of course, but hate? She'd never allowed herself to succumb to that emotion, knowing instinctively that her own soul might be lost in the process. But now, knowing he toyed with peoples' lives, arrogantly thought to alter destiny—

At least there was still time to complete her mission with Oberon, to claim her mother's legacy before the chance was lost forever. She wouldn't let Naill steal that from her.

Talon awoke with his Valken dagger pointed at his throat.

He rose to his elbows and stared down the length of the blade, never having seen the curved talons of the handquard from this angle before. Anger began a slow burn beneath his breastbone, and something else . . . hurt? Nonsense. He'd have to care deeply about Kari to let her betrayal hurt him.

But there was plenty of room for anger. Runagate hell, they'd shared a bed, made passionate love until they were both exhausted and replete. Or had it all been an act on her part?

His gaze shifted upward to meet hers. She flinched visibly from his simmering fury.

"We're about to emerge from the Corridor. I can't risk the chance you might change your mind," she offered as explanation. "It's imperative I get to Verdigris."

"I said I would take you," he growled.

The blade wavered. Then her mouth hardened and she gripped the dagger tighter. "You're a rogue pilot, an adamant loner . . . I have to believe your own hide takes priority."

"What about my word? Isn't that worth something?"

She stepped back. "You didn't exactly swear to it. I need a little insurance. Now, get dressed. We have to land quickly to escape detection from Lochnar patrols."

He couldn't argue with that. Still, highly charged resentment burned through his body. He rose from the bed.

Kari's face paled, then flushed again, as he stood, naked, before her. Her green gaze traveled over him, starting at his mouth and working its way down, then up again. His skin tingled as if she'd brushed her silky hair across every quivering inch. Last night came back in an avalanche of memory, lush in erotic detail. His manhood hardened in a rush of heated blood.

"Stop doing that," she said raggedly.

"Doing what?" he responded casually.

"You know," she snapped, gesturing toward his arousal.

At least she wasn't unaffected. "Sorry, sweetheart, it seems to have a mind of its own." And he'd know exactly what to do with it, if his woman didn't have a lethal blade in her hand.

"Put your clothes on."

The proximity alarm sounded. Corridor exit in five minutes. He'd take care of her later, he swore.

Talon dressed quickly, donning black pants and a sleeveless blue shirt more suited to the warm weather on Verdigris. Then he dropped into the pilot's seat. Kari strapped in as well.

The Sylphs emerged from their niche. Kari concealed the dagger at her side. Beryl perched on Talon's right shoulder, Oberon on Kari's left. They trilled at one another in intimate tones. Just terrific, Talon thought cynically. Now he would have a constant reminder of the mating ritual when he obviously wasn't going to be twice favored by his prickly warrior woman. Damn Kari's fickle femininity, here one minute and gone the next.

Their flight went unchallenged as he guided the *Nighthawk* toward the surface and Oberon's home. The Sylph pointed the way. The rust-colored Tablelands spanned most of the two continents, their flat surface etched by the spidery blue-green fingers of vein-canyons carved out by eons of flowing water.

He lowered the ship between the steep cliffs of the rugged vein-canyon, searching for a place wide enough to land. He had to settle for a ledge fifteen meters above the canyon floor.

Talon set the ship on standby and opened the hatch ramp. The Sylphs disappeared outside with a flip of their wings.

Without hesitation, he rose and went to the storage compartment in the floor, where he'd tossed the weapons the night before. Though not locking the bin had cost him, he couldn't regret the lapse. The availability of weapons had proven a test of trust . . . one Kari had failed. He opened the lid.

Kari leapt to her feet. "What are you doing?" she demanded.

He refused to answer.

"I'm warning you, smuggler, get away from there."

He reached inside the bin. Ignoring the swords—he didn't want to lug the cumbersome blades on their trek through the forest anyway—he retrieved the dagger's sheath and clipped it to his arm. When he stood she was right there, with the sharp end of serious injury poised a centimeter under his chin.

Talon knew his reflexes were capable of a lightning-quick disarming move. But that kind of speed and power lacked control. He would likely break her wrist in the process. Concern for her safety would cloud his mind, risking injury to himself, because the slightest miscalculation—

"You really want to keep me at dagger point the whole way?"

"I told you, I can't risk you changing your mind."

"We're here, aren't we?"

Her lips compressed into a thin line. Talon studied the tense planes of her lovely face, the shadows beneath her eyes. The brackets at the corner of her mouth revealed more distress than hard resolve. What had upset her? And what kind of fool ached to hug and comfort a woman who held a knife at his throat?

"Kari," he said softly, "give me the dagger. I said I would take you to Oberon's home, and I will."

She hesitated, moments when he forgot to breathe.

"Blazes," she said between her teeth, a sound filled with exasperation. She slipped the dagger into its sheath. A tingle raced through Talon's arm when he felt the slight scrape of metal and the click of the magnetic grip. Then she spun on her heel and stalked, stiff-backed and unarmed, out of the cabin.

They had to climb the rest of the way down. No carved steps existed here, no arborlifts to ascend the towering *canopia* trees to human dwelling places. This vein, like so many others that snaked between the colossal mesas of Verdigris, remained unsettled. A good thing, too; otherwise the Sylphs would seek sanctuary elsewhere.

The foursome started for the head of the canyon. The easiest trek lay along the bank of the winding river. Their boots crunched in the loose, red-brown shale. The Sylphs had it easy, flying ahead, flitting in and out of the surrounding forest. Talon's gaze was drawn repeatedly to the massive gray trunks of the *canopia* trees, with their velvety bark and multiple umbrella layers of blue-green leaves. From this angle they seemed to touch the sky, friendly giants, sentinels.

Oberon and Beryl chased each other along the path, engrossed in one another, relishing the freedom. They flashed brilliant color each time they dashed through a shaft of sunlight.

A sudden, terrible revelation struck Talon. Beryl might decide to stay on Verdigris with Oberon. He clenched his teeth, disturbed more than he cared to admit by the prospect of living without his little jewel, adrift in the *Nighthawk* during those long hours in space. Alone.

Selfish bastard, he thought acidly. *Look at her, how playful and energetic she is.* If Beryl chose to stay, he'd just have to deal with it. He couldn't deny her her happiness. He trudged on in silence.

"We're here," he informed Kari an hour later.

She looked around, baffled. "But I thought Oberon said there were many Sylphs here?"

Talon raised his hands, enjoying the drama of the moment.

Oberon trilled loudly. Suddenly the forest came alive. Sylphs detached from their hiding places—tree trunks, fallen logs, huge flowers, vines. They abandoned their camouflage, flashing back to their natural color. The air hummed with the fluttering wings of several hundred bodies, in every conceivable shade of blue, green, purple, and cyan.

Talon watched Kari. Her expression was like that of a child treated to a magical gift. She stood, frozen with amazement, her eyes sparkling with an internal light. She was more beautiful than ever, vibrantly alive, exquisite.

Something painful stirred deep in his chest, sending a searing shaft of longing deep into his soul. He wanted her, desperately. He needed to be inside her, just as he needed the beat of his blood.

Soon Kari would be lost to him forever. He looked away, unable to bear the sight of her, knowing their time together was so limited.

Chapter Thirteen

A breeze caressed Kari's face, stirred by a multitude of wings. The music of Sylph language filled the air.

A particularly bold youngster flew up to flutter just beyond arm's length, his glittering black eyes examining her with the same intensity she devoted to him. His cyan body was no longer than her hand. Kari reached out, unable to resist the urge to touch him. The Sylph's sense of caution prevailed, for he dashed off with a speed that left her blinking.

Smiling, she felt a sudden compulsion to share her joy with Talon. She turned toward him . . . only to find his gaze fixed on something across the clearing, his expression unguarded.

Shock ripped through Kari at the naked pain evident on his rugged face. She followed his line of sight to see Beryl half-hiding behind Oberon, her hand clutched in his as he led her to a pair of regal, older Sylphs. Oberon's parents?

The glory of the moment dimmed abruptly. She'd been so caught up in the anticipation, the hope of healing even part of the pain surrounding her mother's disappearance, that she forgot their quest had another goal. They'd brought Oberon home. Beryl must intend to stay behind, with her mate.

Strangely enough, Kari would miss Beryl's huffiness and petty jealousy. But that paled compared to the wrenching realization that soon she would have to say farewell to Oberon.

How much worse must Talon feel, about to lose his unique companion of several years, perhaps never to see Beryl again?

Kari started toward Talon, aching to smooth the crease from his brow, the brackets from around his sensuous mouth. She was forced to stop when four Sylphs, struggling under the weight of an ornate brown chest, flew toward her. They set the small chest at her feet. Oberon followed, cradling something in his hands.

He hovered before her. His small hands pressed the key into her palm. *"A sacred trust. For Isolde, we did this."*

Kari's throat tightened. This was the moment she'd anticipated, and feared, for thirteen years.

With a warbled signal from Oberon, the Sylphs retreated to the perimeter of the clearing. Except for distant sounds from the forest, all was quiet. Everyone was watching her. She knelt beside the chest. Her fingers fumbled with the key, almost dropping it in the thick grass. Blazes. This was ridiculous. She was terrified of a box. She'd spent years coming to terms with her mother's desertion. Cool logic, practicality, the need to unravel a mystery . . . those should be her motivations.

She looked up, battling feelings that were anything but logical, desperately seeking Talon. He sat on a log, watching her—stern, silent, alone. His brows rose in a what-are-you-waiting-for? gesture. Even from across the clearing, his strength seemed to reach out. Her racing heart calmed.

Kari took a deep breath and opened her mother's legacy.

With reverence, she reached in to touch pieces of jewelry, hair clasps, and a framed miniature of herself. Her mouth turned up in a shaky smile when she traced her fingertip along the back of a carved wooden hairbrush. This was very familiar. She'd once loved to brush her mother's silky red hair.

A folded note, addressed to her, was tucked in one corner.

Kari opened it slowly. Would it say that her own behavior had driven her mother away, no longer able to tolerate a daughter's rebelliousness, the fights?

It was short. Shorter than she wished. But all the important things were there:

Dearest Kari: This disease I've contracted is slowly stealing my life away. I do not fear death. That is why I seek refuge among the Sylphs, dear creatures, who allow me my dignity and the right to die in peace. Far worse is the nightmare of pain I have lived, where your father's doctors seek to keep me alive unnaturally with their vile drugs. Myklar cannot accept the fact of my mortality. As always, I ask myself whether his devotion is truly love, or a dark obsession. This doubt I have carried with me since the day he conquered our worlds, a violent man, yet impressive in his strength and intelligence. I will admit he was never deliberately cruel, unlike his son, Naill. Though Myklar did send my family into exile, beyond the solar system, he spared their lives for my sake. Over the years I have come to see some good in him, and to care for him. One thing I can never begrudge—he gave me you, Kari. The only regret I have in leaving is that I cannot take you with me. Yet I must go alone. I weaken quickly. How could I care for you? I only hope you can forgive me, and that the note I left speaks of my all-consuming love for you, my daughter.

Note? Kari gripped the paper. Isolde must have meant this hidden treasure. *Oh, Mother. If only I'd known of your letter years ago,* she thought with soul-deep sorrow. *Why didn't you leave me something easier to find, when I needed it most?*

With great care she closed the small chest. Isolde hadn't thought her daughter deserving of abandonment after all. Her mother loved her. Her vision blurred by tears, Kari brushed her hands repeatedly over the chest's smooth, carved edges.

Though the letter granted a new understanding and started the healing of old wounds, part of it disturbed her deeply. Isolde had written harsh words about her husband.

Kari had been raised, nurtured, on Father's story of his noble conquest of the solar system. According to him, he had saved the residents from chaos and infighting. While alive, Isolde had never contradicted him. Had her mother remained silent, hoping to maintain harmony in their home, or did she fear Myklar's wrath if she spoke against him? Did this letter contain the truth, or the fevered rantings of a very ill woman? Was Myklar a ruthless dictator, or a gifted leader and caring father?

Uncertainty gripped Kari, firming her resolve not to share her plans to sabotage the ore shipment, not even to warn Myklar of Naill's coup attempt. She was utterly alone in her quest.

Tucking the chest beneath her arm, she stood . . . then took an involuntary step backwards in surprise. Talon had come up soundlessly. He stood close enough to touch. Despite his hard expression, there was a hint of concern in his eyes.

She stared at the sinewy muscles of his shoulders, feeling a sudden, piercing urge to crawl into his arms, to burrow close into his strength and let his rugged masculinity surround and shelter her. She had never met anyone more grounded in reality than Talon. He was an expert at survival.

His arms spread slightly. An invitation, or was pure longing ascribing a fanciful meaning to the gesture?

Guilt coiled coldly in her belly. Talon would shove her away, violently, if he only knew—the Solis family intended to annihilate his brother and his friends in the name of conquest. Kari clutched the box tighter and stepped back.

The expression in his eyes chilled at her reluctance. She felt an answering shiver run down her spine. He spun away.

"I want to see my mother's grave," she said quickly.

He stopped without turning around. "Of course. Ask Oberon to show you the place." The stiffness of his back was like a wall between them. "After that, we're leaving."

On their way back to the ship the horde of Sylphs followed them, disappearing into the forest a few at a time until only Oberon and Beryl remained as escort. Kari watched Talon put on a cheerful front—and knew it for a lie. Beryl grew increasingly quiet and dejected.

Damn all males, their pride and their warped concept of nobility. Clutching her precious box tighter beneath her arm, she hurried to catch up with Talon's long stride.

"You're hurting Beryl's feelings," she stated flatly.

His gaze slanted toward her, then slid away. "What makes you say that?"

"You're doing too good a job of convincing her that you're happy for her . . . staying behind with Oberon, that is."

"I am. This is where she belongs, with her own kind, not someplace where I can't guarantee her safety anymore." With brutal sarcasm, he added, "I'm a hunted man, remember?"

Kari flinched. "Maybe so, but you're so damn encouraging about it, she thinks you don't care whether she stays with you."

"Nonsense. How can you know what she's thinking?"

"Because that's the conclusion I would draw, if I were her."

"What is this, some sort of female thing?"

Kari lifted her chin proudly. "Yes, I suppose it is." Then she dropped behind, retreating before she gave full vent to her temper. Oberon landed lightly on her shoulder. She felt a sharp pang, knowing this would be the last time.

"Are you pleased with your gift, Kari of Khazanjian?"

"Oh, yes, thank you, Oberon. It's a gift beyond measure."

"Happy for you, I am. Where now do we go?"

201

"What do you mean?"

"I can see now why Beryl chooses to travel with Talon. This flying among the stars is exciting. But next time, you must not leave us in the ship. Tired of missing the fun, I am."

Kari savored the Sylph's telepathic message. She wrinkled her nose at the back of Talon's very hard head. Wasn't he going to be surprised.

"Oberon, I think you'd better have a talk with Beryl. She's under the impression you intend to stay here, and her with you."

The male Sylph drew himself up sharply, wings twitching. *"Females are so impractical, listening to their hearts instead of their heads. Why not did she just ask me?"*

He flew off to scold his mate. Beryl didn't seem to mind the lecture. A moment later she was doing flips in the air, warbling gaily, just before she dove for Talon's shoulder.

"I ought to leave you stranded here."

Talon's statement penetrated like a bolt from a crossbow. Kari wrenched her gaze down from a contemplation of the *Nighthawk* and the climb still to be tackled.

"Don't you dare! It would take me days to cover the distance on foot." She relied on a fast trip home to collect her ship and the explosives needed to deal with the ore freighter.

"Exactly. Suits me just fine. Considering your skill and tenacity, every day I get a jump on your pursuit only increases my chances of escape." He crossed his arms over his chest. "I'm sure your training included wilderness survival."

Kari clenched her jaw, stung by his mockery. She'd been about to reassure him that she had abandoned the idea of recapturing him. Now, dammit, she wouldn't give him that satisfaction. No doubt he would arrogantly believe he was somehow responsible for her change of heart. "I must get home as soon as possible. It's the safest place from Naill."

He advanced on her. Though it took all her willpower, she refused to back away. She looked up into his glowering face.

"You have this annoying tendency to phrase everything like an order, Kari. Why don't you try asking for a change?"

She snorted. "It can't be that simple."

"Try me."

His gaze was riveting, intense and expectant. Everything about him radiated energy. He smelled of life—male musk and the earthy renewal of the forest. "Take me with you, Talon," she said hoarsely. One brown eyebrow arched. "Please," she added between gritted teeth.

A muscle twitched across his cheek. He leaned closer. "How far? Exactly how far are you willing to go?" he asked huskily.

Something primitive beat through her blood. Kari shivered, no longer able to discipline her body's response to him. But she could control her mind. She could ruthlessly remind herself that unless she took action quickly to destroy the neryllium shipment, Naill would rip away Myklar's dignity and power, and the solar system would erupt into a one-sided war. Thousands would die.

Talon would die.

How insignificant were her confused longings, her desire, compared to such destruction?

"Only as far as my home," she said firmly while blocking out the sense of loss that twisted deep in her chest.

Talon couldn't purge the image from his mind—her eyes, haunted and pleading, the rest of her face set with stiff pride.

Of the estimated forty-six million humans in this solar system, Kari was the one most dangerous to him personally.

She was also the one woman who enabled him to forget such dangers when he caressed her, absorbed her soft moans into his mouth, and buried himself so deep in her silken sheath that the outside world ceased to exist.

That's what this was about, he thought harshly. Lust, pure and simple. He could control lust. He glanced at her rigid profile as she sat in the copilot's seat. This time he would drop her off, purge himself of this idiotic tendency toward protectiveness, and make a desperate bid for freedom.

He wrapped his hand around the *Nighthawk*'s hoverlift control. As the cruiser lifted free of the ledge, Talon regained his sense of freedom in being one with the ship, which wasn't bound by Lochnar laws, schedules, or even gravity.

The cruiser skimmed the top of the *canopia* trees and shot toward the sky. Visibility had deteriorated while they were on the ground. A thick bank of storm clouds was rolling in . . . the perfect cover for the two sleek black ships that suddenly emerged from the gray mass, dead ahead.

Lochnar patrol ships.

Kari swore, saving him the trouble.

It was too late to avoid being seen. Talon banked the *Nighthawk* hard to starboard and accelerated for the cloud cover. Aft sensors detected a third ship behind the others, hard in pursuit. Then grayness enveloped the cruiser, crippling visibility. He navigated by sensors alone, until they broke free of the rolling clouds and continued heading straight up. Frigid cold crept into the cabin, the heater unable to compensate for their rapid ascent into space.

Talon immediately brought the *Nighthawk* about in a 180-degree turn, targeting the two lead ships. He unleashed a simultaneous burst from the twin ion cannons. A heartbeat later he punched the torpedo launch.

The ship on the right, caught in the ion blast, sparked into a spectacular display of crackling white light. With its shields temporarily disabled, its navigation scrambled, the

Lochnar craft hurtled forward blindly. One torpedo shot in, right on cue, and obliterated the ship.

The other patrol, quicker to react, dodged both weapons. It fired a return salvo. Talon outmaneuvered the threat and bore down on his attacker. He'd used the menacing appearance of the *Nighthawk* before—he didn't hesitate to do so now. The other pilot waffled under the intimidation of a T-class cruiser heading straight for him. His next shot went wide. Talon's shot didn't.

The flare of the blast filled the viewport. Talon swung away from the flying debris. Any sense of victory was lost, however, by what he saw waiting for him.

The third patrol ship had taken advantage of the battle to catch up. The Lochnar pilot fired four torpedoes in rapid succession, each on a slightly different trajectory.

With a tightly executed series of rolls, Talon cleanly avoided the first three, but the spread was too tight to dodge the fourth completely. It skimmed by overhead . . . too close.

The blow struck the *Nighthawk* with the force of a meteor collision. Though not a direct hit, the last torpedo had come close enough to the *Nighthawk*'s electromagnetic fields to trigger its detonation, stripping away the dorsal shield. Orange console lights flashed on, pinpointing damage to instruments the upper shield protected—the communication web, the shield interlacer, and, worst of all, the targeting control for the torpedo guns. Talon bit back a roar of frustration as the last light turned red, indicating a total shutdown of the torpedo launch mechanism.

Then the bow shields flickered and died.

Only the ion cannons were left. Runagate hell; he might as well spit at the Lochnar ship. There was only one chance at escape. He headed for the nearby entrance to the Verdigris-Serac Corridor. The enemy came about, hard in pursuit.

Though the ship had the *Nighthawk* dead in its sights, it didn't fire. Talon was counting on it. No Lochnar pilot would risk torpedo damage to a Corridor station. The cost of repair was incalculable, the demotion in rank nothing short of bloody.

Waiting until the last possible moment, Talon directed maximum power to the stardrive engines to pull away from the yawning mouth of the Corridor. The *Nighthawk* shuddered; its hull groaned. Kari's knuckles whitened as her fingers dug into the armrests of her seat. The ship barely broke free of the radiating power of the grav-well tunnel.

The patrol ship tried to veer off as well. Too late. Smaller, with less powerful engines than the T-class cruiser, the Lochnar craft couldn't escape the embrace of the Corridor. The opposing forces ripped the ship apart. Its demise flashed yellow-white for an instant, then disappeared, the debris sucked in by the pseudo worm-hole.

Talon released a gust of pent-up air. He allowed some of the rock-hard tension to slip from his neck and shoulders. But he and Kari were far from safe. He couldn't stay here.

He circled the *Nighthawk* and headed into the Corridor.

"No!" Kari protested. She jerked forward in her seat. "I have to get to Verdigris!"

Resentment lanced through him, less agonizing than a deeper ache he didn't want to define. He snapped, "Impossible. I've no intention of risking another engagement without full weapons' capability. The forward shields are out, as well. You know we can't make atmospheric reentry without the heat shields. We need repairs. Star Alpha is our only choice."

Kari stared out the viewport, locked in her thoughts. Her whitened knuckles still gripped the armrests of her seat.

She was obviously horrified by the prospect of staying with him a moment longer than necessary.

Though he knew he couldn't blame her, Talon swore under his breath, calling on every familiar invective plus a few colorful Mal'Harith curses he hadn't used in years. Anything was better than concentrating on the spiraling emptiness in his gut.

He was risking everything for a woman who despised him.

A day. She would lose a day by traveling the Corridor to Star Alpha and back again. A serious setback to her mission of sabotaging the neryllium shipment, but not a fatal blow.

Kari analyzed her situation as she paced between the bunk and the starboard bulkhead. She avoided the sullen pilot sprawled in his seat, heels propped on the edge of the console.

Avoided physically, but not emotionally.

She was excruciatingly aware of every centimeter of his masculine length, the sensuous downturn of his lips, the power and sensitivity in the gloved hands that cradled a snifter of Serakian white brandy. Memories of shared passion filled her with an unbearable restlessness. Her stomach fluttered like a flurry of Sylph wings.

She wanted him.

More than that, she wanted him to want her.

As if in a dream, Kari moved to stand with her knee just touching his crossed legs. His heat engulfed her thigh, leaping across her skin like a million tiny sparks. She sensed a ripple of tension travel through his deceptively casual frame. His right biceps bulged as his fingers tightened around the glass.

He continued to stare out the viewport. His efforts to shut her out only spurred her on with fresh determination.

Inclining her head toward his glass, she murmured, "Are you going to keep the brandy all to yourself?" Her voice held a rich, husky depth she'd never heard in it before.

Sourly, he retorted, "I'm not in a sharing mood. This crazy mission of yours left my ship battered and almost got us blown into cosmic dust. I'm warning you, Kari, go away."

"A ship's captain is supposed to see to the comfort of his passengers," she countered softly. "I'd like some of the brandy."

He shrugged. "Help yourself." A jerk of his head indicated the bottle at his elbow.

Kari felt a flicker of irritation. Stubborn man. Determined to crack his shell of indifference, she chided, "Surely you don't expect me to drink from the bottle. What about your glass?"

He raised it in a mocking gesture. "Sorry. It's empty."

"Allow me." She leaned across him to grasp the bottle. The movement brought her breasts directly in his line of sight. His breath caught in his throat. An answering tingle swept through her chest, tightening her nipples.

She straightened abruptly. To cover her nervousness, she curled her hand lightly around the glass. Her fingertips accidentally brushed his. Though she felt them twitch, he didn't withdraw. She poured more of the clear liquor into the bowl.

"May I?"

"Yes," he snarled, relinquishing the glass, "if it will stop you from indulging in this damn game you're playing."

"I don't know what you mean." She took a sip. The smooth brandy permeated her senses. Talon's fierce gaze followed her every move. Adrenaline pumped a jubilant song through her bloodstream. At least he was no longer ignoring her.

"Excellent brandy." She dipped a finger into the liquor, then put it in her mouth to savor the flavor. She didn't anticipate the impact the gesture would have. A growl rumbled from deep in Talon's chest. Something crackled in the air between them, like the charge before a lightning strike.

Emboldened by his reaction, she touched her finger to the rippling surface of the brandy, then reached forward to paint his lower lip with a light caress. He licked the moisture away. She stared, mesmerized by the potent sensuality of his sculpted mouth. Heat curled through her, burning a shimmering path through her buttocks and down the back of her rapidly weakening legs. She extended a wet finger again.

"Try a deeper taste," she said huskily.

His hand shot up to imprison her wrist. His gaze burned with a dark fire.

"What are you afraid of?" she whispered, recklessly throwing out a dare. "That it will taste better this way?"

She drowned in the molten depths of his eyes as he answered her challenge, slowly, deliberately taking her finger into the warm, silken realm of his mouth. Desire gripped her with a sweet, piercing ache. Blazes, she hadn't known something so simple could make her feel as if she was racing among the stars. A moan escaped her lips. Talon abruptly released her and reached for the snifter. "No!" she gasped, barely coming to her senses. "Just one more." Taking his gloved hand in her own, she dipped his middle finger and curled her tongue around it.

Passion erupted on a volcanic scale. He lunged to his feet and pulled her hard against him, devouring her mouth with a kiss that gave every bit as much as it greedily demanded. Impatient hands set the glass aside, then deftly opened her shirt and unfastened her bustier. Both garments dropped to the floor. He swept her into his arms and carried her to the bunk.

"Take off those damn boots before I cut them off," he growled. "Then the pants."

Her lips curled in a smile while she obliged—half from the sultry pleasure of driving Talon to distraction, half from the joy of seeing his gorgeous body exposed with satisfying rapidity as he urgently stripped off his own clothes. The second he was done, she pulled him down to her.

She stroked his back as he lowered himself between her legs. The intoxicating influence of the brandy could never compare to this. Kari had never had such power at her fingertips, even when she was at the controls of the *Arte-*

mis. Talon's rippling muscles, the thundering rhythm of his heart, the gentle strength in the hands that caressed her breasts . . . everything about him filled her with excitement. Her hands curled over his.

The leather of his gloves was soft, nonabrasive against her skin, but it wasn't what she wanted. She craved flesh against flesh, all of him. The wanton touching and intertwining of their bodies lacked the full measure of intimacy. Her nails curved inward, pulling at the zipstraps.

"Don't!" he snapped. His head jerked up.

Kari froze. "I just want to feel your hands against me, Talon." Her voice emerged in a raw whisper.

The anger in his glittering gaze faded. Though the rigid defensiveness eased from his muscles, an element of tense wariness remained. "Not hands such as these, Kari," he said gruffly. "The gloves stay on." He resealed the zipstraps.

A wall rose between them. In recent days they'd shared anger, desire, danger, joy—but the lack of trust was never more heartrendingly apparent.

They stared at one another, old resentments rising anew. The conflicting emotions only made Kari more vividly aware of their nakedness, of Talon's manhood nestled between her spread thighs. Her body betrayed her, pouring out liquid heat. He must have felt the misting of her desire, for his gaze took on a renewed intensity, an animal hunger.

He raised his hips and lowered them again with exquisite care, letting her feel the full length of his shaft rub against the center of her passion. It was a deliberate torment, his own chance to issue a dare, a challenge for her to finish what she'd begun. She wanted to despise him for it. Instead she throbbed with an emptiness only he could fill.

"Now's your chance to refuse me, Kari," he said huskily. "Do you want this?"

Pride urged her to say no. Passion and an incalculable yearning wouldn't permit the word to cross her lips. Her body answered in its own way, arching to capture the tip of his manhood at the opening of her channel.

Talon didn't hesitate. He plunged into her in one swift stroke. She curled her nails into his buttocks, holding him tight inside her.

"Bite me, rake me with those delicate claws," he whispered in her ear, his voice vibrating with intensity. "I can bear it as long as you let me inside you like this. But please, starfire, don't break the skin."

Her curiosity as to why he would begrudge a scratch or two was lost in sensation when he began to move. Desire spiraled out of control when he sought out her mouth, his tongue slipping between her lips to engage her own in a passionate duel.

Their coupling became wild, primitive, a dance of sweat-slicked bodies battling one another in fierce emotion at the same time they shared such sweet sensations that Kari wanted to weep with joy.

She thought herself alone in the feeling, that all Talon cared for was the carnality of their joining, until she heard him growl against her neck, barely audible, "Damn you, Kari. What are you doing to me? Why can't I let you go?" He spoke as if the words were being torn from his chest.

Despite the surface bitterness and resentment in his words, Kari held them close to her heart, sensing a deeper meaning she couldn't yet comprehend. There was an element of defeat there. In a man of Talon's rare courage, such a message was profound. Hope flowered, tentative, unfocused. She clutched at it, even as her body tightened around him.

Her name erupted from his lips in a shout of exultation. Instinctively, she lifted her legs higher. The depth of his powerful strokes touched her very core. Suddenly she was there with him, space and time melding into a brilliant flare of light.

He needed her. More than the primitive release from her body, he needed the complex healing only her soul offered.

211

Kristen Kyle

His body had just admitted it openly, honestly, though she knew he would never say the words. It humbled her that he could conceal such need behind courageous independence.

Talon settled onto her slowly, the rigidity melting from his muscles one by one, until he sagged along her length. He buried his face in her hair, his breath pouring down her neck and shoulder like a hot waterfall.

She stroked his back with a light touch. After a few minutes her chest shook with silent laughter.

He lifted his head, his hooded expression lazy, replete, with a hint of suspicion. "What's so funny?"

"I was just thinking you feel as boneless as a *balcor* playing dead." The smallest of Verdigris's forest predators was capable of going completely limp when threatened.

Talon's mouth slanted in a wry grin. "I kind of feel like one at the moment. Am I crushing you?"

"Breathing is a minor luxury. I like your weight," she admitted impulsively, then blushed at her candidness.

His grin broadened into a genuine smile. She could do no more than gasp as he held her close and flipped them both over, settling onto his back with her nestled along his side.

"Go to sleep, starfire," he murmured.

Kari settled her head into the curve of his shoulder, finding a pillow on a cushion of muscle. She splayed her fingers through the crisp hair of his chest. Deciding to be a little more daring, she hooked her right leg over his, resting it low across his thighs.

His fingers curled warmly around her knee, sliding it higher until her thigh rested intimately against his loins.

Kari sighed. She could grow used to this. Just before drifting off to sleep she drew satisfaction from knowing that there was some measure of trust, however small, in this moment.

* * *

"Forty hours!" Talon exploded.

Kari's heart sank to the soles of her feet. The repair estimate on the *Nighthawk* couldn't possibly be worse. She'd never make it to Avernus by the ore freighter's scheduled launch.

Talon leaned over the console and growled into the comm, "Garek, I don't have forty hours to wile away drinking ale and playing Hazard in the Stargazer. I have to get out of here."

The lead-tech, whom Talon had specifically asked for the moment they'd reached Star Alpha, gazed up at the *Nighthawk*'s cockpit from the floor of the auxiliary bay. Garek shrugged his broad, beefy shoulders beneath the orange jumpsuit. "Sorry, man. I can't start on it for another eight hours. And that's the absolute minimum I can offer, including working around the clock, which you know I wouldn't even offer to anyone else."

Flopping back in disgust, Talon tilted his head back against the headrest. He sighed. "Yeah, I know. Thanks."

"Why are you in such a hurry? Wouldn't have anything to do with this Lochnar bounty on your head, now would it?" Garek asked teasingly. "What did you do now? This one I've got to hear."

Talon closed his eyes. "Oh, life was getting a little dull, so I thought I'd earn the enmity of the Dynast by staging a Narkwar prison break."

Garek gave a low whistle. "And I thought you deliberately steered clear of things like that. Shows how much I know."

"Is it general knowledge that I'm here?"

"Don't worry, I deleted the *Nighthawk*'s landing from the log the minute she touched down."

"Can you hide her?"

Garek grinned. "It wouldn't be the first time. Let me get my equipment detached, then I'll bring over a tow robot."

He disappeared under the cruiser. Kari could hear muffled clanks as he disconnected the diagnostics cables. As soon as his dark head reappeared, she fired her own question into the comm.

"When is the next shuttle to Verdigris?"

Garek turned, fingers pressed to his headset, brows arched in surprise as he looked up at the cockpit window. That was the last Kari was allowed to see.

Talon yanked her onto his lap and clamped a hand over her mouth.

"A lady on board, Talon? You been holding out on us?" Garek prodded with a laugh.

"The tow robot?" Talon reminded his friend, cutting short the conversation. His calm, teasing tone was in direct contrast to the tension Kari felt radiating through his rigid muscles. Garek grumbled something about a certain someone being too private and no fun, just before Talon shut off the comm.

He released his hold on her mouth. "I hate to derail your plans about hopping on the first available shuttle, but you're not going anywhere."

Kari bolted from his lap as if he were swarming with voltaic lizards. Circumvention of a deadly war depended on her getting out of here in the next few hours. She couldn't stay. The *Nighthawk* gave a small lurch and started to move.

"We had an agreement," she whispered accusingly.

"And I still intend to keep it. But I'm not letting you out of my sight until my ship is space-worthy. I've no intention of setting myself up as easy prey for you when my means of escape is crippled. You're still my hostage."

The comm beeped. Talon's breath hissed out between his teeth as he switched it on.

"Hey, Talon, have you heard of the big reward for the Dynast's daughter?"

He stiffened. "What are you talking about?"

"Apparently Kari Solis has disappeared. Run off, or something. Naill Solis has offered twenty thousand value tokens to anyone who can return her safely to him. Know anything about her? No one knows what she looks like, or if they do, they're keeping it to themselves."

"You know I avoid anything that has to do with the Dynast."

"Is that right?" Garek snorted. "Anyway, just thought I'd mention it, in case you were interested. Several people on this station would love to get their hands on that kind of money."

"What about you, Garek?" Talon asked guardedly.

The humor vanished from the lead-tech's voice as he bit out, "Hell, if the little lady wants to bolt, I say more power to her. Her father deserves some grief for all the misery he adds to our lives. And maybe now she'll leave us alone. No more raids."

Their forward momentum stopped. A metallic thunk echoed through the storage bay as the tow robot disengaged. The huge connecting door lowered like a giant eyelid, cutting off the light from the auxiliary bay. The ship's running lights switched on automatically. The glow pushed into the otherwise empty room but was swallowed by the gloom before reaching the steep walls.

"The *Nighthawk*'s secure, Talon. Only a few key people know of this bay. I'll start work on her as soon as I can."

"Thanks for the help, and the warning." Talon turned to Kari after Garek left. "Looks like maybe you'll have to trust me. I may be the only person on this space station you can be sure won't try to deliver you directly into Naill's hands."

He was right. She had no friends here, no one she could count on. She almost hated him for pointing out the obvious.

Chapter Fourteen

Kari watched as Talon clipped a black shoulder strap to his utility belt, then passed it diagonally across the chest of his equally dark flightsuit.

"Come on, Beryl, Oberon. I'm not going to stay cooped up in here for two days," he muttered irritably.

The two Sylphs flew to his back and clung lengthwise to the wide strap, head to toe. They turned the same color as their perch. Kari would have been startled by the transition if she hadn't seen evidence of their camouflage ability on Verdigris.

Escaping from Talon, then finding some way to leave the station without drawing the attention of bounty hunters, was going to be tricky. She had to find the opportunity . . . soon.

"After you, Kari." He indicated the open hatch ramp.

They stepped out into the cool, silent expanse of the storage bay. The slightest sound echoed from the high ceiling. Garek had disappeared. Talon guided her through a service tunnel that led on a roundabout path away from the storage bay.

Cutting over to the main passageway, they had just closed the access panel when a door opened directly across from them. Of all the foul luck, Bhut Camargue backed out of the room, saying, "I said I'd have your money soon, and I meant it. Don't worry."

He started to turn. It was too late to duck out of sight.

When he saw them, his eyes widened, then narrowed just as quickly in speculation.

A shudder of apprehension and distaste passed through Kari. Instinctively, she took a step closer to Talon.

Closing the door, Camargue said with a sneer, "Talon. I'm surprised ya showed your face on Star Alpha. The bounty on your head has jumped to an all-time high."

Talon's hand went to the hilt of his sword. He took a step forward. With soft menace, he said, "Give me something to look forward to. Just try to collect the reward."

Camargue paled and backed away. His jowls trembled as he swallowed audibly. "Uh . . . I was just kiddin'. Wouldn't dream of turning ya in. We smugglers have to band together, ya know."

"Don't count on it. Now, get out of my sight."

With a twisted expression of hate that sent a shiver down Kari's spine, Camargue retreated down the passageway and disappeared around a corner. She was more than happy to head in the opposite direction. They'd taken only half a dozen steps when three other men approached, blocking their path.

Kari caught her breath. She recognized the face of the center man, the thick mane of black hair held back with a maroon band around his forehead. Jhase Merrick. A true smuggler in every sense of the word, perhaps an out-and-out space pirate; rumor had it that Merrick would do almost anything for money. And he was the one man bold enough to stand up to Talon's intimidating reputation . . . and Naill's position of power.

Could she bargain with Merrick, offer him a better deal than Naill's reward? She tensed, torn by doubt. If she miscalculated, he might deliver her straight to her half-brother. In that case her plans, at the very least, would be short-lived.

Her fists clenched at her sides as the pirate and his men drew closer. Before she could say anything Talon spun her into his arms and covered her mouth with a deep, possessive kiss. For a moment she almost forgot where she was, why she was here.

Merrick would pass by. Her chance would be lost. She wedged her hands against Talon's chest and shoved. He released her abruptly. A sharp pressure against her neck sent pain shooting into her head, then everything went black.

Talon swept Kari into his arms when she crumpled. It was the only practical alternative. He'd sensed, in her tension, her readiness to ask the other man for help. He couldn't allow her to reveal her identity to anyone, not even Jhase.

Merrick signaled his two men to move on with a brisk, "I'll meet you at the *Vagabond*." He stopped in front of Talon, commenting dryly, "I knew my reputation with women was more deserved than yours. At least they don't swoon in my arms from a single kiss."

"Don't start with me, Jhase," Talon growled.

Undeterred, Jhase reached forward with a scarred hand. Gentle fingers traced the line of Kari's jaw. His thumb caressed her full lower lip. "Lovely," he murmured.

Talon's teeth clenched against a hot, searing surge of jealousy. "Hands off," he snarled, then regretted his tone when Jhase's gaze, full of knowing laughter, rose to meet his. Jhase was deliberately baiting him. Runagate hell. This damnable possessive streak over Kari was mutilating his self-control.

Talon stiffened when the pirate lifted one of her limp hands to examine her Line tattoo. He knew what was coming.

"And I believed that garbage you told me about avoiding trouble," Jhase scoffed. "Crimony, seems you've found a veritable shipload of it."

"Believe me, I walked into this particular trouble without asking for it."

Jhase shook his head ruefully. "You know, I think you need someone to watch over you, Talon. A partner."

"I thought you'd given up on that idea."

"I'm a persistent man. I'll stick with it until you say yes." He hooked his thumbs in his utility belt and said with obvious relish, "Your worth grows by leaps and bounds, mate. Can't think of anyone else with the balls to abduct the Dynast's daughter. Almost as daring as some of the stunts I've pulled. Now, seems to me you need a place to hide this singularly hot little commodity."

"I was just working on that."

"I can do you one better. I keep a room reserved for whenever I drop by *Star Alpha*." Jhase pulled a key sequencer out of his belt. "Hub seventeen, number fifty-three. Don't get lost." Dropping the key in Talon's breast pocket, he added, "My next shipment is due in Inclement. The Rebels are willing to pay a handsome price for some additional force-field generators. The frequency on this," he continued, tucking a commlink in Talon's pocket as well, "is set to my channel. Call if you feel a sudden need to chat."

Pride urged Talon to say no, but that emotion paled next to the surprise at the genuine offer of friendship. "Thanks, Jhase." It was all he could think to say.

"Yeah, well, I like having you in my debt. Don't think I won't call it in."

Pressing his back against the wall, Bhut Camargue tucked the small, angled mirror back into his pocket. He speculated on the scene he'd just witnessed in the polished surface. Talon and Merrick, together, without coming to blows? It didn't seem possible. He wished he'd been close enough to hear the conversation. Stars, he hated both men and their arrogant superiority.

What had Merrick tucked into Talon's pocket? Were they friends, or was Merrick playing some sly game to collect the reward? Camargue chewed on the fleshy inside of his cheek. There must be some way to turn this to his advantage.

*   *   *

"This information had better be accurate, Camargue. I have neither the resources nor the time to send my men in pursuit of every minuscule rumor," Naill declared in a lazy tone that made no attempt to conceal the underlying threat. He settled back in his chair and stroked his goatee. "And believe me, I've been pursuing too many dead ends over the past couple of days."

A heavy swallow was audible over the comm channel. "I swear it was her, Jemidar Solis."

"I don't recall your being among the select group of bounty hunters to receive a capto-image, Camargue. You say the only other time you saw Kari, she was wearing her helmet?"

"Well, yeah, but it's the eyes, ya know. Those green eyes are hard to forget."

"You're suggesting I take action because of the color of a woman's eyes?" Naill countered incredulously. He was rapidly losing patience with this entire conversation.

"Uh . . . no, Jemidar. There's one other thing."

"What is that?"

"She was with Talon."

Naill stilled. Excitement shot through him like an electrical current. There had been no report on Talon since Boreas, when they'd lost contact with the last of the Interceptors . . . though there was the mystery of three missing patrol ships. Forcing a tone of indifference, he replied, "Indeed. And why should Talon's presence make a difference?"

"Well, ya did put a price on his head at the same time your sister disappeared," Bhut said with sly overtones.

"Half-sister," Naill corrected automatically. "Very astute. I confess, I'm surprised you made the connection." *Stunned, to be precise, and more than a little irritated*, he added inwardly.

"How much are ya willing to pay if I deliver them both?"

"The full bounty, of course. Forty thousand."

Camargue coughed, then cleared his throat. "That leaves just one question: What condition do ya want them in?"

"Why, my half-sister must be delivered perfectly safe," Naill urged in his best devoted-brother tone. He couldn't risk it becoming known that he wished Kari harm. Otherwise, it would be impossible to make her subsequent death look like an accident. "Talon, on the other hand, can be in whatever condition you wish, as long as he's still alive so I can have the pleasure of finishing him off."

"Ya got it. Camargue out." The channel disconnected.

"Slimy, opportunistic smuggler." Naill jumped to his feet and began to pace furiously.

Penn, staying just out of range, offered soothingly, "As long as Camargue serves a purpose, surely you can tolerate him."

"True, but he and his men are amateurs. I'm so weary of incompetence. First the Interceptors fail me; now this." He stopped abruptly and fixed the Gent'Sian with a glare. "I expect better, Penn. What of the mercenary team I sent to Serac?"

"Waiting for any sign of Talon and Jemara Kari returning to the ice planet, as you ordered, my lord."

"And the uniforms? Did you see them properly equipped?"

"Identical to those of Myklar's personal guard."

Naill allowed himself a smile. "Excellent. See that they are immediately reassigned to Star Alpha. There's no need to pay Camargue if we can do the job ourselves."

Talon paused just inside the room and eyed it with a critical, tactical gaze. The wide shaft of light from the open door illuminated the opposite wall. He nodded with approval. Trust Jhase to reserve one of the few rooms on Star Alpha with a rear exit.

He kicked the door shut. He'd have to lay Kari down before he could bolt the door. Before he took another step forward, two small shoves at his back marked the launch of the Sylphs.

Oberon saved him the trouble, turning the small lever that slid the bolt. Beryl switched on the lights. The two flitted around the room, flashes of bright color against the conservative gray walls and the deep burgundy of the furniture and large bed. Talon relaxed. If the Sylphs saw nothing to be concerned about, who was he to worry?

Talon looked down at Kari's serene face cradled against his shoulder. Her fair skin glowed with translucent perfection; her delectable mouth relaxed in a tiny pout. Somewhere between the hangar bay and here she'd slipped into an exhausted slumber.

Well, if she was willing to sleep in his arms, he was enough of a cad to take advantage of it one last time.

After carrying her so far he was too exhausted to even consider undressing. He reclined on the bed, propped up by head cushions, and settled Kari onto his lap. His sword dangled over the edge. Despite the burn of glucose-depleted muscles, she felt too damn good to let go.

"Beryl, turn off the lights," he whispered. She obliged.

In the sudden darkness, he felt the Sylphs settle down at the foot of the bed. The best alarm system in the solar system slept at his feet. It took several minutes for his sight to adjust to the thin thread of light filtering under the door.

With a ragged sigh, he curled his arms about Kari's waist and leaned back, closing his lids over burning, aching eyes. His insides were in turmoil. He wasn't sure what caused him greater pain, the heavy beat of desire or the knowledge that, were she awake, Kari would be doing everything in her power to escape. He ached to kiss her senseless. She wanted to shove him down the nearest refuse shaft.

He wanted to tell her . . . what? That her presence banished the crushing loneliness in his life? He'd never felt more alive than when her green eyes softened as they made love. Or even, oddly enough, when those same eyes scorched him with green fire as they fought. How could he explain to her something he didn't understand himself? Hell, she'd laugh in his face.

"Ouch!" Talon exclaimed, jolting awake five hours later with the pain of someone yanking on his hair.

Kari murmured a sleepy complaint, lifted her head from his chest, then settled back down with a sigh. She obviously wasn't the prankster. Then who—? A wing tip brushed lightly against his ear, clearing up the mystery.

"*Someone comes,*" Oberon communicated the warning.

Talon listened closely. At first, nothing. Then he picked up the sounds of footsteps moving stealthily toward the door. The Sylph had detected the possible threat moments before his own senses would have brought him awake, gaining precious time.

Oberon flew over, dropped to his hands and knees, and sniffed under the bottom of the door. He recoiled instantly.

"Can you recognize the scent?" Talon whispered.

"*'Tis the one who stopped us in the passageway.*"

"The butt-ugly one?"

"*Yes. Smelly, too. What do we do?*"

"Get away from the damn door," Talon hissed. He shook his bedmate urgently as the Sylphs retreated to the opposite side of the room. "Kari, Camargue and his men are outside the door."

She came fully awake in a heartbeat. Jerking out of his arms, she jumped to her feet. Her quick gaze took in the situation. "Brilliant. You got us trapped in this room," she whispered accusingly.

"I'm not that stupid," he retorted in barely audible self-defense. "There's a rear—"

A soft click sounded against the front door.

"Move!" Rocketing off the bed, he yanked open the rear door and shoved Kari into the service tunnel. The Sylphs darted out, just before an explosion ripped into the room.

The concussion slammed the rear door against Talon's shoulder, throwing him against the far wall of the tunnel. He hit, then slid to the floor, fighting the blackness attempting to devour his brain. Through a daze he heard the shouts of Bhut's men, watched Kari wrench the door closed and smash the activator panel with a powerful side-kick. The lock bolted in place with a metallic thunk. Sparks flew from the panel as it shorted out.

"That should hold them. Come on," she shouted, pulling on his arm. "Get up!" He could hear the Sylphs warbling frantic encouragement in the background.

He struggled to his feet, shaking his head. His senses cleared as they ran, until only a slight ringing lingered in his ears. He took the lead then, guiding Kari to an access door that led out of the service tunnel. They had to get into the network of main passageways if they stood any chance of reaching other parts of the station . . . though where they could hide after this, he hadn't a clue.

Talon fingered the commlink in his pocket. Jhase might just be his only way off Star Alpha. The smuggler would be at Inclement by now, but he could make the return trip in twenty-five minutes or less. Reluctantly, Talon lowered his hand. No. He hadn't a right to embroil Jhase in this mess. He'd at least wait until every other avenue of escape was exhausted.

The commotion in the far wing was drawing a lot of attention, including Station Security. Peering through the narrow slits of an access panel, he held Kari behind him until the uniformed men ran past. Then he opened the door and helped her step through into the deserted main passageway.

"What now?" she whispered.

"The main hangar. First order of business is to steal a ship, since the *Nighthawk* isn't space-worthy." She nodded. They ran down the passageway. Oberon and Beryl darted ahead.

They hadn't gone far when the heavy sound of boots

against metal reverberated off the walls. Four Lochnar soldiers stepped out from a cross-passage a short distance ahead. Talon ground to a halt. Kari gasped, a sound of eagerness rather than dread. And no wonder—the men wore the uniforms of the Dynast's personal guard. Myklar had sent his best men after his daughter.

They were cut off from the Sylphs, who fluttered beyond the soldiers' backs. Afraid to do anything that would draw attention to the rare creatures, Talon sent a quick hand signal to Beryl instructing her to stay quiet and meet him back at the *Nighthawk*. She tugged at a reluctant Oberon, drawing him out of sight.

Here was Kari's opportunity to escape. What could be safer than her father's personal guard? She would grab at the chance, of course.

Talon's every instinct clamored that that would be the worst possible choice.

There was something about the soldiers' expressions that went beyond normal military training, even among Lochnar ranks—an icy-eyed, granite-jawed ruthlessness. The lead man smiled, a cold, calculating upturn of his lips, and Talon was suddenly bone-deep certain of his suspicions. These were bounty hunters, or worse. Naill had made sure his agents were properly camouflaged this time, in the one uniform Kari would trust.

There was only one way to compete with that masquerade and keep her from tumbling into Naill's clutches—brute force.

He yanked her back the way they'd come. With a shout, the four men erupted into pursuit behind them. Kari stumbled after him, struggling against his full-out run.

"What are you doing?" she cried.

"Protecting my assets, dammit. Keep up, or I'll drag you."

"Don't, please. I won't tell them who you are," she insisted. "I'll distract them. You can get away."

The passageway dead-ended at a turbolift shaft. Ignoring her, he hit the call button. Thank the stars, the door opened immediately. The car was on this level.

The four men thundered down on them. Kari wrenched her arm free and turned sharply, poised for flight. Talon whipped an arm about her waist and hauled her backward into the turbolift. The door hissed closed.

"No!" she cried, struggling fiercely. "They'll have a ship."

"Kari, I don't trust them," he snapped. He hit the descent button, taking them down two deck levels.

"Of course you don't trust them," she retorted. "They're my father's men, his personal guard."

"But that's just it. I don't think—"

"There's no time. If I don't leave Star Alpha within the next few hours, it'll be too late."

"What the hell are you talking about? Too late for what?"

She turned within the circle of his arms to glare at him. "I can't tell you," she declared heatedly.

"And I won't let you go until you do . . . if then."

He stared down into her beautiful, angry face, choking on the rage and frustration ripping through him because he couldn't force her to give him the one thing he craved most . . . her trust.

The narrowing of her eyes should have warned him. Her strange desperation should have set his defenses on full alert.

She was blindingly fast as she snatched the Valken dagger from its sheath. The blade arced like silver lightning, flashing past the corner of his vision before sinking into the thick muscle of his left shoulder. It didn't hurt—not really—until she pulled it out. Someone gasped. Was it him?

He should take some comfort, he thought distantly, in the horror gripping her face. The look of regret gave evidence of an act that was purely instinctive, defensive, trained into her from the time she was fifteen.

He took the dagger from her slackened grip. His jaw muscles knotted at the sight of the four-centimeter red stain at the tip. Not an overtly serious wound . . . in a normal, healthy man. Dully, he returned the blade to its sheath.

"Talon?" she whispered hoarsely.

He grabbed her wrist with his right hand in a grip that made her yelp in pain. "Nice try, Princess," he snarled, "but you're still coming with me. I'm going to see you safely out of here, despite your best efforts to screw things up."

The turbolift door opened. He dragged her out.

"I'm sorry. I didn't mean for that to happen."

"Yeah, right," he responded with acidic sarcasm. He propelled her toward the auxiliary bay. His only chance now was to make it to the *Nighthawk* and hope Beryl understood his message to rendezvous there.

"Talon, I can't go with you. You have to let me go," she cried, but her struggles had ceased. At least her remorse granted him that one small concession.

"Why? Afraid you'll pay a penalty for turning on me?"

"I would deserve whatever price you demanded, but that's not the point," she said roughly. She leaned back, craning her head to see his wound. He jerked her forward again before she could see the result of her handiwork.

He focused on survival, pushing her down the length of the passageway, turning down another, and yet another. He slowed to a fast walk. With each long stride, the silver tunnels seemed to stretch farther into infinity.

"Talon, you've got to listen to me."

He couldn't, even if he wanted to. It was all he could manage to keep moving, putting one foot in front of the other despite the encroaching weakness and the chill invading his body. His strength was fading. His life was streaming down his back, unabated. The spreading dampness—all the way down to the back of his thigh—told him the extent of the damage.

Pounding steps sounded behind them. He turned sharply, pulling her with him, almost going to his knees.

The fake soldiers had found them. In his weakened condition they looked like a pack of predatory beasts bearing down on their prey.

His gaze riveted on the nearest of the pressure doors that intersected the passageway every fifteen meters. The activator panel was only three steps away, though it seemed more like a light-year's distance. He forced his fingers to touch the cool surface of the cordite. The doors rumbled closed.

"Damn you, Talon!" exploded Kari.

That's appreciation for you, he thought grimly as he transferred the vice-grip on her wrist to his other hand. He was sacrificing everything to protect her, and she hated him for it. Hell, what did he expect from a woman who'd stabbed him?

No time to think about that now. The bounty hunters were activating the door mechanism from the other side.

Quickly drawing his sword, Talon called on the last of his strength and rammed the point deep into the panel. A deadly electrical discharge engulfed the blade. He jerked his hand away, just in time, leaving his Singh Dubh embedded in the wall.

The door jammed just as it started to open, leaving only a vertical hairline crack between the two panels. The twin blades of a pry-lever punched through the gap. A click, a groan of metal, and their pursuers began the process of manually cranking open the door.

He just wanted to lay down and rest, but they were far from safe. He turned . . . and stumbled. Though he lurched to his feet immediately, his stride grew unsteady as they moved away from the door. Everything was going numb. He blinked and shook his head, trying to focus his thoughts.

Kari watched him, concerned. Talon was weakening. Why? The blow she'd dealt him was little more than a flesh wound.

He glanced back over his shoulder, shifting his balance.

Her duty was to take advantage and escape. It was her best chance. Kari planted her right foot hard and swung her weight against him, slamming his back into the wall. His grip on her wrist broke.

Free, she sprinted back toward the widening crack between the door panels, glancing back just once to see Talon sliding slowly down the wall.

The image jolted through her as she ran a few more steps, until her mind acknowledged the horror of what her eyes had so briefly seen. Color . . . red. And quantity . . . an obscene amount, out of all proportion to that minor wound. No wonder he had grown so weak. Talon was bleeding like a gutted tarpan.

And suddenly she knew—why he stayed Neutral and avoided fights, why he was so wary of anything sharp, even her fingernails.

Talon was a bleeder.

Chapter Fifteen

Talon was going to die, leaning against that cold metal wall, hemorrhaging out his life until his blood pressure dropped and he drifted away into oblivion—lost to her forever.

Kari jolted to a stop just before the pressure door and turned, a sob caught in her throat, knowing that to help him would cripple her chance to get to the ore shipment in time. Thousands of lives depended on her success. But right now only the life of this one man mattered above all things.

She raced back to Talon's side.

"Wasting an opportunity to escape, aren't you, Princess?"

"For the last time, stop calling me that," she croaked, forcing words past the crush of emotion in her chest. "You're a bleeder, dammit."

Heavy lids drooped over his eyes. "You noticed, eh?"

"This is no time to be flippant. Why didn't you tell me?"

He grimaced. "It's not exactly something I advertise. In my profession you don't tell the competition, much less the authorities, that you can be defeated by a mere scratch."

"I didn't mean to stab you," she cried out brokenly.

He regarded her doubtfully. "Go on, Kari. It's too late for me. I'll never make it to the *Nighthawk* before I collapse. You've got to get away before those soldiers break through." He gathered her shirt into a bloody fist and urged her close. "I'm certain they're Naill's men. Trust me, just this once."

A groan rumbled from his chest as he leaned his head back against the wall. The defeat in his voice tore at her heart. And why was his goal a crippled, useless ship?

Beryl, of course! The healing power of the Sylph nectar was exactly what he needed, perhaps the only chance of saving his life. She'd seen, firsthand, how well it had worked on her wrist. She had to get him to the *Nighthawk*.

"I'm not leaving you. Now, get up," she snapped.

He didn't budge. "I'll only slow you down. Go."

The pressure door clanked as their pursuers opened it another notch. She had to get Talon up and moving. The only way was to goad him into action. Pulling on his arm, she said derisively, "Look, smuggler, I may be significantly more nimble than you, and a better swordsman, but I can't outdo you in brute strength. Now move, dammit."

"Stubborn, unreasonable woman," he grumbled, but with her help he struggled to his feet.

While he stood, swaying like Verdigrian prairie grasses in a gentle breeze, Kari stripped off her shirt and tied it around his waist. She couldn't have him dripping blood, leaving an obvious trail. Her stomach clenched at the warm wetness across his back.

She ducked under his right arm, laying its heavy length across her shoulders. Talon cocked his head and cast an appreciative glance down the cleavage displayed at the top of her bustier. She almost laughed with joy. If he could still look at her like that, the rogue wasn't too far gone to save.

She struggled to the nearest service tunnel. Though it wasn't much farther to the secret storage bay, he leaned more of his weight on her as they went. Kari had never been happier to see anything than the *Nighthawk* . . . except the Sylphs, who dashed out from their hiding place behind the landing skids.

Beryl's eager flight braked in midair. She flew circles

around them, her worried chirping punctuated by tiny moans.

Kari half-dragged him up the open ramp, then closed the ship. They got as far as the cabin before his legs gave out. He went down and rolled onto his back with a ragged curse.

"Pocket," he rasped, touching the front of his flight suit. "Call for help." Then he lapsed into unconsciousness.

His skin was so cold. Stars in heaven, he was slipping away. She had to stop the hemorrhaging immediately.

She dropped to her knees and unclipped his dagger sheath and forearm guards. Wrenching open the zipstraps of his flight suit, she turned him onto his stomach and pulled the soaked suit down around his waist. The Sylphs crouched on the floor beside her. Oberon had fetched an armful of towels. Beryl warbled softly, a mournful sound that magnified the dread clawing through Kari's nervous system.

The wound steadily oozed blood. In the confinement of the small cabin, the smell was almost overpowering. And it was all her doing. She hated the sight of it, almost as much as she hated herself.

"Can you help him?" she pleaded.

"Wipe the blood away," Oberon communicated solemnly.

While she tackled the gruesome task, the Sylphs fluttered their wings and kneaded their secreted nectar into a paste. Oberon packed the wound with it. He pointed to a clean towel.

"Press."

Kari held the cloth tightly against the wound. Within a few minutes it had soaked through with fresh blood, flowing as surely as the despair that filled her with a dark foreboding.

"It's not working," she whispered desperately.

Oberon pulled the cloth away while Beryl provided more nectar. He repeated the treatment. Kari compressed the wound with another fresh towel. She held her breath, then let it out slowly when a small spot of red spread no further.

A small victory. But Talon had lost so much blood, he could still die. She bound the wound snugly. Finally able to act on his last words, she dug into the breast pocket of his flight suit.

A commlink. *Call for help*, he'd said.

Cradling the precious piece of silver metal and electronics in her palm, she sent a signal. A male voice answered.

"Who's this?" Kari demanded.

"Who's asking?" came the gruff, unrevealing reply.

"Kari Solis. I need to speak to Rand Markos immediately. It's an emergency. Is he anywhere nearby?"

"I might be able to locate him. What's your rush?"

"It's Talon. He's been hurt. We're trapped on Star Alpha. Someone needs to come and get him. Now."

There was a pause. Then another voice, easily recognizable as Rand's, answered in hostile tones.

"Nice try, Jemara Solis, but I'm not buying. I'm not gullible enough to walk blithely into one of your traps."

"But it's not a—"

"Quinn, cut the transmission before they source us."

"No, wait!" she cried out. Panic pressed in on her lungs, pinched her heart. "What can I say to make you believe me?"

"Nothing. Talon's capable of taking care of himself."

"Not when he's bleeding to death, you idiot! Of all the stubborn, misplaced confidence. Your brother is dying! Are you going to come help him or not?"

"What did you say?" Rand countered in a hoarse whisper.

"I said—" Kari stopped abruptly, realizing that she'd hit on the key. Calmly, she repeated, "Your brother needs you."

"How did you know he's my brother?"

"He told me," she lied. Anything to get Rand up here.

"You said he was bleeding. Where's Beryl?"

"She's here with me. We've stopped it, but he's lost a great deal of blood. He needs a transfusion, but I can't take him to the clinic. There are some men after us—"

"Are you on the *Nighthawk?*" Rand interrupted.

"Yes."

"Listen. Talon keeps a supply of blood on board, in the extra preserver-unit. Do you know where that is?"

"Yes, but it's locked. Where does he keep the key?"

The other end of the channel fell silent for a painful moment. "I don't know, dammit."

"Never mind. I'll get in if I have to rip it off the wall."

"Do you know how to administer a transfusion?"

"Yes," Kari responded with confidence. That part of her battlefield training was about to prove invaluable. "Are you coming to get us out of here? A lot of good it will do me if I save Talon, only to have Naill get his hands on him."

"We'll be there in twenty-five minutes."

"The ship's hidden, in a storage annex to the aux-bay."

"I know the place. Sit tight." The transmission went dead.

Kari sat back on her heels, awash with relief. They were coming for him—people who cared for him, who would protect him.

She gently rolled Talon over onto a blanket, then tucked another one around him, desperate to get him warm.

The preserver-unit was indeed locked. Kari slammed both fists against the small door. How was she to get the blazing thing open? Something tugged on her hair. Startled, Kari whipped around, heart pounding. It was Beryl. She pointed frantically toward the storage bin in the floor.

"Is the key in there?" Kari asked breathlessly.

Beryl nodded. Kari almost gave in to the sudden urge to catch the Sylph from midair and hug her. Instead, she yanked open the storage bin. Beryl darted inside, emerging in a flash with a key sequencer hanging from a leather string.

The preserver-unit yielded three celluloid pouches of blood. Kari set up and started the transfusion. The Sylphs produced more nectar to pack around the needle. Kari wrapped the site carefully, saving more of the precious substance for when it was time to remove the needle from Talon's vein.

Oberon and Beryl crouched on the back of the pilot's seat, holding each other tightly. Their worry didn't need telepathy to be understood, but another type of concern was communicated.

"How?"

Kari glanced around sharply, startled by Beryl's voice taking shape in her mind for the first time. A chill sank into her bones. Beryl wanted to know how Talon had been hurt.

Looking away, unable to meet the Sylph's gaze, she said hesitantly, "It was . . . my fault. He tried to prevent me from escaping, and I—I didn't know what it would do to him."

Beryl erupted into chirps of outrage. Kari ducked her head, expecting to feel her hair being ripped out by the roots. Instead, Oberon's voice rose in a furious argument with his mate.

Kari turned. Her mouth hung open in astonishment when Beryl sagged in defeat, then flew rapidly to the alcove and disappeared inside. Oberon rustled his scales in simmering anger.

"What did you say to her?"

He huffed. *"Reminded her of Talon's stubbornness, I did. Said he probably had it coming."*

"No, of course he didn't. I—"

"Hush, Kari of Khazanjian. Too hard on yourself, you are. You brought Talon here, saved him at great cost to yourself. That my mate understands very well. She will forgive. You must forgive yourself." He followed Beryl into the alcove.

Forgive herself? How the blazes could she?

She checked the viewports, confirming that there was

no sign of Lochnar soldiers, fake or otherwise . . . yet. The bay was empty, eerily quiet. She preferred the isolation. Even knowing Garek hadn't yet started work on the *Nighthawk* made her feel safer.

While the first pouch dripped its steady stream of life into Talon's body, Kari slipped his black tunic over her head. She hugged the quivote softness and breathed in his lingering scent. She would pack the blue one for him . . . she wanted this one for herself, precisely because it had been close to him.

She prepared for Rand's arrival by gathering the things Talon would need . . . clothes, weapons. At the bottom of the bin she discovered a pair of exquisitely made forearm guards.

Unlike the plain, pewter-colored guards Talon usually wore, there was not a nick on these. They obviously held too much sentimental value for their owner to wear them in combat. Kari cradled them lovingly in her palms and examined the detailed colored etchings. Valkenbur Line crests, with the differences in the scrollwork meant for Sahr Markos's second son.

As a teenager she'd been fascinated by Conquest history—a fascination that grew with her discovery of something forbidden, buried in Solis records and purged from the regular databanks. Her punishment had been severe for digging too deeply in the computer files and discovering that the *Inquisitor*, Myklar's greatest warship, had been destroyed during one of the last battles. General knowledge was that the *Inquisitor* had triumphed, then later been decommissioned with honors. The truth was that Sahr Markos, a key leader of the Resistance, had plunged his fatally damaged ship into the bridge of the dreadnaught.

Her thumbs traced the shape of the Valken bird of prey, the family's symbol, feeling the multitude of lines in the complex design. The ritualistic introduction of such an intricate tattoo would have damaged a deadly amount of skin on a young bleeder. She could imagine the distress of Sahr Markos and his Mal'Harith wife, fearing the bleeding couldn't be controlled, making the difficult choice to deprive their son of his rightful place in society in exchange for his life. Or perhaps they meant to postpone the tattooing until a treatment could be found. They couldn't have foretold that war would tear the solar system apart a year later, destroying a once proud family.

Her father's war.

Feeling sick with guilt, Kari lifted Talon's head gently. She slid underneath to make a pillow of her lap.

She stroked caressing fingers through his hair. Her hand shook with the aftereffects of terror and adrenaline. She'd almost lost him.

His life was a miracle of survival. How many times had he had these close calls, betrayed by his own body? Bleeders—a rare genetic condition—were perfectly healthy, except for the devastating inability of their skin to close up lacerations. They seldom survived beyond childhood. Sylph nectar apparently contained whatever chemical his body lacked.

Kari swallowed hard against a strangling lump of self-disgust. What she'd thought to be a justified act of defense on her part had, in truth, been the most profound act of betrayal.

Tears burned while she lightly brushed her knuckles over the firm line of his jaw. Talon's continuing unconsciousness worried her. A part of her was grateful for it, however, for she wasn't emotionally ready to face his wrath, or worse, his rejection.

She removed one of his gloves.

As expected, no disfiguring scar marred the back of his hand. Narkwar prison officials hadn't used acid to burn away his tattoos because there were none. How he must have been ridiculed for their absence. A man with no identity. How had he borne it, when one's family Line was a key factor in one's social status, profession, everything?

The answer was sketched out in the bits and pieces she knew of his life. Talon Markos had made his own way— stubbornly, independently, not only carving his niche but gaining the respect and admiration of those around him.

She opened his hand and pressed it to her cheek, then kissed his palm. Why was she consumed by the irresistible urge to touch him, to memorize the shape and feel of his face, to reassure herself repeatedly of the healing warmth of his body?

The truth was pathetically obvious, now that she'd stopped running from it.

Still cradling his hand in hers, Kari leaned back against the bulkhead and squeezed her eyes closed, acknowledging the utter, agonizing irony of loving a man she'd almost killed.

The door to Naill's quarters hissed open. He turned from the communications station to watch his advisor step into the room. Penn's hands twisted together with uncharacteristic nervousness between his bell-shaped sleeves.

"What is it?" Naill snapped in quick concern. Just when things were going so well, so in tune with his plans—

"Your father, my lord. The Dynast has returned from the *Viceroy*. He is on his way to your quarters, even now." Penn hesitated. The lines of his slender throat bobbed as he swallowed hard. "He has discovered that Jemara Kari is missing."

Naill relaxed. "Is that all?"

Penn's thin eyebrows arched, wrinkling his high forehead.

Naill tapped the thin square of a video-slip against his cheek. "Just minutes ago I would have been quite worried about your announcement, but not now, Penn. Not now."

The door opened.

"Father! Greetings. Welcome home."

"Cut the tarpan dung, Naill," Myklar said fiercely as he strode boldly into the room, every inch the leader who had

238

faded away in recent years. "Where is Kari?"

Schooling his expression into one of profound sympathy, Naill answered gravely, "I've . . . been avoiding telling you this. I had hoped to disprove my suspicions by the time you returned. However, I am afraid they've only been heinously confirmed."

Myklar struck the table beneath the display wall with his fist. The weapons on its surface jumped. "Don't play-act with me, Naill. Just get to the point."

"Very well, though I'd hoped to spare you the pain." He paused dramatically. "Kari broke the smuggler, Talon, out of his confinement cell and fled with him aboard the *Nighthawk*."

"You expect me to believe any accusation you make against your sister? Your envy, your rivalry, is too blatant."

Naill held up the video-slip. "Here is evidence to the contrary. It has just been transmitted from Star Alpha."

Myklar's eyes narrowed. "Play it."

Naill inserted the slip into the vid-player. The images were fuzzy, devoid of sound. Regardless, they told a condemning tale. Kari helped a faltering Talon down the passageway, her arm around his waist.

Myklar watched the screen in rigid silence.

"The men I sent to escort her safely home were able to . . . liberate these images from Star Alpha security and transmit them to me. Unfortunately, they could not trace Kari's movements beyond this point. Only the main passageways are equipped with cams. But an unregistered ship, presumably Rebel, did arrive at the space station shortly thereafter. The ship has launched for Serac."

The Dynast's glowering expression, the aggressive stance that had struck fear into the hearts of his enemies, wilted. In that moment Myklar Solis was merely an aging, grieving father.

He pivoted on his heel and stalked from the room.

Naill laughed, savoring the delicious feel of triumph.

He'd just destroyed Kari's credibility . . . with her unwitting help.

Penn cleared his throat. "Congratulations, my lord. May I ask how this affects your plans for the neryllium? Perhaps a coup will prove quite unnecessary, after all. Shall I relay new orders to the crew you planted aboard the freighter?"

"No," Naill answered, sobering abruptly. "As long as Kari is alive, my status is not guaranteed. The little bitch might manage to worm her way back into Father's affections. Besides, why should I wait for a slow transition of power? I can have it all within a few weeks."

"How the hell did this happen?" Rand shouted, furiously demanding an answer to the one question Kari dreaded most.

Talon's brother paced the length of the transport ship's troop hold. His dark blond hair was tousled from raking his fingers through it. His hazel eyes, though clouded with worry, glittered with a visceral anger directed entirely at her.

Jhase Merrick—whom she'd learned was the other voice on the comm channel—stood in the background, one shoulder leaning negligently against the bulkhead, arms crossed over his chest. His gaze shifted alertly between the two antagonists.

Kari glanced nervously to her right, feeling compelled to check on Talon even though he was now safe. He lay on a pull-down bunk, still unconscious. The Sylphs sat on his knees and watched over him. The second pouch of blood dripped steadily, continuing the job of replenishing what he'd lost.

Kari's eyes widened with sudden revelation.

She looked sharply at Rand. "That's your blood, isn't it?"

He stopped and glared at her. Muscles flexed along his jaw, providing the answer even before he spoke. "As you said, Jemara, he's my brother. Quit trying to change the subject, dammit."

"Very well." If she didn't tell him, Talon certainly would when he regained consciousness. "I stabbed him."

Stark incredulity commanded Rand's expression for only an instant before changing to blazing fury. He came at her suddenly, hands outstretched at throat level.

Jhase erupted into motion, belying his casual stance. He grabbed Rand in an Alturian neck lock. Kari backed away, shaken more than she cared to admit by the vehemence of Rand's reaction. As if that wasn't shocking enough, the Sylphs flew to her and perched on her shoulders, one on either side. Oberon spread his wings, rustled his scales, and emitted an ominous warning hiss.

Rand fought against Jhase's grip. True to the technique of the hold, his struggles only tightened the lock on the back of his neck. The high commander paled noticeably.

Jhase suggested dryly, "Kari is Talon's woman. Who are we to interfere if they had a little love spat?"

"His woman?" roared Rand, choking on the words. "Are you crazy? Let me go, Merrick. You don't understand how close he came to dying. I'm going to toss her out the damn airlock."

"Cool off, Commander," Jhase snapped. "I know you don't really mean it. And in case you didn't notice, Beryl is on Kari's side. The male Sylph seems prepared to defend her with his life. You know how hesitant Sylphs are to give their trust. Why don't you acknowledge that maybe there's more to this situation than we know?"

Rand calmed down, though the anger in his eyes didn't fade. "We'll see what Talon has to say when he awakes. In the meantime she's not going anywhere." He shrugged out of Jhase's loosened hold and strode briskly into the cockpit. Oberon huffed and led Beryl back to their spot on Talon's knees.

"Thanks," Kari managed over the hammering of her heart.

Jhase grinned. "No problem. I specialize in rescuing beautiful women. Besides, as jealous as Talon was back on Star Alpha, I figure he'll appreciate my watching out for you. I have a vested interest in earning his gratitude."

Her breath stilled. "What do you mean, jealous?"

"After he knocked you out with that Mal'Harith neck pinch he practically snarled when I touched your face. As vicious as a Valken hawk guarding its mate."

Kari slanted him a frankly skeptical look, despite the hope that leaped to life in her chest. "What utter nonsense."

He looked convincingly wounded, quite an accomplishment for a rogue with unruly black hair and laughing gray eyes. "Now there you wrong me, Jemara. I merely relate what I saw."

"Well, it doesn't matter." She sighed, letting the bitter truth claim her again. "When he awakes he'll hate me. He'll probably cheer while Rand stuffs me in the airlock, if he doesn't insist on the pleasure of scattering my atoms in space himself."

Jhase smiled. "We'll see."

She eyed him suspiciously. "What are you doing here, anyway? You aren't known for taking sides, Merrick."

"You're right. I go where the profit is. I was delivering a shipment to Markos when your call came through. Guess I have a knack for being in the wrong place at the wrong time."

"No, the right place, right time. If it weren't for that commlink in Talon's pocket, I'd have had no idea how to reach Commander Markos. Thanks again."

He shrugged. "How did you know Rand and Talon were brothers? Crimony, that was one hell of a secret. It stunned every man in the room, including his lieutenants . . . and me." He eyed her dubiously. "Did Talon really tell you?"

"No, he didn't. Despite what you think, he doesn't trust me in that way. I figured it out myself when I saw them

together, angry at one another. There was a definite re-
semblance, and something about the way they argued."

"A bold gamble. I like that."

A smile sprang to her lips at his unexpected praise. Then
Jhase raked hair off his forehead with splayed fingers, exposing the ugly, distorted scar on the back of his hand.
Kari froze at the harsh reminder—Jhase, Talon's friend,
was a former convict.

Her smile faded, dying an uncertain, trembling death.
She was sworn to capture this man . . . pirate, marauder,
scourge of Lochnar shipping. Instead, she actually liked
him. What the blazes was wrong with her? She was frat-
ernizing with smugglers, pirates, and Rebels. Then again,
what was that next to the treason of sabotaging an ore
shipment?

Jhase watched her. His grin slanted in a wry twist.

"Consider yourself off duty, Jemara," he advised dryly
as he moved to the far end of the cabin. He lowered a bunk
and lay down with his hands interlaced behind his head.

She sat gingerly next to Talon. His eyelids lifted slowly.
The brown depths of his eyes held no strong emotion. Just
as she was wishing he'd shout out his fury, anything to
free her from this wretched suspense, his gaze shifted
away and made a quick circuit of the cabin.

"Odd; this doesn't look like a Lochnar battle cruiser."

It was logical, of course, that he assume she'd seized the
opportunity to take him prisoner. Nevertheless, resentment seared through her in hot flames. "That's because it's
not," she retorted. "This is a Rebel transport ship, with
Rand at the controls. Surprised?" He opened his mouth,
but she cut him off. "No, don't try to talk. You need to rest
so you won't fall flat on your face the first time you try to
get up."

"Maybe you should do the talking," he murmured meaningfully.

She worked moisture into a suddenly dry throat. "You
want to know why I tried so fiercely to escape? Why I—"

She couldn't finish, even when she clung to sarcasm like a lifeline.

Talon said gravely, "All things considered, I should have expected it. But you did seem rather . . . desperate. I'd promised to let you go, Kari. Didn't you believe me?"

"Yes. It's just—" The portent of war loomed ever closer. "Time wasn't . . . isn't a luxury I can afford."

"So you hinted earlier. This time," he growled, "I want to hear it all."

Her own battle raged inside. Training and years of loyalty to her father squared off against instincts that cried out for her to trust Talon. Not only that; she could no longer hope to succeed at her mission alone. Without allies, she had no ship, no explosives, no time. Jhase's words came back to her: *a bold gamble. I like that.* It was past time to take a few risks.

Digging her nails into her palms, she whispered, "Talon, this is going to seem far-fetched, but I was trying to get away in time to stop a shipment of neryllium ore from Avernus."

His head jerked off the pillow. He lurched up on one elbow. "What the hell are you talking about?"

She caught his shoulders. "If you try to get up, I swear I won't tell you another word."

He settled back, glowering.

"I looked at some of Naill's files just . . . just before I broke you out of the *Regalia.*" She couldn't tell him about the data cylinder. He might demand to see it, read the rest of it. "One file documented a newly discovered supply of neryllium on Avernus. They've been mining it for months. The first shipment is due to launch in twenty-nine hours."

"And you want to stop it?" he asked suspiciously.

"Naill intends to steal the shipment and use it in a coup against Father."

"Runagate hell."

"It gets worse. If Naill succeeds, he won't stop there. He'll plunge the solar system into all-out war with his new weapons capability. His goal is to wipe out the Rebels."

"You've known about this all the time?" he demanded angrily.

"I didn't understand the significance until recently," she hedged.

"This must be the information Bayne intended to sell. We have to tell Rand."

An automatic refusal sprang to her lips. She bit it back, inwardly acknowledging a hard lesson in reality. The Rebels were well equipped to do what she could no longer accomplish on her own. As long as the freighter was blown up, what did it matter? The one thing she couldn't allow was for the Rebels to get their hands on the ore and use it against her father.

"Stars, Rand, you can't possibly place any confidence in what she says," Kjell Timor argued heatedly.

"It's an elaborate trap!" declared Arden.

Murmurs of agreement came from the other four lieutenants around the elongated oval table.

"Well, we're going to have to decide one way or another, aren't we?" retorted Rand.

Kari listened numbly, watching all her plans crumble in the face of their doubt. She'd relayed her story—at least the part she could reveal without producing the cylinder as evidence—but they didn't believe her. Blazes, why should they? She was the Dynast's daughter, their sworn enemy. It was a miracle they'd allowed her into this inner sanctum of Inclement, this Rebel command room, even though they'd isolated her at one end of the table like a criminal on trial. Then again, maybe they just assumed she would never leave . . . alive.

"Can we afford to do nothing?" Talon's quiet question silenced the room.

He sat on Rand's right, looking somewhat pale but vastly improved and heartbreakingly gorgeous. The gulf between them had never been wider, and she wasn't thinking of the physical distance.

"This is neryllium we're talking about," Talon continued, "If it's true, and we don't prevent the ore from being processed, you'll be pitting your swords against phazer pistols."

"And if it's a ruse, Talon? What then?" challenged Kjell.

"I, for one, believe her. I've had personal experience with Naill Solis. He's a ruthless, power-hungry shirker. A coup attempt fits his style exactly. And a threat to her father is the only thing that would motivate Kari to come to us for help."

Kari flushed. How she wished there was true forgiveness in his expression, rather than wry acceptance.

"This is all a moot point, anyway. The hull of a freighter of that class is impenetrable," stated Kjell.

A mutual grumbling rippled through the room.

"I can get you on board," Kari interjected.

Arden, her most persistent detractor, said acidly, "What a nice, convenient place to spring a trap."

Something snapped inside Kari. She jumped to her feet and slammed her palms flat against the table. Every man flinched in surprise . . . except Talon. With raking sarcasm, she growled, "How the blazes did you think I was planning to blow it up myself? Ask the captain to do it, pretty please? You can bet Naill's men will be crewing that freighter. He won't rely on force to steal the shipment. He's an expert at pursuing the most sly, underhanded tactics to accomplish his goals." Leaning forward to emphasis her next point, she said angrily, "But I have the codes to open the shuttle bay on remote." *At least, I hope the codes I found in Naill's files are up-to-date*, Kari thought with a sudden chilling element of doubt.

"And what are they, Jemara?" Rand prompted coldly.

"No way. You won't get the codes until *we*—" she answered furiously, emphasizing the last word, "—get to the boarding coordinates. You're not leaving me behind."

"I wouldn't dream of it," Rand said between his teeth.

"We'll plant the explosives and create a chain reaction that will completely destroy the freighter and its contents. The only question is, do you have sufficient quantity of explosives? The good kind, on the scale of CX-15?"

Rand said, "Will CX-20 do?"

Kari felt her mouth drop open. She shut it immediately with a click of her teeth. "Very nicely. How did you manage to get a hold of the latest stuff?"

"A little bonus in Merrick's shipment. Believe me, I paid dearly for it."

Talon's head snapped up. "Jhase is still here?"

Rand snorted. "He was a few minutes ago, blithely weighing down his pockets with my value tokens."

"Quinn!" Talon bellowed.

The door opened. Quinn stuck his head through the gap.

"Find Jhase Merrick. Tell him not to leave until I have a chance to talk to him."

Quinn nodded and vanished.

"Well, Rand. What's the verdict?" Talon prompted. "Do we go after the shipment or take our chances that Kari is lying?"

Rand leaned back in his chair and crossed his arms over his chest. He lowered his chin in a belligerent pose and glared directly at her from beneath sandy brows. The look was, at the very least, a challenge.

"I'm not sure I believe Jemara Solis, but like Talon said, we could be suicidal by default if we do nothing," Rand stated flatly. "However, if she can get us inside the freighter, I see no reason to blow it up. The explosives will serve merely as a threat. Our goal will be to steal the neryllium shipment for ourselves."

As a cacophony of enthusiastic agreements and worried grumblings broke out in the room, Kari's knees weakened with shock and dread. She sank slowly into her chair, hardly aware of the meeting breaking up around her.

Quinn slipped back into the room between the departing Rebels. Talon told him, "Rand has put you in charge of watching Kari. Don't let her out of your sight while I talk to Merrick."

With a sharp pang, Kari realized Talon distrusted her as much as his brother and the others. But even though her heart was breaking, she had to avert a catastrophe of her own making.

Though she was no longer sure Myklar deserved her loyalty, he was still her father. She could no more allow these men to use superior technology and weaponry against him than she could allow Naill to use it against an entire population.

Chapter Sixteen

The cave that served as Inclement's main hangar echoed with frantic activity. Techs and crews scrambled to prepare every available, battle-worthy ship for the Avernus attack fleet. Despite their urgency, men paused to stare at Talon.

He felt as if he was walking through a gauntlet. He was accustomed to envious glances cast at Beryl, but these men essentially ignored the colorful sight of the two Sylphs flying overhead. Fragments of whispered comments reached his ears.

"Can you believe it? He's Rand's brother."

"Risked his life to bring word of the neryllium shipment."

"Travels with two Sylphs. Stars, he must be rich."

"He must have pretended to be Neutral all this time to cover his true role as a spy."

Word had certainly spread quickly, along with the usual fantastic embellishments garnered along the way. Talon flinched at the touch of awe in their gazes. It seemed the Rebels had not only adopted him as one of their own, they'd labeled him a hero.

Hell, he didn't want to be anyone's hero.

He didn't even have a ship to offer. He agonized, not for the first time, over whether Lochnar soldiers had discovered and confiscated his cruiser at Star Alpha. He felt cut adrift, lost without the *Nighthawk*. There was only one thing he could contribute to the desperate gamble triggered by Kari's stunning revelation: himself. He'd volunteered to lead the sabotage team, partly because he didn't want to let Kari out of his sight.

Jhase Merrick stood beneath the bow of the *Vagabond*, silhouetted by the ship's running lights, feet braced shoulder-width apart. Pirate, master of his own destiny, Jhase wisely remained Neutral, avoiding a potentially nasty fight . . . which made him ideal for the role Talon was about to thrust upon him.

"Well, mate, have you decided to come on as my partner yet?" Jhase called over the racket of clanking metal and loud voices.

When Talon stopped the Sylphs settled on his shoulders. Beryl clung nervously to his hair. He'd already explained his plan to her and Oberon. He intended to stick with it, despite their protests.

Jhase grinned. "Quite a pair of travel companions you have there. Did Rand tell you they flew around us as we carried you off the *Nighthawk*, issuing more orders than a battalion of med-techs? I couldn't understand a thing they were saying, of course, but the gist of it seemed a demand that we be careful."

"I owe you, Jhase."

"I know it. And don't think I won't collect."

"Fair enough." Talon hesitated, reluctant to impose on a man who'd already done more than anyone expected. But there was no one he trusted more. "I have one more favor to ask: watch over Oberon and Beryl while I'm gone."

Jhase's black brows arched. "Will they go with me?"

"Yes. Actually, you're the only one they would consider going with." Jhase looked genuinely astonished. Talon chuckled. "No accounting for Sylph taste. I tried to warn them that you are the scourge of the galaxy, but they wouldn't listen." Oberon warbled softly. Talon paused to listen to the telepathic message.

"What did he say?"

"That he hopes you'll show him more excitement than

I've managed thus far. Says he's tired of being left out of the fun."

"I think that can be arranged."

Scowling, Talon warned, "Don't you dare, Jhase. I'm counting on you to keep them safe."

Jhase raised his hands in a gesture of innocence. "Hey, safe and serene is my new motto."

"Yeah, right," Talon retorted cynically. Taking a deep breath, he revealed his last, and most important, request. "If I don't return, take them home to Verdigris, okay?"

Muscles rippled up Jhase's jaw. "Crimony, I don't like what I'm hearing. That won't be necessary. You'll be back."

"Just promise me," Talon insisted gruffly.

"All right, dammit."

Talon relaxed, satisfied. He dug in the breast pocket of his blue flight suit and held out Jhase's commlink. "I need to return this to you."

The pirate shrugged. "Keep it."

"It's yours. Take it."

Shaking his head, Jhase insisted, "Consider it a good-luck piece. You're going to need one more than I do." He led the way onto the *Vagabond*, calling the Sylphs. They followed, casting back several mournful glances.

Talon forced himself to turn and walk away, battling a horrid, sinking premonition that he'd never see them again.

"What's this Quinn tells me about you assigning a man to guard Kari?" Talon demanded of his brother an hour later. Preparations were almost complete aboard the transport ship. Rand sat at the console, keying in the last of the preflight commands. Talon stood behind his shoulder.

"Well, you can't expect me to give her free run of this ship. I haven't forgotten who she is, even if you prefer to ignore the obvious," Rand replied caustically.

"Who have you put in charge of watching her?"

"Dominic."

"No," Talon said flatly.

Rand pivoted his chair, his eyes narrowed. "You're going to be difficult about this, aren't you? What about Kalfar?"

"No."

Rand surged to his feet. "Dammit. Who do you suggest?"

"Me."

"Sweet everlasting, the woman stabbed you! Forget it."

Talon rubbed the back of his neck. He longed to pace, to ease the knotting in his gut, but he feared it would steal his returning strength. "She did . . . then risked everything to pull me to safety and call the one man guaranteed to mistrust her—you. Explain that to me, because I have yet to figure it out."

"This is crazy. Are you saying you trust her?"

Talon gazed out the viewport, focusing on the empty spot where the *Vagabond* had been. "I don't know."

"But you're sure you don't want any of my men guarding her."

"That's right."

"Son of a tarpan, I don't believe this. You're jealous."

Talon scowled at his brother. "Don't be ridiculous."

"And I didn't think the situation could get any more complicated," Rand muttered ruefully. He sank into the pilot's seat, shaking his head. "We launch in ten minutes. I'll be aboard the *Stormhawk*. Kjell is piloting your transport ship. Just keep Jemara Solis out of his way and out of trouble. I don't even want to hear her name until she gives us those codes. By the way, you look awful. I don't suppose you'll let someone else guard her while you get some sleep?" He paused to examine Talon's rigid expression. "No, I didn't think so. There are several wrist-restraints to choose from back there. Use one."

"I'll think about it."

Rand eyed him gravely, his gaze clouded and worried. "I hope you don't regret this, Talon."

"Yeah. So do I."

* * *

Bhut Camargue's fingers dug into the armrests of his captain's chair aboard the *Concubine*. His excitement grew as another ship, and yet another, left the confines of Serac's atmosphere and headed into open space. By the time the first of the squadron accelerated into the mouth of the Serac-Verdigris Corridor, he'd counted a total of fifteen ships.

Something big was in the works. He hadn't seen that many Rebel ships together since the attempted, and failed, attack on the *Viceroy* during the early stages of its construction. Rumor had it that Rand Markos had lost three ships in the assault. Surely the high commander wouldn't risk another attack on the almost completed station orbiting Avernus.

Yet the Rebels had obviously targeted something significant. Camargue intended to find out exactly what that was.

Naill Solis would be grateful for the information. Camargue smiled, baring his yellowed teeth. The opportunity for profit still dangled tantalizingly within reach, despite the fact that his bungling crew had botched the job of nabbing Talon and the girl.

A thorough search of Star Alpha had turned up no trace of Talon, Kari, or the *Nighthawk*. Camargue could think of only one man his hated competitor would turn to for refuge . . . Rand Markos. Other than his meetings with the Rebel, Talon had always proven an adamant loner.

Eyes narrowed in hostile speculation, Camargue stared at the squadron shrinking into the distance and thought of the unlikelihood of mere coincidence. Talon disappears . . . three hours later a fleet of Rebel ships launches from Serac . . . instinct nagged of the possibility that Talon and Kari were aboard one of those ships. He licked his lips, dreaming of bounty money.

The last of the moving lights vanished into the Corridor. Camargue snapped an order to his pilot to follow.

*   *   *

The door to the cabin hissed shut behind Kari. Her fingers twitched, jabbing her nails into her palms. Just as she wondered, again, why Talon had brought her in here, he engaged the door lock. The sound had a disturbingly final quality.

She was trapped alone with him for the first time since he'd recovered. Fully recovered, that is, with the time to dwell on what she'd done, how she'd nearly cost him his life. Not knowing the direction of his thoughts was eating away at her sanity.

The cabin consisted of little more than a wide bunk, a lav, a narrow closet, and a desk with a small comm station. A lamp over the desk provided the only light in the room.

Talon moved around to face her. The room seemed to shrink around his impossibly broad shoulders. The lamp cast his face into stark planes of light and dark, enhanced by the shadow of his beard-stubbled jaw. His features had never appeared so uncompromising, as if chiseled in stone.

Talon cared nothing for her. He couldn't, not after what she'd done. But she couldn't shut off her feelings. His proximity devastated her senses. Warm excitement unfurled deep inside, pouring molten heat into her veins. She longed to kiss him, but she couldn't bear the look of disdain that would no doubt be her punishment if she tried.

He moved a step closer, all lean, masculine perfection . . . undeniably dangerous. Her fear of him wasn't physical, but in the way she was helplessly drawn to him. The words *I love you* filled her chest to bursting, clamoring to be shared. This urge to bare her soul, when that love obviously wasn't returned, frightened her most of all. Blazes, she had to distance herself from Talon—quickly, decisively—before her self-control cratered and she butchered the straggling remnants of her pride.

He unwittingly provided an opportunity with his first words.

"Why did you come back for me on Star Alpha?"

"Maybe I wanted to make sure the job was done right." She congratulated herself for keeping the quaver from her voice.

"Ah, I see," he murmured. "That explains why you helped me to the *Nighthawk*, why you struggled to stop the bleeding and administer a transfusion. It all makes perfect sense now."

He managed to make her sarcasm sound like child's play.

"You wasted a perfect chance to escape, Kari."

Her face heated, adding to her desperation. "You warned me that those soldiers might be Naill's men. I couldn't take that chance." She tried to look away.

He captured her chin in the crook of his index finger, forcing her to face him. "So what prevented you from stepping around me and running in the opposite direction?"

He watched her intently, as if her answer was of critical importance to him. She reminded herself that he was merely probing for weaknesses.

"I couldn't just let you lay there and bleed to death, okay! Consider it a moment of weakness, insanity, poor judgment."

Golden flecks of fire danced in his eyes. "Poor judgment. There seems to be an epidemic of that lately." A smile tugged at one corner of his mouth.

Without elaborating, he sat on the edge of the bed, then sprawled on his back. He sighed deeply. Kari stared down at him, incredulous. That was it? The interrogation was over?

"You're going to sleep?"

"Unless you have a better suggestion?"

She could certainly think of one, but she feared he was just baiting her. "What's to prevent me from unlocking that door and having free run of the ship after you're asleep?"

"This."

He yanked her down to the bed. Kari sprawled across his body, caught in the circle of his arms. Dismayed by the instantaneous fire that raced through her blood, she braced her palms against the hard muscles of his biceps and pushed.

"Ouch!" he ground out. "Lay down, dammit."

She froze. "Here?"

"I don't see another bed in the room."

"You'd trust me to lay here, next to you?" she whispered.

"This is the best way for me to keep close tabs on you and still get some sleep." His mouth slanted in an endearing, roguish fashion that should be outlawed.

Thoroughly confused and exasperated, not certain whether his attitude stemmed from sincerity or mockery, she glared at him—a silly exercise at best, since her chin was mere inches from his and her breasts were crushed against the solid wall of his chest.

"Why don't you just chain me, like before?"

Tightening his arms around her, he said roughly, "These are your shackles. If you make any move during the night passage, I'll know it. Now, go to sleep. I certainly intend to. I need it." He closed his eyes, then muttered with strong overtones of frustration, "Though I wish I didn't."

If she did slip free, what would she do, where would she go in the limited confines of the transport ship? Kari relented, because she wanted to anyway. She lay down, using his shoulder as a pillow. Resisting the urge to curl her right arm around his waist and hook her leg over his thigh was one of the hardest things she'd ever done.

As she drifted off to sleep, she battled images of flowing rivers of red. There must be a cure for Talon's affliction.

There had to be.

Naill circled the blade of the Haflinger dagger against the oiled whetstone, honing its already dangerously sharp edge.

He hated waiting. But there was nothing more to do for

now. Everything was ready. Everything was perfect. The ore freighter would launch on time. His hand-picked crew manned the controls. All the manufactured evidence was in place to cast the blame for the hijacking on the Rebels.

He wiped the red-tinted blade, then held it up, reflecting the overhead light from its polished surface. A faint reddish beam flashed across his face like a fine spray of blood.

Unfortunately, there would be more tedious waiting beyond the hijacking. Once the freighter transferred its cargo to the old, remote neryllium processing plant on Verdigris—the one he'd secretly reopened after liberating it from two decades' worth of dust and encroaching jungle growth—additional ingredients and six weeks of refining were required before the neryllium was purified into the gel form capable of powering his weapons systems.

He'd put out a call for the last critical ingredients needed—basaelic flakes and larcinium crystals. Smugglers did have their uses, on occasion. He could count on at least one of them scrounging up the necessary materials, for the right price.

The door's call button pinged.

"Come," Naill called impatiently.

Penn stepped into the room, followed by one of Myklar's highest-ranking officers. The Gent'Sian cast Naill a pleased look that on a less serene face might be considered smug.

He bowed. "This officer wishes to speak to you on a matter of some urgency, my lord. It seems the Dynast has left strict orders not to be disturbed, and the Command-colonel feels he must report a potentially dangerous situation."

Myklar, distraught over Kari's apparent defection, was isolating himself from everything. Though it wouldn't last, Naill knew, now was another opportunity to advance his plans.

The incoming message indicator clicked across the room.

"See to that, Penn," he ordered. The Gent'Sian moved to the communications station. Naill forced himself to appear calm. "Yes, Command-colonel. What can I do for you?"

The man stepped forward and saluted briskly by slapping his right fist against his left shoulder. The gold insignia of his rank caught the light, flashing briefly from the drab brown of his uniform.

"Forgive me for intruding, Jemidar Solis. A number of Rebel ships are emerging from the Serac Corridor. They're taking different routes around Verdigris, well away from the *Regalia*, but we think they mean to converge on the other side."

A sense of unease ballooned beneath Naill's breastbone. "Is the *Nighthawk* among them?" he asked impulsively.

"No, Jemidar. Though we've been unable to identify most of the ships, I am certain Talon's craft is not among them."

The timing was too close to be coincidental. If the Rebels entered the Verdigris-Avernus Corridor, their return to normal space on the other side would coincide with the scheduled freighter launch.

Had Bayne talked before he was permanently silenced?

Naill's hand tightened, white-knuckled, around the hilt of the dagger. His carefully laid plans were at risk.

"I want the *Usurper*'s crew scrambled and ready to launch in thirty minutes," he demanded. "I will be taking command."

"Sir, a galaxy-grade battle cruiser isn't designed to launch on such short notice," the officer protested.

"Nevertheless, I want the *Usurper*. She has sixteen torpedo bays and thirty-two ion cannon turrets. There's a promotion in this if you have her ready on time, Command-colonel."

The officer snapped to attention, nodded briskly, then spun on his heel to march from the room.

Penn moved to stand at his shoulder.

"The message?" Naill queried stiffly.

"From Bhut Camargue, my lord. He seeks to inform you of a Rebel attack force that launched from Serac."

"How very informative," Naill scoffed.

"He demands payment. Shall I tell him we are uninterested?"

Naill stroked his goatee. "Is he following them?"

"Yes."

"Inform him that if he wants payment, he must stay close to the Rebels and report back on their movements until we arrive. And tell him there is a bonus waiting if he can confirm that Talon and Kari are aboard one of those ships."

It was a dream, a deliciously erotic dream where warm, masculine fingers combed through her hair in a familiar caress. They teased the edge of her ear, then worked down her neck in slow increments until they reached the side of her breast. The leisurely stroking quickened Kari's body in a heartbeat.

There was only one man capable of invading her fantasies, of taking the sleeping embers of passion and fanning them into an all-consuming inferno. A unique, powerful man, not a dream.

She lifted her head.

Talon looked at her through heavy-lidded eyes. Their brown depths were alight with hunger, not the anger she had anticipated.

Feeling as if she floated in zero gravity, Kari sat up and helped him strip away his shirt. The sight of the bandage marring his otherwise beautiful shoulders grounded her brutally. Old scars took on a new meaning. She pressed her palms over the badges of courage, shaping her hands to the muscles of his chest.

"How did you survive?" she murmured with a touch of awe.

"Sylph nectar." He brushed a lock of hair behind her ear.

Kristen Kyle

"But . . . how did you know? I've never heard of its value as a healant, not until you showed me."

"My father had a Sylph who'd been with him for years. When I was born the few effective methods for stopping the bleeding failed. The Sylph responded to my parents' distress. When the physician had given up hope she closed the wound from the cord."

She traced the thin lines. "Some are darker than others."

"Sylphs weren't always with us over the years. In time most want to return to the forest. Mother would collect their nectar and preserve it in a salve; not as pure that way, not nearly as effective in stopping bleeding."

"It was your mother who taught you the skills to defend yourself," Kari stated with certainty.

"Who better than a Mal'Harith warrior queen?" he said teasingly, but his gaze grew immeasurably sad, distant with memories. "Yes, she trained me. The Mal'Harith embraced the old ways of sword and dagger, even before neryllium became scarce. Most of these scars happened during my training. Mother didn't coddle me. She preferred I learn from my injuries when she was there to treat my wounds."

"You must be so proud of her, as well as your father."

"My father? For martyring himself?" Talon fairly spat the words in a shockingly abrupt change of mood. "Sahr could have ejected in his lifepod . . . instead he crashed his ship in a token gesture that left us bereft and on the run from your father's mercenaries. Such a bloody damned waste. The *Inquisitor* suffered only minor damage." The words spilled from him in an outpouring of bitterness and old pain.

Aching sympathy rolled through Kari in waves, tugging at her heart like sand being washed out from under her feet. How well she knew the agony of a parent's abandonment.

She lay across his chest and caught his face between her palms, forcing him to look at her. "Listen to me, Talon

260

Markos. Your father didn't die in vain. When he deliberately crashed his damaged ship into the bridge of the *Inquisitor* he halted the bombardment against the Resistance forces and enabled them to get away. The damage overloaded the dreadnaught's systems. It blew up later, do you hear me? Blew up! Examination of the wreckage showed Sahr's lifepod eject mechanism had locked. He couldn't escape, Talon, so he took out my father's best battle cruiser at the last. He saved lives. He saved his men."

Talon's heart pounded like a bass drum against her body. With a voice resembling the rough scrape of a blade across a whetstone, he whispered, "How do you know this?"

"My father is very good at covering up his embarrassments—easy enough to do when the only witnesses have fled."

His gaze slanted away. His eyes resembled hammered cinnadar metal. A muscle rippled up his jaw.

"What happened to your mother?"

"All the joy drained out of her after Sahr died," he responded in a flat, lifeless tone. "We went into hiding, always on the run. She was obsessed with our training, though she was harder on me than Rand. She died when I was fourteen."

"So much pain. I'm so sorry." She kissed his chest, then rubbed her cheek against the rigid muscles and hugged his waist tightly. He tensed. "I wish I could take some of the pain away," she forced past a constricted throat. She wanted to say more, to beg his forgiveness for her own role in his suffering, but then he grasped her shoulders and tried to lift her away. She resisted for all she was worth.

"Kari."

She clutched him tighter.

"Kari, come up here and kiss me before I explode from wanting you," he said roughly.

Surprised, she released her death-grip on his waist. He

speared his hands into her hair and gently guided her mouth to his for a deep kiss. Eagerly, she welcomed him, savoring the nubby texture of his tongue as it tangled with hers, cherishing his unique, utterly male taste. Every sensation was all the more precious for being almost lost.

Kari pulled back, eager to be rid of her clothes. His moan of frustration changed to a growl of approval when she peeled away her shirt and bustier. As her pants came off, so did his. The desire in Talon's heated gaze made her feel beautiful and wanted in a way she'd never thought possible.

"Come here," he urged huskily as he grasped her waist and guided her over him. She settled across his hips. The pulsing strength of his engorged shaft nestled between her buttocks.

Kari lifted her hips, impatient for a genuine joining. Her legs tightened around his waist, fearful that if she loosened her hold he would fade into the shadow realm of dreams.

Finally he positioned himself at the opening to her channel. A ripple of pleasure gripped Kari, enhanced by the emotional ecstasy of knowing this was the only way they could get close enough. He belonged inside her, touching her very core. She loved him. She couldn't say the words, for they would be mocked, rejected. That didn't keep her from pouring out her feelings through her body and her hands.

She shifted slightly, trying to slide down onto his hard length and take him fully inside. His fingers curled into her hips, curbing her impatience. With maddeningly slow deliberation, he lowered her onto his shaft, pushing into her in small increments. It was a slow, complete, devastating possession. Kari felt branded as his, inside and out, caught between the heat of his penetration and the masterful caressing of his hands. She reveled in it, because in this one thing she could pretend he wanted her as much as she ached for him.

When he was fully sheathed he whispered in a voice roughened by sensual intensity, "Don't move. I don't think I can stand it yet. Just sit there for now and let me touch you."

And he did, cupping her breasts in the heat of his hands, stroking her nipples with his thumbs until they hardened and strained for more, so sensitized that each brush of his callused skin was like an electrical charge shooting through her. Rogue that he was, he deserved to suffer the same sweet torture. She caressed his flat nipples into hard, tiny buds. Mischievous pleasure joined the other sensations swirling through her when his breath sucked in passionately with each flick of her thumbs.

He lifted her slowly, then sank into her softness again, and then again, bringing them together in a slow motion, filling her as if he wanted each joining to last a lifetime.

His hands stroked a trail of fire down her back. His fingertips brushed over her tailbone and caressed her buttocks. Her body clenched spasmodically, responding to the rippling shockwaves.

Talon groaned. "Runagate hell, it almost destroys me when you do that." His face was drawn, almost harsh.

She stilled. "What did I do?" she asked, afraid she'd aggravated his wound. His answer surprised and pleased her.

"Caress me, hug me inside."

He flexed his hips, pushing deeper. Kari's lips parted on a moan. She writhed, her hips circling of their own will. Talon growled something unintelligible. Then he grasped her hips and started rocking faster. She mirrored his movements, matching the escalating rhythm from below.

She was caught in the tail of a comet. Forcing her nails not to flex into the skin of his shoulders, she clung to him for dear life, riding him as feverishly as he drove into her body. Then his body convulsed, his back arching to lift them both off the bed. Her name burst from his lips in a guttural shout. Kari felt as if she was flying as the wave swept over her, lifting her up into a rush of glittering light and sensation.

Kari lay limply on top of Talon. Her hair streamed across his neck and shoulders. The cool air of the cabin circulated over her skin. She cherished the thrum of his heart beneath her ear and the deep rhythm of his breathing as he slipped into sleep, sounds she'd thought never to hear again.

She was just dropping off herself, when a different sensation pulled at her body. It was the heavy, oppressive feeling of accelerating into the grav-well tunnel of a Corridor, the change in pressure experienced before a ship's gravity compensators made the standard adjustments.

The Rebel force was entering the Verdigris-Avernus Corridor.

She'd been so storm-tossed in the sensual maelstrom of Talon's lovemaking, she hadn't even noticed the return to normal space around Verdigris. They'd been within easy contact distance of the *Regalia*, and she'd been completely oblivious.

Talon had kept her conveniently occupied while the Rebel fleet crossed the dangerous space around Verdigris.

An immeasurable sadness sank its claws into her soul, leaving her raw and bleeding inside. She wouldn't have risked contacting her father. Any message might be intercepted by Naill. But Talon didn't know that.

Now his motive in having sex with her was all too clear. Once again, she'd proven to be a naive, love-sick fool, giving herself to him wantonly, a vessel for his desire, a hunger that was as manipulative as it was potent.

It would be the height of hypocrisy to stay here, in this bed, limbs intertwined in intimate contact. Kari rose, dressed, and retreated to the chair.

Chapter Seventeen

"Target acquired!" Quinn shouted from his position at the transport ship's sensor panel.

Everyone else in the forecabin—Kjell, Talon, and Kari—turned toward the bow viewport.

The bright orange of the ore freighter's launch flares died as the hulking, coffin-shaped craft headed away from Avernus. Talon watched the ship proceed on course at a leisurely pace. The freighter's crew had no idea they were being stalked . . . yet.

The transport's comm beeped.

"Everything ready?" Rand called from the *Stormhawk*.

Kjell sat at the pilot's controls. Talon leaned over his shoulder and answered, "We're preparing to transmit the override code to the freighter's computer."

"You better make this work, Talon." Rand hated how his choice of commanding the planetary attack wing prevented him from leading the assault on the freighter, but something had to be done about the source of the neryllium.

You can't be in two places at one time, big brother. "You'd better disable that facility, Rand, or we're going to be back in this same mess a few weeks from now," Talon countered.

"Don't do anything stupid while I'm gone. You know I dislike the risk you're running by coming on this mission."

"Hey, Kjell has the dangerous part. He's in charge of planting the explosives and dealing with any resistance from the crew. I'm only responsible for playing with the computers, getting us aboard the freighter and onto the bridge."

"You know what I mean. Give me another scare like the one yesterday, and I'll knock your head sideways." Just before signing off, Rand warned, "Watch your back, with Kari around."

"I will."

He saw color mount in Kari's cheeks. She looked away.

Rand still adamantly believed she was a threat, seeking an opportunity to finish what she'd started with that dagger. Talon only wished he could be confident the opposite was true.

He didn't know what to believe, dammit, not after her confusing reversal in behavior last night. What was he to think when she turned his blood to molten fire with sweet, passionate lovemaking, then left their bed sometime during the night to fall asleep, fully clothed, in the desk chair? Runagate hell, it didn't make any sense. Her motives for thrusting a dagger into his shoulder he could understand. But the stabbing hadn't caused him half the pain he'd felt when he awoke to find she'd retreated from his arms.

She'd been distant and chillingly polite ever since. And he didn't have a clue what to say to break down the barriers, not when he didn't understand what erected them in the first place.

He turned away, unable to bear being turned inside out every time he looked at her, wanting . . . something stupid, unattainable, and potentially self-destructive. Wanting her love.

The *Stormhawk* swung away, only dimly visible with its running lights turned off. Eight ships followed, leaving five of the smaller fighters to run escort for the sabotage team on the transport.

Fear for Rand's safety twisted in his gut. The perimeter of the mine would be equipped with Lochnar's best defenses. "Be careful, dammit," Talon muttered between clenched teeth.

"Is that all?" Camargue demanded impatiently.

"We were lucky to pick this up, Cap'n," replied the *Concubine*'s communications officer curtly. "The Rebels have been using channels at the extreme end of the range. I wouldn't have found this, if you hadn't ordered me to scan."

"Well, see if ya can pick up somethin' else. I want to know what's happenin' out there."

"Sorry, Cap'n, they've changed frequency again."

Camargue flopped back in his chair. "Ya idiot. Find them!" he barked. "It'll help make up for losin' Talon and Kari at Star Alpha, ya slimy shirkers."

Muttered complaints rumbled from the other two slovenly members of the crew.

"You'd get better results if you paid what we're worth, you oversized windbag," the comm officer snarled under his breath.

"No, wait," ordered Camargue. "First, open a channel to the *Usurper*. Ask for Naill Solis. I've got somethin' he really wants to hear." He laughed aloud. "I know where they are."

The freighter reached the planned intercept point.

"Jam all transmissions in and out, Quinn," Talon ordered.

The intention was for only the transport ship to dock with the freighter. The small fighters would fly as guard.

"Ready to transmit the code?"

"Any time, Talon."

"Jemara Solis," he drawled, "I believe that's your cue."

Ignoring him completely, she told Quinn the sequence of numbers she'd kept closely guarded until now. Quinn transmitted the encoded Lochnar message to the freighter's computer.

The transport's cabin was eerily silent as everyone's gaze fixed on the freighter. A square of light shone from its port side as the main hangar door opened.

Kjell steered the transport into the bay. Red lights flashed overhead, indicating a detected security breach. So much for the advantage of surprise, Talon conceded irritably. The crew knew they were here.

The sabotage team debarked in a rush of efficiency. Dominic and Kalfar unloaded the eight cases of CX-20. Their job was to plant the explosives strategically close to the stardrive engines, insurance in case anything went wrong in pirating the shipment. Talon, Kjell, and Quinn were expected to gain control of the bridge, and thus the freighter. Kari would go with them to provide the one remaining code for bridge access.

The door barred their way when they reached the bridge, as expected. Kari brushed past him to reach the keypad in the bulkhead. She punched in the other code.

Nothing happened.

She tried again, but Talon knew the fourteen-digit sequence wouldn't work. The crew had managed to change the override code to the bridge. The door was sealed shut.

Kjell Timor slammed his fist against the metal barrier.

"Can we blast our way through?" Talon asked.

Kjell examined the area. "This is the best blast door Lochnar shipping makes. The amount of explosive it would take to punch our way through would risk breaching the hull."

"Perhaps they don't know that," Talon countered softly. A bridge comm was set into the bulkhead opposite the security keypad. He switched it on. "Captain, we brought enough CX-20 with us to destroy your entire vessel. Blowing in this door will be child's play in comparison. My comrades inform me, however, that the explosive force will very likely kill everyone on the bridge. Regrettable, but a consequence that can be avoided if you'll just open the door."

"Grist is the name, and I say you're bluffing," came the hostile reply. "An explosion of that magnitude would destroy all critical controls on the bridge. The prize, you bastards, would be a dead hulk in space, too big to tow, useless."

"Is that your final answer, Captain Grist?"

"Yes, damn you."

"Then we'll have to blow her up, cargo and all."

"Go to hell, you—"

Talon switched off the comm, cutting the tirade short. "Let's give him a few seconds to think about it."

"And if he still refuses?" exclaimed Kjell.

Crossing his arms over his chest, Talon leaned one shoulder against the bulkhead and scowled. "Then we destroy her. What choice do we have? We can't allow the neryllium to fall back into Lochnar hands."

Thank the stars, Kari rejoiced inwardly. Grist wouldn't surrender—the penalty was worse than death. The crew might choose to die nobly for the Dynasty . . . more likely, they would select the option of abandoning ship, leaving the bridge sealed off, inaccessible to the Rebels. A crushing weight lifted from her spirit. The Rebels would destroy the shipment after all. She didn't have to do it herself. She didn't have to betray Talon to accomplish her goal.

A quick succession of five whooshing sounds came from the bridge, vibrating the floor beneath their feet. Kari smiled. That was the sound of ejecting—

"Runagate hell!" Talon exploded, shoving away from the wall with feline quickness. "Why didn't someone tell me this model freighter was equipped with lifepods on the bridge?"

He advanced on her, making it obvious who he blamed for the oversight.

Infuriated by his attitude, Kari shoved at his chest. It was like trying to topple a *canopia* tree. She settled for striking back with a verbal barb. "Why should I have mentioned it? My goal was to blow up this blazing ship, not

269

engage its captain in some stupid contest of dare and counter-dare!"

"Like I said, Rebel," taunted the captain from his retreating lifepod, "you've got yourself a useless derelict, drifting in space. You might as well leave now and limp home."

Talon switched on his forearm guard's commlink, which was set to communicate with the Rebel fighters. "Arden," he ordered briskly, "those five lifepods that ejected from the bow of the freighter—tractor them."

"Done, Talon."

Turning back to the freighter's comm, Talon said coldly, "I suggest you rethink your position, Captain Grist. A full-power blast from our ion cannons is capable of permanently knocking out your lifepod communications. You'll float anonymously in space, too small to be noticed, with no way to call for help and only twenty-six hours of standard life support."

"Only a complete fool would dare face Lochnar retaliation."

Talon didn't honor the taunt with a response. "Arden, can you detect which pod that transmission is coming from?"

"Easily enough."

"Ionize the other four pods."

There was a brief moment of tense silence in the passageway; then the freighter's channel crackled with a string of curses.

Kari shuddered. In her mind's eye she could picture the ion beams shooting out from Arden's fighter, enveloping the pods—otherwise invisible against the blackness of space—in a temporary white glow. Stunned by Talon's display of ruthless resolve, she stared at his rigid profile, realizing anew how dangerous an enemy he could be.

"Well, Captain?" Talon drawled.

"Whoever you are, you're already a corpse." Despite the threat, his voice shook with fear.

"The code," Talon said harshly. "I'm not interested in anything else you have to say."

Kari held her breath. He wouldn't tell. Lochnar military training clearly forbade any compromise in negotiations.

After one last snarling curse the captain relented. He relayed a new sequence of numbers.

Kari's eyes closed in pain. Over the thundering rhythm of her heart she heard the click of the keypad as Talon punched in the revised code. The bridge door rumbled ominously. Kari bit the inside of her lip and opened her eyes. Quinn and Kjell were rushing through the opening onto the bridge.

Stars in heaven, she was right back where she started.

A hand clamped around her upper arm, jarring her out of her frozen state. Her head jerked about, her braid whipping across Talon's chin. Clenched muscles bunched in his jaw. His eyes held all the warmth of ice-slicked stones in a snowdrift.

Oh, yes, Talon was very dangerous. But she couldn't, under any circumstances, allow the Rebels to gain possession of the neryllium . . . regardless of her feelings for him.

He leaned forward, inquiring with soft menace, "Why are you so pale, Kari? If I didn't know better, I'd think you were planning some—"

Another transmission from Arden interrupted. "Hey, Talon, what shall I do with these Lochnar shirkers?"

A muscle twitched across his cheek. "Tractor the pods into the airlock next to the hanger bay. Contact Dominic and Kalfar and tell them to stand watch. They should be finished planting the explosives by now."

"You got it. Arden out."

He pulled her roughly onto the bridge . . . and stopped dead.

One quick glance explained his shocked reaction. Kari sucked in her breath. Half the bridge stations were damaged. Sparks crackled from the directional controls. Of the six life pod launch tubes, three built upright into the bulkhead on either side of the bridge, five were empty.

Kjell looked up from the navigation deck, his expression furious. Quinn's head and torso had disappeared beneath the main console.

Talon groaned. "Okay, tell me the worst. What's the extent of the damage?"

Kjell responded bitterly, "Auto-nav is a total loss."

"Manual navigation?"

"Maybe. I don't know." Kjell kicked the operator's chair in a blatant display of frustration.

Quinn scrambled to his feet. "I'll agree this looks bad, Talon, but it was a hack job. The crew couldn't take the time to do it right. I'm sure I can salvage propulsion."

"What about directional? Moving forward won't help us much if we can't steer the damn thing."

Raking both hands through his blond hair, Quinn answered tensely, "I—I'm pretty sure I can cross-wire something and restore directional."

"Then let's get started."

Talon released her. "Just stay out of the way."

"I can't think of anything I'd like better than to stay out of your reach," she retorted acidly. Massaging the abused area, she glared at him. "You hurt me." She was furious, though 90 percent of her anger was directed at herself rather than him—knowing why she said such things, knowing it was to drive him away, knowing it was to erect a shield to defend herself against a repeat of the emotional hurt he'd inflicted last night.

He had the grace to flush. "Kari, I—"

"Save it, smuggler," she hissed. "No doubt you'll have plenty of opportunities to hurt me again later."

His eyes narrowed. His hands flexed. Though he held back, saying nothing, Kari had the strongest impression he longed to shake her until her teeth loosened. A shiver rippled through her body—not from any fear of violence, but from discovering she was so in tune with him she could almost read his thoughts.

He spun on his heel and stalked away.

Quinn tossed him some tools. All three men went to work salvaging what they could.

If everything had gone as planned, Talon would no doubt be watching her with the same intensity as the Valken bird of prey that represented his family Line. Instead, he lay on his back beneath the directional unit, asking Kjell whether any change he made registered at the main console.

Now was her chance.

Kari eased toward the open door, moving soundlessly. After successfully escaping the bridge and sneaking halfway down the passageway she broke into a run, heading for engineering two decks down.

No one, neither Lochnar nor Rebel, was going to have this ship and its accursed cargo. She couldn't erase the existence of neryllium, or stop the mining, but she could prevent either side from gaining the horrifically destructive advantage that this shipment represented. The best she could offer was a delay; time for the balance of power in the solar system to readjust itself. If not that, then the Rebels at least deserved time to escape annihilation.

Kari approached engineering cautiously. It was deserted. Dominic and Kalfar were busy in the hangar, thanks to the crew's aborted attempt at escape. She slipped into the control room.

One entire wall served as a glass-enclosed overlook into the stardrive section. The restrained power of the units, even at idle, generated a steady hum in her ears and vibrated every surface. Though the eight cases of CX-20 were situated strategically next to each massive engine, they were useless to her. If she switched on the timers, what would prevent Talon or his men from simply turning them off?

She dropped into the chair at the computer console and brought up the freighter's self-destruct routine.

Authorization? The prompt scrolled across the screen.

She typed in her personal code. The image flashed an obnoxious REJECTED in orange. "Damn you, Naill," she whispered furiously. He'd disabled her authorization, which under normal circumstances accessed every function in the Lochnar fleet.

She forced herself to calm down and think. She queried the crew duty roster. Until three days ago the records listed Van Wycros as captain.

Okay, so Grist was not the freighter's regular captain. He was Naill's man, a secret, last-minute change in command. They might have overlooked updating non-routine authorizations, and self-destruct was about as far from routine as one could get.

Kari pulled the data cylinder from her belt and inserted it into the reader. She issued a text search for *Wycros* across all the files. *Please,* she pleaded with growing desperation, *don't let it be in one of the damaged sectors.* The search came back with four hits: three documents and one data file.

She opened the data file . . . and found hidden treasure. "I've got you now, Naill," she whispered with satisfaction. The file listed all Lochnar officers and their authorization codes.

Returning to the destruct routine, she typed in the code string belonging to the freighter's rightful commander.

The computer accepted it, then issued the next prompt. *Delay time?*

Thirty minutes.

Do you wish to disable the warning system? Yes/No.

Kari hesitated, then typed *yes* with trembling fingers.

Do you wish to lock in the non-abort option? Yes/No.

Such a deceptively casual question. Her stomach turned over. If she responded in the affirmative, no one could stop the chain reaction that would implode the engines, creating a massive explosion that would obliterate everything in the near vicinity. On the other hand, once she warned the Rebels, giving them time to escape, they would attempt to force her to stop it. She couldn't give them that option.

Yes. It had never been harder to punch three simple keys.

The computer completed the routine. The screen returned to normal. The only change was a red indicator light shining on the console. Blazes, she thought with amazement, when it asked to disable the warning system, it really meant it.

She ejected the cylinder and stored it safely in her belt again. Goal accomplished. She'd just put in place a destructive power unrivalled by anything in the solar system.

Standing abruptly, Kari started to return to the bridge to provide the Rebels adequate warning for evacuation. She stopped dead in the doorway. A subconscious urging held her back. Turning, she stared at the computer screen. The significance registered like the first rays of blinding light as the sun crested the mountains of Avernus.

It was right here, at her fingertips. She had access to the complete store of Lochnar medical data, not the abbreviated, screened version released to secondary facilities. Could there be information concerning treatment for Talon's condition?

There had to be.

Hastily, she dropped into the chair. The search she conducted returned with a list of eighteen files . . . big ones.

Blazes, she didn't have time to read through these now! But there wouldn't be another chance to get this information to Talon. After today she'd never see him again . . . he'd get rid of her as fast as possible, if he didn't kill her first.

She would have to download all the files. Frantically, she searched the room for a data cylinder, wrenching open every cabinet. Nothing. On the last one, she let out a hoarse cry of frustration. What was wrong with this stupid crew? Didn't they ever download any files?

Countdown was at twenty-seven minutes.

You have a data cylinder, you simkin. The words, lurking in her subconscious, clamored for attention.

Maybe there was room on her cylinder for both. Quickly she reinserted it and compared available space. The worst immediately became apparent. Because of the damaged sectors, the current download would have to overwrite everything in order to fit, and then just barely. She swallowed convulsively.

If she wrote over Naill's files, she would destroy the only evidence of her half-brother's malicious scheming. This was her sole means of justifying to her father why she sabotaged an exceedingly valuable freighter and its cargo—her only hope of going back with some honor, some status other than traitor.

Eighteen files. The number, the size, promised valuable information. There was something in these files that could help Talon, perhaps save his life someday. She was certain of it.

Though a chill washed through her, Kari didn't hesitate any longer. She keyed in the command for download.

She ejected the cylinder and headed back to the bridge, bracing herself to face the first of many consequences for her actions, a choice that she would make again, because she had to.

"How are we doing?" Talon said between gritted teeth.

He'd just discovered Kari was missing, and he wanted some indication of the status of repairs before he went in search of her. This mission was taking too damned long. Every additional minute increased their chances of discovery and failure.

A soft step sounded behind him. He spun around.

"Kari?" His rough tone carried a wealth of warning. She didn't respond.

"Talon," Kjell called from where he bent over the sensor readout. "The *Viceroy* is coming around in orbit."

"How long until they're in range?"

"Fourteen minutes."

"They shouldn't be a problem. To them, we're just another freighter en route. Contact Arden. Send the fighters farther out where they won't draw undue attention."

Kjell opened the channel and issued the orders. Just before he signed off, Arden's voice cut sharply through.

"Lochnar battle cruiser emerging from the Corridor!" the lieutenant yelped, then added with an undercurrent of dread, "Stars, it's the *Usurper*."

Kjell swore.

"Call Rand back," instructed Talon grimly. "We can't let five fighters face a ship with that kind of firepower. It would be suicide."

"What about us?"

"Transmit an emergency call for help to the *Viceroy*."

"Do what?" Kjell exclaimed in disbelief.

"And send it via the standard Lochnar channel so the *Usurper* will intercept the signal."

Kjell relaxed and smiled. "I get it. A call for help will make them think the freighter's crew is still in control. A clever ploy to buy us some time."

"Then let's make it count."

"Don't bother," Kari interjected gravely. "Time is the last thing you have. In twenty-four minutes this ship is going to disintegrate."

Chapter Eighteen

"That's where you've been? Setting the timers on the CX-20?" Talon bit out. He switched on his wrist-comm. "Dominic—"

"Don't bother. He can do nothing. It's not the explosives I tampered with. I set the freighter's self-destruct."

Talon fixed his gaze on Kari's pale face. He took a menacing step forward and snapped, "Stop it. Now."

"I can't."

"And if I said we're not leaving? What then?"

"Then we'll all die. I disabled the abort. Not even I can stop it now."

"Is she serious?" Kjell exclaimed.

"She's serious," Talon stated in a flat, hard-edged tone.

"Dammit, I knew it was a mistake to bring her along. We should have forced her to tell us the codes. Rand needs to know about this." Kjell hurried to the comm station.

A mistake. Definitely. A hard knot of bitterness settled like a dead weight in Talon's gut. She'd betrayed him yet again.

Kari retreated slowly, hands raised as if to ward off a blow, a strange posture for her . . . until Talon realized he was advancing on her with threatening intent. She backed into the one remaining lifepod launch tube. The solar-protective material of the spacesuit hanging there crackled as she sank into it.

His hands slammed against the frame of the shallow closet, trapping her. The muscles of her slender throat corded, but she met his accusing glare with a familiar bold defiance.

"How long?" he snapped.

"Twenty-two minutes. Talon, I—" She swallowed hard. "We've got to get off the ship, now."

His chest couldn't ache any more if he was trying to draw breath in an Avernian sandstorm. "First you're going to tell me why, dammit," he managed to say.

"I can't let the Rebels have the neryllium," she cried. "What else do you expect me to do? He's my father!"

"Let's see if I've got this right." He leaned closer, until the warmth of her flushed skin countered the angry heat of his breath. "You sought Rebel assistance to prevent Naill from staging a coup, and even though we're risking our lives, you can't allow a weapon to fall into Rebel hands which might, in turn, be used against your father." His mouth twisted in a sneer. "How very Lochnar of you, Princess."

Her chin jerked up a notch. "Is there someone else who deserves my loyalty? Tell me! Who?"

Me! he wanted to shout in response to her challenge, but how meaningless would her trust be if it weren't freely given, how empty her loyalty when she didn't feel he deserved it? Instead, he snarled, "Apparently not."

She turned her face aside. "Then get away from me," she whispered hoarsely.

Every muscle in his body drew taut, battling the urge to grab her chin and force her to face him again. If he did, he'd succumb to this raging, primitive urge to claim her mouth in a brutal kiss, to brand every part of its silken lining with his tongue, bind her to him forever . . . even if it meant keeping her prisoner again. But if he did, his soul would be lost.

Talon shoved away. He said acidly, "Did you also arrange for the *Usurper* to join this little party?"

The slap cracked against the side of his face, snapping his head to the side. He had only a fraction of a second to be grateful she hadn't used her fist when she struck an even crueler blow with her words.

"Bastard," she hissed.

Shaking with rage, Talon yanked off one of his gloves and jerked his fist up between them, defiantly exposing his secret shame. "How right you are, Jemara. With these bare hands, I'm as close as a man can get to the dishonor of bastardy without being sired outside the law."

She looked down her regal nose at his smooth skin, which was marred only by the white tracks of rigid tendons. "You expect me to be shocked? Appalled?" She shrugged. "I've already seen your hands, smuggler, missing Line crests and all."

Shock jolted through his body. "When?" he demanded.

"When you were unconscious. Right after I saved you from bleeding to death," she reminded him through clenched teeth.

"Right after you stabbed me," he corrected bitterly. He spun away. Hell, he wanted to hit something, to do violence in a dramatic way that went light-years beyond slamming his fist against the wall.

Blowing up the *Viceroy* would be a good start.

The perfect tool of destruction was at his fingertips. If this damned freighter was doomed to explode, he was going to make sure it took down the Lochnar space station with it—and all the future threat it posed to the Rebels.

He looked up. Runagate hell, during the heat of the argument he'd forgotten they had an audience. Kjell, as expected, was the embodiment of tight-jawed fury. Quinn's worried gaze flashed between the two combatants. Talon flinched. The boy's look of dismay reflected something deep within himself, an outcry, a fierce denial—

He slammed an internal door against it. It should be easy to get Kari out from under his skin, now that he knew for certain what a faithless little schemer she was.

"Quinn, get Jemara Solis out of my sight," Talon growled between clenched teeth. "Take her to the transport. She's fulfilled her usefulness."

He should have followed his own advice and refused to look at her. Most of Kari's color drained away, leaving her as vulnerable-looking as the fragile *chaotti* blossoms capable of crumbling in a stiff breeze. The glittering green light of her eyes, so characteristic of her pride and energy, seemed to cave in upon itself.

Quinn muttered an apology and took her arm. Kari went meekly, for the first time . . . ever. She didn't look back.

He didn't think he could feel any more pain. He was wrong.

Kjell moved up beside him. "Only nineteen minutes left. Let's get out of here, Talon. There's nothing more we can do."

"And go where, Kjell?" Talon retorted. "The *Usurper* is blocking escape through the Corridor. You know as well as I that she'll stay there until the opposition is crushed. Unless I do something everyone out there is going to die . . . Rand, Arden—" His throat closed off, refusing to utter the one name that shifted his protective instincts into star-drive. What the hell was the matter with him? Why did his emotions feel raw, as if all the skin had been flayed from his body? He retreated into sarcasm, adding, "Do you think using this freighter to blow up the *Viceroy* would serve as a sufficient diversion?"

Kjell gave a long, low whistle. "I can't think of a better one. You intend to ram it into the space station?"

"Not exactly. The *Viceroy*'s crew would only shoot down the freighter at a harmless distance if they perceived it as a threat. No, I intend for the commander of the *Viceroy* to invite it in, with a little coaxing from Naill's greed. The one thing Solis will not do is allow his precious shipment to get away."

"But you heard Quinn. This thing can't be steered without manual control."

Talon turned away to gaze out the viewport.

"Stars, you can't stay on board this ship!" Kjell protested, quickly grasping the significance of Talon's lack of response. "Start her on an intercept course, then let's get out of here."

"At this distance, without directional lock?" Talon reminded him gravely. "You know the slightest fraction of a degree miscalculated and she'll be kilometers off course by the time she reaches the *Viceroy*. Besides, fooling the station's commander will require some last-second maneuvering."

"This is tantamount to suicide, man!"

"I'll use the freighter's shuttle to get away just before she blows." A feeling of déjà vu nagged at Talon, though he knew he'd never been in a similar situation before.

Kjell's scowling expression, reflected in the viewport, was frankly skeptical. Nevertheless, he gave a brisk nod. "You're obviously not going to listen to me. And heaven knows it'll require some desperate tactics to get us out of this mess." He gripped Talon's shoulder with one hand. "Before I go tell me something I can do for you."

One last thing. The unspoken words passed between the two men in silent understanding. Kjell knew the risks; the chances of Talon coming through this alive were slim.

He hesitated. It was strange to have someone other than Rand show concern for his welfare. "See that Jemara Solis is returned safely to the *Regalia*."

"Are you crazy? Just let her go, after what she's—?"

"Swear to me, Kjell," Talon interrupted, spinning around.

The Rebel reared back at the sudden show of anger. "Okay. But how can I get her there without risking my own capture?"

"I trust your ingenuity to find a way. Unless you want someone else to pocket the reward for her return?"

"I'm already working on an idea." Kjell moved to the bridge exit. He turned in the opening, his expression grim. "Good luck. Try not to end up like your father, dammit."

Kjell's words stunned him. Like Sahr . . . martyred.

Talon managed a crooked smile. "Because you don't want to face Rand's wrath if I don't come back?"

"No; because it'll piss me off, you thick-skulled idiot."

With a sharp turn on his heel, Kjell was gone, leaving Talon more alone than he'd ever been.

Talon watched the transport speed away from the freighter.

Fourteen minutes.

He had to make the most of every second. The precise moment he reached his target was a crucial factor that separated success from failure. It was time to move in.

The 180-degree curve of the freighter's viewport provided an excellent view of the *Viceroy* against the backdrop of Avernus. He stepped up to the main console. The stiff material of the spacesuit, which he had donned in accordance with his plans, crackled as he moved. The helmet dangled from his right hand.

As he eased the propulsion control to maximum, Talon resolutely refused to look aside at the telltale flashes of light surrounding the *Usurper*. The battle raging inside himself was more than sufficient distraction.

Try not to end up like your father. Kjell hadn't fully realized the impact his words carried. Sahr Markos had died in a similar situation. Talon had spent years despising his father's choice and mocking the concept of martyrdom. Kari's revelation had begun to change that.

How blind he'd been. That kind of choice—the same decision he now faced—didn't revolve around something so fleeting as a cause. It involved people, friends at risk.

He could even feel a measure of the agony his father must have experienced at knowing he'd never see his family again. Talon's long-held bitterness faded, allowing forgiveness, and an undefinable measure of sadness, to fill its place. He'd wasted so many years nursing resentment against his father . . . a child's anger, with no place in a man's understanding of the infinite complexities of responsibility. He could only be grateful that, if his plan didn't work and he perished in the freighter's explosion, he wasn't leaving anyone vulnerable behind.

The memory of the hurt, lost, defeated look on Kari's face hit him like a body blow.

He rubbed his cheek, remembering how she'd slapped him rather than ball up her fist. It was a woman's response to insult, so out of character with her warrior-side that the instinctive reaction couldn't be anything less than genuine.

She'd reacted to his accusation concerning the *Usurper* as if he'd wounded her deeply. Could he have misjudged her?

No. Hadn't she brought the suspicion on herself?

Then why was guilt clawing its way through his insides like a burrowing scale lizard? She'd been the one to betray him by setting the self-destruct!

The conflicting emotions built to a screaming crescendo in his head. With a roar of rage, he flung the helmet against the bulkhead. It ricocheted off with a sharp clang, then bounced across the floor until it wedged under the weapons console. He stood with chest heaving, heart pounding.

The explosion of temper succeeded at one thing—it unraveled the horrid knot of tension in his body. He felt numb in its aftermath, coldly functional, like an automaton.

Thirteen minutes.

He needed more power for the propulsion systems. A last sensor scan for life signs showed none but his own. Kjell had taken the captured freighter crew with him. Talon resolutely retrieved the scratched helmet and put it on. When the seal had tightened and oxygen flowed coolly around his face he shunted all power from the freighter's life support. The bridge lights shut down, enveloping everything in darkness. The ship pushed forward at greater speed. A heartbeat later the red emergency lights came on.

There was only one way to get the *Viceroy*'s crew to override normal precautionary procedures and tractor in a rogue freighter—a direct order from Naill. The would-be Dynast wasn't stupid, but he was compulsive and, Talon suspected, rather prone to panic when things didn't go according to plan. He counted on Naill's loss of self-control when he made it look like the precious neryllium shipment was about to slip between his fingers.

He estimated six minutes to prep the shuttle, and another three to return to the bridge and pull his planned, last-minute maneuver. He was cutting it very close to the edge.

He was starting to leave the bridge when a flash of dark red caught his eye. His heart gave a lurch. Then he realized it was only the one remaining lifepod, nestled upright in its launch tube. The deeply tinted window of the sleek, capsule-shaped pod reflected the red emergency lights.

At first he'd thought it was Kari, with the distinctive way light brought out the fiery color in her auburn hair. His fingertips tingled with the memory of sliding his hands through the soft paradise of her hair, of stroking her cheeks with his thumbs while he looked into eyes that went so deep he once believed they could reach inside him and touch his soul.

All the pain came rushing back, all the longing for something infinitely precious, something lost.

Now, when he wasn't sure whether he'd be alive or dead twelve minutes hence, he could admit he'd left something crucial behind. Kari, and his heart with her. Regardless of everything she'd done, he loved her.

She hated him.

She hated the supreme effort of will it had taken to show a brave front while Talon carved her heart into tiny pieces.

She despised herself even more. How could she have

given herself to Talon so freely, not only her body, but her hopes, the fostering of dreams long denied, of tenderness, passion, love—

And he'd thrown it all back in her face.

She's fulfilled her usefulness. His words had been the knife that inflicted the wound. The disdain in his expression rubbed in a generous helping of salt.

He'd used her. Just like everyone else since her mother died, including her own father. She was sick of being used. No more. Within minutes Naill would receive his pay-back for the childhood cruelties and the recent attempts on her life. Father would soon learn she was no longer his puppet, when she refused to succeed him in his despotic role. That left only Talon. For the level of pain inflicted, his was the greatest crime of all.

Kari gripped the back of the copilot's seat, shaking with undiluted fury as the freighter receded into the distance.

From his position in the captain's chair, Kjell ordered quietly, "Full stop, Quinn. This is far enough. Bring her about one hundred eighty degrees. Magnification six."

The upper-right quadrant of the bow viewport showed an enlarged view of the freighter. It was heading straight for the *Viceroy!* This couldn't be right, Kari thought.

"How much time?" Kjell asked.

"Six minutes," whispered Quinn.

Her fingernails cut into leather. Why the blazes didn't Talon launch the shuttle and get off the freighter?

Kjell sat forward in his seat. "Scan the comm channels. See if you can pick up any transmission from the *Usurper.* I want to know what's going on, dammit." Quinn hunched over the console. Silent, tense seconds ticked by, until suddenly a voice boomed across the speaker.

"What is it now, Camargue? I'm rather busy at the moment, in case that fact has escaped your notice."

A jolt rammed through Kari at the clearly recognizable voice of her half-brother. Stars in heaven, Naill was on the *Usurper.*

"Uh, sorry, Jemidar," answered Camargue, "but ya told me to report on any Rebel activity. I tracked 'em here and intercepted some of their audio. I'm sure Talon and Kari, and a Rebel sabotage team, are aboard that freighter."

Into the stunned silence, Kjell whispered furiously, "Why, that backstabbing little son of a tarpan. I'll remember this, Camargue. Count on it."

Naill, not realizing their conversation was being pirated, finally responded, with undeniable smugness in his voice, "Excellent, Camargue. You have done quite well, surprisingly."

"Does that mean I've earned the reward? All forty thousand?"

"When Kari is delivered, and Talon is captured . . . or dead."

"Turn it down, Quinn. I've heard enough," Kjell hissed. "How much farther does Talon have to go? It sounds like things are about to get nasty."

Quinn checked his instruments. "Time and distance from target are a good match. He'll get in close enough . . . if they don't shoot him down first."

Kari's breath froze in her throat. Talon intended to catch the *Viceroy* in the blast? This was insane!

"Four minutes."

The freighter drew dangerously close to the mammoth space station.

"Now, Talon. Now, dammit," Kjell urged, hands clenched in white-knuckled fists on his knees.

"He's doing it. He's veering off!" Quinn shouted excitedly.

The freighter shifted its course, adjusting to a vector that would take it between the arms of the station and out into open space. And the *Usurper* was too far away to do anything about it.

Kari moved around the chair, mesmerized, drawn irresistibly toward the viewport. She sensed the Rebel commander rise, but he made no move to stop her. Where could she go, anyway?

"What's happening on the *Usurper?*" Kjell asked quickly.

Quinn turned up the volume.

"—a direct order." Naill's enraged voice invaded the transport's bridge again. "Lock one of the *Viceroy*'s tractor beams on that freighter before it moves out of range."

"Jemidar, please, we don't know what's aboard—" responded someone from the space station.

"Don't question me," Naill interrupted furiously. "A group of shirker Rebels are aboard that freighter, particularly one barbarian named Talon. They're attempting to steal a very valuable shipment. I'll take it out of your hide if they succeed! Carry out your orders!"

"Yes, Jemidar."

"And shoot down any craft attempting to launch from the freighter. *Usurper* out."

Kari's hands seemed a foreign extension of her body as she pressed trembling fingertips to the viewport.

The green light of a tractor beam lanced out from the *Viceroy*, capturing the bow of the fleeing craft, bringing it back around. An instant later a blip of light marked the launch of a shuttle from the ensnared freighter.

A dozen impact torpedoes shot out from the *Viceroy*, fired at maximum spread by the Lochnar crew in a desperate ploy to find a target. Kari's hands curled into fists against the cold glass. She bit down on her lower lip until she tasted blood. She strained closer to the window, her heart pounding as her whole body urged the shuttle to greater speed. The torpedoes wouldn't find their mark, she prayed—

The shuttle exploded in a spectacular flare of yellow-white.

Kari froze. The air whooshed out of her lungs as if she had just received a brutal kick to the chest. The chill of space was as nothing compared to the icy emptiness that engulfed her like a shockwave.

Talon was dead.

"No," she croaked. The whisper barely slipped past the grip of horror around her throat.

"Son of a tarpan!" Kjell burst out, his voice vibrating with helpless rage.

"Stars," Quinn said hoarsely. "He must have loaded some of the CX-20 on the shuttle. That was too big of an explosion for a torpedo blast."

With their words, the numbness was obliterated by a fiery burst of agony.

"No!" Kari screamed, pounding the viewport with her fists. "No! Talon!"

Kjell's arm snaked around her waist like a band of durasteel. He hauled her back. She struggled desperately, irrationally terrified of breaking that last link, of losing sight of the tiny, drifting bits of wreckage, the flares of light winking out as the last pockets of flammable gases were consumed.

Kjell's anger-laced strength proved the greater.

"Damnation. If I didn't know better, I'd think you cared about Talon. A little late for that, isn't it?" he snarled.

"Look!" Quinn cried. "The *Viceroy* is continuing to tractor in the freighter."

The Rebel second-in-command froze, intent on the drama being played out.

Kari stilled as well to whisper accusingly, "You don't care that he's dead, as long as your war goes on."

"On the contrary," Kjell responded acidly, "I care that he didn't die in vain. I sure as hell wasn't the one who sent him there." His arm jerked, tightening in a cruel grip.

Let him do his worst. The agony inside was so much greater than any punishment Kjell could inflict. She was responsible for Talon's death. She had set the freighter's self-destruct, with devastating consequences. Bile rose in her throat.

"The tractor beam has brought the freighter to full stop, two kilometers from the bay," said Quinn.

"Will it be close enough?"

"I don't know, sir. They're launching a boarding craft. One minute to destruct."

Kari barely heard the young Rebel as he continued to count down the seconds, so intense were the plaintive cries in her head. *This couldn't be happening. No, please, no. Not Talon.*

"Detonation!"

The freighter exploded. The blast ripped outward, triggering other explosions on the station. A chain reaction of destruction engulfed half the *Viceroy*, turning it into a twisted mass of glowing metal.

Kari watched silently. Some remote, still functioning corner of her mind was amazed at how little she cared, even though Naill's threat of a coup was nullified for now. The *Viceroy* was severely damaged, facing months of expensive repairs.

The *Usurper* abruptly broke off its engagement with the Rebel fighters, heading away from the Corridor and toward the crippled station, which had shifted out of its standard orbit and was drifting downward at a vector that would soon plunge it into the planet's atmosphere.

Kari numbly allowed Kjell to drag her out of the cabin.

"Come on; the freighter crew is locked up in the brig. I'll have to secure you in the captain's cabin." Between gritted teeth, he added, "I should kill you for what you've done."

Kari's reaction was instantaneous and born of despair. She rammed her elbow down onto his forearm, targeting the vulnerable nerve that lay just beneath muscle. His grunt of pain was timed perfectly with the loosening of his grasp. She pivoted violently, ripping free of the circle of his arm, and grabbed his sword as she sprang back. It came away in her hand, sliding out of its scabbard with a grating scrape of metal against metal.

Kjell froze, hands outspread, braced for attack. His face registered shock when she immediately turned the sword around and handed it to him hilt first. The instant he grasped it, she stepped up until the sharp tip pressed deeply into the soft flesh beneath her breastbone.

"Then do it," she hissed. When he didn't oblige, didn't answer, she shrieked almost hysterically, "Do it!"

A multitude of expressions rippled across his face, from anger to confusion to something akin to sympathy. Then he straightened from his crouched, battle-ready posture and sheathed the sword. "I can't. I promised Talon I'd return you safely to the *Regalia*, and your father."

All the strength leeched out of Kari's limbs. Her legs crumpled. She sank to the floor. As her head hung limply, hot tears flowed down her cheeks, falling away to burn the backs of her hands like tiny brands. It should be the heat of her own blood flowing freely, emptying her worthless life onto the deck.

Until a few moments ago she'd reconciled herself to the concept of existing without Talon's love, knowing, at least, that somewhere in the galaxy he would be hale and hearty and very much alive. That all that gorgeous, hard-edged, robust masculinity would be out there, taking risks, piloting the *Nighthawk*, propping his feet on the console while sipping white brandy, arguing with Beryl—

The emotional equivalent of a broadsword twisted deep in her gut. Kari wrapped her arms tightly about her waist and curled around the pain.

Now she didn't even have the reassurance of knowing Talon was alive. It hadn't taken Naill's sadistic machinations to destroy her beloved. She'd done it herself.

"Open a channel to Arden," Kjell ordered the instant he reentered the transport's cockpit.

Stars, he wanted to get back to the cut-and-dry business of commanding a ship. No more of the wrenching uncertainty caused by having a distraught woman offer her life at the tip of his sword. No more watching her curl up on the captain's bunk, not caring that the room went pitch black when he locked the door.

He never would have believed it possible if he hadn't had the evidence thrust in his face. Kari Solis loved Talon, despite their antagonism. And now that he knew what signs to look for, in retrospect, he recognized a lot of Talon's behavior as signs of love. If possible, the realization made Talon's death even more tragic.

Quinn established the connection. Arden's voice came on the line, full of enthusiasm and the cheerful flush of victory.

"Hey, Commander, I don't need any coaxing," the lieutenant joked. "I'm setting a course for home right now."

Kjell winced. "One last task before we go. We've got a traitorous little weasel who needs to be disposed of: Bhut Camargue. He's responsible for the death of one of our men."

The brief silence was potent. "Who?" Arden asked roughly.

"Talon."

Arden responded with a string of curses.

"I found the *Concubine*," crowed Quinn in triumph. He rattled off the coordinates.

"Do you read that, Arden?"

"Yeah, I sure do. I'll take care of the lousy shirker."

"No!" interjected a deep voice vibrating with fury. Rand had returned and picked up on their transmission. "This kill is mine. Do you understand, Kjell? No interference."

Kjell closed his eyes with a sigh. He hadn't meant for Rand to find out this way. "He's all yours, Rand." He waited until Markos disconnected, then said, "Arden, fly backup, but keep your distance unless any stray Lochnar fighters come around. It'll piss him off if he knows you're watching out for him."

"Got it." The comm clicked, breaking transmission.

"Quinn, open another channel to Camargue's ship." The boy looked startled, then nodded grimly and quickly obliged. Kjell took a deep breath. He was going to enjoy this. "Camargue, this is Rebel Commander Kjell Timor."

"Timor," Camargue acknowledged with a sneering tone. "What do ya want?"

"My comrades and I were just speculating on what brings you to this sector," Kjell commented mildly.

"Business," snapped Camargue with blatant impatience.

"In the midst of a battle?"

"That's right."

"You contacted the *Usurper* a short while ago, Camargue."

There was a long pause. "So? Smugglers run shipments for the Dynast now'n then. Ya know that."

"Nice try, but we heard the details of your little deal with Solis. Were you aware that Talon was Rand Markos's brother?" There was a distinct gulp at the other end of the line. "Consider yourself enlightened. By the way, I believe you're familiar with the *Stormhawk*," Kjell continued conversationally. "You might want to take a peek out your starboard viewport."

There was a choked-off cry of horror before the comm erupted in a burst of static.

"Ship destroyed, Commander," Quinn whispered.

"Of course; Rand never misses." Kjell sank into the captain's chair. "Unfortunately, it won't take the pain away." He rubbed his hand across his face. He'd misjudged Talon for years. Now, when he'd discovered the man, the hero, beneath the surface, it was too late. He'd lost a good friend. "Take us into the Corridor, Quinn," he said wearily.

"Commander," Quinn cried, "the *Stormhawk* is rendezvousing with our other fighters. They're heading back to Avernus."

Kjell leapt to his feet. "Dammit, Rand."

"Where are they going?"

"To finish the job at the neryllium mine, what else? Has the crew of the *Usurper* spotted them?"

"I don't think so," Quinn answered guardedly. "They appear too involved in evacuating the remaining personnel from the space station. I think they're scrambling to restore retro-rocket capability to the surviving section before the orbit deteriorates any further. Anyway, they have not engaged a pursuit."

Kjell ground his teeth. "Why did I get stuck aboard this damned transport ship, with no weapons?"

"You volunteered, sir," Quinn offered innocently.

"Thanks for the reminder, kid," Kjell retorted dryly. "Get us out of here. There's nothing we can do to help now . . . nothing except fulfill a promise to a friend when we near the *Regalia.*"

Chapter Nineteen

The electronic bolt slid back with a muffled clank. The door swung open, allowing a biting draft to sweep into the already cold room, bringing with it the stench of unwashed bodies and despair. Kari resented the interruption, for it disturbed the numb, spiritless state to which she'd retreated . . . but not as much as she despised the snide tone that cut across her peace.

"How is the detention cell, Kari? Comfortable?"

Naill's vindictiveness was expected. After all, it was very much in character for him to grab the first opportunity to torment her since her ignominious return to the *Regalia* two days earlier.

"Quite comfortable. You should try one some time," she answered flatly. There was no sarcasm in the response, no inflection whatsoever. How could she put any feeling into the words when she was dead inside?

A muscle twitched under Naill's eye.

There were compensations for being locked up. She hadn't seen his gloating face since he'd paid Dominic and Kalfar, posing as bounty hunters, for delivering her safely to the bosom of her loving family. Myklar had left strict instructions that no one was to speak to her until he ordered her brought before him.

"It is time," Naill said, confirming her suspicions.

She stood, ignoring the stiffness of muscles neglected while she'd sat motionless, for hours on end, staring at the black walls. She squared her shoulders and moved through the door.

It didn't bode well, the fact that Father had ordered her confined, guarded, shunned. Nevertheless, she walked boldly down the *Regalia*'s passageway, challenging Naill and the four armed soldiers to keep pace with her long strides. Whatever fate Father decreed, she deserved that and more.

Not for aiding the Rebels, or for the damage to the *Viceroy*, but for a betrayal greater than everything else combined.

Evidently dissatisfied that he hadn't struck a nerve, Naill tried again. "Father has been deciding what to do with you."

"No doubt you've been offering a multitude of suggestions."

"Actually, I haven't felt the need. He is still furious over the loss of the freighter and the damage to the *Viceroy*. Then there is the small matter of treason. Tsk, tsk, Kari, I really thought you would be more circumspect." He laughed and stroked his goatee. "I am so glad you weren't. I am really enjoying this. Yes, I feel quite confident that the punishment shall fit the crime."

What punishment is sufficient for plotting Father's over-throw? Kari thought. She dared not utter the challenge aloud, however. If Naill suspected she knew of his foiled plans for a coup, and intended to reveal them in Myklar's presence, she'd never reach the audience chamber alive.

Instead, she shrugged.

Naill reddened, then retorted, "You won't treat this so lightly when you stand before Father and feel, firsthand, the ruthlessness that enabled him to conquer a solar system."

"Give it up, Naill. Nothing you may devise can hurt me." *More than I've already hurt myself,* she added, deep within the wretched emptiness where her heart had been.

* * *

"Before you say anything, I want you to know I no longer choose to be Heir to the Dynasty." Kari straightened her back and looked her father straight in the eye. "I refuse to have any further part in your oppression of the solar system."

"From your actions, Kari, I managed to surmise that much for myself," Myklar snapped.

He pushed up from the only seat in the audience chamber, a huge chair carved of black calamani wood, and began to pace. His burgundy tunic added the only splash of color to the austere room. His boot heels clicked on the polished marble floor. The silver-veined black and gray tiles distorted his reflection. Curtains of gray Taki silk, although draped along the walls in generous folds, added no warmth to the stark decor.

Naill stood a short distance behind Kari, his sly expression making no secret of the fact that he eagerly awaited her downfall. The four guards had been ordered to wait just outside the large double doors.

Abruptly, Myklar stopped and took a deep breath. "You are not helping your case, Kari, with such defiant statements."

"My intention is not to be defiant, only to speak the truth. I won't beg for leniency."

He glowered at her from beneath bushy brows. "You may wish to, once you hear where I intend to send you," he said ominously. Rather than finish his threat, he declared, "Naill is Heir now."

Earnestness roughened her voice as she urged, "You may wish to reconsider that decision once you hear what I have to say. I destroyed the ore shipment because Naill was in the process of hijacking it. He planned to use the phazer fuelant to arm a coup against you."

"Little liar!" Naill shouted, jarred out of his smug, superior attitude. "You won't save yourself by falsely implicating me. She is lying, Father."

"You are repeating yourself, Naill," Myklar said stiffly.

He glared at Kari. "This is a very serious accusation. Do you have proof?"

Kari stood with hands locked behind her back, feet braced shoulder width apart. Though she knew her position was crumbling, she raised her chin proudly. "I did have irrefutable evidence, but it was destroyed. Father, I wouldn't try to deceive you on something this important—"

"You have done nothing but betray my trust," he interrupted, his voice shaking with wrath, "ever since you helped Talon escape from the *Regalia*."

"That decision I will never regret. Naill planned to torture him to death. Surely that was not your intention?"

"Why not?" Myklar threw back at her.

His face held the petulant expression of a thwarted child. She had hurt him, butchered all his plans for her future, and now he was striking back. Then again, maybe he would have personally supervised Talon's torture once he returned from the *Viceroy*. In retrospect, there was no way of knowing. But one thing she had learned in recent days—the characteristics she once admired in her father as strength were just cleverly disguised forms of cruelty. Despite the pain of disillusionment, she embraced the eye-opening truth.

"You can't let Naill be Dynast, not after planning a coup."

"Don't believe her, Father!"

Ignoring Naill, Myklar asked angrily, "What choice do you give me?"

"There is always a choice. You could dissolve the Dynasty and give these people back their freedom."

Naill snorted. "Those shirker Rebels would create chaos out of freedom. They haven't a clue how to order their lives. Everything would deteriorate into civil war, chaos, poverty."

"You underestimate them!"

"Enough!" Myklar's voice boomed across the room, silencing their hostility. "No. I created this Dynasty out of a dream of order, and of my seed carrying on after I am gone." His voice hardened as he finished, "I shall not sacrifice all I have built for a daughter who has betrayed me."

Myklar wouldn't listen, didn't want to listen. Naill was all he had left. A shadow of sorrow passed over her already grieving heart. "Then I guess there's nothing more to discuss."

"Except where I have decided to send you. You shall go to Turliss, to assist the researchers at the lab."

Avernus's barren, mineral-rich moon . . . the most dreaded duty in the Lochnar Dynasty. He was banishing her.

"Are you not going to ask how long you will be assigned there?"

"No, Father," she said dully. "It doesn't matter, because I don't intend to come back even if you allow it."

His unyielding expression cracked, revealing a glimmer of dismay, even vulnerability. "Kari—" Myklar began in a thickened voice, then faltered.

Kari felt a flicker of sympathy, but little more. Though this whole situation distressed her father, she knew that love and loss were not the main emotions with which he struggled. He was primarily torn by disappointment. Banishing her was like cutting off his sword arm. Despite declaring Naill his Heir, Kari knew her half-brother had not been, and never would be, her father's first choice. His grand plans for generations of capable rule had come to naught.

Thank the stars she had learned the truth before sacrificing her future to a role of arrogance, cruelty, and abysmal ignorance. From the very beginning she had been groomed for a purpose—his purpose—and manipulated to the point of concealing the truth about her mother. With the frantic desire to earn his approval gone, purged, it was amazing how little she felt for this man. She still loved him, but the emotion seemed rooted in filial devotion rather than true affection.

Then again, everything inside her was so empty, she doubted she was capable of feeling anything at all.

Talon, the plaintive whisper welled up inside, louder and more desperate than the constant echo that reverberated through the deepest part of her soul, haunting her days and invading her dreams at night.

"Do you have anything more to say?" challenged Myklar.

"No. I did betray you, Father, though I had my reasons. Of all the decisions I've made in the past few days, there is only one I would change. I can't go back to being what I was. Since you only want the most loyal of followers around you, it only makes sense to banish me."

Myklar's mouth worked during her speech. The whiskers across his chin twitched. "Then so be it," he snapped. "You will leave immediately. Naill has offered to take you straight to Turliss aboard the *Usurper.*"

"Why so melancholy, Kari? You should be accustomed to losing by now."

Blazes, Naill was full of himself, Kari thought with disdain. He strode alongside her down the passageway, the four soldiers marching behind. "Don't flatter yourself. You may have won, but your triumph is clouded by deceit. And the Rebels will guarantee it is short-lived. As for being melancholy . . . no. I was just regretting the loss of something I had to leave behind on the *Nighthawk.*"

"And what would that be?"

"A chest of my mother's belongings, including a letter."

Naill's expression registered surprise. "Another letter?" he exclaimed.

She stopped dead and pivoted on her heel to face him. "What do you mean, *another?*" Suddenly her mother's last written words about leaving a note took on new meaning. Had there been two? "Mother left a message for me at the house, didn't she?" Kari demanded furiously. "I was meant to find it the day she left!"

Naill's mouth twisted in a sly grin.

"Damn you, you took it!"

"Yes, I found her maudlin good-bye note. I destroyed it. The opportunity to see you suffer was too good to pass up."

Kari was about to go for his throat, despite knowing that the four guards would only pull her off and wrestle her to the floor, when an achingly recognizable voice interjected.

"Solis," Jhase Merrick said.

Kari spun around, her heart thundering.

Jhase ignored her. He greeted Naill with a nod, a casual greeting that few would have gotten away with.

The shock of seeing the space pirate broadsided her, mutilating her defenses and reminding her brutally of every bittersweet moment with Talon. The acute sense of loss she'd kept locked away, until she had the privacy to mourn, burst upon her with a fiery agony that threatened to char her flesh from her body. Her throat locked. Unshed tears trembled on her lashes.

Jhase's gaze shifted to her. She thought she saw something flicker in his eyes, but then he looked away, disinterested . . . or pleased by her evident suffering. She was his enemy, because he was first and foremost Talon's friend. And she was responsible for Talon's death.

"Do you have the materials I requested?" Naill asked.

"I never fail to acquire a commodity for which a customer is eager to pay," he drawled. "The hold of my ship is full of crates of your chemicals. Penn just transferred the first installment on the payment to my account."

"The balance is not payable until delivery."

"There's no need to remind me, Solis. I'm on my way back to the *Vagabond*. I'll see you at the rendezvous coordinates."

"Excellent. Until then."

He eyed Naill coolly. "Remember our agreement: skeleton crew only."

"You are being overly cautious, Merrick."

"Perhaps. Then again, that's how I've not only survived but thrived in my business for so long. If sensor scans detect more life-signs aboard the *Usurper* than we agreed upon, I'll turn right around and sell your shipment to the next highest bidder."

"It sounds as if you don't trust me."

Jhase's only answer was to bare his teeth in a smile that held no warmth or humor. "Seventeen hundred hours. Don't be late."

He didn't even spare her a glance as he turned and walked away. She was caught between two worlds, betrayer of both, belonging to neither. Nevertheless, curiosity prodded her out of her wallowing grief and encouraged her to discover what that discussion had been about.

"What is Merrick doing here?" she asked as Naill pushed her forward again.

"I have arranged to buy a shipment of . . . materials from him."

"He mentioned a rendezvous," she hinted.

"He wants to transfer the cargo, directly from his ship to the *Usurper*, in space link. Insists on not bringing it aboard the *Regalia*. He has the gall to imply he doesn't trust me. Can you imagine that?" Naill stroked his goatee. "The fellow has courage for saying so to my face, I will say that much for him."

"Discriminating fellow. It's unfortunate he's not very finicky about who he does business with," she said dryly.

"Few smugglers are." He gave her a sly, sidelong glance. "Merrick is motivated by profit, much like your friend Talon."

Kari struggled to hide the pain, keeping her face impassive, for she knew Naill eagerly watched for a reaction to his thrust.

Kari rose from the bunk as Naill entered the *Usurper's* brig. The white glare of overhead lights shone painfully in her eyes, preventing her from seeing his face clearly; a small blessing until he stepped close to her prison. The semitransparent force field of her cell stretched between them.

The battle cruiser had been underway for nearly twenty minutes. Now it lay motionless in space. She'd recognized the sounds of docking. They must be transferring Jhase's shipment, before entering the Verdigris-Avernus Corridor.

"Aren't you wondering what I'm purchasing from a notorious smuggler?" Naill taunted.

"No."

He scowled. "Larcinium crystals and basealic flakes," he finished, despite her refusal to rise to his bait.

That did get her attention. "Those are ingredients in processing phazer fuelant."

"Exactly." He arched his dark eyebrows in a look of mocking sympathy. "You don't think I intend to wait until the old man dies, do you? Your sabotage of the freighter may have delayed my plans for four, perhaps six months, but my engineers will soon be extracting more ore. Even the Rebel's attack on Avernus won't stop me."

A charge of excitement shot through her. "Then Rand Markos succeeded in destroying the neryllium mine?"

"Minimal damage only," he retorted. A flush mounted into his lean cheeks.

"Liar," she whispered, deriving satisfaction from a little taunting of her own. "I can tell by your expression that, even if the mine wasn't destroyed, the damage was substantial."

His eyes narrowed ominously. What he would have done next she was never to know, for the sounds of a scuffle came from outside the brig. Startled, Naill spun around.

Jhase entered the room, stepping over one of the guards slumped on the floor.

"What is the meaning of this, Merrick?" Naill exploded.

Jhase grinned. "I believe you have something that belongs to a comrade of mine. He's rather obsessed with the idea of reclaiming what is his."

Another man loomed in the doorway behind the pirate. Kari squinted against the blinding lights and cursed the fact that Jhase blocked her view.

Naill gave a ragged gasp. "No, this can't be. You're supposed to be dead, dammit!"

The newcomer's answering chuckle stole the breath from her body. Jhase moved aside to let him pass. Tears suddenly hampered her vision, making it impossible to focus on the man's face, but only one rogue moved with that smooth, predatory grace. Hope glittered through her, surging through her bloodstream. It was a miracle, a blessing, the very gift of life. Either that, or she was losing her mind.

"You really ought to check the reliability of your sources, Solis," Talon countered as he shut down the cell's force field.

Free, she launched herself against his chest. She didn't care if his instinctive reaction was to push her away in disgust. All that mattered was that she touch him, reassure herself that he was gloriously real and not some tortured fantasy.

His chest was a reassuring wall of strength as he absorbed the impact. Her arms locked around his neck. She rained frantic kisses across his smooth-shaven cheek to the corner of his jaw, then buried her face in his shoulder.

"I don't care if you hate me," she said hoarsely, "I have to hold you. Please don't push me away yet. I have to feel you, to convince myself that you're real. I thought—" Her voice broke on a sob.

His hands slid up her back, scattering her thoughts with an internal storm.

Looking up into his handsome face, she said, "I love you." Husky, fervent, the words vibrated with all the joy and passion she felt. His hands clutched fistfuls of her shirt just beneath her shoulder blades. Part of her was appalled by her open admission, the blatant vulnerability, but it felt so good to reveal what was slamming around inside her heart that she said it again . . . and felt renewed. "I love you, Talon."

He engulfed her in an embrace that squeezed the air from her lungs and lifted her toes from the floor. She didn't care if he cracked her ribs, as long as he held her locked in his arms this way . . . like he wanted her, like she was his salvation.

"Crimony, Talon, she's going to pass out if you don't let her breathe," Jhase muttered.

She laughed, a shaky sound that changed to a soft moan as he lowered her slowly to the floor, letting her rub against his arousal. His brown eyes smoldered, promising decadent things. His mouth tilted in a sensual smile that demanded a kiss. Oh, blazes. All she wanted now was to be alone with him, strip him out of his flight suit, touch him . . . but this was hardly the time or place.

"How did you survive, Talon?" she blurted out, asking the next most important thing on her mind. "The shuttle was destroyed."

"I wasn't on the—"

She didn't allow him to finish. With frustrated passion that seemed as limitless as the boundaries of the universe, she captured his face between her hands and kissed him.

"The shuttle was a decoy . . . the life pod—" he murmured against her lips.

She kissed him again, cherishing the warmth and silky texture of his firm mouth, his masculine taste. She'd experienced what it felt like to face the future without him, and she never, ever wanted to confront that horror again.

His words finally registered. Her eyes flew open. She leaned back and stared at him. "The life pod, from the bridge?" He nodded. "Then why didn't you radio Kjell for help?"

"The explosion stripped away all the pod's comm gear. The concussion wave knocked me on a wild tumble through space. By the time I regained consciousness, the transport was long gone."

"Then how did someone find you?"

He held up a small commlink. "Recognize this?"

She took it from him and cradled it in her palm. "Jhase's commlink. The one I used to call from Star Alpha."

"And to think, I almost gave it back to him," he teased.

After the stress of the past two days, his irreverence caused something to snap inside. Stepping back, she slapped the commlink against his chest. He winced. Catching the sharp-edged object before it fell to the floor, he returned it to his pocket.

"How can you joke about something so serious?" she cried. "You could have died! Maybe you should carry his commlink with you from now on, you reckless maniac! Someone has to watch out for you."

He caught her face between his hands, kissed the angry words from her lips with a tender assault, then had the audacity to grin at her. "Want the job?" he asked huskily.

Her anger abruptly melted away.

Jhase cleared his throat, drawing Talon's attention. "I think you two are forgetting you have an audience. And don't you think it's about time we were getting underway? My men have loaded Penn and the former crew of the *Usurper* onto a shuttle and bid them farewell."

Talon looked around sharply. "Where's Naill?"

The pirate shrugged. "Gone," he said simply.

"What?" Talon exploded. He jerked away, apparently ready to go in pursuit.

Kari latched onto his arm with all her strength. He would have to drag her bodily to move another step. "Oh, no, you don't! I'm not letting you out of my sight. Ever again."

His frown appeared more bemused than angry. He didn't try to pull away. "How could you just let him walk off, Jhase?"

"Actually, he ran, as if a catamount were snarling at his

heels, the moment you two began enjoying this touching reunion. The ship's console registered launch of a second shuttle." At Talon's scowl, he added defensively, "You don't think I'm going to be responsible for kidnapping the Dynast's son, do you? It's bad enough I'm stealing this ship." Jhase looked around at the polished metal walls and said speculatively, "I wonder how much Markos will pay me for a Lochnar battle cruiser?"

"Not you, Jhase . . . us."

"Does this mean you've finally come to your senses?"

"Yeah . . . partner. But this one," Talon added, rapping his knuckles on the *Usurper*'s bulkhead, "is for free."

Jhase's jaw dropped. "Free? You must be joking!"

"Nope. You know Rand can't afford your price. This will be our gift to the Rebel cause."

"Crimony," muttered Jhase sourly, "this ship is worth a friggin' fortune. Hey, where are you two going?" he exclaimed as Talon swept Kari into his arms. "Never mind; stupid question. Crew's quarters are down that passageway, to the right."

"You claim to be a better pilot than me, so prove it by taking us home. I need to fetch the *Nighthawk*."

"Good idea. Then we can start building our shipping empire."

"Not until after I seek out some much needed privacy for a wedding trip. Afraid my interest in another partnership takes precedence over yours, Jhase."

Kari's hold on his neck tightened. "Do you really mean it?"

"More than I've ever meant anything, starfire. Marry me. I love you," he said huskily. "Be forewarned, if you say no, I'll only kidnap you again. And this time I'll never let you go."

"Hmm . . . tempting, but I think I'll simplify things by saying yes."

"There, you see?" Jhase called after them. "I'm doing a good job of teaching you to be a pirate already. Capture a ship, plunder its riches, and seduce the women."

Kari looked up at Talon, laughter sparkling in her eyes.

He grinned back, then called over his shoulder, "I'm only interested in one woman, Jhase, and I've found her. All I want to capture now is her heart."

Her hand curled lovingly against his cheek. "You have it, smuggler."

Chapter Twenty

Ten days later

Talon emerged from the med-lab at Hibernix, the new Rebel stronghold on Serac. He stared at the inside of his bare forearm. Kari jumped up from the bench where she'd been waiting in an agony of impatience and worry. The creased frown between his brows made her feel much, much worse.

Dear heavens, the treatment hadn't worked!

The Sylphs sprang from their perch on the back of the bench and followed as she ran to him. The pounding of her boots echoed in the cavern. Talon looked up from his dark contemplation, his expression distracted as she jarred to a stop in front of him and grasped his wrist.

"Let me see," she insisted.

The warm weight of his outstretched forearm felt good cradled in her palms. The thick muscle, the roughness of masculine hair, contradicted the vulnerability that had cursed his flesh since birth. Kari looked closely, bracing herself against more of the disappointment that had settled in her belly like a massive stone.

Where the intravenous needle had fed the last of the three prescribed treatments into his bloodstream, she found a scab.

A genuine scab.

Her chest constricted with relief, excitement, gratitude . . . and exasperation. She dropped his arm, clutched the

309

front of his tunic in her fists, and pulled herself up onto the balls of her feet until she met him nose-to-nose. "You simkin! Why were you frowning so fiercely? I thought something had gone wrong. Don't scare me like that, ever again!"

His gaze warmed. "Were you worried for me, starfire?"

"Yes," she growled.

He gave her a quick, hard kiss, knocking her back on her heels. Then, in a tone that set her teeth on edge because he could sound so practical when he'd just sent her equilibrium into a spin, he said, "I was examining the med-tech's handiwork with your pirated cure. I still find it hard to believe. Look." He picked off the scab.

"Why the blazes did you do that?" she exclaimed in astonishment, releasing his tunic. Beryl's warble quavered as fresh blood appeared. The Sylphs flew in circles overhead.

"I like to watch the bleeding stop on its own." He flashed Kari an unrepentant grin. "It's a new experience for me."

She rolled her eyes and groaned. Then tenderness welled up inside, for she loved him all the more for his boyish excitement over something that should be so mundane but wasn't. It was a miracle of genetic research, a renewal, a chance not to live in dread of an accidental scratch or a minor wound.

His free arm curved around her shoulders and pulled her close. Slipping her arm about his waist, she watched with him as the slight trickle of blood thickened, slowed, then stopped.

Responding to the tug of his arm, she gladly turned into his full embrace. She enveloped his rib cage in a powerful hug. When he grunted in mock discomfort she squeezed even tighter and cherished the chuckle that vibrated through his chest.

Kissing his neck, she whispered, "I'm so happy for you."

"I'd rather you be happy *with* me. Are you finally ready to go through with our marriage ceremony?"

"You know I only wanted to postpone it until the treatment was complete. I was afraid the formula wouldn't work."

Talon heard her muffled confession drift up from beneath his chin. "You were afraid I'd be angry with you if it failed," he said. She nodded, rubbing her forehead against his collarbone. He smiled and stroked her back. "How could I be angry over a gift freely given, at great sacrifice to yourself? Over a hope I didn't realize even existed until you pulled that data cylinder out of your belt on the *Usurper?*"

"But that's what seemed most cruel of all, to offer hope where there had been none before, then see it snatched away."

"Well, we don't have to worry about that now. It worked. But, regardless of how it turned out, I'd still love you, Kari. Desperately," he growled in a tone roughened by desire. "No more concern that sleeping with me will adversely affect the treatment, okay? I can't stand the torment."

She looked up. The sight of tears trailing down her cheeks left him feeling rather frantic. Would he ever grow used to the rare sight of his warrior woman in pain? Probably never. He cupped her cheeks in his hands, slid his fingertips into the warmth behind her ears, and wiped away her tears with his thumbs. His reward was a tremulous, feminine smile that brightened the gloom of the cave and lightened his heart.

"Why are you crying?"

Her mouth quirked higher at one corner. "I don't know."

"Infallible logic. I like that," he teased.

"I love you," she said softly.

"Marry me. Now. I can tell you I love you all day for the rest of my life, but right now I'd prefer to demonstrate it."

She chuckled. "You are an impatient sort, aren't you?"

"When it comes to making love with you, damn right. The alderman said we could come by and see him any time."

Her eyes widened suddenly. She stepped back out of his arms. "Wait!"

"Runagate hell, now what?"

"I bought a gown to wear to the ceremony. I have to go back to the *Nighthawk* to change first."

His brows arched. "A gown? Now, that is intriguing. By all means, my lady," he drawled, eyeing her customary breeches.

She grasped his hand and headed for the *Nighthawk*, which awaited them in the adjoining cavern. Snatching a package off the bunk, she disappeared into the lav with an instinctive knack for feminine mystery.

"I prefer your hair loose," he called after her.

While he waited in an agony of suspense, he changed into his best tunic. It was woven of brown quivote, matching his hair, and embroidered with gold thread. He called Rand, Jhase, Kjell, and Quinn on the commlink and told them to meet him at the alderman's temple.

The lav door opened. He was struck speechless.

Beryl chirped excitedly. *"Like it very much, I do."*

Oberon flew to Kari and perched on her outstretched hand. He touched her face as if she were a fragile treasure. *"Your beauty rivals the fairest flower."*

Kari blushed, obviously pleased by their flattery.

Irked that the Sylphs had drawn Kari's attention away from himself, Talon scolded, "Hey, you two, it's my opinion that matters in this case."

Beryl huffed. *"Then share it, you big shagya."*

He moved forward. Oberon obligingly flew aside, taking Beryl with him to the pilot's seat, where they perched and wrapped their arms around each other. Talon took Kari's hands and spread them so he could get an unobstructed view.

It pleased him that she'd chosen a Mal'Harith gown. The deep green quivote made her eyes shimmer like dew-painted leaves. Slender sleeves hugged her arms. The neckline dipped down in a *V* that displayed a tempting amount of cleavage without being immodest. The flowing, calf-length skirt was caught up with a gold clasp on one side, revealing a shapely expanse of leg to mid-thigh.

"You look incredible," he said raggedly. Just when he was ready to kick himself for saying something so simple and foolish, not the least bit poetic, she smiled brilliantly.

"Do you really think so?"

"Beyond my humble ability to describe." Sincerity and passion deepened his voice. "You are an exceedingly stubborn woman, however. I said I wanted your hair loose." He touched the artistic sweep of auburn hair she'd piled on top of her head, then reached for the pins.

She danced out of reach. "I thought you'd enjoy the privilege of taking it down . . . later," she said saucily.

This new, playful Kari, walking away with a flirtatious glance over her shoulder and a gentle sway to her hips, made him look forward to a lifetime of discovering her infinite complexities. He repaid her with a wolfish leer and followed. The Sylphs trailed behind.

Talon sighed with satisfaction when he returned to the *Nighthawk* an hour later with his wife. Kari's future was now inexorably linked to his own. A wave of possessiveness swept through him, feeding a hunger that went deeper than desire.

She stood with her back to him, staring at the spot where the Sylphs had disappeared into their arbor. He stripped off his tunic and boots. Clad only in his breeches, he wrapped his arms around her waist from behind. When she snuggled back against him, however, the sad, faraway look in her eyes remained.

He lipped the edge of her ear and murmured, "What's wrong?"

She rubbed her cheek tenderly against his jaw. "I was just thinking that I might not ever see Verdigris again, now that I've been banished from my home."

"The time will come. Besides, I'm your home now."

She smiled. "Wherever you go, I will go; is that it?"

"Damn right. And you have friends here." At her snort of disbelief, he insisted, "Quinn adores you, Kjell respects you; that was evident enough from their enthusiastic well-wishes at the ceremony. Even Arden has changed his tune. And if Jhase ever kisses you like that again, I'll knock him back on his ass."

"What about Rand?"

Talon flinched. "Trust me, he'll come around. You certainly caught his attention after the ceremony. What did you say to him to earn that look of astonishment?"

"I asked him to locate the best tattoo artist available."

Dazed by her thoughtfulness, he watched as she lifted his left hand and kissed the smooth skin. A surge of love filled his chest to bursting. Wrapping her tight in his embrace, he said hoarsely, "Rand will soon figure out what I already know . . . that I'm the luckiest man alive."

"Remember you said that when you have to sit still for five hours and your hands hurt. As for Rand, he looked mighty grim for a man who not only crippled the neryllium mine but stole a shuttle full of stockpiled ore before they blew everything up."

"It's not a large quantity of ore, but it's a start. And it buys us time. Between the neryllium and the *Usurper*, we stand a fighting chance. We're not just targets anymore." He nuzzled her neck and pressed kisses against her warm, scented skin, enjoying the tremors that rippled through her.

"Talon, you know I can't think when you do that."

"Good. You're talking too much as it is."

"But both sides are preparing to escalate the war."

He sighed, realizing she was too troubled to let the subject rest. "It's the Rebels' chance to secure the freedom we've been denied for over twenty years."

"And what about your role?"

"We've just reached the crux of the matter, haven't we?"

She turned and flung her arms about his neck. "I don't

want you to fight. Despite everything, Myklar is still my father."

"And what if Naill is the one attacking us?"

"Well, that's a different matter entirely. Do you think we can steal the *Artemis?* If not, maybe Rand can find me a ship—"

"No!" he snapped, cutting off her willingness to volunteer. "Believe me, we'll be far too busy smuggling the supplies the Reivas need. Let the war be Rand's concern."

"That's all I wanted to hear," she said happily. Then she stunned him yet again by slipping out of her gown and letting it drop around her ankles. With trembling hands, he unpinned her hair. She watched him with glowing eyes. He spread its silky warmth across her bare shoulders, then swept her into his arms and carried her to the bunk. Eagerly answering the siren call of her welcoming arms, he peeled off his breeches and carefully lowered his length over her.

"This time," he whispered, nipping her chin, "you can scratch me all you want, love."

Her smile held all the allure of an experienced temptress. Just as he was wondering what mischief she plotted, he felt the light scrape of her nails up the sides of his thighs, across his hips, and back down over his buttocks. His breath sucked in hard.

"I'll keep that in mind," she said softly, then pulled his head down for a drugging kiss.

Futuristic Romance

Love in another time, another place.

On Wings of Love — Saranne Dawson

"One of the brightest names in futuristic romance.
—Romantic Times

Jillian has the mind of a scientist, but the heart of a vulnerable woman. Wary of love, she had devoted herself to training the mysterious birds that serve her people as messengers. But her reunion with the one man she will ever desire opens her soul to a whole new field of hands-on research.

Dedicated to the ways of his ancient order, Connor is on the verge of receiving the brotherhood's highest honor: the gifts of magic and immortality. All will be lost, however, if he succumbs to his longing for Jillian. Torn by conflicting emotions, Connor has to choose between an eternity of unbounded power—and a single lifetime of endless passion.

_51953-4 $4.99 US/$5.99 CAN

Futuristic Romance

Star-Crossed

Saranne Dawson

Bestselling Author Of *Crystal Enchantment*

Rowena is a master artisan, a weaver of enchanted tapestries that whisper of past glories. Yet not even magic can help her foresee that she will be sent to assassinate an enemy leader. Her duty is clear—until the seductive beauty falls under the spell of the man she must kill.

His reputation says that he is a warmongering barbarian. But Zachary MacTavesh prefers conquering damsels' hearts over pillaging fallen cities. One look at Rowena tells him to gird his loins and prepare for the battle of his life. And if he has his way, his stunningly passionate rival will reign victorious as the mistress of his heart.

_51982-8 $4.99 US/$5.99 CAN

DON'T MISS OTHER STAR-STUDDED *LOVE SPELL* ROMANCES!

Sword of MacLeod by Karen Fox. When his daughter leaves their planet to find their family's legendary sword, Beckett MacLeod is forced to enlist the help of the best tracker in the galaxy—and the most beautiful woman he has ever laid eyes on. But Beckett has no patience for the free-spirited adventurer—until one star-studded evening she gives him a glimpse of the final frontier. Raven doesn't like working with anyone, but being in desperate need of funds, she agrees to help Beckett, thinking the assignment will be a piece of cake. Instead she finds herself thrown into peril with a man whose archaic ways are out of a history book—and whose tender kisses are something from her wildest dreams.

_52160-1 $4.99 US/$5.99 CAN

The Dawn Star by Stobie Piel. Seneca's sinewy strength and chiseled features touch a chord deep inside Nisa Calydon—reminding her of a love long gone, of the cruel betrayal of a foolish girl's naive faith. But she's all grown up now, and to avert a potentially disastrous war, she has kidnapped the virile off-worlder to fullfill her responsibility. But the more time she spends with the primitive warrior, the less sure she becomes of how she wants this assignment to end. For behind Seneca's brawn she finds a man of a surprisingly wise and compassionate nature, and in his arms she finds a passion like none she's ever known.

_52148-2 $5.50 US/$6.50 CAN

Dorchester Publishing Co., Inc.
65 Commerce Road
Stamford, CT 06902

Please add $1.75 for shipping and handling for the first book and $.50 for each book thereafter. NY, NYC, PA and CT residents, please add appropriate sales tax. No cash, stamps, or C.O.D.s. All orders shipped within 6 weeks via postal service book rate. Canadian orders require $2.00 extra postage and must be paid in U.S. dollars through a U.S. banking facility.

Name _____

Address _____

City _____ State _____ Zip _____

I have enclosed $_____ in payment for the checked book(s).

Payment <u>must</u> accompany all orders.☐ Please send a free catalog.